LEE STONE

THE NEW **CHARLIE LOCKHART** THRILLER
FEARLESS

DEDICATION

To those who served at Camp Bastion in Afghanistan where I started writing this book, and to those along the Camino who helped me to find the Way.

MORE BY LEE STONE

Charlie Lockhart Thriller Series

Fearless
The Smoke Child
Helter Skelter
The Road North

Bookshots (with James Patterson)

Break Point
Dead Heat

ACKNOWLEDGMENTS

Thank you to Darren Brophy, my unlikely tour guide.

i

CHAPTER ONE

Quetta, Pakistan. November 2009.
"Hey kids, rock and roll, Nobody tells you where to go, baby."
– REM, Drive.

The Tourist sat on a beaten up chesterfield in the shadows at the back of the tea shop. It was nearly time to make his decision. But not yet. It was best not to rush. The man who had offered to take him over the border into Afghanistan would not be back for an hour, so he had time to lean back and mull things over.

His name was Charlie Lockhart. He imagined the old sofa he was sitting on had once gleamed in the corner of an important office, its unyielding leather buffed up by cheap labor and expensive polish. Now it was a wreck, with bits of its guts hanging out of long slashes in the leather skin. Its mahogany color had faded, and dust had blown in through the open front of the tea shop and settled in its buttoned indentations. As he ran his hands through his dark hair, Lockhart realized that the dust had begun to collect on him too. His hair felt thick and unruly and his fingers got caught up in it. He looked up at the cracked mirror on the wall to his left, and even in the subdued light he seemed to have turned slightly gray.

The creaking fan above him circulated a smell of spiced lamb through the warm air in the shop, but it did little to cool him down. His skin felt salty, as if he had walked out of the sea and dried in the sun. He wore sturdy boots and good socks, but the rest of his clothes were cheap loose cotton. He hadn't seen rain since Istanbul, weeks ago.

He liked traveling light, and had nothing with him except his beige rucksack which was slouched against the side of the sofa, its sturdy buckles threatening to inflict another injury on the old chesterfield's thin leather.

255

The bag contained a few well traveled shirts and a pair of shorts he wore for swimming. Beneath them was a book called *The Hidden Words*, a Tunisian jug and a few other trinkets from along the way. He had wrapped his clothes in plastic bags in case the rain had leaked into the rucksack during his winter weeks through Europe. Now, despite the dust and heat of Quetta he had kept them wrapped, because he knew that he would get drenched again before he got home.

His other belongings were simple. A phone. A passport. Cash. A simple medical kit.

None of the clothes in his bag had been there when he started his journey. He had swapped and traded as he went. Locals had swapped practical cotton shirts in return for things that were Western, expensive, and useless. So now the clothes Lockhart wore reminded him of the places he'd been. Which made him happy.

Once, he had offered his quilted jacket to a motorbike salesman in Marrakech in return for a cheap NYC baseball cap. Lockhart had needed a hat, and it was far too hot to need the coat, even at night. He kept everything he owned in the pack on his back, and he didn't want to be weighed down with anything unnecessary.

Back on the sofa in the teashop, Lockhart smiled, remembering the motorbike salesman. The guy had been so pleased with the swap he'd thrown dinner into the deal. He closed his shop on a whim and gave Lockhart a hair-raising journey through the narrow streets of the old town on the back of his noisy dented scooter.

The whole place had echoed of Ozymandias, hot red walls reduced to sun bleached pinks, and crumbling buildings that echoed of more splendid times. They had raced past Arabic and French road signs and narrowly missed the ornate Victorian street lights that protruded alarmingly into the narrow thoroughfares.

The scooter had wound through tight alleys, flung around sharp blind corners and juddered over rough pavements. Mostly they rode in shadow, but occasionally they'd been bathed in the low-slung late evening sunlight. When they eventually arrived at the salesman's house, his sister greeted them at the door. Lockhart had taken to her immediately. She had a healthy radiance which made it hard not to stare at her, but Lockhart had acted as politely as a good guest should.

She was pretty, perhaps twenty-two or twenty-three. She was a serene collision of worlds; European and African, traditional but liberated. Her hazel eyes were enquiring and knowing all at the same time.

Likewise, in conversation Lockhart found that she was a deft and assured host, engaging without prying. She found common experiences and interests between the three of them, and as they ate Lockhart felt like all three of them could have been old friends.

The salesman's sister had cooked a traditional tagine of lamb and prunes, different to the Berber cuisine that Lockhart had become used to in Morocco. The lamb was flavored with onions garlic and ginger; it was warm and comforting. It was sweetened with cinnamon and honey, and there was a hint of orange blossom in the dish which was a touch of an Andalucían recipe that had been passed down from mother to daughter since their Moorish ancestors had retreated from Spain. Somewhere in their blood, and in their souls, the salesman and sister understood what it meant to travel, and to wander through the world and to sleep under the stars, and so they had welcomed Lockhart into their home.

The trio sipped sweet mint tea and shared stories and easy laughter as they relaxed on plump patterned cushions on the terracotta-tiled floor. Slowly the sky had darkened above the open courtyard at the center of the salesman's house. Candles flickered in alcoves in the walls.

Moments like these were gifts saved for strangers who had traveled as far as Lockhart. They were a just reward for the miles he had journeyed. It had pleased the motorbike salesman that his guest understood the encounter for what it was; a simple gift on the long road.

Lockhart had slept well that night, resting under the stars without moving from where they had eaten. Feeling comfortable on the cushions under a huge potted palm tree in the middle of the courtyard, he had covered himself with his jacket and fallen into a peaceful sleep. The wide leaves had swayed and lullabied as the Mediterranean and Atlantic winds had jostled for position above him.

The next morning, neither the salesman nor his sister had been anywhere to be seen. The courtyard had been empty except for a skinny black cat which had taken to sunbathing on a square of terracotta which was already warming in the sun.

The calm air was broken by the sound of a small fountain away in the shadows, and the distant rumble of civilization on the other side of the thick wooden courtyard door. His coat, which had been folded under the tree, was gone.

As Lockhart stretched, his arm had knocked the peak of the NYC cap, which the salesman had evidently perched on top of his head while he had been sleeping. Lockhart had laughed out loud, imagining the salesman and his sister swapping the hat and the coat without waking him. The deal was done.

Alone in the courtyard, his heart had felt light, but even so he spent five minutes in the courtyard unpicking the stitching on the embroidery until he could remove the New York logo from his new cap. It had seemed like a prudent thing to do. Then he had stepped out of the heavy wooden door back into the labyrinthine streets to see what the new day would bring.

*

Back on the old sofa in the tea shop in Quetta, Lockhart smiled as he remembered the motorbike salesman and his sister. He drew strength from those memories, and the miles he had already walked, and he wondered what encounters lay ahead.

He loved the feeling of evolution and change. Swapping his clothes was like shedding his old skin and blending into his ever-changing surroundings. The day he set out on his adventure he had felt like a stone dislodged from a riverbed, and even now he sensed that he was at the mercy of the current which pushed him along and buffeted him from side to side.

He knew that if he sat on the sofa for long enough, the current would decide for him.

The mint tea on the low wooden table in front of him had cooled; droplets of condensed steam were rolling down the inside of the glass back towards the vivid green leaves, failed in their attempts to escape.

Lockhart's stomach was beginning to growl because of the constant smell of roasting Sajji wafting through the teashop from the street sellers outside. He had developed a taste for the delicately spiced lamb when he first arrived in Quetta along the long road from Kan Mehtarzai.

North Pakistan was hot and poor and political and wise and backwards all at once. Quetta itself was full of danger and mystery. A border town just a few miles from Afghanistan, it sat in the dust like a magnet for travelers and smugglers and zealots and drop outs alike.

The light from outside the tea shop was glowing orange, and the shadows cast from the tables at the front were lengthening. They grew towards Lockhart, like the legs of a giant spider trying to reach inside and hook him out from his comfortable seat at the back of the shop. Even the shadows could tell that he had been sitting there for too long. Even the shadows were growing restless.

So Lockhart needed to make a simple decision which direction to take. North, South, East or West. Except that the decision wasn't simple at all once he started to think about it. The four different compass points held four different destinies. When he stood up from the beaten sofa, he would have to choose between those different directions and different futures. He reminded himself that this was why he was here. To search for his destiny. To change his future.

Lockhart had arrived in Quetta on his journey to New Delhi. It was not the most direct route, but he decided that going directly through Afghanistan would have been foolhardy. He was looking for adventure, not spoiling for a fight.

But sometimes when you are looking for one thing, another thing comes along to find you instead. And so it was that opportunity had found Charlie Lockhart, sheltering at the back of the tea shop in Quetta, away from the prying eyes of the afternoon sun.

CHAPTER TWO

Santa Barbara, California. Early December 2010.
"Just because you're paranoid don't mean they're not after you"
- Nirvana, Territorial Pissings.

It was late November and the war veteran looked out of place on State Street. The purple Jacaranda blossom which carpeted the sun-bleached sidewalk in summer had long gone, but the air was still warm and fragrant.

Santa Barbara was a gentle wash of warm terracotta and manicured streets; the kind of hushed place where you can hear your shoes scuffing on the jet-washed sidewalk as you make your way along.

The name on the veteran's tags was David Barr. He wore them under a khaki shirt and combats, although he was no longer in official uniform. His right trouser leg was rolled up to show that it was only partly occupied. Barr didn't have much below his right knee.

His wheelchair was cheap and rickety but he was agile in it when he needed to be. He had fallen on hard times but he still had a warrior's soul. Over the months, his hair had grown long and his heart had grown bitter. His wiry body held still, but from behind lank unkempt locks, his cornflower eyes darted about wildly. He looked like he was spoiling for a fight, as though he might spring up from his chair and lunge at a passer-by at any moment.

Mostly, local people kept out of his way. Every ointment had its fly, they figured, and David Barr was theirs. He was noisy and unsightly in their pretty town, but they were liberal and compassionate folk. They pitied him.

Which he despised.

Most people in the town assumed he was a Vietnam vet, but David Barr hadn't been out of the Army more than twelve months. He looked much older than his 32 years, mostly because of the nagging fear which hung about him all the time.

His disability embarrassed people and the people of the town hated catching his eye. They squirmed to look at a man who had lost his leg for his country. They knew they had it better than him, with their comfortable small-town lives. Most of them felt sorry for David Barr. Some of them felt grateful for his service. None of them wanted to swap places with him anytime soon.

So they turned a blind eye and a deaf ear as he berated them from the other side of the street. Occasionally a cop would move him along, but always in an apologetic and conciliatory fashion, feeling guiltiest of the lot.

Even with the pity, Barr liked it better in Santa Barbara than Los Angeles. When he had first gone into hiding, after things went sour in Kandahar, he'd slept for two weeks crammed between the concrete blocks under a bridge near the wide basin of the Los Angeles River. Despite the dry weather, the concrete wept a greenish slime that bled from a joint in the corner of his hole.

Barr had no problem sleeping rough. During his infantry days he had dealt with far worse. He had survived the South African bush for three weeks, learning bushcraft from a bunch of Zulus. The command chain had decided that soldiers were too reliant on technology, so they had stripped Barr of everything except his canteen and his knife and the clothes he stood up in, and sent him out into the wilderness. He had loved every minute.

The Zulus taught him to appreciate nature. He learned to trap and kill snakes and to use the ribs from the snake to make a fishing hook. When he got it right, the Zulus would nod and smile. They showed him how to navigate using the stars. They showed him how to watch and listen to animals to find out where there was water. They taught him which plants would feed him, which would heal him, and which would kill him.

Los Angeles was a different world though. Here in the sprawling metropolis, nature had been tamed and broken. The once beautiful *Río de Nuestra Señora La Reina de Los Ángeles de Porciúncula* had been encased by man in concrete walls and trenches. As if to wound her more, gangs had scrawled all over the concrete. Threats and warnings; turf wars for a putrid, God-forsaken place. Every surface was a violent clash of aerosol signatures suffocating one another.

Life's wreckage flowed and rolled down into the man-made basin; pram wheels, smashed orange boxes, food wrappings, misery, and broken people. Barr knew it was a place where nobody would come looking for him.

Unlike the Zulus, nobody under the bridge wanted to befriend him.

Sure, all the hobos checked him out, but they were all on the make. Until he finally hit rock bottom, while he still had more than them, they would covert the few things he had left. Which didn't amount to much.

Barr had fallen a long way already. A year ago, he had been sitting in a truck with three hundred million dollars in the back of it. The keys had been in his hand. The tank had been full of fuel. He could have driven that damn truck anywhere, but he didn't. He gave the keys to a stranger who had appeared out of the desert and disappeared just as quickly, leaving Barr in a lot of trouble. Barr knew that the guy must be rich or dead by now.

During the day, Barr's missing leg helped to earn him enough loose change to eat. He didn't have a drug habit, and he didn't drink, so the money he made went on food and Pepsi. The begging kept him occupied. Stopped him from thinking about the places he would rather be. The people he would rather be with.

His self-imposed exile was tough, but the alternative was worse. If the people who were hunting him found him, so be it. But the men who had followed him back from Afghanistan wouldn't think twice about hurting his family. Barr refused to take the danger home to his wife and daughter, so he stayed away from his family, his home, his bank account, and his friends. Even if they found him, they wouldn't touch his family. Barr would make sure of that.

At night, he was tough enough to cope with the trouble that street life brought. He kept to himself mostly, but when that didn't work, the fact he could unexpectedly spring out of his wheelchair was enough to scare the shit out of most people.

The first two months in L.A. passed with little incident. He got used to the cold at night, the constant moving around, and the slow degeneration of his clothes. No hardship for a soldier. But just like in combat, things can change quickly on the streets. One night under the concrete bridge, Barr had been settling back into his slimy concrete hole. A gnarly old guy had been drinking cheap vodka nearby and had stumbled over to Barr, determined to talk. Barr had sat and listened. He threw in the odd non-committal phrase here and there, never questioning too deeply and never giving away too much of himself.

The other rough sleepers had a small fire going in an old oil drum, and as its embers slowly died, the old drunk stopped talking and Barr eventually fell asleep. Under the bridge he dreamed that he was chasing a woman and a girl across a dusty desert. He thought he knew them, and he called their names, but the wind was against him and they couldn't hear. He chased them over the sand until his legs ached and his lungs burned. Their faces were covered except for their eyes; but he knew them. Eventually he caught up with them and held them both close to him. He felt the satisfaction of having them near, remembering their smell and the warmth of their skin.

When he could resist no longer, he lifted the veil from the woman's face, but saw straight away that her hair was too short to belong to the woman he remembered. Much too short in fact. Suddenly she was growing; growing so fast that her billowing black dress engulfed the young girl beside her. She grew bigger until she towered over him and her facial features transformed from soft and feminine to hard and angry and masculine.

Barr woke up in a sweat to find the gnarly old man in front of him. The old guy whipped out a handgun and pointed it straight at Barr, muttering some indecipherable demand. A stupid thing to do to a man with Barr's training.

Despite his age, the old guy was well built. He was nowhere near as big as the man in Barr's dream, but imposing all the same. Especially because he was right in Barr's face. His breath still smelled of vodka, and his face was menacing, glowing in the dying embers of the oil drum.

Barr didn't think. He saw the gun and a decade of military training did the thinking for him. Barr's good leg kicked up at the rugged old man, winding him. His hands pushed the gun away from him and then twisted the guy's wrists until they gave way. The old guy sank to his knees trying to go with the pressure; drunk and ungainly.

Barr's hand closed around the gun, pushing the old man's fingers over the trigger. In a moment it was over; two shots rang out and the old drunk lay twitching on the concrete. He was face down, his gaping mouth drooling into the green slime.

Accusations flew between the few people under the bridge. They were suddenly scared of Barr, scared of the gun. Scared at his will to use it in anger. From what Barr could piece together, he had fallen asleep and some time later the dead guy had returned with murderous intent having finished his vodka. He had wanted Barr's jeans and assumed he was an easy target. Nobody had stepped in to stop him.

There was time for David Barr to move on. The other souls under the bridge were high as kites and would make the worst witnesses. Besides, the police wouldn't be breaking their balls to work out why there was one less homeless gun-toting alcoholic on the streets of L.A. after that night. Even so, Barr took the time to drag the body into the river before beginning the long journey up the coast to Santa Barbara. He covered his tracks. David Barr was a survivor.

CHAPTER THREE

Quetta, Pakistan. November 2009.
"But as sure as God made black and white
What's done in the dark will be brought to the light."
- Johnny Cash, God's Gonna Cut You Down.

Opportunity was sitting in front of Charlie Lockhart in the shape of a man called Ajmal. Hours ago, Ajmal had been relaxing on the chesterfield at the back of the teashop when Lockhart had walked in. Lockhart had felt the man's eyes weighing him up when he first arrived in the shop. He didn't understand Dari or Pashto, but Lockhart had a manner which put strangers at ease quickly, and he blended in easily to most places. He had a warmth and confidence about him, which usually attracted friends as surely as it repelled trouble.

A few choice phrases in Arabic, and a couple of nods towards another customer's order, and the owner of the shop understood what Lockhart wanted to drink. He headed off to the far corner of the room to prepare his sweet mint tea.

The man on the chesterfield was dressed simply in near-white shalwar kameez and brown Kabuli sandals. There was nothing remarkable about him, except that Lockhart had the impression that he was trying to catch his eye. He turned around and inspected him. He had closely cropped hair and was probably fairly wiry underneath the loose material of his outfit. He was about five foot eight and couldn't have weighed over ten stone.

"Aya ta pohe-gi?" he asked, looking straight at the tourist.

The man was asking him whether he understood Pashto, which mostly he didn't. But he had understood the question, so it was hard to know how best to answer. He let the man on the sofa work out for himself if he could speak the language.

"Ta la cherta ragh-ley?" Lockhart had asked with as much confidence as he could muster.

"Where am I from?" the man had laughed. "The same place as you, by the sound of it."

Lockhart stared at Ajmal as he recognized the inflections in his voice.

"Birmingham?"

"Alum Rock," replied Ajmal.

Lockhart shook his head and smiled. Alum Rock was one of Birmingham's run-down districts.

"I don't live anywhere near Alum Rock," he said, deadpan.

"You know what I mean," Ajmal laughed. "We're three thousand miles from England. People out here would think we're virtually neighbors!"

Ajmal and Lockhart laughed, amazed by the chance of their meeting. It was strange, but Lockhart had become open-minded to coincidence and fortune during his travels. As the men got to talking, Lockhart learned that Ajmal had apparently come out to Pakistan nearly a year ago for a family wedding and had never got around to going home.

The way Ajmal told the story, he had never wanted to come to Pakistan but his family had insisted. He didn't really know any of his Pakistani relatives, and hadn't enjoyed the wedding much, except for when an attractive henna-covered second cousin mistook him for the groom and spent a happy ten minutes rubbing scented oil through his hair at the Mehndi ceremony.

"Well, I wasn't going to put her straight," he said with a mischievous smile.

After the wedding, Ajmal had taken off around the country, visiting various relatives and seeing some places his grandparents had told him endless stories about back in the three-bedroom Victorian terraced house he shared with them in Birmingham.

When he was a kid, Ajmal used to sit on the floor in the small front room of the family home and eat chicken and rice from a cheap Formica table while his grandparents sat on a hideous brown sofa behind him. His Grandma, Dadi, would ruffle her hand through his hair as he tried to eat, while his grandad, Dada, would tell stories about what it was like growing up in Balochistan years before.

A magnified picture of Quetta hung in a cheap metal frame on the wall behind them, and as his grandad told his stories about his hometown, he would point out parts of the distant mountain, blurred corners of the Main Street, or buildings that were jostling as if to get a prime spot in the photograph. There was one building towards the right-hand side of the picture which Ajmal's grandad would always stand up to show him. On the right-hand side of the plain square frontage there was a small, dark, and very unremarkable window.

"That is where I first set eyes on Dadi" he would explain to the young boy, and Ajmal's grandma would beam and nod her head, although she had heard the story a thousand times.

"Look how small the window is," he would implore Ajmal. "If I hadn't looked up through that tiny window, I would never have seen your Dadi, and then your father would never have been born and neither would you."

"It is incredible Ajmal. Our fate and your very existence have squeezed through this tiny little window right here!" and he would tap his finger against the picture for a moment, losing himself in the magic of it all.

"So, I bet I can guess where you went when you first arrived in Quetta?" Lockhart asked Ajmal, looking at the cracked mirror behind the damaged Chesterfield. He could imagine the picture of Quetta on the wall back in Ajmal's home in Alum Rock.

Ajmal nodded and smiled, partly because it embarrassed him he had predictably sought the house with the little window so soon after arriving in Quetta, and partly because he was pleased that Lockhart had understood how much his grandad's story had meant to him.

"The house was broken down when I arrived, and there were cattle living inside. I was frustrated because someone had stripped the place out. The floorboards were gone, along with the ceiling."

"The shell of the house was still there though and I could see the window that Grandad had seen Grandma through, but the staircase was gone and so I couldn't reach it."

Lockhart asked Ajmal what he had done next, although he could guess the answer. He had learned a lot about people on his travels; the things which made us similar, and the things which made us unique. Ajmal was not unusual. He was someone who followed his heart and was a slave to his feelings and emotions.

"I couldn't reach the window, so I ran to the marketplace," he explained, and Lockhart could see from the distant look in his eyes that Ajmal was re-living the excitement of that moment.

"There was a fruit stall selling everything, man. There were boxes of plums, peaches, and pomegranates, and rows of apricots and olives and cherries. The guy who ran the stall was sitting in the shade on top of a stack of empty fruit crates and I thought I could pile them up and stand on them, so I asked him if I could buy them."

Apparently, the seller had been a wily old man and he could see how impatient Ajmal was to get back to his window.

"These are not crates," he had answered as he sat chewing on pistachios and almonds. "This is my chair, and chairs are very expensive today."

Despite Ajmal's best attempts at bargaining and pleading, the market man had been unmoved. Eventually he had agreed to relinquish his seat and in return Ajmal had purchased an entire box of apricots at something of an inflated price.

"I ran back to the cowshed with all of my crates, and a box of apricots balanced on top," laughed Ajmal between sips of his mint tea. "I must have looked like a complete idiot!"

"When I got back, I stacked the crates on top of each other and climbed up to the little window to look out. I ate a handful of sweet apricots and I watched the dusted street for an hour as the light started to fade, and I imagined my Grandad down there, looking up at the window. I imagined the destiny of my family passing through this tiny square in front of me. Even though he was three thousand miles away, I felt closer to Dada at that moment than ever before."

Ajmal knew all of his Grandad's stories by heart, and Lockhart had time to listen to them. After another hour, the first shadows started to form outside the shop and afternoon slowly began to ebb away. Ajmal sat up a little straighter on the Chesterfield, adjusted the loose cotton of his salwar, and pitched in with a proposal for Lockhart.

"After the wedding when I went visiting my family, I needed some transport and the only thing for sale was a truck. It didn't cost much, but I fixed it up and painted it. We did a lot of miles together, me and that truck. It wasn't comfortable, but it was reliable, and when I got to Quetta, I couldn't bring myself to part with it."

"So I kept it, and then I bought another one. And now I have a truck depot just outside Rawalpindi with about thirty drivers working for me. I have bought up tankers, busses, trucks—and tomorrow is a big day for me, because I'm taking a convoy down the Chaman Road."

Everyone knew where that road led. Lockhart took a sip of his tea and studied the man on the sofa.

"How far along the Chaman Road is this convoy headed?" he asked after a moment. He suddenly felt like they were playing poker.

"We'll go to the border, and then across into Afghanistan. We are setting out in the morning for Kandahar, and I'm a driver short. An Englishman would be helpful when we arrive at the American base, *Insha'Allah*. Can you drive?"

As he sat in the teashop Charlie Lockhart noticed the flow of the river and the current pushing him along. It was time to make his decision.

CHAPTER FOUR

Santa Barbara, California, December 2009.
"Your eyes are burning holes through me.
I'm gasoline. I'm burning Clean."
– REM, Electrolite

David Barr had flown straight out of Afghanistan on the night that the job had gone wrong. He had used his contacts to get stowed away on the back of a C17 transporter to Cyprus, and then traveled on using civilian papers which he had forged before he left Kandahar Airfield. Los Angeles had been an obvious choice. Big, brash, and a million miles from his home and his family. He could feel the hot breath of serious trouble on the back of his neck, and he didn't want to lead it back to the people he loved.

But after shooting the old man, Barr fled L.A. just like he had fled Kandahar. Self defense or not, he felt troubled that he had killed the alcoholic under the bridge. Not *guilty*, exactly. But troubled. It wasn't the first time he'd shot another man, and he had seen enough innocent deaths in Afghanistan to keep him awake for a lifetime.

The man under the bridge had been waving a loaded gun in his face and deserved everything he got. Barr was more bothered about the practicalities; about the fact that the body would wash up somewhere, and that the police at the very least might come looking for him. He badly needed to stay off the radar.

So he fled the scene and left the City of Angels in the same way as he arrived; in the middle of the night, with his cap pulled low over his face, hoping not to be noticed. The good thing about living rough was that he had nothing to pack and nothing to arrange. He just moved on, a hundred miles up the coast to Santa Barbara.

When he first arrived, he had been edgy, and nervous. He had considered ditching his wheelchair in case he was recognized, but without medical help his legs had deteriorated to the point where he couldn't get along without it. He had thought about smartening up and taking a job, but that would have meant paperwork and credit checks. If he opted back in to normality, he was sure that trouble would find him.

So he continued his broken life on the streets. His wife and his daughter would mourn him, but at least they would be safe. Nobody would go looking for them. Nobody would kill them. Life became a waiting game, and Barr learned to be patient. As long as one day he could get back to his family, he would continue to live his empty life on the streets. As the guys on ESPN always said: *It's the hope that kills you.*

It was only when the air turned colder that Barr realized he was spending a second winter in Santa Barbara. A full year away from his daughter. He wondered if he would recognize her if she walked up to him in the street. These days young girls were ushered quickly past him by their protective mothers. Barr didn't blame them.

He was still thinking about his daughter when he was shaken from his thoughts by a sense of danger. Although his mind was miles away, his eyes still constantly swept the street. Force of habit. He spotted a giant of a man about half a mile away, dressed in a dark jacket and standing head and shoulders above everyone else around him. Barr's blood froze as he recognized the hulking shape. Was it really Tyler? After thirteen months of hiding, had his past finally caught up with him?

He had seen Tyler only once before, in his office in Afghanistan, but he knew exactly why he was in Santa Barbara. Tyler would interrogate him for as long as it took to discover what had happened on the road to Herat. And when he realized Barr didn't have the answers he wanted, he would kill him anyway.

When Barr saw him, he wheeled straight off State Street and into the shadows. Hitching a lift was out of the question, so he pulled together every dollar he had stashed away in his pockets and headed for the cab rank. He threw some green at the guy with the biggest-looking car, and grabbed the back door. He deftly transferred himself onto the back seat and glared at the driver in the rear-view mirror, waiting for him to pack away his chair into the trunk. No arguments.

Thirty minutes later, he was on a fast train back to Los Angeles. He knew the game was up. The giant and his boss were onto him. When they didn't get the answers they wanted, they would kill him. At least he'd stayed away from his family. The sacrifice had been worth it.

CHAPTER FIVE

Quetta, Early November 2009
"Words that flow between friends, Winding streams, without end."
- Mercury Rev, The Dark is Rising.

It was getting late by the time Ajmal returned to the tea shop. He had spent much of the afternoon on the phone to the office in Rawalpindi, checking the latest details about his fleet of trucks.

He was bringing prosperity to the people of Quetta with his trips into Kandahar. His drivers were getting well paid for the dangerous trip, and those who got cold feet would find ten men behind them, ready to take their place.

The women worried about their men going over the border, but enjoyed the luxuries they came back with. And mostly the men *did* come back. Besides, Ajmal had taken special measures to ensure that his cargo would get through to Kandahar without much trouble. He was employing mechanics and accountants and boys to stack the trucks. All of them were profiting from the trips to Kandahar.

He hoped that he could convince Lockhart to drive with him. He would put him two trucks from the front, and the chances were that he would lead the convoy by the time they arrived at Kandahar. If anyone would trigger a roadside bomb, it would most often be the first truck, so he would keep Lockhart a little way back.

Ajmal was not stupid though. He had cut deals and reached agreements with people who mattered. Many of the people along the Chaman Road disliked convoys reaching the Americans, but most would have received instructions to turn a blind eye to Ajmal's group of dusty trucks. *Sometimes you have to dance with the Devil*, he though.

As he entered the shop, it took a moment for his eyes to adjust to the darkness before he spotted Lockhart on the sofa.

"*Salam Alaikum*," he said in his English accent as he reached out to Lockhart. "How's it going mate?"

They shook hands as Ajmal sat down, and they both knew at once that the deal was already done. Lockhart wouldn't still be sitting there if he wasn't interested in the journey to Kandahar.

They spoke for a while about the plan for the next day. They would set out early in the morning, driving through the dawn up into the mountains. They would stop briefly at Chaman at around ten in the morning and aim to be at the main gates of Kandahar Airfield by 3pm. Lockhart would take the third truck and be sure to stay twenty meters behind the vehicle in front. He would keep his doors locked at roadblocks. He wouldn't get out of the cab. If the truck in front drove straight through, so should Lockhart. Child's play.

Now that Lockhart had decided, he felt happy. Afghanistan would be dangerous, but he figured this was a chance to get right to the heart of the country as an anonymous truck driver. A chance to see what the place was all about. In the dust and the noise of thirty vehicles, nobody would notice him. Once he got to the military base, he could work out his next move, and Ajmal could find someone else to drive the truck back.

Lockhart could feel the river of fate sweeping him along, pushing him towards his next adventure.

The two men left the tea shop together and walked out into the open road. Lockhart left the owner a generous tip; he had stayed far longer than two glasses of mint tea warranted.

Quetta was not a big place, and fairly soon they were outside the house that Ajmal's Grandfather had lived in many years ago. Lockhart saw for himself the tiny window that Ajmal had described. Inside, the house had been lovingly restored, and a first floor and staircase had been reinstated. The walls were whitewashed and newly plastered, and there was a smart new kitchen.

After resisting the smell of the sajji lamb all afternoon, Lockhart had purchased some on the way home, and the two new friends sat and ate together in Ajmal's house.

"We should rest now," Ajmal eventually decided. "Tomorrow will be an early start for us both."

He showed Lockhart to his room, which was simply furnished but pleasant enough. It had a small window in the corner, and it wasn't until Lockhart was in bed that he realized that it was the window that Ajmal's grandfather had pointed to a thousand times in the picture above the sofa in Alum Rock. The window he had seen Ajmal's grandmother through. The window that Ajmal's family had traveled all the way to Quetta to find.

Lockhart smiled and felt happy for his host. He felt sure that Ajmal's Grandfather would be proud to see him in the old family house, bringing prosperity to people in the town that he had kept in his heart for so long.

Charlie Lockhart watched the stars through the window as he drifted off to sleep, ready for an early start on the road to Chaman in the morning.

CHAPTER SIX

Mandhi Sar, Afghanistan, Midday, November 2009.
"This is what you get if you mess with us. And for a minute there, I lost myself, I lost myself." - Radiohead, Karma Police.

Charlie Lockhart was seconds away from death. The truck in front of him was smoldering, and in his mirrors he could see two more vehicles on fire. It amazed him how quickly things could switch from mundane to pure terror.

There were four men outlined on the horizon to his right, about fifty meters away. Three of them had fired their grenades. The remaining silhouette had lifted his launcher to his shoulder and was aiming straight at Lockhart's truck.

Lockhart thought back to his decision in the tea shop. He had chosen to be here today, and he couldn't blame anyone else for it. He thought about the billions of people shuffling about the earth at that exact moment. Nothing would really change if he was gone.

Until this point, Lockhart's day had gone fairly well. Ajmal had woken him up at dawn as the first light began to glow in the tiny window. They had met with the convoy, and Lockhart had been given the truck he would drive into Afghanistan. It was not what he had been expecting. Every inch had been customized; arches swung across the trailer, and the cab was adorned with shining mirrors and Islamic slogans. Only the dust muted its brightly colored paintwork. Ajmal had chosen a truck with tinted windows for him so he would not be easily recognized as a foreigner.

The front of the cab was already dusted over, and one of the regular drivers had written something into the grime. When Lockhart asked Ajmal what it meant, he explained that it was the Arabic phrase meaning *"without fear"*.

"They just think it's strange that you would come on this trip for an adventure," Ajmal explained. "They think you're Fearless."

"They think I'm an idiot," suggested Lockhart.

"Yep, they think you're an idiot," agreed Ajmal with a laugh. "Come on, Fearless man, are you ready to roll?"

The air conditioning in the cab was feeble, but they had left a crate of cold water on the passenger seat for him. Three of the trucks in the convoy were crammed full of bottled water; it was a precious commodity for an army that couldn't stomach the local supply. Locals in Afghanistan drank from wells contaminated with e:coli with no ill effects. But the US Army spent over one hundred million dollars each year on bottled water alone. Ajmal figured they wouldn't miss a few crates for his drivers.

Ajmal told Lockhart that he could open the windows whenever he wanted, but he got the impression that it wouldn't be a good idea. After the drivers had said their prayers and their goodbyes, the convoy rumbled out of Quetta along the Chaman Road. Nobody waved them off.

The edges of Afghanistan and Pakistan smudged into one another. By the middle of the morning, the convoy stopped at Chaman, the last town before crossing the border. The dusty trucks parked up in the town's schoolyard, all judders and hisses and sighs until the last engine fell silent.

At the weekend, Afghan FC used the schoolyard to play football matches in the Pakistan Premier League. Lockhart imagined the crowds and the noise and the passion, the crunching tackles and the plaintiff yells: But today the place was empty. No footballers and no schoolchildren. A couple of dogs wondered about, looking for mischief.

After twenty minutes of stretching their legs and gossiping, the drivers climbed back into their cabs and started their engines like a badly tuned diesel orchestra. One or two pointed to the hand-scratched *Fearless* sign on the front of Lockhart's cab and laughed as they passed.

There was a bang on the window. It was Ajmal, his hands shielding his eyes from the sun as he squinted to see through the mirrored glass. Lockhart wound it down.

"Hey, Fearless!" Ajmal greeted him.

It struck Lockhart that in the last twenty-four hours; he hadn't told Ajmal his real name, and Ajmal hadn't asked. It didn't matter. It was safer to be anonymous.

"The front truck won't start, and I don't want it holding us up once we get over the border," Ajmal scanned the horizon as he spoke. "So he's holding back. You'll be rolling out second, ok?"

Lockhart nodded as he started up his engine. The dust was kicking everywhere, and the noise made it difficult to talk without shouting. Ajmal let go his grip of the wing mirror and jumped backwards from the footplate. He was as sprightly as a mountain goat.

He raised both fists to the air as he landed in the dust, still facing Lockhart.

"Fearless!" he yelled to Lockhart, as though it was a battle cry. Lockhart laughed. There were probably guys in the convoy with worse nicknames, he guessed. He wound up his window to keep out the dust and kicked the truck into gear, rumbling out of the schoolyard and over the border.

There was a symbolic archway between the town of Chaman and Spin Boldak in Afghanistan. Driving under the arch meant passing over the border. As the trucks passed under the arch, Lockhart could see very little else to signify that the convoy had passed into another country.

NATO had erected surveillance cameras along the border partly because the road was an important supply line for the Americans at Kandahar, and partly because it was an important route for the Taliban.

Other than the archway and the cameras, the convoy flowed from one country to another with minimal ceremony. Most of the vehicles were brightly colored, and the Pakistanis in Chaman turned to look at them as they passed. Two miles later, Afghans in Spin Boldak did the same. But as Ajmal had predicted, the trucks encountered no problems as they passed along the way.

It was two hours later, deeper into Afghanistan when it happened. They had just driven through Mandi Sar, the last town marked along the road before Kandahar. Many of the drivers were already scanning the horizon for a first glimpse of the massive Airfield.

Lockhart heard the first explosion in front of him, followed soon after by two behind, some way further back. He could see smoke in both of his mirrors. As he looked to his right, he saw the attackers. Eight men, four spotters, four shooters and four long tubular grenade launchers. They aimed the final Rocket-Propelled Grenade right at his truck. He braced for impact, as if scrunching up his face and clenching his shoulders higher would somehow compensate for him being smashed into by an RPG.

Time slowed down. Lockhart thought about the scratched Arabic name in the dust which caked the front of his truck. *Fearless*, the Western adventurer, driving a truck into the dangerous desert because he had nothing better to do. The new name had stuck quickly among his fellow drivers. Right now though, he wasn't living up to the name. He was scared as hell.

The first grenade had hit the cab of the leading truck, and there was no chance to save the driver. Lockhart had listened to Ajmal's instructions and had kept a distance between him and the truck in front, so he could maneuver around the burning vehicle, and he put his foot down as he tried to get past it. Keeping moving was the only chance of saving himself and the convoy behind him.

He focused on the road ahead, trying to squeeze around the burning truck while staying on the road. He knew that there would probably be IEDs either side of the ambush. They would shoot the front truck, and the back truck, and fence in the sides with improvised explosive devices, so that the trucks would be at their mercy. Standard procedure. So Lockhart sacrificed a small amount of speed for precision. He wasn't hanging around.

From the corner of his eye, he saw the flash of the weapon discharging and ducked down in the cab as he rammed the accelerator. He heard an almighty thud as the RPG smashed into the side of his truck, and dust unsettled and flew around his cab. And then there was nothing. For whatever reason, the grenade hadn't gone off. It must have been Lockhart's luckiest day.

As he settled back into the seat, a man with an AK47 stepped out in front of the truck, aiming the barrel of his gun straight at the windshield.

There are times to submit to the river of fate, *thought Lockhart,* and there are times to make your own luck.

He pushed harder on the gas, acting on instinct, and aimed for the man who was trying to shoot him. A single round escaped from the AK47 and smashed the truck's wing mirror clean off. Then the gunman hit the front of the truck and disappeared under the wheels with a thump. Lockhart heard a thud as the back axle passed over him.

He assumed that none of the convoy would stop for the gunman, considering they were trying to escape from the attack. They might not even see him in the dust that was kicking up as they all sped up. There wouldn't be much left of him by the time they had all made their escape. Road kill.

Charlie Lockhart was now leading the way, the fearless idiotic Westerner out in front. He knew it was a straight road to the Airbase from here on. No stopping. In the isolation of the cab, he realized that he was shaking. He had just run a man down in cold blood. He was angry at the fact that three drivers had just been killed. Angry that the gunman had wanted to kill him too. In a primal moment of revenge, he had felt satisfied by the sickening sound of the gunman being crushed under his truck.

Overwhelming emotion burst through him; elation at survival, guilt for leaving the dead drivers behind; shock at the stark reality of his own peril. Then suddenly, and just for a moment, he shook and sobbed like a boy. It felt good. After a few seconds he wiped a couple of tears from his eyes with a salty thumb. The momentary collapse had convinced him he was still human, and now he could get back to business.

He stared at the long straight road expanding before him, which felt more dangerous now, and he felt more exposed at the front of the line.

Now he was focused on survival, not adventure. *Welcome to Helmand Province.*

CHAPTER SEVEN

The Road to Kandahar. November 2009.
"Faces look ugly, when you're alone."
– The Doors, When You're Strange

An hour later, Lockhart was consumed by the desert. The fine particles of sand had made their way into every part of the cab. His dark hair felt thick and matted and looked almost gray with the dust. His skin felt dry and hardened and his lips cracked. The air con had lasted well, but even so the footwell was strewn with empty bottles of mineral water.

The convoy had been driving for hours and he had consumed liters of water, but in the heat and dust he hadn't wanted to pee. Which was just as well, because a comfort break on a convoy like this would have been a stupid idea. And peeing into a bottle that he'd only just drunk out of seemed wrong to him, no matter where he was. The Englishman hung onto the idea that manners were important, even when nobody was looking.

Still the convoy trundled on - thirty vehicles, minus the three trucks that had perished in the rocket attack. The dust they kicked up must have been visible from outer space. In the distance, the wind swirled and eddied and created mini tornadoes with the sand. Ahead there was nothing; just the flat beige landscape stretched on for miles with no discernable change.

Occasionally, adobe dwellings would rise out of the floor apologetically, their mud walls and roofs perfectly camouflaged until Lockhart was almost next to them. Nobody came out to see them with flags or flowers. The dust cloud advertised the convoy hours before the trucks arrived, and when your world has turned to war, it pays not to be too curious.

With nothing to see and three vehicles already destroyed, Lockhart began to rely on something halfway between intuition and paranoia. Since the attack, he had been more cautious as he led the others along the road to Kandahar. He stopped for any bump in the road, any disturbed earth, discoloration, mound, box, dead goat or shit heap. Stopped. Considered. Looked for trip wires. Scouted for dodgy looking farmers who might plan to detonate something by remote control. But always eventually he drove on. As he had to.

As he made slow progress across the desert, Lockhart remembered walking along the Camino de Santiago, a one-thousand-kilometer pilgrimage route across northern Spain. That journey had been slow and troublesome too.

His problems had started as he climbed over the mountains into the Najara valley, and the first drops of rain had begun to fall. He was miles from civilization. He had pulled on his poncho and soldiered on through unforgiving torrents, darting between lemon trees and almond trees and olive trees. None of them offered him much shelter.

Within minutes, clay paths had become fast-flowing streams between plump red Rioja grape vines, and everything smelled of freshly disturbed earth. Despite the poncho, Lockhart had been soaked, and the wet fabric of his clothes began to cut into him as he marched on. His feet got the worst of it, and by the time he reached the shelter of the Refugio at Torres del Rio huge blood blisters covered both of his soles.

He had dumped his rucksack and hobbled out to find a bar. Luckily the only place he could find had an open fire, which was well stoked and already blazing, and he sat down to dry off.

He must have looked a sorry sight, because the barman brought him over a hot drink and some Morcilla de Burgos, to save him hobbling to the bar. The old guy had not been so quick on his feet himself, and Lockhart had appreciated the kindness.

The barman wore a cockle shell on a rough twine around his neck, and behind the bar there was a picture of him carrying a rucksack, beaming in front of the twin towers of the Cathedral at Santiago. Evidently, he understood the pilgrim's pain.

"Ultreya" the barman mumbled as he handed the warm dish to the wet traveler. Lockhart looked at the barman blankly as he tasted the warm blood tapas. It was just what he needed.

"Ultreya," the man repeated slowly and deliberately, pointing at Lockhart's bloody feet. Lockhart wasn't sure whether he was pausing for effect or struggling to put his thoughts into broken English.

"It means that you must go on to the end, one foot in front of the other. Be stubborn and go one step at a time. To make one step is easy, and if you keep making small steps, you will surely reach your final destination. Ultreya!"

Back in his dusty cab in the middle of the desert, Charlie Lockhart smiled. He remembered the wet clothes, the warm fire and the simple pleasure of listening to that ancient wisdom. His right foot pushed a bit harder on the gas, and the low gear whined at a slightly higher pitch.

And so the empty water bottles piled up, the dust rose, and the trucks rumbled on towards Kandahar Airfield. *Ultreya,* thought Lockhart, and he knew that he would reach his destination.

CHAPTER EIGHT

KLA AM NewsTalk Studios, Downtown Los Angeles
"There's a radio tower, it's egging you on.
Back to the place where you never belonged.
Where the people thrive on their own contempt.
Whatever meaning is long gone spent."
- REM, Low Desert.

There was dirt underneath Rachel White's fingernail. She noticed as it hovered above the red plastic fader on her mixing console. The dirt pissed her off. It hadn't been there when she started the show, but now it was.

Six minutes and fourteen seconds to go.

She pushed the fader about half an inch off its backstop, and immediately the atmosphere in the studio changed. The music which had been blaring out of the two speakers hanging from the ceiling cut out automatically, but the treble continued to rattle out of the various pairs of headphones laid out for guests.

The tiny red square just above the fader started to glow in the gloomy room, as did several red "On Air" boxes on the walls inside and outside the studio. The background to the computer screen in front of her changed to red. The countdown showed three seconds before she had to talk again.

These were the things that her studio guests noticed in their excitement when they arrived to go on air; the flashy shiny things. The eight flat-screens facing the presenter, the glowing red lights and the heavy muted atmosphere. Rachel had seen the flashy shiny things a million times. What *she* noticed these days was the smell of burning circuit boards kicking out of the back of a hundred of pieces of kit, the lack of natural light, and most of all the fact that dirt collected in every groove and corner of her mixing console.

She didn't like the way the grime slowly transferred onto her skin during the show. Three hours of talking to late night callers was grime enough.

The cleaners were too shit-scared to go anywhere near the broadcasting equipment in case they turned it on and accidentally ended up talking to a million listeners. Or in case they made the music stop. Or in case they made the whole thing blow up. Or because they were just fucking lazy. Whatever the reason, the upshot was that the place was unclean and slightly oppressive, in Rachel White's opinion.

The adverts ended, and silence crashed in. Rachel exhaled, loudly enough for the microphone to pick up the noise. *Loud enough for effect.* Her smoke rushed up and swirled and eddied into the air in front of her. The smoke became air, and the air became smoke. Bleeding. The heavy arm of the studio clock thudded forward, inevitably.

Six minutes and eight seconds to go.

Behind the triple-glazed window, Rachel's producer looked up from her papers. She had heard the presenter exhale at the end of the ad break, and on instinct she had looked into the spot lit studio and rolled her eyes. Rachel was smoking in the studio again. Fuck it.

It would be the producer who would get the call at home tomorrow, from the morning team, complaining about working in a room that smelled like an ashtray. The producer made a mental note to leave her phone on silent when she got home.

Rachel White had been hosting the late-night phone in for the last three years, and at the start it had been a struggle. It felt plastic. It felt like an act. During the day she had fun, met friends, worked out. At night she became aggressive, argumentative, edgy.

Eventually though, as sure as water cuts through rock, the nightly outpouring had worn her down. Rachel was lost in the part. Moody, unfair and unkind. Bleeding.

"David, Line Seven."

Husky.

The wind was blowing into the caller's face, making his eyes water and sting. Way below him, the bright the neon *Staples Center* sign glared up at him from the gray corrugated roof of one of L.A.'s most famous addresses. The playoff final had just finished, and jubilant Lakers fans were swarming around the circular building and out into Nokia Plaza and the surrounding streets. David Barr's military training had not let him down; he had chosen his moment carefully for maximum impact.

The second hand slammed forward again, but Rachel waited. She had instinct, and she sensed that this would be a good call. He was outside, which meant he'd called the show on a whim. Breathy, which meant he was emotional. Probably going to be a ratings winner.

Five minutes and fifty-eight seconds to go. Network news wouldn't wait.

"David? Hello?" she pressed. Tone was everything; different voices unlocked different situations. Rachel had perfected her armory. Harsh, playful, bored, disbelieving, caring, whimsical, enthralled, enraged, impressed, conspiratorial, furtive. Each emotion that her voice conveyed would unlock a reaction in her callers. They were here marionettes.

The producer's note on Rachel's MSN told her that David Barr was a US Army Captain, and she knew how to deal with military men. With the end of the show breathing down her neck, she needed to keep this caller on a tight leash. Controlled.

"David, talk to me."

Urgent. Instructive. She figured he'd be used to following orders.

There was a pause as Barr cleared his throat and prepared for the last phone call he would ever make.

"I'm on the fifty-second floor of the Marriot and I'm about to jump."

Fuck. Five minutes and thirty-seven seconds to go.

CHAPTER NINE

Fifty-Second Floor, Marriott Hotel, Los Angeles.
"And we choked on all our dreams, We wrestled with our fears
Running through the heartless concrete streets."
- Levellers, One Way

Five minutes and thirty-six seconds to go.

The smoke from Rachel White's cigarette still hung in the air but she was already stubbing out the butt and leaning forward towards the microphone. Focused. Why the hell had he decided to jump when she only had five minutes of the show left? Damn it.

If time ran out, she could offer to head out to the Marriot, to talk to him. It would be a great cliff hanger ending. She could use the old trick of making her producer host the last couple of minutes of the show as she herself began a mercy dash across town. She could broadcast from the back of a cab on a scratchy cell phone en route. She'd done it before.

Tune in tomorrow to find out if he jumped...

But even as the idea came into her head, she discounted it. The Lakers had just beaten the Celtics in game seven, and the whole place would be grid-locked for another two hours. Which made her think David Barr was probably an attention seeker, having chosen tonight of all nights to stand on a rooftop next to the Staples Center and call a radio station.

Actually, Barr wasn't standing on the rooftop. He was sitting. It had taken him some effort to get where he was, too. He had taken the lift to the top floor and then pulled himself out of his chair at the foot of the stairway that accessed the roof. The chair had toppled as he'd hauled himself out, and for a moment he thought he might wake up one of the penthouse guests, but nobody came.

His arms had grown stronger over the past year as he had wheeled himself through Santa Barbara each day, and now he used that strength to drag his body up to the top of the short flight of stairs and out into the cool night air. He had crawled across the rough bitumen flat roof which had cut into his hands, but he'd been careful not to rip his new suit. Then he had used all of his energy to pull himself onto the low wall, which guarded the edge of the building.

He used the last of his strength to drag his useless legs over the edge and then stopped to catch his breath. Gravity would do the rest.

The second hand on the studio clock slammed forward again.

Rachel White figured that the next five minutes would be great radio. Maybe she could talk him down; maybe she could keep him talking until the cops arrived. Either way, she was confident that the whole thing would eventually be an anti-climax. If you're determined to kill yourself, why would you bother to phone a radio station? It seems like overkill. In the last three years, four callers had phoned up threatening to jump. None of them had gone through with it.

She weighed up her options as shrewdly as she could.

"If you're really at the top of the Marriot, tell me what you can see."

David Barr looked down below him.

"What do you want me to tell you? I can see Boston fans weeping. I can see the top of the Staples Center with a massive neon sign on it. A Herbal Life sign. Who gets to read those signs?"

"People who are thinking about throwing themselves off buildings, maybe?" Rachel offered. She was walking a tightrope, she knew. Trying to engage him, connect with him. Trying to hint at compassion without selling out her audience. Without breaking out of her persona. Shackled.

"I'm not *thinking* about throwing myself off," Barr corrected her. "I am *going to* throw myself off. There's a car on fire down there, and people coming out of the Nokia theater, and I can see Lakers fans… Jesus, that's Jack Nicholson!"

"Really?"

"No. How the hell could I see that? I'm fifty-two stories up."

Rachel smiled, despite herself. She couldn't work this guy out. She figured that he had a sense of humor, and he sounded relaxed and confident. So why was she more worried about him than any of the others who had threatened to jump? There was no anger in his voice, no bitterness, no sorrow. He didn't sound desperate. Her heart sunk as she hit on it. He sounded *resigned* to it. Not good. Not good at all.

Four minutes and forty seconds to go.

Rachel reached for her mouse and dragged the news jingle into a play-out window on her computer. Then she dragged in a Pearl Jam track, just in case this thing finished early. Abruptly. Violently.

I'm Still Alive.

Ironic.

"OK, smartass," she smiled, "I believe you, and you're playing around up there on the roof. So, what's the deal?"

David Barr thought about how to answer. This moment would be his eulogy, and he had prepared well for it. Earlier in the day, he had poked his finger through the small tear in the seat of his wheelchair and fished around inside it. His fingers grappled with the edge of his plastic card and then pulled it out into the daylight.

He was a disciplined man, and he hadn't touched the visa card since before Kandahar. It had molded itself to the contours of his buttock over the months, and David Barr laughed to himself thinking he might have created a new form of biometric identification. He wanted to laugh. His heart felt light. He had been playing a losing hand for a full year, and now he felt a strange relief course through him as the end game approached. He had submitted to his least worst fate.

Tyler and his boss, a gnarled old war dog called General Lang, were well connected. They would watch his bank account for sure. It's possible that after a few months they had realized he would not pop up on the radar. They might even have wondered whether he had the money at all. But with three hundred million dollars missing from the US treasury, someone would still keep an eye out for David Barr.

He had withdrawn cash at an ATM in the departure lounge of the Tom Bradley terminal at LAX. At least they might waste a few minutes trying to work out if he got on a plane. He had chosen a machine that didn't appear to be overlooked by CCTV and taken five hundred dollars out of his account. As he had typed in his pin number, he felt sure he had just alerted someone to the fact that he was still alive, and that he was in Los Angeles. It wouldn't take them long to find him.

He pulled his cap a little lower over his brow and checked the balance which had grown to over $110,000 as his various pensions and allowances has dripped into the account untouched over the last thirteen months. He withdrew another five hundred, just because he could.

After stuffing the cash in his pocket, he had wheeled back through the terminal feeling more acutely than ever that he was on borrowed time. Outside the airport, he picked up the Green Line bus to Union Station. The bus driver helped him through the indignity of boarding public transport, kneeling his vehicle and then helping the veteran to truss his chair safely to the inside wall of the transport.

Barr was grateful that the driver didn't fuss. He was too busy being embroiled in a good-natured argument with a vivacious woman on a seat further back.

"Now you jus' listen to me, sugar pie," she hollered at the driver as he went about his work. She had a melodic voice that rang out theatrically. She would have made Aretha Franklin jealous. She didn't care who was listening. She was playing up.

"I think there's something wrong with your head if you think the Lakers are gonna win tonight!" she shouted down the isle, goading the driver as though he were her big brother.

"Nyesha, that's the dumbest thing I ever heard" he shouted back over his shoulder, all smiles as his hand held tight to the wheel. The bus rattled and juddered as they journeyed along the elevated airport ring road. "You keep saying things like that, and I will put you right off this bus!"

"Who's this Kobe Bryant anyhow?" she roared back at him. She looked around the bus at her fellow passengers who had been listening to the debate for a few stops. She was no shrinking violet, but she was infectious. Most of the passengers were quietly encouraging her.

"Woman, I'll put you off this bus, and you'll have to walk home!"

"Ko-bee Bryant!" she emphasized. "The man's got plasters all over his fingers, he looks like Michael Jackson!"

People around her laughed.

The bus driver eyed her up in his mirror. He shook his head. She was loud, argumentative, opinionated, distracting; and he hated the days when Nyesha didn't get on his bus. Sometimes he'd take a bit of extra time loading his passengers' heavy suitcases, if he knew she was about to clock off. He didn't know where she lived or what she did once she got off his bus. He didn't know much about her at all, if he stopped to think about it.

"Hey you!" she called, her throaty voice slicing effortlessly through the noise of the bus. "Hey, army man!"

David Barr was warming to her. Maybe it was because he had a thousand dollars in his pocket, or maybe it was because he knew that he'd set his end game in motion and that time was limited and precious, but he thought her voice sounded like birdsong. Usually, he'd spit an insult back at anyone who shouted 'hey you' at him, but not today. Not on this bus.

He turned his head and gave her his full attention, fixing his cornflower eyes on her.

"You're a Boston fan with me, right?" she implored. He was getting dragged into the game, but he didn't mind. His blue eyes twinkled back at her. Nyesha thought he could have been handsome, if he'd cut his hair.

"Ma'am, I'm a long way from home but I will support the Lakers all the way just to see how mad you get!"

She shrieked.

"Everyone I meet today is a damn fool," she called, emphasizing the word 'fool' as she looked into the driver's mirror, laughing. She started to gather up her belongings.

"Nyesha, you've gone too far now with this Celtics nonsense. I'm putting you off this bus at the very next stop; I don't mind *how* far you've got to walk!"

The driver brought the bus to a stop. The hydraulics hissed, and the doors opened as Nyesha navigated her wide hips like a metronome between the rows of seats towards the front.

They both knew that this was Nyesha's stop. David Barr had the feeling that she got 'thrown off' the bus on a fairly regular basis. She ruffled the driver's hair on the way past him and called her goodbyes over her shoulder to nobody in particular.

"See you tomorrow, Mr. Lincoln," she said as she breezed past the man at the wheel, all charm and lashes and perfume.

The rest of the journey had passed with little excitement; Barr had transferred between the bus and the subway with minimum fuss, passing through the airy East portal of Union Station under the watchful gaze of the ten colorful Angelinos in the gigantic City of Dreams mural.

A red line and a cab journey later, he was outside Prada on Rodeo Drive. Captain Barr had worn the same clothes for most of the last three hundred and eighty days. It was the price he had paid for anonymity. For safety. But now that someone knew where he was there was no need to pretend. No need to hide. It would all be over soon enough now, and he might as well look good when the end came.

So, he wheeled himself towards the door, with his year-old clothes, his long hair, the bad smell and his creaking wheelchair. The security guard was hesitant. There was no way that a man who looked as bad as David Barr should be coming into the store, and yet he didn't want to be the bad guy manhandling a crippled war veteran in the street. Barr decided for him. As the guard went to open his mouth, Barr reached out to him and handed him a fifty-dollar bill.

While the guard tried to work out why he'd just been given the best tip of the month by someone who looked like he hadn't bathed for a year, Barr wheeled past him and into the store, the chair creaking and straining over the threshold of the doorway.

Inside, he thought it best to take control of the situation. His combat training had taught him it was prudent to tackle the biggest and strongest first, so he approached the most experienced (and most horrified) looking assistant, wheeling his chair between her and any obvious means of escape.

"I need a suit, what can you do?"

The woman looked him up and down, her gaze settling on the fleshy end of his thigh sticking out of his trouser leg, and the gap below it where most people would expect to find their lower leg. Everything that ought to be below David Barr's left knee was buried in a cardboard box in a desert somewhere outside Basra.

She pointed timidly at his leg, and at his wheelchair. "Will you need…" she looked perplexed, "pants?"

"Of course I'll need pants, for Christ's sake!" he barked. "And stop looking at me like I'm Julia fucking Roberts."

After that, the woman was relatively helpful and together they found a sharp suit in next to no time. He got the feeling that she was keen to conclude their business as quickly as possible, and he couldn't blame her. As he sat in the middle of the perfumed boutique, he glimpsed himself in one of the many mirrors, and he realized how far he had sunk. The price he had paid just to stay alive. To stay hidden.

"Are we taking the suit home, or wearing it?" she asked, in the airiest tone she could muster.

David Barr was direct. "Ma'am, let's be honest. We both know that I smell of sweat and piss, and I'd prefer not to transfer that smell to my new suit. Perhaps you could double-bag it for me?"

The suit cost considerably more than a thousand dollars, so he was forced to pay by card. It wouldn't matter now. All six sales assistants clustered around the visa card reader, and none of them disguised their shock when the sale went through without a problem. They thanked him, and he wheeled his way out of the shop. He hadn't reached the door before he could hear air freshener cans behind him.

The security guard was quick to hail a cab for him; partly because a man who looked like David Barr wasn't good for business, and partly because he was keen to earn the fifty-dollar tip he'd picked up from a guy would didn't look like he had fifty dollars to his name. *Guilt is a great motivator*, thought Barr.

The cab took him to the Marriot after a short stop at an electrical store where he grabbed a pre-paid mobile phone. He knew he wouldn't find a salon keen to tackle his tangled hair, so he bought a pair of clippers and did the job himself once he got to his hotel room.

He shaved and scrubbed. As the stubble and the grime came off, his cheeks looked hollow after his time on the streets, but he didn't look so bad. The cleaner lines on his face framed his cornflower eyes much better, and when he shaved off thirteen months of matted hair from his scalp, he became the man he remembered. He looked in the mirror at an old friend. Out of hiding, for one night only.

And now, up on the Marriot roof, the night was nearly over. It was time to pay the price.

Four minutes eighteen seconds to go.

The woman on the end of the phone was waiting for an answer. She obviously had listeners in Los Angeles because a crowd had gathered below him, with some people pointing up towards him. The plaza below was filling up with cop cars too.

"So, the deal is that I'm in trouble, Rachel."

"Well, if you weren't before, you are now," she chuckled, trying to break the mood. Trying to connect. "But, hey. Everyone's in trouble sometime or other."

"The thing is, I screwed up. I made a mistake in Afghanistan, and now someone wants me dead."

"A lot of people screw up, especially during a war," said Rachel, as she considered all the possibilities. "It doesn't mean they can't get a second chance."

Time was slowing down, or maybe her thoughts were speeding up. It amounted to the same thing. She wondered whether he was suffering from some form of paranoia, maybe bought on by post-traumatic stress. That wouldn't be good.

"But you know, trouble comes and goes. Maybe you can ride this thing out?"

She was reaching.

"Not really," said the guy at the end of the phone. "I lost some money for a bunch of pretty serious guys."

"David, how can this be making sense to you? How can it be worth killing yourself for cash? I mean, how much are we talking about?"

Rachel had an iPhone full of experts, including plenty of financial advisors. This could be a quick fix before the news after all. But she needed him to give her a steer.

"Did you lose some money to these guys in a poker game or something? How much are we talking about? A grand? Two?" she pushed for an answer. Time was tight.

He took a deep breath and used his arms to shuffle himself further over the edge of the building.

"Three hundred million US dollars, give or take."

Three hundred million?

Rachel White looked at the clock and recalculated her strategy, allowing for the fact that David Barr was evidently insane. *Three minutes forty-five seconds to go.*

CHAPTER TEN

Ground Floor Lobby, Marriot Hotel, Los Angeles.
"Sweet dreams are made of this, Who am I to disagree?
I've traveled the world and the seven seas.
Everybody's looking for Something."
- Eurythmics, Sweet Dreams.

The man in the black jacket crossed the hotel lobby as quickly as he could without running. Even so, he was conspicuous. Over seven feet tall, broad and muscular, he had a square jaw and a foreboding presence. He didn't look entirely comfortable in civilian company.

He went straight for the elevator, which he had to stoop to enter. He was no Samaritan, but he had a life to save. There were things which David Barr needed to tell him before he could be allowed to kill himself. They had waited thirteen months to find him, and now Tyler needed to get to the roof, quickly.

CHAPTER ELEVEN

KLA AM NewsTalk Studios, Downtown Los Angeles. December 2010.
"The Lights are getting dim; will I pay for who I've been?"
- Tori Amos, Happy Phantom

Rachel had decided to ride the call out until the news, and then record the rest of it after the show. Her producer was already setting another studio up for recording so they could hit the news on time and then continue the conversation ready to play out at the start of tomorrow's show. Good plan.

"David, how can anyone owe three hundred million dollars?"

He exhaled without answering. He couldn't answer that question without doing serious damage to the reputation of the army and to his country. Corrupt officials, stolen cash and friendly fire? The press would have a field day. And nobody would believe him.

"Do you have a family?" asked the woman at the end of his mobile phone.

From the inside pocket of his new jacket, Barr pulled the photograph of the auburn-haired woman and the girl in the green dress. He traced the contours of their faces with the tip of his finger back with them for a minute. A last minute.

Two minutes, fifty-nine seconds to go.

Before he could answer the question, he saw something moving on the opposite side of the roof. As he turned, a tall guy in a black coat came fast through the shadows towards him. Tyler. His weapon was already trained on him, his hand steady and his eyes cold.

Barr knew that Tyler worked on impulse and that he wasn't always smart. Barr's trained eye could make out the weapon in Tyler's hand and saw that the safety was off. Tyler hadn't come to talk. He'd been hunting Barr for one reason: to convince him to give up the money which he didn't have. Convince him any way he could. But he was too late.

Barr had made his decision thirteen months ago. Nothing was more important than the two women in the photograph in his right hand. He had spent thirteen months alone, wondering how his daughter had grown, thirteen months wondering whether his wife had given up on him. Thirteen months staying away, to keep Tyler away. And now it would end, and they would be safe. They would be safe soon, because the huge man was only ten paces away.

Ninety seconds to go.

The studio was tense now. Rachel didn't feel like she had the call under control. By now she should have nailed him, but he didn't fit the model. Suddenly she knew that this guy might actually do it, and about four hundred thousand listeners would hear him do it. And blame her. *Focus, for Christ's sake.*

"David, why did you call me, if you've already decided to jump?"

Barr felt sorry for her. Who knows what happens to a radio host who lets someone die on their show? Probably good for publicity. Probably bad for the soul.

"Ma'am, I'm afraid there's not enough time to explain."

He started to shift his weight further over the edge of the building. The pain from the bitumen cuts in his palm kept him focused, and a rush of night air blew around his neck, which felt super-sensitive since he had buzz-cut his hair. It was a long way down, and his body was exhibiting all the signs of fear, his pupils were wide, his hearing acute, his heart rate was up and his breathing was fast. But David Barr was a soldier, and he knew how to operate under pressure.

The woman on the other end of the phone was reasoning with him, but the time for talking had passed. Tyler's arrival was a comfort to Barr, because Barr knew he would witness his final moment and no doubt report back to General Lang. He had no more energy for running. No more energy for hiding. If Tyler hadn't shown up to see him die, Barr was certain he would have heard it on the radio or seen it on the TV news. It's not every day a guy kills himself live on air. Barr had the whole thing locked down because he'd only get to do this once. If his family were going to live, Tyler had to see him die.

Tyler was closing in, breaking into a run. The moment had come. As the soldier leaned forward, he took one last deep breath of Californian air and pushed against the ledge with his right hand. He fell from the building and into the night.

CHAPTER TWELVE

Birmingham, England. January 2010.
"I've been watching your world from afar,
I've been trying to be where you are.
And I've been secretly falling apart, unseen."
– Aqualung, Strange and Beautiful.

Daud had spent the morning studying. These days he was spending more and more time on his own, partly because his brother was on the other side of the world and partly because he was sick of talking to other people about him.

"Any word from Ajmal?" people would ask. Daud knew that they were just fishing for gossip. His blood would boil at their soft words and their kind eyes and their vicious hearts.

In his darkest moments, Daud wished Ajmal was dead. Then he'd have a body to mourn. Then he would know his brother was at peace. After all, they couldn't hurt him once he was dead. And the questions and the gossip could die with him, too.

But in his heart, Daud didn't really want his brother to be dead. What he really wanted was to bring him home, nurse him better, calm his soul, and then find out what he had been doing in Afghanistan. The boy he grew up with, the boy he knew better than anyone else. The man he didn't know at all, apparently.

Since the day he was born, it had been in the stars that Daud would be a pillar of his community. He was the oldest son of an oldest son. Someone to look up to, a role model. He should have been a role model to his younger brother, Ajmal. But now Ajmal was beyond his reach. Beyond anyone's help. More and more, Daud's soul felt angry and his heart felt clouded.

This must be how it goes *thought Daud*. The heart searches for healing, but when the world grows cruel, it settles for revenge instead.

It was Friday and Daud was standing at the entrance to the mosque with a bucket in his hand, collecting money from the people as they streamed out after prayers. He was collecting for poor families in Pakistan who had recently been devastated by flooding and disease. When he wasn't at work, Daud had busied himself by collecting money for good causes and organizing aid trucks for his appeal. It was good to be busy. Good to be helpful.

Since the news about Ajmal though, he noticed people had found it harder to meet his eye, and that after prayers several people found it easier to talk to his bucket than to him. Pretty much everyone asked the bucket how the aid effort was going; several asked the bucket whether there was any news about Ajmal. Nobody asked Daud about himself or the rest of his family. They didn't even ask the bucket about that. Vicious hearts.

So Daud kept his eyes to the ground and his thoughts to himself and as he shook his bucket, his heart began to dwell on revenge.

CHAPTER THIRTEEN

Fifty Second Floor, Marriot Hotel, Los Angeles.
"Is something wrong?" she said. Well of course there is. "You're still alive," she said. Oh, and do I deserve to be? – Pearl Jam, Alive.

Things hadn't gone to plan for David Barr. He hadn't accounted for the blood which had been spilling from the bitumen cuts in his right hand. It had slowly congealed into an oily mess on the wall next to him as he had been talking to the radio host. As he had made his final push off the wall, his palm had slipped in the blood and for a second he had lost momentum. It had been enough time for Tyler to reach him.

Barr's neck had jolted backwards as he stopped mid-air. Tyler's huge hand had clamped down on his forearm. Mentally, Barr counted the five seconds it should have taken him to die. But he was still alive, caught in Tyler's grip, only half a floor nearer to his destiny.

Tyler looked down at him, checking that he'd got the right person. Just in case there was another one-legged man trying to jump off the other side of the same roof. Tyler's hand was rough and dry, and his grip dug into Barr's arm. Barr felt his skin stretching, complaining, and the rest of his body trying to break away from the snare.

Between them, the men had two free hands. Barr was using his left hand to grip his mobile phone. He could hear Rachel White's tinny voice calling his name from the earpiece. Tyler was still holding his Beretta M9 in his right hand.

As Barr watched, Tyler put down the gun and pulled him higher, back up towards the ledge. He might not have been the smartest guy, but he had impressive strength. He used his free hand to grapple with the buckle on

Barr's watch. Barr did not understand what the man was doing until he pulled the watch up over his hand, threw it across the roof, and began examining Barr's wrist intently.

Fifty-three seconds to go.

Then Barr understood. The man clutching his forearm was looking for a tattoo, because he was looking for Fearless. And as he hung in the air, Barr realized that Tyler thought he was Fearless. But Fearless was a ghost; he had arrived in Kandahar with no paperwork, no story, and no real name. Then he had disappeared in a puff of black smoke, presumed dead, along with three hundred million dollars. An idea started to form in David Barr's head. A glimpse of survival. Not for himself, but for his family.

When Tyler saw the bare skin on Barr's wrist he grabbed at the dog tags around his neck, checked the name, and let go. For a brief second, Barr's eyes were level with the small ledge that he had been sitting on a moment ago, and he stole one last glance at the blood-smeared photograph of his wife and daughter.

As Barr felt the metal chain of his dog tags snap behind his neck, gravity did its worst. He plunged downwards and his stomach slammed into his chest, but he used all of his strength to pull his mobile phone to his mouth.

In the studio, Rachel White had been listening to the sounds of scrabbling and scuffling and was hopeful that the LAPD had arrived on the scene and grabbed the guy before he could jump. But now suddenly, the sounds at the end of the phone had changed. Wind was whistling into the mouthpiece and she had a dreadful feeling in the pit of her stomach. Then clearly she and her audience had heard him speak. He wasn't shouting exactly, but it was horribly clear that he was calling out as he fell.

"Charlie Lockhart is Fearless!"

Barr started to repeat his message, just to be sure, but halfway through the sentence there was a sick, heavy thud and the line cut dead. The mobile phone hadn't survived the fall any more than David Barr had. High above, Tyler was already moving off the roof. Barr didn't have the tattoo. But Tyler had a new target.

Eleven seconds to go.

The volume monitors in front of Rachel White fell to zero and the shock of what had just happened hung in the air in the studio. There was silence, and she had no desire to break it. She felt heavy; Every tiny movement was an effort. She half-heartedly pushed the news fader up and waited for the bulletin to save her.

Across town, a huddle of basketball fans and cops had formed at the foot of the hotel. In the middle, broken on the paving slabs, darkening blood was already finding its way through the torn lining of Barr's new Prada suit. The heavy second hand in the studio slammed into the top of the hour. Inevitably.

And Captain David Barr was dead.

CHAPTER FOURTEEN

Main Gate, Kandahar Airfield. NOVEMBER, 2009.
"What the hell am I doing here? I don't belong here."
– Radiohead, Creep.

Kandahar Air Field centered around a weird cream-colored terminal that dated back to the nineteen sixties. Back then it might have looked space-age, but by the time the ISAF forces took control of it, it looked strikingly bizarre, with its round domes and curved stilts that stuck out like the legs of a giant sun-bleached spider. As the war raged around it, it retained its ornate green plastic sign, which read: "Welcome to Kandahar Airport."

There was a large square building to one side of the space age spider, which once served as a passenger terminal. On the airfield, people referred to the place as TLS, the Taliban's Last Stand. Some archways around the sides of the building showed signs of damage, and there were bullet holes in the cream facade.

Now it was the nerve center for the ISAF military base, and hundreds of thick black communication wires and power lines emanated from it, so that the giant bleached spider looked like it was sat in the middle of a giant black web. Brown humvees buzzed around it like flies, kicking up dust as twenty thousand Western personnel went about their business.

It was late afternoon when the convoy from Quetta reached Kandahar. The worst of the midday sun was gone, which was good because Lockhart figured he'd be sitting in the cab with his engine off soon, and that would mean no air conditioning. But there was still plenty of time to go through the laborious task of getting through the main gate before darkness fell.

The trucks in front of Lockhart had stopped. Slowly, they were making their way through the security systems at the front gates. The ISAF forces called it *the sink*. The waiting place where explosives or contraband could sink through their hiding place and be sniffed out by the dogs.

At the front of the queue, the trucks panned out into six lanes, each one separated by a three-meter blast wall made of sand and sack cloth and metal mesh. Until a truck was passed as safe by the guards, it would stay quarantined between the thick sand dividers.

The guards, mostly soldiers from the Afghan National Army, would check the cargo, the cabs, and the chassis of the vehicles. Sometimes, they would 'sweat' the drivers, taking them off to one side for an hour or more, just to see how they reacted. Then they would send in the dogs, after any explosive or contraband had had a chance to seep through its hiding place.

The result was a long queue and slow progress. Security on the base was paramount, and there was no fast-tracking. No nodding and winking. Everyone got stopped, and everyone got checked.

*

Just after six pm, Lockhart drove through the outer gate and into the US control of Kandahar Air Field. He didn't know much about the place, except for Ajmal's description; there were twenty thousand ISAF troops here, hundreds of aircraft, robust security, and a chance to buy Western food.

The camp blended into its environment; the blast walls were made of sand and matched the dusty ground. The gray concrete walls were of the same hue as the natural terrain, and most of the military vehicles were colored to blend in, as were their drivers' uniforms.

The whole place looked temporary, but impressive. A testament to man's ability to take a strip of desert where the temperatures reached forty degrees in the shade, and turn it into a hospitable place within a matter of weeks. Nothing was dug in, nothing felt rooted. Lockhart imagined that the place could be gone almost as quickly as it had arrived should there be an appetite to leave. Bits would be packed up on low-loaders and moved on to the world's next conquest. What was left could blow away on the wind and return to the dust.

Lockhart hit the front of the queue and watched carefully to see what the guards would ask him to do. An Afghan in a dark green uniform, a makeshift dust mask, and Ray-Bans indicated that he should drive into one of the bomb-proof bays. He pointed the way with his AK-47. Lockhart guessed that the ANA soldier had been working in the sun all day, because he didn't look as alert as he should.

Even behind his Ray-Bans, Lockhart could see that the soldier wasn't giving him proper eye contact, not evaluating him properly. He clunked the truck into first gear and began to move slowly forward.

The system reminded him of the "nothing to declare" lane at a seaport customs check. Everyone would be scrutinized enough to make the most virtuous souls feel guilty. Even so, he was looking forward to the process for two reasons. First, it would be in stark contrast to the last few hours of queuing, and secondly because it would be the last stage before he could get out, stretch his legs, and find out what Kandahar Airfield offered.

Lockhart rounded the tight bend and entered a wide sandy courtyard, overlooked by two guard towers and policed on the ground by about 40 ANA personnel. Suddenly, the guard was not waving his AK-47 but pointing it straight at his cab. Pointing and shouting. Lockhart wanted to comply with his instructions, but it was impossible to understand what the man was saying.

He thought about what Ajmal had told him to do at checkpoints; go slowly, take your time, dip your headlights, keep your hands in view. He did these things, but the soldier still yelled. Others began to take an interest in his truck. The Afghan soldier was shouting instructions to him, but he didn't understand. He came to a dead stop.

All the soldiers hit the floor. With several soldiers now pointing their weapons at him, including the teams in the guard tower, Lockhart put his hands in the air. As he did so, the soldier who had originally ushered him into the courtyard beckoned him out of his cab.

When lots of people are pointing guns at you, the sensible thing is to do everything slowly and deliberately. Lockhart knew that. He leaned out of his window and opened the cab door from the outside rather than risk getting shot by a twitchy Afghan soldier as he fumbled by his side for the door handle. The handle clunked, and the door swung open. Carefully, he placed his boot onto the footplate and eased himself out of the truck.

The guard had retreated somewhat and was poking his head round the end of the nearest blast wall, frantically beckoning Lockhart towards him. Lockhart was happy to move away from the truck and out of the sightline of at least some of the soldiers.

As he reached the blast wall, three Afghan soldiers grabbed him and pinned him to the ground. They looked nervous. A higher-ranking US soldier had joined them from a nearby building and was speaking directly to him as the others searched him roughly, jostling him about in an undignified manner. He acquiesced. Not that he really had a choice.

The three Afghans were angry. They were pointing at the truck and demanding some sort of answer, from what Lockhart could gather.

When he turned and looked at the truck, he understood at once what had happened. His lucky escape during the ambush at Mandi Sar had been luckier than he knew. The RPG, which had mysteriously clunked against the side of his truck, had just reappeared. It was stuck in the side of the truck that Lockhart had been driving for the last sixty miles.

The US soldier who had joined them had the two stripes of a captain showing on his uniform. He was in his late twenties and had a capable air about him. Like every other soldier in the front gate holding area, the captain wore a sandy-colored flak jacket and helmet and dark glasses which protected his eyes from the sun and the constant dust. They also offered him a sense of reassurance in combat situations and a sense of detachment when he was interrogating suspicious drivers.

The soldier saw the man in front of him as something of an enigma. He was too white to be an Afghan, too well nourished to be a vagrant, and his hair was too long for him to be a soldier. In fact, his hair was too long, period.

"Do you speak English?" he asked. His tone was neither aggressive nor friendly.

"I *am* English," replied Lockhart, picking himself up and dusting off the motorbike salesman's baseball cap which had fallen off during his brief tussle. "Welcome to Kandahar, eh?"

"The trouble is that you seem to have driven into the holding area with an RPG attached to your vehicle," explained the captain in unequivocally simple terms.

"Yes, but these guys have proven beyond doubt that I don't have another one strapped to my body so maybe you could assume that I didn't put it there deliberately?"

The stranger was assertive, but not aggressive, the soldier noted. He also made a fair point. He was pretty composed for someone who had just been taken from his cab at gunpoint and rolled about in the dust by three guards.

"What's your story?" the captain asked. His keen eye noticed that the driver's cap had the faintest outline of the letters N Y C on the front. The fabric was darker where the sewn-on letters had prevented it bleaching in the sun. Maybe the man understood local sentiment towards the US and had removed the letters for his own safety. In which case, he wasn't dealing with a complete idiot, at least.

"We were ambushed at Marni Sar," replied Lockhart.

From behind the blast wall, he could see several soldiers walking past in a hurry, sweating with sandbags, securing the side of the truck that was carrying the unexploded RPG. Others were instructing the nearest trucks to reverse back out of the holding area. The routine was well rehearsed.

"I'll need some details," said the captain. "Follow me, but stay low. The grenade on the side of your truck has a kill distance of about ten meters."

Lockhart was not a soldier, didn't follow orders, and had never been fond of people who told him what to do. Having just been rolled ignominiously through the dust, he planned to walk away from the scene with as much dignity as he could.

He drew himself up to his full height. The soldier didn't look like he gave a shit either way.

"Just so you know," he said, "the *kill radius* is ten meters, but if that grenade goes off I'd say you're still in the 'fuck you up pretty badly zone' at the moment."

Then he moved on at quite a pace, probably compensating for his limp. Making a point. They navigated through a maze of blast walls until they arrived at the front gate complex; a series of prefabricated buildings incorporating a small canteen, an armory and a central briefing room. As they pushed through the side door into the air conditioning the temperature dropped by about twenty degrees, and it took a moment for their eyes to re-adjust to the shade.

Lockhart followed the soldier through the main briefing room and both men removed their shades so that they could better navigate the various desks. Maps on the wall showed the complex layout of the front gate and the holding areas, the sink and the rejection lane.

A cabinet on the wall contained about two hundred mobile phones which had been confiscated from local drivers on their way into the Airfield. They had been tagged and stored ready for collection by the drivers when they left the camp.

The office was almost empty - half finished cardboard cups of coffee sat cooling on the desks. Everyone was outside, dealing with the grenade that the fearless Westerner had inadvertently bought into their midst. The captain swept through the office, slaloming the desks deftly despite his limp. Through another set of doors, they headed into a smaller interrogation room, and beyond that into his own private office.

Inside there was a simple desk and a plastic chair. On the walls were more plans of the main gate and another map that marked the main layout of the Airfield. A window looked into a small courtyard on the opposite side of the building from the holding area. There was an air conditioning unit behind the desk, and a rack of walkie talkies were charging in a large black plastic wall unit. There was a framed picture on the desk, a girl wearing a green dress and a woman with auburn hair gazing out at them.

Next to the desk was a recycling tub, three quarters full with blue water bottle lids. There were similar bins all over the camp. The soldiers were getting through more than a hundred million dollars' worth of bottled water each year, and Lockhart wondered what happened to all the little blue caps that were collected up. *War is an industry* he thought.

The soldier indicated that the driver should take a chair in front of the desk. Time to talk. Lockhart sat down and the solider did the same. Then he gave a loud sigh, pulled off his leg, and placed it on the desk in front of him with a thud.

He rubbed the sore flesh below his knee and ran his hands through his closely cropped hair. He leaned back on his plastic chair as his cornflower blue eyes studied his enigmatic guest.

"Sir, my name is David Barr and I am a Captain with the US Army. Welcome to Kandahar Airfield."

CHAPTER FIFTEEN

Main Gate, Kandahar Air Field.
"Deputy Sheriff said to me Tell me what you come here for, boy.
You better get your bags and flee.
You're in trouble boy, And now you're heading into more."
– Simon and Garfunkel, Keep the Customer Satisfied

As they sat in the clean office at the front of the airfield, Captain Barr considered the man in front of him. His picture matched his passport, but it was hard to believe that he was a tourist who was in the wrong place at the wrong time.

All sorts of strange people turned up at the front gate of the military base. Local villagers would arrive with the sick and wounded regularly. When possible, the military hospital would treat them, but this year the trauma bays had seemed to be almost constantly filled.

Sometimes the gate turned up someone unusual, but never tourists. Barr had been on duty for one such arrival last year. A crazy English guy had arrived at the gate announcing that he wanted to join the SAS. He thought if he walked through Afghanistan, it would prove that he was tough enough to join up. He was beyond dumb. When he arrived, he was badly burned and dehydrated. Barr had instructed the Afghan authorities to detain him on mental health grounds and then deport him back to Europe.

However, the guy in front of Barr seemed much more sensible. Likeable even. They had been talking for about an hour while Barr decided what to do with him. The man seemed keen to learn about the history of Afghanistan, explaining that he was a tourist and that he hadn't originally planned to come into the country.

No shit, thought Barr.

Barr told him about the Americans and the British, and the Russians, and the Pakistanis and the Chinese and the CIA and the Mujahidin. The tourist had seemed interested and intelligent. Barr figured that the guy was brave too, judging by the way he had conducted himself at the gate. Weighed against all of that, he was unregistered and anonymous. Potentially, the stranger could prove a very useful combination.

Barr was the gatekeeper to the Camp, which was an important job. He took his responsibility of keeping the camp safe seriously, but he was also running a few deals on the side. In the right circles, he was known as the camp's fixer. If you needed something that you couldn't get through the stores, Barr could usually find it. What's more, he had the ability to smuggle it through the camp's security.

Barr did well out of the illegal side lines, earning a bit of pin money here and there. The camp was officially dry, but Barr made sure there was enough alcohol seeping in to keep people sane. The extra cash meant more generous gifts for his wife and daughter when he got home. But now he had been tasked with something huge; Something bigger than he wanted to get involved with. Smuggling into the camp had become routine, but a couple of men had approached him about transporting some cargo out of the camp up to Herat, in the North.

They were serious guys. One was an Air Force one-star General. His name was Ben Lang. The other a muscular Warrant Officer who didn't do much of the talking. They were careful not to mention what the cargo was, and Barr was smart enough not to ask. They had offered him a hundred thousand dollars to drive the shipment out of the camp and up to a contact at Herat. From there, it would be helicoptered out of the theater of war. That, he was told, was all he needed to know.

The money sounded good, besides which these guys weren't the kind of people he could say no to. But trying to navigate to Herat in the dark through Afghanistan was suicide. Even if he made it, the odds of him getting back without being spotted were almost zero. Which meant that the man in front of him could be useful. Very useful, in fact.

"So, Charlie Lockhart," said Barr, looking up from Lockhart's passport. "You're brave or you're stupid. Which is it?"

"Who knows?" Lockhart shrugged. He wasn't sure himself. "Some of the drivers called me Fearless, but I felt pretty scared during the grenade attack."

"That name will stick," said Barr, evaluating Lockhart. "You drive into Afghanistan for fun, get hit by a grenade, rolled over by the ANA in the sink, and then you just stroll along with me and drink my coffee without your hands even shaking."

Lockhart didn't answer. He wasn't sure whether it was a compliment or an accusation. It was true that his hand was steady.

"I think the name suits you," continued Barr. "Fearless."

A compliment then.

Barr explained to Lockhart that as he was not military personnel he had no right to stay on the Airfield, but offered to find him a room for a few nights while he worked out his next move. Lockhart didn't have a better offer, and he thanked the captain for his help.

So Barr processed Lockhart's paperwork and then filed it away in a draw in his office. Then he handed him an ISAF badge on a lanyard.

"Stick this round your neck," he said. "It's a standard contractor's ID and will let you stroll around the non-restricted parts of the camp. Stay away from the flight-line though. Nobody likes civilians staring at their aircraft."

Barr told him to report back in a few hours to find out where he was sleeping, and that he could swipe the card in the dining facilities to get fed.

"I'll pick up the tab," he added congenially. "You can leave your bag here while you grab some food."

Lockhart felt like the comment about his bag was more of an instruction than a request. Barr was a gentleman, and after an hour of conversation and coffee, it felt rude to rummage through the guy's bag. But rules were rules, and it needed to be done. Barr had one last instruction for Lockhart as he headed off to dinner.

"Hey Charlie," he called after him. "I'm the only person who knows that name, and it would be better for all of us if it stayed that way, ok? Keep your passport to yourself and I'll smooth everything else out."

Lockhart looked down at his ISAF badge and laughed at the name Barr had written on the front:

Fearless.

CHAPTER SIXTEEN

Custom hotel, LAX. December, 2010.
"Now the ground shifts beneath my feet
The faces that I greet never know my name."
- Badly Drawn Boy, Pissing in the Wind

The lobby of the Custom Hotel was unusual, with a flock of full-sized stuffed sheep grazing in one corner, and a hanging cage of stuffed birds singing in the other.

The girl on the front desk had long blond hair and pale skin and wore an elegant dark suit which emphasized her slight figure. She had the ability to look busy while still being approachable, and she kept a careful eye on the comings and goings of the hotel.

She was polite to the guests, but to keep herself amused she would imagine what they did for a living. Sometimes it was easy. At the moment she was certain that she had three sets of air crews staying and a group of Mexican baggage handlers. There were also a group of open-source software geeks who were easy to spot.

Usually the receptionist was discreet, but as the man in the black jacket swept past her, she couldn't help but stare. His stride was purposeful, but it was the sheer size of him that was entrancing. He was well over seven feet tall and looked athletic. He had arrived two nights ago with no luggage, but his clothes looked immaculate. His hair was cropped short, and he was freshly shaven. The receptionist assumed he was a seasoned hotel bum who found it easy to travel light. According to his passport, his name was Jason Tyler. The document told her he was French, but his accent told her different.

There was something about his manner she found unnerving. He didn't acknowledge other guests, and he never stopped to take in the view. He had walked through the lobby four times while she had been on the desk, and he hadn't caught her eye once. It was midnight, and she had noticed him arrive in a taxi about ten minutes earlier. He was heading for the poolside bar. He was in luck, thought the receptionist. The bar was staying open late because the large TV had been showing the Lakers match all night. They had just won the play-off final and there was a party atmosphere by the pool.

The underwater lighting was throwing up subtle undulating shadows; its shimmering blues and greens were in sharp contrast to the warm orange tones of the mood lighting at the tables surrounding the water. The television was still showing highlights of the game, and the scrolling headlines were reporting a suicide near the Staples Center.

The bar was well stocked, and the staff were smart. Tyler ordered bourbon over ice, which they served quickly and with a smile. The girl who fixed his drink was pretty, and he considered sitting at the bar for a while, but it had been a long day and instead he moved to a sofa in the shadows. There were questions that he would have liked to have asked David Barr before he fell from the roof, but at least it was done. Easier all round for everyone.

Tyler was sure now that Barr hadn't stolen the money, but there was no question he had been part of the fuck-up. So there had to be some retribution. Rules are rules. The US Army might have been relaxed about three hundred million dollars disappearing, but his boss wasn't.

Tyler had expected Barr to be a dead end. He had made no contact with his family since he returned from Afghanistan. Hadn't contacted anyone else either. The trail had run cold, and killing him had only been a matter of tidying up.

But just as the end had come, everything had changed. According to Tyler's boss, Barr should have had a tattoo. All of their information said that Fearless had a tattoo, but when he checked, David Barr's wrist had been clean. No ink. No tell-tale laser removal scars. Nothing.

And why had Barr called out a name as he fell? What did it mean? Another bluff? It was possible that Fearless had been Barr's cover story. Possible he had never existed. But with Barr plunging to the ground, what did he stand to gain by revealing a name? It was perplexing and irritating.

Whatever the answer, Tyler had phoned his boss from the hotel room as soon as he arrived back, and told him the name. After he finished the call, he had felt trapped inside the hotel room so he had headed over to the bar. As he watched the other guests celebrating the Lakers' win he sipped on his whisky and tried to relax.

A dying man has no reason to lie, thought Tyler. He didn't understand people very well.

The air felt warmer by the pool than it had done hours ago on top of the Marriot, and there were several girls in the bar who were all legs and lipstick. Once Tyler sat down, people stopped staring at him. They didn't notice his size, and he was less intimidating slouched back in the sofa.

The group of Mexican baggage handlers were loud; playing pool and passing round a bottle of tequila. The Lakers had won, and Mexico was doing well at the soccer world cup. Good times.

A scuffle had broken out between them at one point, and they had knocked a girl to the floor. Her lip bled, but it was superficial. Tyler took a passing interest, weighing up the situation, but he didn't care for any of them and none of it was his problem. So he didn't stand up.

As the night drew on the music became louder and there was the occasional sound of rolling bottles and smashing glass. It wasn't the relaxed drink that Tyler had hoped for, but the ambiance was mostly good-natured and besides, he usually drank in much worse bars than this.

The ice had barely started to melt in his second glass when two reasonably attractive girls slunk over to his sofa. They were dressed for a party, but their clothes were cheap. To compensate, they'd displayed as much of their young bodies as they could, without getting arrested. Young and poor; they were pressed for time. Tyler figured they had about six years between them to find a man who would make them old and rich. After that, their elastic would give and they'd have to work harder on their conversational skills. Not that Tyler was any kind of conversationalist, but he'd reached an age where he appreciated a girl who had something interesting to say.

Strictly speaking his sofa was a generous two-seater, but Tyler had sat squarely in the middle and spread out. It wasn't like the place was packed, so he figured nobody would mind. Not that anyone would say anything if they did. People usually left Tyler alone.

Judging by the lack of finesse with which the girls crashed down either side of him, he guessed they'd been drinking since the start of the Lakers match. Tyler was in good shape, and his face was taut enough that it hadn't yet succumbed to gravity. All the same, he was old enough to be their father. Probably.

Both girls leaned in. A pincer maneuver. Cleavage everywhere. Tyler felt more irritated than flattered. The girl to his left whispered in his ear with a few suggestions about what might happen if he bought them a bottle of vodka. Her friend nodded and winked, eyes wide and pupils dilated. Reactions slow and judgment impaired. It was in Tyler's nature to notice these things. When he didn't rush to the bar, they moved on. He went back to his drink and closed his eyes.

Behind him, the surface of the swimming pool undulated gently, echoes of the pulls and swirls of the mid-afternoon swimmers. History sloshing around in a basin of water.

Three of the noisy Mexicans came over and sat on the sofa next to Tyler, with some demand about arm wrestling. Usually, that would have been enough to upset him, but he made allowances because they were drunk. He asked them politely to fuck off.

They were insistent though, and aggressive. *This was what happened when he wasn't standing up.* The other Mexicans had finished their game of pool and come over to join their friends on the sofas. Evidently, they had all been drinking hard. Tyler buttoned his black jacket and necked down the last of his bourbon. He had a feeling he'd be leaving soon. The Mexicans explained to Tyler that he would be leaving when they'd had their arm-wrestling match. They dictated their terms. A very bad idea.

"Don't worry," drawled the drunkest. "You can go home if you beat Kasper."

He pointed with his bottle of tequila at the fattest of them, who had already rolled up his sleeve. As if to convince Tyler to engage, the fat guy called out a few insults about Tyler's mother.

Tyler hadn't seen his parents in a decade.

He shrugged, lifted his massive frame from the sofa, and walked over to the fat guy. A few of the Mexicans noticed his height for the first time. And his height didn't disguise his breadth. He was barreled and brawny.

Without bothering to say anything, Tyler grasped the fat guy's outstretched fist and took the strain. The Mexicans whooped and encouraged their man. The giant in the black jacket was slow and controlled as he started to exert pressure on the Mexican's arm. It shook with the strain but soon enough Tyler had him beaten. There were plaintiff cries from the surrounding group. They'd had their fun, and they'd have to let Tyler go. But it was too late for that now. Tyler was going nowhere.

Emotionless, he continued to push at the arm in front of him. Anger began to flow into his body, coursing through his veins at the way these wet-back fuckers had ambushed him. His grip tightened around the man's thumb as he bent it back. The crowd fell silent and only the music masked fat Kasper's cries. He twisted from his chair and onto his knees to stop his joint from giving way.

Tyler didn't stop.

Pain shot through the Mexican's arm, and even over the music his friends could hear the first bone crack. The guy with the almost empty bottle of tequila smashed it over the back of Tyler's head. It shattered, but Tyler didn't flinch.

The group of men who had seemed so boisterous a moment ago now looked like frightened kids. They were sobering up fast, and remembering that they were baggage handlers, and not gangsters. They saw no emotion in the tall man's face, but Tyler was enjoying his work. The fat Mexican's wrist was next to snap, and then his elbow.

Tyler considered pulling out the Mexican's shoulder, but it seemed excessive, so he released him and straightened his jacket. As he turned to walk out, there was a glint of steel as one of the Mexicans pulled a knife. Probably the most stupid of them all.

Instead of backing off, Tyler stooped a little, so that his eyes were level with his assailant. They shone brightly, and he looked demonic as the refracted light from the pool played across his face.

God, he loved combat.

The Mexican was about six foot three and was not used to being the shortest man in a fight. Still, he took a wide stance and kept his blade steady. He hoped the man in the black jacket would stand down, but he was ready to slit his throat if he didn't. Tyler kept his hands by his side and spoke to the loaded Mexican quietly. He was measured and calm.

"Over my left shoulder there is a security camera," he explained. "If it wasn't there, I would take your blade and push it into your eye, right up to the hilt. Do you understand me?"

The Mexican nodded and then stole a glance over the tall man's shoulder. It was true. The camera was there with its red LED blinking down at him.

The camera captured the Mexican's face twisting up in pain as his momentary glance upwards allowed Tyler to bring his hands up to the blade and push back on the Mexican's wrist. The knife fell to the floor with a clatter of metal, and the man with the black jacket brushed past him, ready for a few hours of sleep before he caught his plane.

CHAPTER SEVENTEEN

Kandahar Airfield, November 2009
"Freezin', rests his head on a pillow made of concrete, again"
– Pearl Jam, Even Flow.

The gradual realization of danger is an ugly feeling. The moment you notice the tiger's eyes in the bush; a desperate clawing for hope, a split second of denial, and then the ice-cold comprehension that mortal peril is upon you.

Lockhart had been idly exploring the military base at Kandahar when the low sound of the alarm started to rumble. Earlier in the day Ajmal had told him it would be another twenty-four hours until their trucks would be ready to head back to Quetta, and as dusk had fallen he had wandered around the base and see what was on offer.

The cloudless sky had turned pitch black, and thousands of freestanding streetlights cast a moody glow up into the infinite darkness. Most of the air missions flew under cover of night, and the runway was busy. Impossibly heavy Hercules and Chinooks shook the floor as they lumbered off into the night, and the afterburners of fighter jets shot down the runway like fireworks. Lockhart had been poking about near the Dutch PX when the alarm began.

He had wondered if he was imagining the noise, but the wail of the siren got louder, and its pitch got higher. There was no mistaking it now.

Kandahar Air Field was surrounded by three-meter blast walls, and ditches beyond them, and razor wire fences further out still. They had designed the perimeter to keep people out, but Lockhart couldn't help feeling that it was penning him in. Like a prison.

Earlier he had walked to the heart of the camp which was a huge dusty square surrounded by western shops. The Boardwalk, as it was known, looked like it had been put up in a hurry, with rough splintering wooden walkways which creaked as uniformed packs of young men sauntered past in heavy boots.

Charlie Lockhart had sat alone outside the Canadian cafe, listening to a group of Brits who were also feeling trapped inside the wire. They were waiting to fly out of Afghanistan, but the ancient Tri-Star which was booked to take them home had broken down on the tarmac at Brize Norton, another world away.

Around the wooden walkway, freight containers had been lined up and converted into coffee shops and restaurants. TGI Fridays gleamed as small groups of soldiers were shown to leather booths by civilian servers. Pizza Hut was closed, having been hit by a rocket-propelled grenade one Saturday night a few weeks ago. The side of the steel box had been ripped away; its jagged edges were twisted back on themselves revealing the charred black interior.

Two US soldiers who had been assigned administrative jobs on the base slung their weapons over their shoulders while they queued up for ice cream. Then they sat in the shade and sipped on Tom Horton's coffee while they talked about how they'd prefer to be outside the wire facing the enemy. They watched the Canadian airmen playing hockey on the polished concrete rink in the square and complained bitterly about their frustration at not being posted in some shitty patrol base in Sangin.

Lockhart could read people well, and he could tell that although secretly each of the men was pleased to be out of harm's way, they were racked with guilt as they sat in the middle of Afghanistan with a three-meter blast wall between them and the enemy. Next to the US soldiers' table was a small square granite monument, dedicated to those who had fallen outside the wire.

The boardwalk had been calm, but now as Lockhart stood in the dusty street outside the Dutch PX, the siren was becoming deafening. It was shrill, and it was echoing all around the camp. A harsh female voice sliced through the air, much louder than the humming generators or the distant thunder of planes.

"We are under attack. This is not a drill."

The stark warning was repeated every ten seconds as the siren continued to wail. Several soldiers nearby started fumbling with helmet straps and pulling on flak jackets. They lowered themselves quickly to the floor and lay face down in the dust. They pushed their legs together and folded their arms around their faces. Lockhart had no helmet, but he copied the soldiers. He got down on the floor, coughing as he inhaled the dust in the confusion, and closed his eyes.

The chatter of camp life had muted, and the alarm had stopped. Apart from the generators gurgling in the background, everything was quiet. None of the soldiers called out. Everyone was listening for the sound of approaching doom.

It was a beautiful moment. Charlie Lockhart felt an absolute calm running through his body, and an absolute clarity in his mind. He had never felt so relaxed. As he lay prone in the dust, the reason for his desire to travel became obvious. He wanted to grow. He wanted to test himself and learn what kind of man he was. He wanted to throw himself to fate and see where chance steered him.

Ask not for whom the missile screams; it screams for thee.

Fate had put him here, in this spot at this time. He wasn't a soldier or a doctor, or a contractor earning six figures of tax-free cash. He didn't need to be here. Nobody had ordered him to be here. It was his choice to submit to the river's current. He hadn't swum against it.

Kandahar was a dramatic place. Days were dusty paths and bleached dry earth. Nights were jet black skies and pin sharp stars. Beautiful, treacherous mountains surrounded the Airfield.

As Lockhart lay face down in the dusty street, four men were standing next to a beaten-up Land Cruzer in the mountains overlooking the Airfield. Each had a rocket grenade launcher on his shoulder. The first had launched his weapon, and the others were waiting for the first smoke plumes to orientate their own attacks.

Lockhart glanced up. Couldn't resist it. The soldiers were still facing the ground, silent and still. Kandahar Airfield was the size of a large town, and the chances of the grenade hitting him were miniscule.

He imagined what would happen if it landed right next to him. It would be quick, he decided. He wasn't frightened. As he had wondered across the world he had learned that his life had been rich and privileged, and that he was a small and insignificant part of the teaming mass of life on the planet, and that nothing lasted forever. Ozymandias. He lay there still, in the dust, and waited. Every scuff of movement was amplified. Every sense was heightened. Every emotion was simple, pure and intense. Seconds passed. Nothing happened.

Lockhart could hear himself breathing.

And then it came. The screech lasted for less than a second. Much less probably. It passed over his head like he was being run over by an intercity train at full speed. About forty meters in front of him, it hit a concrete blast wall and obliterated. Shards of vicious concrete and hot metal carved through the air above him, and dust flew. A second screech followed, and a Humvee exploded, sending a diesel plume high into the air. Even with his head down, Charlie Lockhart knew he was in trouble.

CHAPTER EIGHTEEN

LAX Departures. December 2010
"Go on go on and disappear, go on go on away from here."
– The Cure, Inbetween Days.

There was money behind Tyler, and when he arrived at LAX, they had already booked a ticket for him. He picked up some essentials as he headed for the first-class lounge and spent a few minutes in the executive bathroom shaving and making himself look presentable.

His French passport roused no suspicion on his way through, but even so he preferred not to hang about in airports for too long. Especially when he was fleeing the scene.

He was looking forward to getting some sleep on the flight. The phone had rung almost as soon as he got back to his hotel suite last night, and they had given him an update. It was exciting news and better than Tyler or his boss could have hoped for. There were things to do, and Tyler hadn't slept.

As Tyler pulled the sharp new blade across his jawline in the first-class bathrooms, the housemaid back at the Custom Hotel entered the room he had checked out of that morning. She slid her electronic card through the reader and pushed her trolley in through the door before her. She didn't call out because the room number was on her printed sheet. Mr. Tyler had checked out two hours earlier, heading for the airport three miles down the road.

As he finished shaving, Tyler heard the final call for the London flight, threw the razor away, and dabbed his face with a soft towel from the pile in front of him. He checked himself once in the mirror, more cautious than vain, and set off at a pace to board the plane.

Back in the hotel, the maid was confused. There was nothing to suggest that Tyler's room had been slept in. She looked down at her crumpled printout and then back at the number of the hotel room door. The bed was immaculately made, with just the slightest indentation where someone had been sitting next to the phone. The stationary was not touched, the blinds were in their proper position, and the bathroom was spotless.

When she looked closely, she noticed that one of the three miniature bottles of shower gel had gone, but the shower itself was clean and dry, and there was no evidence of the discarded bottle in the empty bin in the bathroom. The one in the bedroom was empty too.

As Tyler boarded the plane, a stewardess in a smart red uniform showed him to his comfortable seat, apologizing that he had got mingled in amongst the business passengers. He reassured her it was his own fault for running late, but he didn't return her warm smile. He didn't like fuss. Didn't enjoy standing out.

Traveling first class was not ideal. He preferred the anonymity of business or coach, and he didn't give a damn for *a la carte* menus or free champagne. Or status. It was simply that his huge frame didn't fit into the smaller seats. For Tyler, first class was closer to necessity than luxury. He settled into his seat and drank the champagne, anyway.

Over the years, Tyler had been more accustomed to rough-and-ready transport than pampered civilian travel. To him, flying was usually about being flung about in the back of a C-130 with a pair of yellow ear defenders rammed in to block out the racket, clinging on to the rough red nylon netting as the pilot plunged downwards to their landing point at the last moment.

In the subtly lit cabin, an apologetic steward went through the safety routine, buckling straps and pointing at doorways while everyone ignored him. Everyone except Tyler, who took his safety seriously. It was the only reason he was still alive.

*

The maid at the Custom Hotel was having a good day. She was ahead of time thanks to the room that hadn't been slept in, and was planning to sit out the back on the old patio chairs catching a bit of warm sun for a few extra minutes at lunchtime. She whistled down the corridor and said *Buenos Dias* to everyone she passed.

She reached the next room on her list and swiped her staff pass through the card reader. She pushed backwards through the door. The stench of stale alcohol hit her immediately. *How the hell did these Mexican guys get up for work after all their partying?* Her trolley complained as she pulled it through the doorway, and she left it half in and half out, propping the door open to get some air into the room. As she turned, her knees gave way and she let out a scream.

The baggage handler was lying rigid on the bed, laid out as if by a mortician, in a pool of his own blood. There was no sign of a struggle. A cheap flick knife had been forced and twisted into his right eye, buried up to the hilt.

*

Tyler exhaled as the rubber of the front tire lifted from the tarmac runway, and he felt a cushion of air lift the heavy plane into the sky. He settled back and tried to get a couple of hours' sleep before Dallas.

CHAPTER NINETEEN

Kandahar Airfield, Afghanistan.
"We got John Coltrane and a love supreme, Miles says she's got to be an angel" – U2, Angel of Harlem.

Outside the Dutch PX, smoke was billowing from the wrecked Humvee. Dust turned the air into a thick soup, pouring into everyone's lungs. Charlie Lockhart felt adrenalin burst from the center of his chest, flooding through his veins. He wanted to run, but the air was thick with debris and so he kept his head down. Staying low, he shuffled closer to a blast wall about two meters to his left. There was a ditch behind it which offered a natural shelter and he slid into it on his stomach.

Silence descended as quickly as the dust fell to the floor. Logic told Lockhart that the generators must still be humming but his ears were ringing after the explosion. The Humvee was burning furiously, but there was no sound of licking flames. The muted scene was claustrophobic.

Slowly, his hearing started to return, like he was emerging from underwater. He saw the soldiers across the street scrabbling up, coming together. One of them had reached a shelter point where several concrete slabs surrounded a ditch and was beckoning his friends to stay low and come to him.

Lockhart was considering a mad run across the street to join them when he felt a hand grabbing his collar and pulling him along the floor. He was dragged out of the ditch and into a building behind the blast wall he had been using as cover.

Inside the building, the woman who had pulled him out of the ditch manhandled him unceremoniously back to the ground. She pushed him under a table. His hearing was coming back now and he could make out the sounds of sirens some distance away. Scores of vehicles were heading towards the scene, checking for casualties and securing the area.

The woman squeezed herself under the table next to him. She was mid-twenties, curvaceous and seemed to have spent more time on her appearance than was strictly necessary for military purposes. From the dazzlingly white teeth, he guessed she was American. Her accent confirmed it.

"You should get yourself a helmet" she chastised. Her body felt warm next to his, and despite the dust and the smoke and the sweat, he found himself conscious of her closeness. Maybe it was a reaction to the near-death experience. Whatever the reason, he wasn't convinced that the American was feeling the same way.

She explained that another grenade could rip through the skin of the building, so they stayed low under the table waiting for the all clear to sound.

They heard two bloodthirsty Thunderbolts roar off down the runway to eliminate any further threat from the men with the grenade launchers. Armored vehicles full of vengeful warriors and hopeful forensics teams were leaving the main gate too.

The American brushed against Lockhart as she twisted round under the table to face him, her eyes sweeping across him as she did. Slowly, she drew her hand towards him and ran her fingers through his hair.

"You're bleeding," she said, rubbing his blood between her fingers as the all-clear siren wailed through the base. "Stay there."

She shuffled out from under the table and strode across the room towards a large green medical cabinet attached to the wall on the opposite side of the room. Ignoring her instructions, Lockhart shuffled out.

The room was clinical and anarchic all at once. The outside of the blast wall was regulation gray concrete, but its hidden reverse was an orgy of spray paint. As Lockhart looked out at it, the bright pinks yellows and oranges were in complete contrast to the regulation beige buildings and vehicles, the dusty roads and the dowdy uniforms. Manga drawings mixed with colorful patterns, Celtic signs, and Arabic slogans.

The room itself was well lit and much more cluttered than any other Lockhart had experienced in Kandahar. Trestle work surfaces ran around the outside of the room, and a dark Afghan rug covered most of the floor.

In the center there was what looked like a shining leather dentist's chair. It was hinged in four different places and had a heavy cylindrical metal base. Around it, there were several chrome stacking-shelves on plastic wheels, full of rubber gloves and sterile metallic instruments. There was a metal sink and a first aid cupboard.

A full height angle poise light was aimed at the chair casting long shadows around the room, and a thick roll of blue paper sheets was waiting to be turned and torn. A round chrome practitioner's chair with a cerise seat rested near to the dentist's chair.

It looked like a torture chamber, except for the cartoon drawings and mystic charts pinned to the wall, alongside black and white posters of Dizzy Gillespie and Miles Davis, all lost in smoke and magic. There was an impressive looking iPod dock on one table, and two large wooden speakers which stood four feet tall in each corner.

Lockhart was still soaking in the room when the woman turned back round from the medical box, with several sealed packages from the trauma kit. She had rinsed his blood from her fingers and gloved up, ready for action. She offered him a latex-clad hand.

"Kirsten Miller," she said.

Lockhart shook her hand. His father had once told him that a gentleman should squeeze a woman's hand with the same pressure as she squeezed his own. Miller's hands were delicate for a soldier, but her touch was assured and her handshake was as firm as it was feminine. She didn't release his hand, and it took him a moment to realize that she was waiting for him to reveal his name too.

"Charlie," he said reluctantly, remembering Barr's instructions. "But people I'm with call me Fearless."

Miller raised a well-plucked brow.

"You're the guy with the grenade stuck to his truck, right? I heard about you."

They carried on talking as she went to work, her blue plastic fingers rummaging through his hair. The cut was superficial, but it had bled quickly like most head wounds. She made him lean over the sink as she washed the blood out of his hair. The water was cold and his scalp started to sting. Lockhart was careful to conceal his discomfort because Miller seemed like the kind of girl who would not be impressed by any signs of pain.

The water ran into the metal sink in reds and browns as dust and blood and concrete washed out. He noticed that Miller's hands had slowed up, and her actions began to feel more intimate. He could feel her breasts and hips brushing against his back as she went about her work.

Suddenly the door slammed open and a medic in desert combats, helmet and body protection leaned into the room. It felt like she had crashed in from another world. Beyond the vibrant mural on the blast wall there were emergency vehicles with blue lights flashing, soldiers on high alert, and a Humvee still throwing flames into the air. Chaos, compared to the calm inside.

"Any casualties?" the medic shouted, as her eyes settled on the couple at the sink. She lowered her voice as she recognized the woman. "Kirsten… everything under control?"

"We're all good here, thanks. I didn't see anyone injured in the road either." Her voice was low and calm. "Jesus Christ, it landed close though."

Miller didn't turn around or pull away from Lockhart as she spoke to the medic. She carried on working his hair without missing a beat as the medic closed the door behind her.

After a while, Miller stopped the tap and reached for a fresh towel from on the table. She pulled off her gloves, rinsed her hands, and dried them as she walked over to her iPod. As she walked back to the sink, a mournful piano struck up its first notes. Her gentle hands persuaded Lockhart to turn around from the sink, and she began to scrunch his hair dry with the towel.

Miller took her time drying the stranger's hair. She cupped the nape of his neck, her skin touching his for the first time. She had a husband at home. She didn't have a husband in Afghanistan. Ella Fitzgerald's heavenly voice wrapped around them like a warm duvet as Lockhart pulled Miller into his arms.

They didn't kiss. Instead, their foreheads touched, and they began to giggle like children; slowly at first until they were laughing like old friends as they hugged one another. They had come close enough to death to say that they'd cheated him, and the cheating felt good. Being alive felt good.

After a while, they headed outside, and Lockhart sat in the doorway, massaging Miller's shoulders as she leaned back into him. She was rolling a cigarette, lost in the ritual. He was staring at the stars, amazed by their brightness. The Humvee had burned itself out, and the air was still and calm. Billie Holiday was singing about the bubbles in her champagne as Miller took her first drag and blew out for an eternity.

CHAPTER TWENTY

Central Mosque, Birmingham. August 2010.
"Like a phoenix rising needs a holy tree, Like the sweet revenge of a bitter enemy." - U2, Hawkmoon

Even after a year, few members of the mosque would associate with Daud because of the shame his brother had bought to the community.

Daud didn't mind. His main reason for going to the mosque was not to atone for Ajmal's actions, nor to defend them. Besides, he did not understand what his brother had been doing when he was bagged, cable-tied, and dragged off on a C-17 to Guantanamo in the middle of the night.

Daud went to the Mosque to reflect and to ask questions. Maybe he was questioning himself, or maybe he was questioning Allah. He had faith and wisdom in equal measure, so he was happy to believe that he could do both at the same time. Allah might be a supreme being, or he might be Daud's internal construct. Either way, he hoped for a few answers.

As he drove towards the Central Mosque along the Belgrave Middleway, he cast a rueful eye towards the rough gray square of concrete surrounded by floodlights on the other side of the busy duel carriageway.

Only a few short years ago it had been covered with AstroTurf and the two brothers used to play hockey together there. Daud was two years older, bigger and stronger, and always had a new trick to teach Ajmal. They were good times, but now the green carpet had been ripped up, the floodlights were smashed and they had taken his brother from him.

Daud himself had no interest in Holy Wars, nor the rights or wrongs of Western aggression. He didn't really care about the motives of the Taliban or America's thirst for oil. He found the world's conflicting viewpoints on liberty, capitalism, pornography and a million other subjects tiresome.

As a Muslim living in the West, he had grown up listening to these arguments every day, and he had grown bored with people's entrenched opinions and closed minds. What was the point of being so passionate about something that you lost your ability to question your own threadbare mantra? Daud never understood that.

What distorts life from its perfect path is us, thought Daud. Our emotions; greed, fear, jealousy, envy, pride, lust. It doesn't seem to matter whether we live in the East or West; we are united in our ability to mess up what could otherwise be a perfect world.

So Daud had never been a pacifist, or a jihadist. He'd never rejected his faith, but he'd never been a zealot either. He'd just tried to create a quiet, harmless and reasonable life for himself. He wasn't pious, but he tried to do well by the people around him. As Shakespeare put it, he was a man more sinned against than sinning.

Daud's brother had always been thoughtful too. Impetuous sometimes, ambitious in so much as he was keen to please his family, but a calm soul with a good heart. *Ajmal couldn't be a terrorist.*

And yet, Daud had no way to be sure. Neither did he have any way to protect his little brother as he had done all his life. Daud had terrible ideas of what the Americans would be doing to him in Guantanamo. He'd heard stories from Tipton about torture in the camp. His mind was full of images of his brother being beaten, force-fed, drugged, and maybe worse.

Sometimes, happy moments would enter Daud's life, and immediately guilt would come rushing into his mind like a tsunami, sweeping the happiness aside as he remembered Ajmal languishing in some lawless place in Cuba.

The feeling of impotence had enraged his usually peaceful soul, and over time his heart had hardened as he sought a way to help his brother. And now something had happened. A name had emerged. Daud could not free his brother, but at least now he could avenge him.

He had learned the name of the man who had handed him to the Americans. With a cold fury at his core, Ajmal's brother began to plan.

CHAPTER TWENTY-ONE

Kandahar Airfield, Afghanistan.
"Moi je t'offrirai des perles de pluie, Venues de pays où il ne pleut pas"
– Jacques Brel, Ne Me Quitte Pas.

The wind had changed, and the smell of the burned-out hummer had eventually become overwhelming. Miller and Lockhart had moved back inside the strange room with its jazz posters and its dentist's chair. Jacques Brel had taken over from Ella Fitzgerald, and it reminded Lockhart of Laurent, an eccentric old French flat mate he had lived with years ago.

The camp was dry, but Miller rustled up two tumblers and a bottle of Jack Daniels from somewhere. They clinked glasses and Lockhart lay back in the dentist chair, letting his eyes wonder around the posters and charts on the wall, before settling back on the woman sitting next to him.

"What is this place, anyway?"

Miller explained that as well as working in Kandahar's hospital, she ran a tattoo parlor on the side. She explained that she mostly worked for favors like the rug, the iPod and the whisky. Occasionally money exchanged hands. When Lockhart asked her whether her tattooing was legitimate, she looked at him innocently and explained with a smile she was a great doctor.

"What's your blood type?"

"A-B negative," Lockhart answered. "But I don't think I'll need a transfusion after tonight's scratch."

"That's rare blood; you're about one in a hundred." Miller sounded impressed, as if his blood type had been a matter of his own choice.

"What if you needed a transfusion? How would I know what to give you?"

Lockhart understood at once. Miller made money tattooing blood types onto soldiers and contractors. Not legal, not officially condoned, but the authorities tolerated it because it was useful. Lifesaving, potentially.

Soldiers who came into the hospital in need of blood would usually have their blood type written on their helmets or on their body armor. But recently the severity of some IED blasts had charred the details and made it difficult to get blood into them without either waiting for medical files or taking a gamble.

The tattoos worked much better, unless the roadside bombs obliterated whichever limb had been marked. That was happening more and more, and now some patrols were going out having already fixed tourniquets to each of their limbs, ready to tighten up, in anticipation of getting something blown off. It was morbid, but Miller could testify to the fact that it had saved at least three lives while she had been in Kandahar.

"Let me do you?" Miller asked. "You'd be my very first A-B negative."

Lockhart looked at her, feeling like a rare butterfly.

"Not until we've finished the bottle," he said. Miller smiled and poured them another drink.

CHAPTER TWENTY-TWO

D-Fac Number 4, Kandahar Airfield.
"Oh the sun beats down and melts the tar up on the roof,
And your shoes get so hot you wish your tired feet were fire-proof."
– The Drifters, Under the Boardwalk

Like every meeting place on the camp, the dining facility was protected by a tall concrete blast wall around its perimeter. The queue for food snaked round the outside of the building and along the inside of the blast wall. There were four main dining facilities on the airfield and twenty thousand hungry mouths. They were busy places. The inside of the facility was bright and bustling, with soldiers coming and going from table to table. Charlie Lockhart got through the main doors and swiped the card that Captain Barr had given him.

There were about five hundred people seated inside the dining hall, being fed by an army of chefs. In the center of the room was a cold buffet, with meats, cheeses, salads and breads. Local contractors working for the catering firm were serving roast beef, pork and chicken from the hot buffet with steaming vegetables. Further down there was a selection of curries and pastas. One wall was lined up with refrigerators full of bottled water and pallets of Coca Cola. It was like home from home.

The lights were bright, and the mood was fairly cheery. Above the tables, there were flat screen televisions showing breaking news from back home.

The food was good, and because he had nowhere else to go, Lockhart took his time and watched the television screens as he ate. He had attempted to disconnect with home life during his adventure, but information was a drug.

As he reconnected with news that seemed unimportant compared to his recent experiences, he fiddled absently with the bandage covering the new tattoo on his wrist. The material had turned a dusty shard of beige. Nothing stayed white in Kandahar for very long.

Miller had painted a tiny tattoo on the inside of his wrist, with his blood type and the word خوف دون written underneath it.

"It means without fear," she said. Lockhart had liked it immediately. After two dangerous days, it felt like a well-earned battle scar. He was smart enough to know that one day the memories of the attack on the convoy, the exploding concrete blast walls, and all the beautiful memories of the desert would become dulled by time. The tattoo would be a souvenir; a momento mori.

Right now, the tattoo itched like hell, but Miller had assured him it would calm down within a couple of days. He thought about her for a moment. She had a good soul and honest, intelligent eyes. Not to mention that she had a great figure, and she smelled better than anyone else he'd met in Afghanistan. But he had promised himself that he wouldn't become too attached to anyone while he was traveling, and he could tell that she wasn't the kind of girl would appreciate it, anyway. It had been a fun night, no more and no less. Another memory to savor.

Finishing his meal, Lockhart decided that he would walk by Miller's tent tomorrow and see if she was about, but if she wasn't that would be fine. She'd understand, too.

As he was leaving the dining facility, Lockhart caught sight of Ajmal ducking inside the blast wall and out of sight. Lockhart doubled back on himself and quickened his pace so he could catch up with his friend; perhaps there would be news about when the convoy was heading back. Besides, he needed to tell Ajmal that he might not want to head back to Quetta with the convoy.

But by the time Lockhart rounded the corner of the building, Ajmal had vanished. Lockhart checked both sides of the blast wall, but he definitely wasn't there. Half way along the wall there was a metal ladder which led up to the roof of the canteen and as Lockhart looked up, he saw a flash of Ajmal's Salwar disappearing over the top.

Lockhart didn't stop to think. On impulse he headed towards the ladder. He was three steps up when a soldier called out to him.

"There's someone on the roof," Lockhart yelled. He wasn't sure why, but he knew something was wrong. The soldier was already calling others, and Lockhart could hear someone shouting into his radio. By the time he was on the top rung of the ladder, he could feel the vibrations of heavy boots clambering up behind him.

He could see Ajmal standing dead still in the middle of the roof, with something in his hand. As it glinted in the sun, Lockhart realized that Ajmal was holding a mirror. He called out, but Ajmal ignored him, focused on the mountains beyond the outer perimeter.

Lockhart realized what was happening at once, and in horror he broke into a run. There were five hundred men below them, eating lunch and watching television. All of Ajmal's focus was on the mountain, but Lockhart bounded across the roof at full speed. As he leaped into the air, he realized that he might run out of roof, but it didn't matter. If he didn't act, he would be dead anyway.

His shoulder hit Ajmal square in the ribs. He knocked the mirror from his hand, and it fell to the floor and smashed. Ajmal hit his head as he fell and Lockhart tumbled past him rolling perilously close to the edge. A marine who had followed him up the ladder was right behind him. He lunged out and caught Lockhart by his boot to stop him going right over. A second Marine had drawn his weapon and had it trained on Ajmal who was lying crumpled at his feet. He had a scruffy hand-drawn map in his hand.

The alarm was already sounding around the camp and the men on the roof wondered whether Ajmal had signaled to the grenade launchers in the mountains before Lockhart had smashed his mirror. They would know within a few seconds. The marines had seen the tactic before: a local contractor up on the roof using a mirror to guide in the rocket-propelled grenades. The soldiers watched the sky but nothing happened.

After two minutes, the Marines man-handled Ajmal off the roof. He was handed to some military police at the bottom of the ladder. He glared furiously at Lockhart through the window of the military police jeep. He was still glaring as they hooded him. Anger and frustration left him wide eyed and angry as they drove him away. That was the last Lockhart ever saw of Ajmal. *So much for neighbors* he thought. He deserved everything he would get.

The group of soldiers helped Lockhart down the last few rungs of the ladder. Not because he needed help, but because they wanted to congratulate him. Word had quickly gone around that he had almost thrown himself off the roof to save the five hundred men in the dining facility. And he was a civilian.

The highest ranking among the group of soldiers was a USAF Lieutenant Colonel who stepped forward from the small crowd.

"What's your name?" he asked. Lockhart remembered the advice that David Barr had given him on the front gate. Somehow it seemed like a good idea to stay as anonymous as possible.

"Fearless" he replied.

The colonel looked confused. Then he reached out and examined the contractor ID that Lockhart was wearing around his neck. When he saw the same name on the badge, he looked back up and smiled.

"Well, I guess the name fits."

The crowd laughed, and the remaining Military Police started taking witness statements about the mirror, the insurgent, and the man called Fearless who had saved five hundred soldiers that afternoon.

CHAPTER TWENTY-THREE

Kandahar Airfield, Afghanistan.
"I have held the hand of the devil; it was warm in the night."
– U2, I Still Haven't Found What I'm Looking For.

People survive in this place by staying anonymous thought Lockhart as he watched the packs of men moving around the Airfield. They don't make choices for themselves, but they stay in the middle of the shoal and let the river flow along its course. They think it's safer. Lockhart knew that he didn't belong in the middle of the shoal. He thought one of the worst pieces of advice he had ever been given was that the things you are searching for are always in last place that you look. Well, obviously. Why would you keep looking once you've found them? Lockhart hadn't worked out what it was he was looking for; let alone where to find it. So, he kept moving on and kept his heart open to opportunity.

Despite all of this philosophizing, he still arrived outside the tattooist's room with no real idea how he got there. He had been half daydreaming and half planning his next move. Lockhart knew that it was time to move on. Kandahar was locked down and bleached out. He was a tourist, and he wanted to feel real life, and vibrancy, and fun and enjoyment. He was looking forward to reaching a country where he could have a beer and talk freely.

Over the months, his soul had been nurtured by the people he had met on his journey. He had loved the conversations, the arguments, the meals. He had learned about the things that made people different and the things that made us all the same. He wanted to get back on the road.

The tattooist wasn't in her room, but Lockhart pulled a small glass jug from his rucksack and placed it outside her door. She liked presents, and he thought it would look nice on the top of one of her huge speakers, rattling from side to side as Harry Edison or Nina Simone let rip.

On a scrap of paper, he carefully copied the Arabic script from his new tattoo; خوف دون. He rolled the paper and left it in the top of the glass jug and smiled as it reminded him of notes his mum used to leave on the doorstep about how much milk she wanted delivering. Back in the day.

He walked alone to the dining facility, swiped his card, and washed his hands. He picked a green salad from the buffet and grabbed a glass of dark syrupy grape juice and scanned the room for a table. As he made for a vacant table in the middle of the room, a soldier stood up and beckoned him over to join him.

It was Captain Barr from the front gate. He was eating on his own and had almost finished his meal, but he didn't seem to be in a rush to head off. Instinctively, Lockhart shook his hand as he reached the table. Even though Barr was almost a stranger, he was the only person in the room that Lockhart recognized.

"I heard you've been living up to that name of yours?" he asked Lockhart, pointing at his contractor ID.

Lockhart shrugged his shoulders.

"Well, I guess it leaves you without a ride back out of the country?" Barr continued.

Lockhart looked up; he sensed that Barr was about to offer him a choice.

"The thing is, we've impounded the other trucks from your convoy, and we're questioning the other Pakistani nationals," Barr continued slowly. "But I guess you've earned our trust by almost throwing yourself off the roof to save a bunch of guys in the canteen."

"Well, I thought I might see if I could get a lift back to Pakistan with another convoy," said Lockhart. He had traveled for long enough to learn the art of improvisation.

"Would you like to see Herat?" asked Barr. "I need a delivery taking there tonight, and I need someone I can trust to do a good job. Herat is full of history, and it's safer that Kabul right now."

Lockhart was smart enough to know that "safer than Kabul" didn't mean much. Even so, it would be better than heading back to Quetta. Now that he had started along this path, he didn't particularly want to turn back. *Make a choice and stick to it,* he thought.

"How about using a couple of your men?"

"I need someone I can trust not to ask questions" said Barr, and he held Lockhart's gaze long enough for him to understand that the enterprise wasn't entirely legitimate.

Before Lockhart could ask any more questions about the consignment,

Barr explained his terms in a low voice so the Marines on the next table wouldn't overhear him.

"I'll have a Mastiff ready for you at the main gate first thing tomorrow morning. It'll be loaded already, and you just need to drive it to Herat. Don't stop for anyone or anything, don't tamper with the cargo, don't use the official comms. There will be a pre-tuned radio on the passenger seat, use that if you need anything. Your contact at Herat will guide you in once you get close to him."

Lockhart looked at Barr. He knew that war was an opportunity, and there would be plenty of people working their side line while they were in Afghanistan. As gatekeeper, Barr had the perfect chance to skim a bit from the smugglers and make some decent cash. He earned a few dollars; the smugglers got rich, and the people inside the wire got alcohol, or whatever they needed. Barr was right. Lockhart didn't need to know the grubby details.

"I can offer you two thousand dollars for the job, and transit documents for a swampy flight at Herat. You'll be out of the country by tomorrow night."

Lockhart wondered why Barr was smuggling things *out* of the Airfield, but decided not to ask too many questions. He could choose not to help, but as a result he would probably be deported back to the UK or left to fend for himself outside the wire. Neither option sounded great.

CHAPTER TWENTY-FOUR

Highway 1, Afghanistan. November 2009.
"The 18-wheeler and the payback dives,
Gravity pulls on the power lines.
A jetstream cuts the desert sky,
This land could eat a man alive."
- REM, Low Desert

By the time the sun was properly up the next morning, Lockhart was alone on the Herat road, and he was happy. He had traveled thousands of miles on his own before he arrived at Kandahar, and he liked his own company. After a while he had found the military base oppressive. Apart from Miller and her makeshift tattoo parlor, everything was geared towards conformity and routine, and Lockhart had not set out on his journey to find either of those. So, he was glad that he was moving on and glad to be on his own.

In the back of his armored Mastiff were about 30 blocks wrapped in durable blue shrink-wrap plastic. Each block was about the size of a small hay bale. As promised, Barr had left a two-way radio on the passenger seat and had buzzed him for an update twice already.

Lockhart wasn't too pleased that he was smuggling something elicit between the two military bases to ensure his own safe passage from Kandahar, but needs must when the devil drives. Besides, the whole country seemed lawless, so it didn't hurt him to be pragmatic. He could use the proceeds to fund the rest of his otherwise wholesome trip. Everything he had heard about Herat sounded enticing and he was looking forward to wandering around the place later.

He wondered what was in the blue blocks crammed into the back of the Mastiff, but he remembered David Barr's warning about not interfering with the goods.

Lockhart had met Captain Barr at the front gate as planned before first light, and with minimal fuss he took the wheel and headed out of the base through the main gate area. With Barr orchestrating, Lockhart and his Mastiff were led down the overflow channel away from prying eyes and out onto the freedom of the highway.

Soon the sun was strong, and Lockhart was driving straight into it. He was careful to keep his wits about him. After his experience with the truck convoy, he knew how dangerous the roads in Helmand were. Still, despite his best efforts, the glare of the sun made it difficult for him to see too far ahead.

The view from the road was barren. Lockhart wondered why so many civilizations had spilled blood over the place. He understood that it was strategy and politics and oil and opium, but to look at the prize it all felt senseless. Empty and pointless.

There was little of interest to see along the road. Occasionally, huge puck marks in the sand dunes either side would tell a story of conflict. Some scars were new, but others told older tales of Russian helicopters and stubborn Mujahidin.

After about an hour driving, Lockhart rounded one of the few corners on his journey, as the road passed between two fairly pronounced undulations in the otherwise flat landscape. As the road expanded back out towards the horizon, Lockhart spotted three unmarked jeeps blocking the path in front of him. They were beaten up and dusty. They didn't look official.

Instinct told Lockhart to check his mirrors to see if there was anyone else coming to block his exit. He saw nobody behind him, or on top of the high ground, but thought better of turning away. Where would he go if he turned back, anyway? He would be a sitting duck if they aimed at him while he turned. Besides, he might trigger a mine or some old ordinance if he strayed from the well-worn road.

He slowed the Mastiff to a crawl and stared into the sun, trying hard to see what was happening in the road in front of him. It wasn't until he was about a hundred and fifty yards away from them they revealed their weapons. A rocket-propelled grenade came flying at Lockhart before he'd had time to think, and exploded just in front of him, close enough to rock the Mastiff. Suddenly, the radio on the passenger seat crackled and David Barr's American accent filled the cab, all jovial and reassuring.

"How's the road trip so far, dude? Did you take any pictures?"

Lockhart had bad news for Barr's investment. It was about to go up in smoke. He explained the situation over the radio; the jeeps, the grenade, the options. But as he was talking, his voice was drowned out, even through the thick glass of the armored Mastiff.

A pair of light gray American A-10 Thunderbolts screamed so low over Lockhart that the cloud of black smoke belching out of the missile in front of him split into two. He heard the screech and dull thuds as they aimed round after round into the white jeeps in front of him. Sand sprayed and metal twisted and charred.

As the Thunderbolts approached, Lockhart had seen several silhouettes franticly scrambling behind the dusty windshields, grabbing at their AK47s on instinct. As if a Kalashnikov would help them. It took about three seconds before the two of the jeeps, the men and the AK47s were all twisted together in a deep crater about a hundred meters ahead on the road.

One guy had escaped from the only jeep that wasn't hit directly. He was running hopelessly into the sand, anywhere. But the A-10s were ruthless. They screeched back around and came in for a second swipe. One plane took out the remaining jeep, and the other aimed at the fleeing driver.

Although the driver had just unleashed a missile in his direction, Lockhart still felt sorry for him. It was hard not to, given the hopelessness of his situation. Lockhart could imagine what the driver was thinking, scrabbling in the sand, looking for an escape, for hope, for a way to cling to life. Half of him already knowing his fate, half of him refusing to believe it.

He was up against millions of dollars of military hardware. Generations of science and funding all focused on the eradication of enemies. The A-10 was efficient. The pilot released one burst of five massive shells. Not in anger or haste, but coldly and clinically. Like pest control.

As Lockhart watched, the driver disappeared into the sand. Completely. One minute he was there, the next he had gone. There would be no corpse or gravestone or dignified mourning. No trip home on a C-17, no flag-draped coffin. Just heat and flying sand and blood and nothingness. Another puck mark beside the Herat Road.

Although the driver would have killed him a moment ago, Lockhart couldn't help but mourn the human life snuffed out. Just for a second. *This is what you get if you mess with us.* Lockhart embraced his sorrow. It held him back from the abyss. It was what made him human.

The A-10s could destroy tanks, and the thin rolled metal skin of the jeeps had been no resistance at all. Lockhart could see why they were nicknamed Thunderbolts, but they were ugly machines. Boxy and cheap looking. Not ergonomic like a Typhoon or a Raptor. They looked like gigantic Airfix models which had been stuck together by a ham-fisted eight-year-old whose parents didn't love him enough to help him out. For all of that, Lockhart was glad to have them on his side.

The ruthless way in which they had cleared the road ahead was impressive and chilling in equal measure. Problem deleted. Lockhart was glad that his Mastiff had been recognized as a friendly, even if his business wasn't entirely official. It was heavily armored and should have survived an attack by a few guys in the jeeps with their AK47s. But if the A-10s hadn't recognized him he could have been burned up in friendly fire without too much trouble.

As the smell of burning fuel mixed with the exploded ordinance, Lockhart felt enveloped and cocooned by the chaos. The worst was over, and he was untouched. He felt a moment of calm wash over him, and he exhaled properly for the first time in a couple minutes as his rough hands twisted and broke the blue seal on another bottle of mineral water. David Barr's voice crackled through the speaker asking for an update.

Charlie Lockhart was a man of integrity, but not in a pompous Etonian way. He liked to do right by the people around him. He believed in karma. He wasn't a soldier, and he didn't have to slavishly follow orders. The desire to rip open the mysterious blue blocks in the back of the Mastiff was becoming stronger. It wouldn't be long.

As he swallowed, he considered his options. The first sip from the bottle always tasted best. A red LED glowed on the side of the oversized walkie talkie on the passenger seat, and his unofficial comms crackled into life again. It was Barr sounding more urgent now. Never a moment's peace.

Lockhart reached into the back of the Mastiff and tore away at the corner of one of the bales. As the blue plastic skin stretched and gave way, Lockhart caught the smell of fresh ink and paper. New bank notes. Thousands of them, millions possibly. The denominations were high, too.

Lockhart considered his situation. Nobody knew he was alive. The pilots would report the ambush to Kandahar. He had a truck full of a serious amount of cash, which serious people would want returned. He couldn't drive back to Kandahar without arousing suspicion, but anyone taking delivery of that much money wouldn't want to be traced. They'd be sure to kill him when he arrived in Herat. Lockhart realized that they had chosen him for the job because he was anonymous and expendable.

So: Take the money and run, leave the money and run, or deliver the money to someone who would almost definitely kill him? Lockhart ruled out option three.

He put the Mastiff into gear and drove out of the smoke. As he edged around the burning crater where the jeeps had been moments ago, he threw the walkie talkie into the flames and began to drive on towards Herat. *Easier to run when you're rich,* he thought.

CHAPTER TWENTY-FIVE

Front Gate, Kandahar Airfield.
"Instant Karma's gonna get you, If I don't get you first."
– U2, I Believe in Love.

David Barr's office was silent and dusty. The light was fading in the courtyard outside his window, and the only thing which broke the silence was the constant hum of the air conditioning unit.

Suddenly, the door slammed open and the huge Warrant Officer poured himself through the doorway with his hands high, ready to strike at anyone he found in the room. General Lang walked calmly in behind him.

His eyes shot around the room. Barr had not answered his phone when they had called from the other side of the Airfield. It was risky to be anywhere near the front gate during their private operation, but Lang had felt that with so much riding on the shipment they should come over and ensure that Barr had come good on the job.

The phone was on the desk, and the office looked the same as it had done last time they had visited. There were maps and charts tacked on the walls along with a walkie talkie charging unit.

Ten minutes earlier, Barr had been sitting at the desk, trying to contact Lockhart on the radio. The front gate had been warned that an incident had occurred outside the Airfield, and that insurgents had ambushed an ISAF Mastiff on the Herat Road. The pilots had requested information about any vehicles that had recently left the camp because a single vehicle on the road by itself seemed highly irregular. The reports were unclear about whether the vehicle had survived.

Barr knew that there was three hundred million dollars of cash inside the Mastiff, and that losing the shipment was not an option. He was ruined. If the Mastiff had survived, he would have to explain how it had passed out of the front gate with the cash. If it had been destroyed, General Lang would undoubtedly hold him responsible. As he had discovered over the last few weeks, the General was not a reasonable man.

Lang's gaze fell on the picture frame on the desk. It was empty. Never a good sign.

"He's gone," he called to Tyler. "Get after him."

Both of the men in Barr's office had made more money from Afghanistan than they could make in a lifetime back home, but even so they could feel their biggest pay check slipping away. Burning to ashes on the Herat road.

CHAPTER TWENTY-SIX

Qal'eh Mir Da'ud, Herat.
"You never count your money when you're sitting at the table; there'll be time enough for counting once the dealing's done."
– Kenny Rogers, The Gambler.

Lockhart had thrown caution to the wind and was speeding along the road towards Herat. Watching the jeeps being obliterated in front of him had been his third brush with death in three days. He felt like he was getting used to it.

He remembered the old chesterfield in the tea shop and the time he had taken to drink his mint tea, deciding which road to take. He had chosen to come into Afghanistan, and now he had to live with the consequences. Now, he had to find a way out.

As far as he could work out, he didn't have any friends in the country. He had let the Americans think he was dead, and he was driving a military Mastiff which would not make him any new friends among the locals in Herat. On the plus side, he couldn't even imagine how much money he was hauling behind him. Lockhart knew that the people who tell you that money can't buy you friends are usually poor and lonely themselves. The money would help him escape. All he needed was a plan.

He mulled the situation over. He would need to change vehicle at some point. The Mastiff was fairly resistant to roadside bombs because it was well armored. On the other hand, an American vehicle driving around on its own was likely to be a magnet for trouble. He would need to change his clothes too. During his travels, he had weathered a bit, but he still looked painfully western. Something local and scruffy would help him blend in, at least from a distance.

He would stock up on food and water at Herat, hopefully in one hit, and then he'd head for the border. The closest border would be Iran where there would be fewer bullets and bombs, but he wouldn't be extended a warm welcome. Lockhart planned instead to continue north through Herat and up into Turkmenistan.

Checkpoints would be a problem, because they'd want to search his truck. He would have to keep a stack of dollars up front, to bribe a quick passage through.

Lockhart felt that the plan was taking shape by the time he arrived on the outskirts of Herat. Then saw something remarkable. On the horizon, a few hundred yards from the Herat road, was a Russian tank. It was old and rusted, covered with a shiny, cheap looking paint, something between green and mustard yellow. It looked putrid compared to the refined hues of the modern ISAF forces.

As Lockhart drove closer to the tank, another appeared and another. Then an army of dark green missile launchers, their cabs and their silos painted in a dark green that would have been better suited to northern Europe. They had all been driven to this place and then left behind when Gorbachev had come to power and ordered the Russian withdraw.

There was something spooky about the deserted machinery, and Lockhart imagined what they would have looked like when their diesel engines were fired up in anger.

Afghanistan had been a cold war playground. These Russian tanks had rumbled over the border in 1979 to help the failing left-wing Afghan government. Nearly half of all Afghans were displaced to neighboring Iran or Pakistan. In response, conservative Islamist factions had come together to form the mujahedeen, dedicated to fighting the Soviet forces. Funding poured in from the US, China, Iran, Pakistan and Saudi Arabia.

The brief history lesson that David Barr had given to Lockhart on his first night at Kandahar was running through his head. These missile silos were for launching stingers, the same sort which the CIA had provided to the mujahedeen to help shoot down Soviet helicopters. The same sort that was now threatening US aircraft.

Even during the Cold War, superpowers were gentlemen, choosing to have their conflicts in Godforsaken countries in the middle of nowhere. The Americans armed one side, the Russians the other. Locals died, but the world's press didn't dig deeply enough to unravel the story. Besides, their readers had no idea where Afghanistan was. Chickens and eggs. Now they were home to roost.

Lockhart could see about two hundred tanks and a hundred missile trucks. There were also piles of spent munitions and beyond the military graveyard there were a thousand used cars and trucks waiting to be stripped for parts. Although his Mastiff was newer and better than anything else in the graveyard, it would still be a brilliant hiding place.

As he drove into the midst of the old tanks, a scrawny man in a dark blue shalwar kameez came running up to him, waving an AK47 and looking hopping mad. *Brave guy*, thought Lockhart. Although he wasn't carrying a weapon himself, most people would assume that anyone in a Mastiff would be armed to the teeth. Lockhart ignored the angry-looking guy and chose a parking spot. Then he turned off the engine and waited for the man to catch him up.

By the time the angry guy caught up, Lockhart was already out of the Mastiff. His plan was to make the Afghan believe that he had several well-armed friends in the back of his transport. It seemed to work because the guy lowered his gun and began to speak in more reasonable tones. He pulled off the scarf which had been keeping the dust out of his face and asked Lockhart what he wanted.

He spoke decent English and Lockhart asked him how much it would cost to buy one of the old trucks. He produced a wad of new dollars to help with the negotiating. The man looked crestfallen.

"No trucks," he said. "But I have a very good four by four."

The blue bales of cash would never fit in the back of a jeep. No truck, no deal. The man looked around his scrapyard, keen to make some decent money. He did not understand why a guy with an armored Mastiff would want to buy an old truck, but he was sure that the soldier had plenty of money so he wasn't arguing. He also wanted to get the deal done quickly, before village tongues started wagging. It wasn't a good idea to do deals with soldiers.

Lockhart looked around the graveyard for the biggest thing he could see. He spotted a beaten-up old coach. It was yellow and looked like it might have been a school bus in a previous life. He pointed it out to the owner.

"Does it work?"

The man nodded and smiled. Apparently, it worked very well and was a very good price. Car salesmen were the same the world over. Lockhart was not convinced. The vehicle was parked towards the back of the graveyard, almost half a mile away.

"If you can drive it over to me without breaking down, I'll take it." offered Lockhart. "Park it alongside, between me and the road."

Within twenty minutes, the man was back, proudly sitting at the wheel of the coach. It was about thirty years old, but it had started first time and had had no dramas on the way across the graveyard. Several of the red velvet seats had collapsed, but the driver's chair was comfortable enough. A dusty plastic fan stuck on the windscreen told him that the air con wouldn't work. No real surprise. Outside, it looked fairly roadworthy. The electrics worked, and there was nothing hanging off the bottom.

Lockhart didn't haggle too hard, and they agreed a price of eight thousand dollars, as long as the man could fill the tank before he left. He offered to up the price to ten thousand dollars if he could provide a crate of bottled water and thirty suitcases before sunset. The man looked confused, but he said he could manage it.

Lockhart kept the keys to the Mastiff, in case the man came back with anything or anyone other than the suitcases. Within an hour, he returned in a pickup truck with an assortment of tatty old cases strapped precariously to the back. He was alone.

The man had found him a stack of water bottles, the seals of which were unbroken. He also handed him a set of shalwar kameez and a woolen pakol hat like his own. There was a scarf to cover his face from the dust and to keep him from being recognized. Ten thousand dollars was a lot of money and the salesman didn't want to see his best customer being kidnapped before he came back to buy more trucks.

"If you are staying long, grow your beard," he advised the stranger. Lockhart thought it was good advice, but he was already planning to leave Afghanistan that night.

When the salesman left the graveyard, Lockhart spent the next hour loading up his coach. There were thirty shrink-wrapped bundles of cash like the one he had opened. Each fitted snuggly inside a suitcase with little room to spare. He cased them up, and slung some of them in the luggage compartments and others in the overhead lockers on his coach. He jammed the open bale underneath the driver's seat and then covered it with a dusty rug he had found at the back of the coach.

The ten thousand dollars had made no dent in the cash under his seat, and Lockhart couldn't even work out how much money he was sitting on top of as he bumped and hissed his way out of the graveyard and back onto the road to Herat.

Lockhart's best guess was that Kandahar was a distribution point for contractors' wages and US funds for rebuilding the country's roads, schools, and hospitals. He guessed that the money had been creamed off from the huge amount which was flowing through the Airfield until they had a gigantic haul, and then they had tasked David Barr to smuggled it out. If Barr had any sense, he'd be running as fast as Lockhart was. If Barr had any sense, he'd have a plan too.

CHAPTER TWENTY-SEVEN

Mary, Turkmenistan.
"Will the wind ever remember, The names it has blown in the past?"
- Jimi Hendrix, The Wind Cries Mary.

Charlie Lockhart had driven solidly through the heat of the day and now the light was fading. By the middle of the morning he had crossed the border into Turkmenistan, and the roads had become better as the day had progressed.

The yellow bus had served him well so far, but it had rattled like hell along the dust roads outside Herat. As the roads had improved, the deafening juddering which had accompanied each mile had slowly subsided, and the ride had become more relaxing. Sixty miles an hour was about as much as the bus could do before the metalwork started to complain and bits of the coachwork threatened to fall off.

At lunchtime, he had stopped at a town called Shark. There was a serene-looking lake nearby, and the place was packed with intricately carved buildings and sun cracked silver trees. Lockhart took time to look around; it felt good to be a tourist again.

Turkmenistan was arid, and dust kicked up behind his bus as he drove further into the country. Things were changing though, and grass had started to spring up either side of the road.

It felt good to be out of Afghanistan. The country had a rich and beautiful history, but war had ravaged it. Locked it down. The Afghanistan that Lockhart had seen was little more than a flat packed America, reconstructed in the middle of a desert, surrounded by razor wire, flooded in fluorescent light. Filled with Pizza Huts and TGI Fridays and cocooned from the reality beyond its perimeter.

By the time he arrived in Mary, Lockhart knew that he was two hundred miles away from Afghanistan. He felt two hundred miles safer, but the money was already becoming a problem. It was weighing on his mind. There was no way that Lockhart could keep it. It should build hospitals and schools, but it was sitting in blue bundles in suitcases at the back of his bus. Lockhart promised himself that he would use what he needed to get home safely, and the rest would end up where it belonged.

Mary itself was originally an oasis town on the Silk Road, but the modern city was grim. The British Machine Gunners and Bolsheviks had clashed here in the early part of the last century, blowing chunks out of the place. Now Mary lived off cotton and gas, and consequently it was industrial and ugly. It was a great place to disappear for the night.

The bus had been easy to drive along the wide straight desert roads, but as the city streets became tighter, Lockhart had to concentrate more and more as he maneuvered round corners. It wasn't fun, and he pulled off into the courtyard of a shabby-looking motel at the first opportunity.

The guy on the front desk looked suspicious of a Westerner turning up in an old bus with no passengers. He spoke very little English and was short-tempered. Most of his neck was red raw. Either his razor was old and blunt or his washing powder was cheap and scratchy. Or both. He kept rubbing away at the skin absent-mindedly while he demanded to see some identification from the stranger before him. Lockhart kept his passport to himself. There was no reason to make it easy for anyone who came looking for him.

The motel owner seemed lost in thought as he continued to rub at his neck. Probably planning how to part the tourist in front of him from a few extra dollars. Lockhart pulled out a wad of notes he had removed from the open blue bale under his seat. The motel owner's eyes widened. They were fifties, and Lockhart could have hired the room for a fortnight for just two of them, but he peeled off four and handed them to the guy behind the desk. From that moment on, the passport was forgotten, and the motel owner couldn't do enough to help. He took Lockhart's keys and parked the bus out of harm's way, turning it around, ready for departure the next day. Lockhart made sure he locked the luggage compartments and went to check out his room.

There were thirty rooms in the motel, and the owner showed Lockhart to the best of them, stooping and bowing along as if he were welcoming royalty. Lockhart began to regret his generosity when the man insisted on presenting the room to him, turning on each tap and pointing proudly at the water flowing from it, next the shower, then an explanation of the buttons on the remote control for the air conditioning. By the time the owner had flicked through the satellite TV channels, Lockhart was ready to physically eject him from the room.

When the man finally bowed and scraped his way backwards out of the door, Lockhart sat down on the bed and had a look around the room. It was a perfectly good room, clean but dull. A framed print of Genghis Khan was nailed to the wall. He had apparently visited the ancient city in 1221. The motel was about ten years old and had probably never been beautiful. It was already showing signs of wear and tear. But it was a good place to stay for the night; Discrete and anonymous. As a tourist, Lockhart had learned never to stay in the best hotel in town. The best hotel was always a magnet for tourists, terrorists, pickpockets and beggars. *You always sleep well in the third best hotel in town.*

He thought about lying back on the bed. He had been sitting down all day, and it had worn him out. Instead, though, he showered and pulled on a fresh shirt. Eventually, he took his discarded clothes down to reception to see if they could be laundered overnight. At first the receptionist was dubious about whether his clothes would be ready in time for his early checkout, but a twenty-dollar tip seemed to ensure that his bundle would be next into the machine. She stuck his name onto the netted wash bag and threw it under the desk. She pocketed the twenty and smiled at him for his kindness. Turkmenistan was a place where money talked, and Lockhart had plenty to offload.

The lobby was air-conditioned, and when Lockhart walked back out into the last of the sunlight, it was like walking into a greenhouse. The motel owner watched him go, still rubbing his neck. Still sore from lunchtime. He watched Lockhart stroll up towards the market, took a breath, and shook his head. It was the second time today that trouble had checked into his guest house, and it was time for him to pick a side.

He had been sweating on a decision since the tourist had arrived an hour ago. Finally, he reached for the phone and called the number that he had written on a scrap of paper earlier. He pulled it out of his top pocket and looked at the number. He didn't recognize his own writing; his hand had been shaking uncontrollably when he wrote it.

The giant had been pinning him against the wall by his throat when he gave him the number. He had been looking for another Westerner and had left the cell phone number for the owner to call if any strangers checked in. An hour later, Lockhart had shown up with his empty bus.

It was a problem that the motel owner could do without. Tyler's rough hands had crushed tighter and tighter around his throat as he explained the consequences of him not calling the cell phone if another westerner arrived. He had explained the consequences for the owner and his guests and his family. Then he had left as quickly as he had arrived, probably to scare the shit out of the rest of the motel owners in Mary. The owner shuddered, took a breath, and dialed the number he'd been given.

The marketplace was only around the corner from the hotel, and although some of the stalls were packed up and empty, there was still plenty of trading going on when Lockhart arrived. The place was a permanent structure with a fixed roof that gave shade from the sun. The traders displayed their goods on long concrete blocks which rose about three feet from the ground and were as thick as they were long. They reminded Lockhart of the blast walls he had crouched behind outside Kirsten Miller's tattoo parlor during the missile attack in Kandahar. These were worn and chipped by daily life though, unlike the freshly molded military versions.

The market traders covered the concrete tops with colorful rugs and displayed their goods on top. All of them were women and their clothes were bright and eye-catching. Their heads were covered, but their faces were open and warm.

Lockhart hadn't shaved since he left Kandahar and his beard was beginning to disguise his face. He wore a slightly beaten hat which he had found on the driver's seat of his coach, and was still wearing the cotton trousers that the scrap dealer in Herat had found for him. A market girl in a bright red sack dress spotted him instantly as a tourist and beckoned him over to her. She began to talk him through the fruits and vegetables on her stall, pointing and nodding at various items which she thought he would like. Lockhart promised the girl that he would come back later and then pushed deeper into the market to look for money dealers.

Turkmenistan was totalitarian, and in towns like this, Lockhart knew that there would be black market traders hungry for dollars. Currency was power. Lockhart knew that dealers couldn't be trusted, but he found them easily and there was no fuss. Within five minutes he had a wad of local notes to spend in the market.

There was a tea shop right at the heart of the marketplace, with an amazing array of bottled syrups on the counter. The bottles were different shapes and sizes, and the purple and yellow and orange liquids inside clashed violently with one another as they jostled for attention on the concrete counter. Behind them were bottles of water and piles of fresh lemons and apples. An electric urn was steaming away to one side.

A beautiful young girl with hazel eyes observed him from behind the counter. All Lockhart wanted was a place to sit and watch the market for a while. He was enjoying soaking up the exotic feel of the place. The air was perfumed by a spice stall a few meters away, which had nutmegs and cinnamon scenting into the atmosphere.

Behind the counter, an old woman pushed gently past the beautiful girl. She had the same hazel eyes, but they were milked by heavy cataracts. Her manner was brisk but not unkind. Years of work had bowed her back, and her face had become lined with life's slow lessons.

The girl's skin was olive, but the old woman's was darker and more weathered. She wasn't much over four feet tall and had trouble reaching some of the items on her counter. Still she looked proud, and the young girl seemed to know better than to interfere with her work. Lockhart wondered how many years of working in the market it would take before the elegant young woman began to look like her grandmother.

The old woman didn't waste time with language, but pointed at everything on the counter until she got to the grape syrup and Lockhart indicated that she had found what he was after. She was efficient and brusque, and Lockhart imagined that in another life she would have made a good New Yorker.

He held out some local currency, apologetic for not understanding the price. The woman carefully took the right amount, unabashed. She rummaged around in her pocket and gave him change, which he left on the counter. Despite her business-like manner, when the transaction was complete, she gave him an ancient smile which lit up the whole market.

There were two plastic seats at the side of the stall, and the old woman invited him to sit down to drink. The girl offered him some fresh bread which he accepted gladly, and he sat watching the business of the market for the next few minutes. The young woman tried to strike up a conversation with him, but he couldn't understand her. She turned towards her grandmother and shrugged in embarrassment, and all three of them laughed. She went back to her grandmother's tuition, removing one bottle at a time and cleaning it methodically. Lockhart went back to idly studying the buyers and the sellers.

Things felt different; more dangerous than before. Maybe it was because the military paranoia of Kandahar had rubbed off on him, or maybe because of the close calls he'd had in the last few days. Whatever the reason, something didn't feel right. He couldn't settle. He was halfway through the sweet grape juice when he realized. He was watching the girl writing the names of the infusions on the labels of the bottles. Just like the woman in the motel had written a name on his washing. Not his room number, but a name. *Fearless*.

There was only one way that she could have known the name: someone had reached the motel before him. Somebody was already here, in Mary. Somebody was looking for the bundle of dollars hidden in the bus.

Lockhart looked carefully through the marketplace and saw a guy in a black jacket standing a good foot and a half taller than anyone else in the market. Tyler was working his way into the market from the other side, heading towards the moneymen in the shady center of the place. He stood out a mile, but so did Lockhart; they were probably the only Westerners in the town. The only reason Tyler hadn't spotted Lockhart was because he was on his phone, head down and animated. He was zipping through the crowd towards Lockhart's motel. If he didn't change direction, it wouldn't be long until Tyler walked straight past the tea stall where Lockhart was still sitting.

"Hey," Lockhart called to the girl behind the counter. She looked over her shoulder and he placed a fifty on the counter. Enough for a couple of hundred drinks at market prices.

"Drinks for everyone," he pointed around at the people nearby. He gave the girl another hundred dollars for herself. Maybe she'd have some fun with it before she eventually turned into her grandmother. The girl latched on and started calling to the customers around the stall. Word went around quickly, and Lockhart slipped away as the customers started to draw to the tea shop like it was a magnet. Lockhart did the same at the spice stall, and at the edge of the market again he pressed money into the palm of the girl with the red sack dress and began handing out her fruit.

Tyler spotted the movement like a big game hunter. Watch the birds, and they'll tell you where the beasts are. *Watch for the patterns and you'll find your prey.* Something was happening, so he needed to react. He reached for his weapon and waded into the crowd. He was huge, and he tore through them. But the more people he shoved past, the more people he found in front of him. Word was spreading along the street outside the covered market. There was a crush. Everyone wanted something for nothing, and Tyler was swimming against the tide. Lockhart slipped out of the marketplace and into the open street.

Deep inside the market, Tyler's rage was kettling. He was punching people out of his way and trampling them down. But it was like swimming through tar. Suddenly, he broke through to the eye of the storm. An old woman was handing out grape juice as fast as she could. Jamming up the place. Losing him three hundred million dollars. She smiled at the giant and offered him a plastic cup. Tyler shot her right between the eyes. A ribbon of blood flicked across the clean bottles on the counter as the old woman dropped like a stone. The brown-eyed girl screamed as her grandmother hit the floor. It did the job. The crowd split like a flock of birds speared by a hawk.

Lockhart heard the shot, but there was nowhere to hide, so he tore up the street without looking back. Tyler moved fast for a big man as he burst out of the marketplace. Locals scattered all around him as he scoured the street. Lockhart had a hundred yards on him and kept the pace. By the time he rounded the corner to the hotel's courtyard, his lungs were burning, but it was his lucky day. The motel owner was shunting the bus around in the courtyard. Lockhart flew through the open door and pulled the owner from the driver's seat. He hit the gas hard, and the bus lurched forward onto the street.

As Tyler rounded the corner, he saw Lockhart at the wheel of the passing bus. He sprang full length at the open door and grabbed for the chrome handle just inside. Lockhart sped up; tearing back down the street towards the market as fast as the bus would go, pulling Tyler with him. The motel owner was standing at the front of the bus, trying to make a decision. Then suddenly he picked a side all over again, leaning forward and stabbing his finger at the button which closed the bus's pneumatic door. It slammed closed like a shark's mouth over Tyler's muscular arm. But the soldier hung on. His feet dragged along the tarmac as he kept a grip of the bus.

Lockhart could see tendons flexing in Tyler's forearm as the door hissed and complained, halfway between open and shut. Tyler was winning. As the bus sped past the market, an angry crowd came running out, trying to get hold of the soldier to avenge the innocent old woman from the tea stand. Lockhart leaned forward and hit the button to re-open the pneumatic door. He came off the gas to allow the crowd to catch up, and he slammed his foot into the side of the motel owner. The guy toppled out of the open door straight on top of Tyler. The weight was too much even for the giant. He released his grip on the handle and both men fell away from the bus, rolling into the baying mob. As Lockhart's eyes flicked up to the rear-view mirror to check their fate, he saw two things.

The first thing was that the angry crowd had closed in on Tyler and the motel owner. Tyler was swatting them away, more focused on his main task of strangling the guy who had just fallen on top of him. Keeping his promise. The second thing that Lockhart saw in the rear mirror was that there were about twenty startled passengers sitting in his bus, all wide eyed and staring straight back at him.

CHAPTER TWENTY-EIGHT

Gun Quarter, Birmingham. September 2010.
Across the lines, who would dare to go over the bridge, under the tracks
that separate Whites from Blacks? – Tracy Chapman

The man driving the white ford transit parked up three streets from the
Crown and Sceptre. He killed the engine and pulled the keys from the
ignition. He left the goods safely hidden in the back and put the keys under
the wheel arch, just in case things didn't work out.

As he set off towards the Crown, he pulled a pack of Superkings from
the pocket of his leather jacket and lit up, sucking in the warmth. His hair
was pulled back from his face; he'd reached an age where he didn't need to
shave it to look menacing.

It was an hour since the phone call, and the guy should be in the pub by
now. Unless he was a chancer, or worse still a cop. Most likely a chancer,
judging by the shaky conversation they'd had earlier.

The man had been loading the last of his crates into the back of the van
when his phone had vibrated. Number withheld. He ignored it.

It was three in the afternoon and the fish market in Birmingham was
closing. Everything was wet and washed off, but the stench of fish hung
around the place. The mobile had rung for a second time. Withheld.
Ignored.

The third time it rang, the fishmonger was hurtling down the Aston
Expressway out towards the motorway. This time, the number had flashed
up, so he had picked up the call. The guy on the end of the phone had
sounded nervous and naïve.

"I need a gun."

The fishmonger had been inside enough courtrooms and prison cells to know better than to get involved in that sort of conversation on the phone.

"Who gave you this number?" the fishmonger had shouted, over the din of the juddering chipboard panels inside the transit van.

"Mo," the reply was hesitant. "Mo gave me your number. You know Mo? The security guy?"

The fishmonger knew Mo, and he was an alright guy. He was fat and sweaty, busting out of his uniform, but happy to put the boot into anyone who messed with the vans during the day. He was also happy to turn a blind eye to late night activity in exchange for a bit of lobster. Yes, all in all, Mo was all right.

"Do you know the Crown and Sceptre, in Smithfield Street?"

"No," said the voice on the phone, curtly. Defensively. The fishmonger had already put the guy down as Asian, and figured he was probably Muslim. *Probably never set foot inside a pub.*

"Well, sort your shit out, find a map, and I'll see you there in an hour."

The fishmonger had only been to the Crown and Sceptre once before. It was a tiny backstreet pub in Birmingham's Gun Quarter. The kind of place where there's always a deal going on. The kind of place where nobody ever notices anything, and nobody asked questions.

The weather had turned wintery in the last couple of weeks, and by the time the fishmonger arrived in the Gun Quarter the late afternoon sky looked threatening. All the same, it took him a moment to adjust his eyes to the gloom inside the pub as he slipped through the heavy green doors into the bar.

The front room was dark, and the carpet was soaked in years of beer and ash. Daud was in the corner with a coke and a scowl. The fishmonger had guessed right; Daud didn't drink, and he was uncomfortable in the pub. When he looked around the place, he didn't feel he was missing out. Broken men coughed and wheezed from their chairs to the bar and back again. Bulbous noses, bronchial lungs and hard stares. Cast off like clinker.

Things were unraveling for Daud. He was the first son of a first son, a proud family of good men. But first Ajmal had gone off the rails, then the community he had worked hard for had ostracized him. Now Daud's heart lusted for revenge, and here he was buying a gun from a stranger in a pub.

In his pocket he had three thousand pounds. It was money which he had collected at the mosque for families suffering in the Pakistan floods. It was charity money that people had thrown in his bucket, and he was spending it on a gun to avenge his brother. *The brother that everyone else at the mosque seemed to have forgotten about.* Daud justified it to himself. He told himself that it was his duty to seek revenge for Ajmal. But deep down in his soul he knew it was wrong. Deep down, he knew that his soul was lost.

CHAPTER TWENTY-NINE

Ashgabat, Turkmenistan.
"Many rivers to cross, But I can't seem to find my way over."
- Lorraine Ellison, Many Rivers to Cross

As the dust and the crowd from the market consumed Tyler and the motel owner, Lockhart drove the bus on. The motel owner would be fine; Everyone in the marketplace was on his side. Lockhart was worried. He had expected someone to chase after him, but the huge man who had chased him from the market had already been looking for him in Mary when he arrived.

Lockhart could think of two possibilities. Either there was a tracker inside one of the blue bales, or else the soldier had guessed the route that Lockhart would use to escape. As he drove, Lockhart thought about it. He had headed past Herat and gone for the border. He had tried to get out of Afghanistan as quickly as possible. That was the obvious thing to do. Then he had avoided Iran, which would be predictable. Instead, he had chosen the biggest road on the map and followed it to the first big city on the route back to Europe. He had made it easy for Tyler.

Just as Lockhart was thinking about taking a detour, one of the passengers tapped him on the shoulder. It was an old guy who spoke a little English. Apparently, he was the best linguist among them. He explained that their regular bus had broken down so the motel owner, ever the entrepreneur, had sold them tickets to hitch a lift with him.

There were about twenty of them in all; mostly women wearing bright clothes, a few men dressed more soberly, and a large woman who looked like she was in mourning wearing a black burka.

"Where are you all going?" Lockhart called over his shoulder.

"Ashgabat," said the old man. "Same place as you."

"Ashgabat," the crowd all nodded and repeated when they heard the old man mention their destination. Some of them started fumbling around with grubby looking local currency and waving it towards Lockhart.

Lockhart could have kicked himself. He was planning to go to Ashgabat next. It was the next big city along the main road. Which mean Tyler would know exactly where he was going, too. And now he couldn't change his plan because he had a bunch of locals waving their money at him from the back of the bus.

"Not tonight" Lockhart shook his head. He grabbed the map that David Barr had given him back in Kandahar. He pointed to a town about sixty miles away. The old man craned his neck to see what Lockhart was showing him.

"Tejen?" he asked.

"Yes," said Lockhart, nodding his head. He had grabbed about four hours sleep on the road north of Herat last night, but he had been driving for hours and there was no way that he was going another three hundred miles tonight. "Tejen tonight, and Ashgabat tomorrow."

The old man looked at him for a moment and then turned to the other passengers and explained the news. Lockhart braced himself for a tough conversation, but it was non-negotiable. If they didn't like it, they could walk. After a minute, the old man turned back to Lockhart at the wheel. The passengers seemed fairly happy with the deal. The man explained one of the passengers had family in Tejan, and that they could sleep in the community hall for the night.

They arrived an hour later and the woman who had family in Tejen got off the bus first. She disappeared inside a municipal building for a moment. It was painted a terracotta color, but the paint was peeling in patches, revealing the concrete underneath. It didn't look like the Ritz, but it had been a long day and Lockhart was ready to sleep just about anywhere.

The woman emerged from the building and beckoned the passengers in. Once they were all off, Lockhart went to park the bus out of sight. He was happier staying here than in Ashgabat. It was suitably anonymous, just a dot on the map. Lockhart was careful where he parked.

The Russians say that sailors should trust in God, but keep rowing towards the shore. Muslims have a Hadith that believers should trust Allah, but to tie up their camel. There is a similar Jewish fable. It all boils down to the same thing: fate is quicker to help people who help themselves.

In a way, it would be a blessing if somebody drove off in the night with the yellow bus and its payload of dollars. But Lockhart felt a duty to return the money to Afghanistan, and he also needed the bus to get himself home. So, he tied up his camel, parking the bus so tight to the side of the building that nobody could get into the luggage compartments.

Lockhart wondered how much money was in the suitcases. Judging by the number of fifty-dollar notes crammed into the one blue bale he had opened, he estimated that there must be much more than a million dollars in each bale. There were thirty bales. He'd spend whatever it took to get home safely, but he couldn't wait to get rid of the rest. It was dangerous and would only bring trouble. He locked the doors and headed after the passengers.

There were several dormitory rooms in the building with rickety metal bunk beds crammed into them. They had thin mattresses on top, which had been worn down by myriad travelers. The men and women separated, with none of them complaining about their unexpected overnight stay. Lockhart and the old man ended up sharing a room by themselves. The only problem was the woman in the black burka who insisted on having a room to herself.

The other passengers guessed that she wanted some privacy in grief. None of them wanted to upset her, so they arranged for her to sleep in the smallest room on her own.

Lockhart lay on the bed and thought about his next move. His priority was to get as far from Afghanistan as possible. He had known that someone would come after him; he just hadn't realize that they would arrive so quickly, or that they'd be so formidable. Whoever he was, he seemed to know where Lockhart was heading. Lockhart wondered again whether there might be a tracker buried along with the money. Was it bleeping away now, outside against the wall of the building?

There was nothing he could do about it. There was no way for Lockhart to check inside the tightly baled notes. Unwrapping the packages would be a disaster. He would just have to take his chances and hope that he was being paranoid. He did his best to forget about it.

Someone had folded a pile of blankets on top of one of the bunks, and Lockhart grabbed one each for him and the old man. There were no bed sheets, so he slept in his clothes, draping the blanket over him more for comfort than for warmth. After his long journey, it felt like heaven. Lockhart fell into a deep sleep.

He woke up eight hours later, soon after dawn. The old man was shaking his shoulders. He was leaning over Lockhart whose bleary eyes struggled to focus on him for a moment.

"Ashgabat?" he asked, smiling like an impish child who had just woken his father from a well-earned night of rest. It was a good idea to get back on the road early. Lockhart nodded and groaned and used his stomach muscles to pull himself up.

"Okay," he said with a smile to the old man. "Let's go to Ashgabat."

CHAPTER THIRTY

Tejen, Turkmenistan
"Now I been out in the desert, just doin' my time
Searchin' through the dust, lookin' for a sign
If there's a light up ahead well brother I don't know
But I got this fever burnin' in my soul"
– Johnny Cash, Further on Up the Road

By the time Lockhart and the old man got outside, the rest of the passengers were all ready to get going. The sun was shining, and the bus was still parked behind the building, unscathed. Lockhart couldn't help wondering where the man from the marketplace was waking up this morning. Was he still in Mary, or had he traveled through the night to Ashgabat? Lockhart shook his head. He didn't even know whether the danger was lying in front of him or behind.

There was some good news though. Lockhart figured that the crowd of passengers around his bus might be useful. A guy driving an empty bus across a country would look far more suspicious than a driver with a coach full of passengers. He needed to head towards Ashgabat anyway, and the locals would complete his disguise perfectly. He ushered them all back onto the bus.

None of them had much luggage apart from one clumsy woman who had two scrawny caged cockerels. The birds looked annoyed rather than alarmed as she bashed them against nearly every seat she passed as she made her way to the back of the bus. Lockhart turned the key, and the bus shuddered into life and purred as it idled. It sounded happy to be back in service after its time languishing empty in the Afghan bone-yard. Eager to please.

By midday, the bus was halfway to Ashgabat, having managed the tarmac road with no problems. They had passed more camels and green grass, but most of the horizon was dusty and dry. From time to time they would drive through vast areas that had been irrigated by the Russians, and the roadside would burst into color; poppies and grassland and cereals sprung up from the sand. Wild seeds, blown on the wind for hundreds of miles, had been lucky enough to land here, and clusters of alien color had taken hold.

After thanking him profusely as they boarded, the passengers who had commandeered his bus had paid no further attention to their driver. He had kept an eye in his rear-view mirror, enjoying their company. Strangely, the bus shuddered and jolted less with their ballast. The hum of their conversation was soothing compared to the rattle of yesterday's empty carcass.

The passengers had paired off as the journey had worn on, and all of them except for the widow were deep in conversation. They talked, laughed, and nodded at one another as Turkmenistan's Mountains rose and fell in the distance.

As he drove, Lockhart wondered about what was happening back in Kandahar. David Barr was small-time and Lockhart figured that he would be in big trouble for losing the consignment. Kandahar would be a dangerous place for anyone who fell in with the wrong crowd. Even worse if you fell *out* with them.

For all the contentment that his new passengers brought, Lockhart still felt uneasy. Perhaps it was just coming to terms with his perilous situation; the vast quantity of cash under the floor of the bus and the certainty that someone would come after him to retrieve it.

There was no sign of the huge soldier in front or behind. But even as he drove along the straight road to Ashgabat, Lockhart felt as though he was being watched. They hadn't passed another car for twenty minutes, and he could see nothing behind him in his mirrors. There was no obvious cause for alarm, but as a tourist, Charlie Lockhart had learned to listen to his intuition and his heart.

By lunchtime, they reached a small town called Tejan. Lockhart parked in the marketplace and the people behind him spilled off the bus, keen to stretch their legs for twenty minutes. A couple stayed close by, in case the unfamiliar driver tried to depart without them, but the others wondered in amongst the market traders.

Only the widow hung back. She didn't seem keen to get up from her seat, but Lockhart made it clear that he was locking the bus and that she needed to get up. As she rose from her seat, he was again taken by her size. She didn't speak as she passed him, and Lockhart wondered whether that was normal for someone in mourning. His travels had made him enjoy different cultures and traditions, but he still felt uneasy around people who covered their faces.

Before Lockhart had decided what to make of the widow, she was gone, lost in the market. He didn't trust her, but she was not his problem. Whatever her story, she would be off the bus in Ashgabat in four hours' time. But twenty minutes later, when the passengers returned to the bus, the widow was nowhere to be seen.

The rest of the group piled back onto the bus, again they nodded and smiled at Lockhart as they boarded. The woman who had bought the two chickens along was beaming. She had apparently exchanged the birds for a hungry-looking goat, which she pulled onto the bus by one of its horns. For a moment Lockhart considered whether goats ought to be allowed on his bus, and then smiled at his own British lust for regulation. He clapped as the woman pulled her new prize along the aisle, and the passengers joined in, laughing.

They waited for five more minutes, but the widow didn't resurface. The mood felt lighter without her, and it became clear that she had no friends on the bus. The goat and the passengers grew restless, and eventually Lockhart resumed his seat at the front and turned on the engine. His fuel gauge needle was about half full, and a red light on the console flashed briefly but then went out. The hydraulics hissed as he closed the door, a sound which made Lockhart feel like he was five years old, a kid pretending to drive an imaginary bus at school.

As they drove out of the marketplace, and the passengers were settling down, they hit an almighty sandstorm. Something was kicking up a huge amount of dust just a few meters up the road to their right. Suddenly, as the people on the bus strained to see what was causing the storm, two masked men appeared from within the cloud. They were working quickly together, pointing sticks and calling short instructions to one another.

They looked young and strong, and on high alert. Their eyes swept up and down the road for dangers. They were wearing traditional Turkmen clothes, and one carried a rolled-up rug on his back. The other was carrying a large water vessel as he scrambled from side to side, arms outstretched, preparing for whatever was about to emerge from the dust.

Then from behind them, hundreds of sheep came swirling like a shoal of fish across the road, with a black mongrel dog chasing behind them. Near to the dog was a third man on horseback.

Lockhart remembered the old Turkmenistan saying which had been framed on his wall in the hotel room, below the picture of Genghis Khan; *Water is a Turkmen's life, a horse is his wings, and a carpet is his soul.*

Shepherds had probably bought their flocks here to market since the village began. They would sell a few and exchange a few and then head back out to pasture for another week. Lonely work.

Inside the bus, the passenger with the goat looked crestfallen. If she'd been in the marketplace when the new sheep had arrived, she might have got a better deal. But if they had traveled with their regular driver, he wouldn't have stopped in this village at all. *So much of life is about being in the right place at the right time*, she thought. Then she reached into her pocket and retrieved some grain that she offered to her new goat. It nibbled and licked at her hand gratefully.

Despite the dust and the commotion, the bus kept rolling forward. Lockhart remembered a piece of advice Ajmal had given him back in Quetta before they set out on the convoy.

"If something strange is happening, assume that it's something bad. And if something bad is happening, don't stop driving."

The advice had served him well during the attack at Marni Sar. Suddenly the flock of sheep in the road in front of the bus panicked and split in two. A dark figure thrust out from the middle of the dust cloud, sending the flock off in different directions. It was the mysterious widow, but she didn't look like the sedate woman the passengers had seen earlier. She was running full pelt through the dust and the startled animals. Her strides were forceful and muscular and she was clawing at the air to get back towards the departing bus. As she ran alongside them she banged on the doors heavily with her palm.

Lockhart was about to open the door when two more figures burst out from the dust away to the right, running at full speed towards the woman. Lockhart hesitated for a moment. He had suspected the woman before, and now his instincts had been proven right. The men chasing her were uniformed police, and although they hadn't yet drawn them, they were reaching for the holstered guns on their hips.

Lockhart had to make a decision.

This really wasn't his problem, and with millions of dollars in the luggage compartment, he didn't want to get embroiled in a local dispute. He was about to press harder on the gas when the widow tore away at her veil and banged on the window again. It was a shocking revelation. Not only was the widow a man, but she - or rather he - had been hiding a full beard under his black veil.

"I'm a journalist," he yelled with an accent that Lockhart couldn't place. "Open the fucking door!"

The dust was getting into the widow's lungs now that he had removed his veil, and as Lockhart opened the doors he fell into the bus coughing and spluttering. Lockhart could see the policemen yelling in frustration and shaking their fists at the bus as the sheep slowly swirled back into a single flock around them.

Lockhart kept an eye on the road as he rumbled forwards, but glanced occasionally at the man who had now slumped into the first seat in the bus and was regaining his breath.

"Thank you," the man gasped. "Thanks very much."

He looked frightened rather than dangerous, but Lockhart didn't trust him as far as he could spit.

"Take off your clothes, please."

The journalist's laugh faded as Lockhart gave him a hard stare.

"You've been hiding a beard from me and the rest of these passengers all morning, and unless you want to get off the bus, I want to know what else you're hiding."

The man reached into his burka and pulled out a blackberry and a camera and an iPhone.

"That's all I've got," he said, placing them on the floor in front of him. "Satisfied?"

Lockhart stopped the bus sharply, and the doors opened again, the hydraulics startling the goat. The widow looked around the bus, but was met by hard stares. A few hundred meters back, the policemen straightened up as they heard the hiss of the brakes.

Reluctantly the man removed his dark robes, revealing a pair of beige combat trousers and a dark brown top. Lockhart started the bus again as he asked for the man's passport. The journalist complied.

"Which newspaper do you work for?" Lockhart asked, as he studied the man's credentials and tried to keep driving in a straight line. He was Spanish.

"I'm a stringer. I get calls from British agencies or newspapers, and if I like the sound of the story, I take it on."

Lockhart was piecing the guy together. Most likely, he was employed to report on stories that were too dangerous, too sensitive, or too illegal for staff writers. He was traveling on a Spanish passport and working for the English media, which meant the odds were that the story was political. Which meant he had probably been working over the border.

"Iran?"

The Spaniard looked at the bus driver. The guy was obviously fairly astute to have worked out where he was traveling to. But who was he? If he was a fellow journalist, or a mercenary, or a tourist, why the hell was he driving locals around on a beaten-up bus?

"Yes, Iran," he confirmed, realizing he was in no position to ask questions at that moment. "And I'm finished now, heading home."

Lockhart suggested that he should put the burka back on so as not to draw too much attention to them.

"I can take you to Ashgabat but then you're on your own" he said, and he indicated that the Spaniard should head back along the bus to his original seat.

As he was getting to his feet and adjusting his burka, the Spaniard noticed the bright blue package tucked underneath the driver's seat. He had no idea what it contained, but he wasn't a journalist by chance. He had a curious mind and a sharp wit.

Smuggler, he thought as he hid his beard and took his seat at the back.

By mid afternoon the road had begun to run alongside a vast and tranquil river, and the land either side seemed more fertile. On the other side of the river just a few miles away was the border with Iran. At the nearest point, the bus drove within two miles of the boundary but continued along the M37 towards Ashgabat. Although all the passengers seemed suspicious of the bearded journalist, he sat quietly as the journey continued.

In the end, the trouble came from another passenger. They were about half an hour from Ashgabat when she started speaking hurriedly to the woman next to her. She became agitated and began calling out to the rest of the bus. Lockhart turned his head to see what was happening, and the woman with the goat started shouting at him.

Lockhart stopped the bus at the side of the road. The journalist turned out to be helpful after all because he could translate the girl's cries.

"She's having a baby."

Lockhart had no intention of helping a Turkmen woman give birth in the back of a clapped-out school bus while being cheered on by a group of freeloading passengers, a goat, and a Spaniard dressed as a woman. He got back to the driver's seat and started up towards the city at full speed.

"Ask one of them to point the way to the hospital," he called back to the Spaniard. "We can drop her off there."

The man in the burka translated and sure enough an old man shuffled to the seat nearest the front and as they entered the city he began pointing left and right as they got to each junction. The woman had started making some alarming noises.

As the streets became more urban and busier, Lockhart was too focused on getting the girl to the hospital to notice that the city was modern and crowded. It was full of neon lights and communist bronzes and mausoleums. Suddenly, as they rounded a corner, the bus-load of passengers stood up at once. Apparently, it was their stop.

Despite the drama of the pregnant woman gripping them for the last twenty minutes, they didn't want to miss their stop. Lockhart couldn't help but laugh. The old man dutifully stayed in his seat and the journalist stayed on at the back, but the other fifteen people and the goat alighted from the bus and headed off down the street.

The hospital was minutes away, and the three men helped the girl into the main entrance. She had been traveling alone and Lockhart suspected someone would need to accompany her. He realized that they had more chance of getting a poor girl into a city hospital if he had a few dollars in his pocket. As he turned to reach under his seat, he realized that the journalist was behind him. It was too late for pretense now, and Lockhart reached into the blue bale under his seat and pulled out a stack of fifty-dollar bills.

The journalist looked at Lockhart, knowing that it was a good time to ask a question because the driver was in a hurry. The skill to getting the story is knowing when to ask the question.

"Smuggler?" he asked. "I'd love to hear your story."

Lockhart pulled about a thousand dollars from the pile and handed them to the journalist. The guy in the dress didn't think twice about taking them.

"No," said Lockhart as he handed over the cash. "I'm no smuggler. I don't want to tell my story, and I don't want to see you again. Understand?"

The journalist hitched up his burka and stuffed the money into his combats without counting it. Lockhart noticed that his knuckles were cut and that two of his fingernails were black. He wondered what kind of journalism the bearded Spaniard specialized in.

Without saying another word, the man straightened his veil and sauntered off up the street. Despite the need to get the pregnant girl inside, Lockhart took a moment to watch the journalist disappear into a café further along the road. His veil was back on, and he didn't look back.

The old man had offered to stay with the girl, which was helpful. Lockhart paid the front desk enough money to see that he was ushered straight in for an audience with the hospital director. He explained that the girl should be well looked after, and he paid twice the hospital's usual fee to ensure that she stayed in the best room.

Then Lockhart made a substantial donation to the hospital funds. The money in the suitcases had probably been meant for hospitals before it was stolen from Afghanistan. The hospital director was beside himself with excitement. Lockhart wondered whether he was pleased for his patients or whether he was planning on taking his cut. He looked like he was a decent guy. Lockhart wanted to think he was happy for the patients.

He had hardly finished counting out the money when there was a knock at the door. A nurse spoke quietly to the director, and he beamed.

"It seems to have been a quick labor," he smiled. "Your passenger has given birth to a very healthy baby girl!"

Lockhart didn't go and see her. He didn't know the girl who had gone into labor on his bus. While throwing a few dollars at the hospital director felt like the right thing to do, he didn't feel it gave him the right to intrude on her personal moment.

The director acted as a translator as Lockhart spoke to the old man who had helped to get the woman to the hospital. He pulled out another two hundred dollars and gave them to the old man. He explained that he should ensure that the woman's husband and family could be sent for. He told him to keep the rest for himself for his troubles.

*

Two streets away, the journalist sat in the café and pulled out his Blackberry. He wrote what he knew. The driver was definitely English and had a fresh tattoo. The only point of his driving from Mary to Ashgabat would be to escape from Afghanistan back to Europe. He was smuggling US dollars which meant he was involved in something big. The journalist could smell a story. All he needed to do was to work out which would pay him best; writing a story about smuggling or asking the driver for a cut of the cash in return for staying silent. He typed the registration plate of the yellow bus into his Blackberry, and thought about his next move.

CHAPTER THIRTY-ONE

Leaving Ashgabat, Turkmenistan.
"Everybody here comes from somewhere,
That they would just as soon forget and disguise."
- REM, Supernatural Superserious

Since setting out to travel the world, Charlie Lockhart had learned about people and he had learned about nature. Over the last few days he had followed the direction of the birds and watched the few clouds in the sky beginning to change shape. At night when he rested he could smell the salt on the air as he got closer to the Caspian Sea.

After leaving the old man and the young girl in the hospital, he had returned to the bus and driven out of the city. Ashgabat had a million inhabitants and he could easily have hidden amongst the churning humanity. But it stood to reason that anyone fleeing Afghanistan would end up in Ashgabat after two days, so anybody looking for him would be sure to scour the city. The yellow bus didn't blend in so well.

So, he kept driving through the city and out of the other side. He stopped once for fuel and then took the main road west towards Turkmenbasy, which was three days away on the Caspian coast.

Soon the capital city was small enough to fit entirely into the bus's rear-view mirror, and Lockhart was back surrounded by poverty and emptiness. The bus had begun to rattle again, pining for the passengers who got off in the city. The sun was losing the will to hang in the sky, and the view along the road became obscured as the shadows lengthened and the light began to glint off anything reflective up ahead. The tranquil waters of a Russian irrigation canal suddenly turned to fire as the falling sun cast onto it.

Despite his glasses, Lockhart drove pretty much blind.

As the blaze of pinks and oranges was subsiding, he made out something in the road ahead. He was on top of the silhouette before he could see that it was a small boy clutching a football, staring straight at him. Instinct kicked in, and Lockhart pulled everything at the right-hand side of the wheel. The bus began to turn, its locked wheels scoring black lines along the tarmac. The boy didn't move as the bus missed him by inches, the wind from the wing mirrors ruffling his hair as it passed.

Lockhart felt the back of the bus starting to lose traction and flail outwards, so he released the brakes and the bus straightened up clear of the boy and plowed straight into the dusty field at the side of the road. The windscreen smashed as the bus scoured into the unforgiving dry earth. Lockhart's head hit the steering wheel, and for a minute everything went black.

As he started to come around, Lockhart could feel blood on his forehead. There was an insistent banging coming from the door of the bus, and without thinking he released the hydraulics and it hissed open. He was immediately aware of the sound of the boy's high voice, shouting at him angrily.

Lockhart looked up to see that the boy must have been seven or eight years old, wearing a bright red replica football shirt. Lockhart tried not to let his football prejudices cloud his judgment. The boy stood in the doorway, shaking his fist at the driver of the bus that had almost run him down. He had learned some English, because he kept shouting "Sixty-Three, Sixty-Three" at the top of his voice.

Through the smashed windscreen Lockhart could see a woman, presumably the boy's mother, skirt gathered up, running across the arid field. Behind her was a small courtyard and a collection of low-slung buildings. A donkey was standing in the courtyard looking startled by the yellow bus which had disturbed the tranquil sunset.

The woman had now crossed most of the field and was waving her fists around just like the boy. She yelled as she ran, her long skirt bundled up in her hand. It soon became clear though that she was not angry with Lockhart. As she clambered through the open doors, her sound filled the bus. She was deeper and far louder than the boy. She grabbed him by the ear and shook him. He looked baffled. She yelled and scolded him, pointing at the bus, and the road, and the driver.

He didn't understand her words, but Lockhart could see in her eyes the emotions of every mother who comes close to losing a child; relief, rage and guilt all pouring out on top of each other. The boy didn't look at the driver, but got off the bus and meekly trotted back to the buildings across the field. The donkey watched him with idle interest as he passed.

The woman watched him until he disappeared from sight, her shoulders falling and her composure returning. She turned to the driver and pulled her wild hair from her eyes. Then she took Lockhart by the ear just as she had with the boy. Except more gently. More professionally.

"So sorry," she said in a clear voice. "You are bleeding from your head. Come with me, I am a doctor."

Lockhart didn't want to bring the family any trouble. He insisted on moving the bus out of sight of the road and diligently picked up any recognizable bits of bright yellow bodywork which had shaken loose during the accident. The doctor put this slightly odd behavior down to concussion and waited for him to clear up. The head wound was not so serious, but she had heard about concussion patients becoming disorientated and aggressive, so she waited for him to park his bus behind her house out of sight.

The light was dying outside and as Lockhart entered the house it didn't take too long for his eyes to adjust. The man of the house stood up to meet him as he walked in. He looked as though he had not been designed to work the land, but the land had molded him as best it could. He had clear honest eyes which picked up the glow of the small fire burning in the corner of the house. He held out a hand and Lockhart took it. His handshake was firm and dry, surprisingly strong considering his frame. He introduced himself as Jeyhun.

"Sorry for auto-bus," he said, pointing towards the back of the house. His wife was the linguist in the family, but Lockhart appreciated the sentiment.

"No problem," replied Lockhart, looking around for the rest of the family. "Where's Pele?"

Jeyhun laughed but didn't answer the question. The men fell into silence, as Jeyhun busied himself with the fire. The doctor soon emerged with the boy alongside her. She was running her hand through his hair gently. The boy with the football shirt stepped forward towards Lockhart sheepishly with his hands clasped in front of him. Lockhart felt sure they had been rehearsing next door. He played his part and sat stony faced in front of the boy.

"Sorry for auto-bus," he said, in the same tone as his father.

Lockhart smiled and gave the boy a wink. The boy's face lit up, and he skipped to his dad. He was off the hook. His mother had a small metal bowl full of water. She began to boil the water on the fireplace in front of the stranger. She had an electric kettle next door, but she was worldly enough to know how westerners worried about disease in strange countries, so she boiled up the water in front of him, so he could see.

She had a bright green first aid box which reminded Lockhart of Miller, the tattooist from Kandahar, and for a moment his mind wondered back to her. He wondered if she had liked the glass jug he had left for her, and whether he had made any lasting impression on her at all. The smell of disinfectant and a stinging forehead bought him back to the moment, and the doctor looked at him closely.

"I should really tell you my secret," she said, as she carefully mopped at his head. "I am a doctor of philosophy rather than medicine; I studied in Baghdad, but I should be able to deal with a cut like this."

Lockhart smiled. He had enjoyed his time in Baghdad.

"My name is Rosalina and my husband here is Jeyhun."

"Yes, he told me," replied Lockhart. He guessed that the woman had been teaching him English and that she would be pleased that he had been speaking the language. She seemed more cosmopolitan than her husband, and her surroundings. Her eyes lit up a little in the firelight. Lockhart had guessed right.

"Oh, he told you, did he?" she said, and she chuckled. "He speaks very good English when he tries."

*

Less than a mile away, Tyler had been scouring the road for any sign of Lockhart. He was rewarded as the sun set on a narrowing stretch of the main road out of Ashgabat. He slowed as he approached a hollow in the road. He sensed danger and realized that the earth to the right-hand side of the highway was freshly disturbed. He was trained to spot roadside bombs, and he hit the brakes hard. Then he remembered that he had left Afghanistan, and that life here was safer.

He was about to set off again when he spotted the glass in the road. Safety glass. He knew that safety glass was most likely to be from a bus or a truck. His eyes scanned the field, and he made out wide tracks heading towards a low house about a hundred meters from the road. There was a warm light coming from the windows and smoke coming from the chimney. Someone was home. His gut told him he was in the right place, so he pulled off the highway into the hollow and waited patiently for nightfall.

Tyler had been chasing a ghost for the last three days. He had been traveling for hundreds of miles with no idea who or what he was chasing. He had found the stranger in the marketplace in Mary, but he couldn't be sure he had the money. The bus he was driving was big enough to stash the bales in, but where had he found the passengers? It was a mystery.

It was over two days since Tyler had found the empty Mastiff in the boneyard in Herat, with no sign of the driver or the cash. He and General Lang had been planning the shipment for months, and they had risked everything to get the consignment out of Kandahar. In return, he'd been left with an empty vehicle in a scrap yard in the middle of nowhere.

The cash wasn't legal. But then lots of illegal things happened in the middle of a war. Tyler and Lang had been creaming money from the civilian contracts in Afghanistan and stashing away millions of dollars. They had carefully planned the trip to Herat for months; the moment they would flee the country with their hard-stolen currency. Now someone else was running away with the stash.

As Tyler sat in the car, just outside Rosalina's cottage, he mulled over the last couple of days. Remembered the rage which had flooded into his body as he had stared at the empty Mastiff in the boneyard. Standing amongst the broken vehicles, he had controlled his temper for a moment, his mind straining to keep control of his anger like an archer's fingers holding back the taut string of a bow. Release was inevitable. His brow furrowed, his turned to the local guy running the bone yard.

"Tell me everything about the man who left this truck here," he demanded, all calm and menacing.

Where was David Barr? Had he even been here? Barr had been tasked with getting the cash to them on the border with Turkmenistan, and Tyler had planned to shoot him when he arrived. Until they crossed the border, Tyler and General Lang would have had complete deniability.

Now though, Barr had disappeared. He had told them he had found a ghost driver to do the job for them. He said it was a civilian who had no knowledge of the operation and who was not known at Kandahar. Tyler had never seen this mysterious stranger and couldn't be sure that he really existed. Frustrating.

The owner of the bone yard had been wide-eyed. He shrugged and smiled apologetically at Tyler. Maybe the owner didn't know much about the man who had left the Mastiff behind, but the shrug and a nervous smile were enough to unleash Tyler's fury. He kicked out at the man, hard and high. His smile disappeared as he fell to the ground. Tyler's gun was in his hand, and he aimed where the annoying smile had been.

The first bullet took out the man's teeth and ripped through his cheek and the back of his throat. Hatred gripped Tyler as he fired again and again. The violence released his anger, and he felt good as he continued to empty his magazine as accurately as he could towards the man's face. He was definitely dead by the time the second round hit him, but the bullets continued to pulverize his soft flesh and smash through his bone.

Tyler fired again and the man's eyes ripped and his face caved in. The fourth and fifth bullets went into his neck and spine until his whole head gave way and came away from his body. Tyler ignored the decapitated corpse and continued to fire at the head, which bobbed about as more metal dug in. A few stubborn bits of sinew kept it within a few inches of the rest of the dead man's body.

When all the bullets had gone, Tyler stamped on the remaining bits of skull and brain, mashing them into the dust. Then he regained his composure and caught his breath, and phoned Lang to break the bad news and to work through the plan. Dust clung to his bloody shoes as he paced back and forth next to the headless corpse.

"So, are we looking for David Barr, or this Fearless guy?" he asked, agitated.

Lang explained to Tyler that they were looking for the money, nothing else. He would stay in Kandahar for a few hours to see if he could flush out Barr there, and Tyler would head for the border and see if he could pick up tracks.

"Whoever he is, he's got to be in a truck because of the cash," he explained. "He'll be about 4 hours in front of you. Any signal?"

Tyler had been looking for a GPS signal from the bales of cash since he arrived at the boneyard. There were occasional bleeps, but nothing concrete. His hunch was that Fearless was a smokescreen that Barr had invented to gain some time while he made off with the money himself. But he did what Lang told him and headed north of Herat and over the border. Now as he waited in the hollow near the isolated house, the journey seemed worth it. Tyler had found the yellow bus and was waiting until nightfall to get some answers.

*

Inside the house, Rosalina was introducing Lockhart to her son.

"His name is Nazar" she said, and she looked at the stranger enquiringly. She had introduced her entire family, but he had not mentioned his name yet. His quick actions had saved her son's life, and he had reacted calmly and fairly. He had a thoughtful face and his eyes were alert but kind. She had been studying him closely as she attended to his cut and he seemed like a good man.

The stranger looked straight at her, and their eyes were so close that she felt that their souls connected. He spoke simply and honestly.

"It is best for you and for your family that I don't tell you my name. I am traveling from Afghanistan and I don't want to be followed."

Rosalina lived in a country where the state insisted on conformity. She had traveled through places which frowned at educated, liberated women. She understood the need for discretion and was pleased that the stranger had been as honest as he could.

"Sometimes things have to remain hidden," she said, understanding. "Sometimes even our words have to remain hidden."

Her last comment was wistful and had been mostly to herself, but Lockhart was better traveled than Rosalina had imagined, and he understood what she meant. Ever since Baghdad Lockhart had kept a copy of The Hidden Words in his rucksack.

"Especially when you are traveling through the seven valleys?" Lockhart offered. Rosalina looked at him, and he held her gaze. After a moment she glanced at her husband and her son, and then she turned back to Lockhart.

"Yes, you are right. We *are* traveling through the Seven Valleys. We are a

Bahá'í family, but they do not tolerate our religion here. It has to stay secret."

"Hidden?" said Lockhart as he reached into his rucksack. The woman smiled and nodded. When Lockhart pulled his well-traveled copy of The Hidden Words from his bag, she looked astonished.

Although Bahá'í taught its followers about the oneness of humanity and even encouraged mixed marriages, Rosalina had never met a western follower before.

"I'm not Bahá'í," the stranger told her, as if he had read her thoughts. "But I have been to Baghdad just like you, and I was given this book as a gift. I have been reading it while I have been on my journey."

Baghdad was the place where Bahá'í began in the nineteenth century, when Baha'u'llah wrote the Hidden Words and the Seven Valleys. It was a boiled down essence of a religion, in which the voice of God handed down pearls of wisdom in Twitter sized sound bites. There were seventy-two verses in Arabic and a few more in Persian, and they spoke simple but profound truths. Lockhart liked them.

Before he had set out on the road that very morning, Lockhart had read the sixty eighth verse. It spoke of people around the world being made from the same clay so that nobody was better than anyone else. He guessed from their names and their general appearance that Jeyhun was Turkmen and Rosalina was Russian. Lockhart wondered how long they had been Bahá'í.

As Rosalina finished attending to the cut that Lockhart has sustained in the crash, she spoke to Jeyhun and Nazar over her shoulder. Her husband headed off to the kitchen and the boy began lighting candles around the room.

"We should show signs of unity through our deeds and our words and our actions," she said softly to Lockhart. "We walk with the same feet and we eat with the same mouth."

Lockhart was impressed. He could recall the verse that he had read earlier in the day, but Rosalina was evidently a true believer and knew all the Hidden Words by heart.

She took the book from Lockhart and ran her finger along the spine, feeling its texture. She had never seen a translation into English before and the foreign type on the weathered pages made her marvel at the way the word had spread. She spoke to the stranger about the valleys of love and contentment and wonderment, and all the others which made up her journey towards God. His face looked warm and friendly in the candlelight and she found him easy to talk to.

The smell of pumpkin dumplings started to waft in from the kitchen, and the house felt warm and cozy. Lockhart thought this was the best thing about traveling, the way strangers could become instant friends, and the warmth of a night in their homes.

Soon Jeyhun returned with dishes full of Manty dumplings and Plov; a simple dish of meat and carrots and rice. It was the first time that Lockhart had eaten food cooked with cotton oil, and he didn't think it added much to the flavor. But the fields were full of cotton, so it was sensible to use its oil for cooking.

The food was simple, but the company was nourishing, and soon enough the fire became embers and Jeyhun put Nazar to bed. He returned to the room with another Bahá'í scripture. Their church had no clergy or priests, but once every nineteen days they would come together to celebrate their religion. Other times they would share prayers together, and in Turkmenistan that meant meeting in secret.

Rosalina asked Lockhart if he would join them in a prayer before bed, and she began to read from the book in words that Lockhart didn't understand. It didn't matter though. Her tone was low and honeyed, and the glow of the embers and the shortening candles began to make him sleepy. After a few minutes, Rosalina closed the book and Jeyhun found some rugs for the stranger under their roof. His quick reactions had saved their son, and in return they had fed him and given him shelter. The doctor knew that the stranger would leave first thing in the morning; she could tell that he had a good heart but a restless soul.

The couple were soon gone, and Lockhart settled down in front of the dying fire. He was far from home and unsure of what tomorrow would bring, but the food and the fire and the talking had calmed him. He fell into a deep and happy sleep which would have lasted until dawn, if he hadn't been woken by the gunshot.

Tyler's mood improved as he walked outside through the dark. Everything that he and Lang had done over the last few months had gone perfectly to plan, right until the last moment. Now it was time to get things back on track. The sun had set behind the ramshackle house, and he had begun to move towards it. He was cautious because he had shot all of his ammo in anger in the boneyard, and would have to rely on other methods when he reached the house.

He was only halfway across the field when a bright light illuminated the road behind him. Instinctively, Tyler hit the deck. He watched the vehicle slow down to a crawl. Then whoever was driving pulled the four by four off the road and killed the lights. A tall woman in a dark burka and a veil got out of the driver's side and started running stealthily towards the house.

As she disappeared around the back of the buildings, Tyler edged closer to see what was going on. The woman was trying to open the door of a yellow bus, which was parked just out of sight of the road. She was having trouble with the door and eventually threw her head back in frustration. She removed her headscarf and ran her hands through her hair, cursing. She had a beard. Tyler had seen some strange things, but he didn't know what to make of it.

The bearded man thumped at the door of the coach, far too noisily in Tyler's opinion. Sure enough, within a couple of minutes another guy emerged at the door of the house. He saw the bearded man and started shouting. The intruder took fright and hitched his burka around his waist and began running through the field. The man in the doorway had a rifle of some description and it suddenly rang out in the night.

There was no town for miles in any direction, so the night was the darkest black and the silence was stifling, and when the shot rang out Lockhart snapped awake instantly. The noise was still ringing as his wits came about him.

For a moment he was disorientated, but he quickly remembered his bearings. He was sure the shot had come from outside, so he headed for where he remembered the front door to be, and he called out. Lockhart scoured the yard but could see nothing under the stars. Then there was a commotion at the back of the house, and Jeyhun came through the room behind him. He was holding an ancient rifle.

"A man in your auto-bus" he breathed, his eyes wide and bright in the starlight. Full of adrenalin. His brow furrowed as he scanned the horizon for any sign of movement. As Lockhart watched, a silhouette broke from behind a nearby tree and ran across the open field. Jeyhun was trying to train the barrel of the rifle onto the moving target.

His finger twitched, and a shot rang out into the silent air. Jeyhun was not a natural marksman, and the bullet ricocheted off a wall and rung around the courtyard. The man kept running, but the quiet was ripped apart by a scream from the donkey. Either a bullet or some shrapnel had given him the fright of his life.

The intruder kept running back towards the road as Jeyhun fired off another shot. By now he was a hundred yards away, and the shot was more in frustration than anything. Even so, the man cried out and fell to the ground, but quickly he got to his feet and limped on to the road. Lockhart thought it was more likely that he had fallen and twisted his ankle than been hit.

Soon enough, there was the sound of an engine roaring to life and a pair of high beam lights dazzled the two men standing in the porch. The stranger swung his vehicle round; it looked like a meaty four by four, but before they could get a good look at it, the car and its driver were gone.

Tyler watched as the man with the beard drove away, figuring that he was probably Fearless, coming to reclaim the bus he'd hidden earlier. Being as he didn't have a weapon and the man in the house was armed, Tyler followed the beard. He could come back for the bus later now that he knew where it was hidden.

The guy in the burka started his jeep and hit his main beams. Tyler followed behind in his own vehicle, driving on night goggles and no headlights. Within two miles Tyler had gained on the car in front and was close enough to be less cautious. The guy wouldn't get away from him now. Tyler hit the lights and pushed the gas so that his bumper touched the one in front, planning to run the ghost driver off the road. Just then though his phone bleeped.

It was General Lang with news that David Barr was in Turkmenistan. Lang had reported him missing and as a matter of procedure his name had been flagged with civilian airlines. A call had come in to Lang five minutes ago. David Barr was booked to fly out of Ashgabat first thing in the morning, en route for Bangkok.

"He's paid someone to pull us onto some dusty Turkmenistan trails while he gets out by plane overnight," he told Tyler over the phone.

Tyler looked at his watch. It would take him four hours to get back to Ashgabat, and the flight left in six. It would be tight. He told Lang that he wanted to check out the hidden coach before he left, but the General insisted that he get back to Ashgabat at once to reach Barr before he checked in.

"Things will be much harder if he banks the money, and once he finds a way back to American soil" Lang said. "While he is in Turkmenistan, we have a window of opportunity - and we should take it."

Tyler hit the gas again and ran the bearded guy off the road in a fit of anger more than anything else. Then he turned his own car back towards Ashgabat as he watched the jeep roll onto its roof. As he drove back past Rosalina and Jeyhun's house, he wondered what was inside the yellow bus, but he sped on towards the airport. Orders were orders, and Tyler trusted Lang's judgment. Besides, he didn't have time to get embroiled with an armed man tonight.

CHAPTER THIRTY-TWO

The Road to Turkmenbasy
"A voice inside my head said don't look back,
you can never look back."
- Don Henley, Boys of Summer

The donkey had not made it through the night. Jeyhun's bullet had torn through its back and it had bled to death. Lockhart had helped Jeyhun to deal with the animal's carcass before Nazar woke up.

When they returned to the house, the men were dusty and sweaty, and Rosalina had already prepared bread and tea for breakfast. The men took time washing their hands and then joined the woman and her son to eat. Apparently, Nazar had slept through the excitement and seemed not to have noticed the missing donkey.

As they broke and shared the bread, Lockhart suddenly remembered the boy shouting at him in the road the previous day.

"What is sixty-three?" he asked.

After the shooting in the night, Lockhart couldn't sleep and had lain awake chewing over the events of the previous day; the passengers on the bus, the strange journalist dressed as a woman, the girl who gave birth, and eventually the boy playing football in the middle of the road. He remembered the boy shouting the number at him, and he wondered if the boy might have been referring to verse sixty-three of the Hidden Words. So, in the middle of the night, Lockhart had reached into his backpack, found a tiny torch, and pulled out his book of The Hidden Words.

VERSE 63: O YE PEOPLES OF THE WORLD! Know verily that an unforeseen calamity followeth you, and a grievous retribution awaiteth you.

It seemed unlikely that the kid was pointing him to that. All the same, after the gunshot in the night and the stranger trying to break into his bus, the verse hit home. Lockhart felt like calamity had been following him, and he planned to stay one step ahead. Lockhart watched the boy chewing at his bread.

"Why did you shout out sixty-three yesterday, Pele?"

Nazar smiled, he liked the man calling him that name. Rosalina translated the question, and he answered her quickly and earnestly.

"Sixty-three?" she said, and she smiled too. "Very good, Nazar."

The boy looked even more pleased, and Rosalina explained that he was juggling with the football and counting his keep-ups.

"He wants to be a footballer, and I want him to learn your language," she said. "I let him play as long as he calls out his score in English. Sixty-three was his world record, so he was angry that you and your bus interrupted him!"

After breakfast, Lockhart thanked the family and packed his rucksack into the coach. All the blue bales were safely stowed away in their suitcases in the luggage compartment, except for the one under his seat. Rosalina gave him a sheet of paper with her name and address printed on it, and then he set off back up to the road. The windscreen was a mess, but he had little choice but to keep going forward until he reached somewhere big enough to swap vehicles.

The morning passed easily enough with straight roads and very little traffic. The road had moved away from the river, and the land had become dry and cracked. As the sun rose higher, Lockhart passed a natural spring jetting into the air at the side of the road. It was surrounded by mud and lorry drivers cooling off in the water.

The thought of spending a few minutes in the cold water was appealing, but the words of Verse Sixty-Three were on his mind. Were calamity and retribution following him? It couldn't be a coincidence that someone had been creeping around the back of the remote house in the middle of the night. But who had it been? Had someone been watching as he had hidden his bus behind the building?

He was sure that the journalist in the burka had seen the money under the coach seat. Maybe it was him. That wouldn't be so bad. He only knew about the money under the driver's seat, and Lockhart could probably lose him without too much trouble. The good thing about traveling light was he wouldn't be easy to track.

A flock of birds flew across the clear sky in front of the coach, the first Lockhart had seen for days. He had been traveling the world for a long time, and he felt tuned in to changes along the way. He felt like he could smell the salt on the air coming through the bus's smashed windscreen. He would reach the Caspian Sea by the evening.

As he drove along, Lockhart thought about the other possibility; that it might not have been the journalist who had found him at Rosalina's farm last night. Maybe the man who had followed him from Afghanistan had found him again. Maybe retribution was breathing down his neck.

CHAPTER THIRTY-THREE

Kandahar Airfield.
"Leading you down into my core where I've become so numb."
– Evanescence, Bring Me to Life

General Ben Lang was sweating more than usual as he made plans to leave Kandahar Air Field. He and Tyler had been building up their millions by skimming the aid and reconstruction money that flowed through Kandahar for redistribution for the last year. Sometimes they renegotiated contracts with local firms and pocketed the saving; other times they simply stole what they could get away with.

Last summer, Lang and Tyler had done a deal with the company that supplied bottled water to the camp. They had used their business skills plus a bit of coercion, threatening contractors' families, but the net result was a fifty million dollar saving each year. They passed on a five million saving to the US Army which kept their superiors happy, and they stored the rest in a hanger in a remote part of the base. It was a full-blown industry, and the two men were ruthlessly making money.

Until they smuggled the money out of the camp and out of the country though, it was nothing more than a pile of paper in a hanger in a desert. So, they planned for months, ready to ship one big load out of the camp and into a Swiss account. At the last count, Tyler would make about one hundred million dollars, and the General would have double that. Even in corruption, rank counted.

Four days ago, the Mastiff was loaded with the bales of cash and the two men had made their plans to disappear. Lang deployed Tyler on a fictitious job in Herat, ready to meet the cargo. Once the cargo was delivered to Tyler north of Herat, the plan was to shoot the driver and drive the Mastiff to Ashgabat where a private plane would be waiting to take him to Zurich.

Lang had been in the flight ops room when things had fallen apart. The men in the room were on edge, knowing that they had a general in their midst. They diligently monitored the air traffic in the skies overhead, each performing his duties by the book. One of them suddenly spoke up.

"Sir, two of the A-10s are reporting that a Mastiff is being held up by a group of other vehicles on the Herat road."

There was some confusion. There was no record that any US vehicles were traveling along the Herat road, and the idea that a single Mastiff would travel unaccompanied so late in the afternoon seemed unlikely. One of the men asked whether the Mastiff could be civilian.

"Well, we don't know who is in the Mastiff," Lang lied, "but we can be damn sure that the people in the jeeps are hostile, so let's engage them first."

Nobody argued with the General. The Thunderbolts were sent back to destroy the jeeps, and Lang listened to the radio as the pilots reported that the jeeps had been destroyed.

"It's very smoky down there," one of them called in. "We're unsure about collateral."

So, Lang left the room knowing that the jeeps were destroyed, but unsure whether his money had been obliterated with them. He spent the day feeling clammy and restless, waiting for news from Tyler. At first the news was encouraging. It looked like the Mastiff and its cargo had survived the ambush. Tyler tracked it to the bone yard where the trail went cold.

So, Lang's best guess was that if the money had left Afghanistan, it would have been driven through Turkmenistan towards the Caspian Sea. Lang had set Tyler after the cash like a faithful bloodhound, but so far, he had come up with nothing.

The mysterious driver that David Barr had conjured out of thin air seemed to have vanished as quickly as he'd appeared. He'd taken the money with him. Then there were hours of waiting. Occasional reports from Tyler with news of possible sightings, but nothing certain. The tracking device was proving to be muffled and useless.

Then the phone call came. David Barr had booked a flight from Ashgabat. Lang had made the call to pull Tyler away from the bus he'd been following. He'd turned him one-eighty and sent him hurtling back to the airport. But it was all in vain. Six hours later Tyler had reported in with a text message. Two of the most miserable words Lang had ever read on his cell phone:

WRONG BARR

The General had made the call, and he had called it wrong. Tyler knew bitterly that he had been in the right place. If he'd sprung the yellow truck, he would have found the cash. Now he was tired, and he was twelve hours behind Fearless. He didn't blame Lang. The General made a lot of calls, and he got most of them right.

Back in Kandahar Lang began closing things down on the Airfield as Tyler plowed through Turkmenistan looking for the money. Tyler was a hard man to control, but he was ruthless and smart. He was an excellent soldier and a fine tracker, so if anyone could find the money, Tyler was the man for the job.

CHAPTER THIRTY-FOUR

Turkmenbasy Highway
"Smack, crack, bushwhacked,
Tie another one to the racks, baby."
– REM, Drive

Charlie Lockhart had driven the bus for about an hour after leaving Rosalina and Jeyhun before he passed a crumpled Jeep at the side of the road. It had come off the highway at some speed, and the scores in the earth leading up to it looked fresh. Lockhart couldn't help wondering if it belonged to the person who had been sniffing around his bus the previous night. The front tires had blown out, and the airbag had deployed. There was no one inside, and no obvious signs of blood or trauma. Lockhart kept driving, resisting the urge to have a mooch around the broken car. *Ultreya* he thought, and kept moving forward.

He was now only three hours from the coast, and the port town of Turkmenbasy. He had planned to drive there without stopping, but near the halfway point of his journey, he arrived at a temporary marketplace. A group of trucks had arched out from the road in a horseshoe, each facing their cabs outwards and selling goods from their trailers. Lockhart pulled his bus up next to one of the trucks, and got out. Locals were rummaging through the sacks of cotton, onions and potatoes, and the drivers were haggling over price. The place was loud and exciting. Lockhart felt like a tourist again.

He approached two brothers who looked to be in their mid-twenties. They were trying to sell tomatoes to a group of skeptical looking middle-aged women. Lockhart jostled his way to the front of the crowd and beckoned one man over. The man didn't speak English, but he called his brother to help.

Between them, the two men realized that Lockhart was offering to buy the tomato truck from them. The truck was their livelihood, so they would not let it go easily; but eventually Lockhart offered an amount which was too good to turn down.

While the men offloaded their tomatoes, Lockhart found another trader who was prepared to sell him a donkey. It was lively and looked healthy enough. Lockhart led it back to the tomato brothers and offered them his yellow bus in return for them driving the donkey to Rosalina and Jeyhun's house. They agreed, and Lockhart gave them the address that Rosalina had written for him. He knew it would please them to see a replacement for the animal that he and Jeyhun had buried that morning.

Finally, the two brothers helped Lockhart to transfer several heavy suitcases from the bus to the truck. They covered the cases with boxes of tomatoes and covered the tomatoes with a sheet of tarpaulin. Lockhart grabbed the open bale from under the driver's seat, along with the beaten-up cap which he had grown fond of, before handing the keys to the elder of the brothers.

He watched as the brothers disappeared over the horizon in the yellow bus, the donkey visible through the back window, and dust kicking up on either side. Then he started the engine of his new truck, settled into his new driver's seat, and rolled back onto the road to Turkmenbasy.

Within two hours, he reached the port. The ferry dock was hidden like a dirty secret in the back of beyond, but eventually Lockhart found the place and parked his truck.

It was ramshackle, the sea air having gnarled away at anything metal, and the sun and the wind having bleached and sanded the remaining wooden shacks. Lockhart bought a ticket from a surly Russian-sounding woman in a small cabin. She took his money, pointed at the ship behind her, and wrote a time for him.

The boat sailed once a day, and it was leaving in 40 minutes. Luck was on Lockhart's side, and he felt the river of fate pulling him along once more. He got the truck through the maze of crates and boxes waiting to be loaded onto the boat, up the ramp and on-board. The ship would sail for two days to Azerbaijan.

Lockhart parked the lorry deep inside the ship and wondered how the old handbrake would cope as the boat rolled around on the Caspian Sea. They walked round to secure the back of the vehicle. There were millions of dollars hidden under his tomatoes, and he didn't want prying eyes spotting his cargo. Then he found a small sack amongst the produce and filled it with some vegetables. He hadn't eaten all day, and now that he had made it to the coast he realized how hungry he was.

He filled the sack to the brim - the stuff would only waste in the back of the truck, and there were sure to be other hungry travelers on the ship. As it turned out, there was nowhere to eat or drink on the boat so he was glad of his stash. The thought of eating nothing but tomatoes for the next two days did little to lift his spirits, but as the boat bobbed unsteadily out of Turkmenbasy harbor Lockhart felt glad to be on his way back towards Europe.

As the sun started to fall from the sky, Lockhart felt cold for the first time in weeks. The horizon started to burn pinks and oranges, but the boat was exposed to the wind which had picked up across the flat sea, and the spray whipped into his face. Lockhart ducked back through the heavy rusty doors to fetch his only warm top from his rucksack. He headed down the stairs to the back of the boat where his truck was stored.

As he arrived at the truck, he thought he spotted a shadow darting away from his vehicle. Immediately, he chastised himself. He was supposed to be a tourist, and he was supposed to be traveling through the world with an open heart. His journey had taught him to trust in the friendship of strangers, to give and receive gladly. He had learned that when he treated people well, they were kind in return.

Since Afghanistan, he had found himself more guarded. *Perhaps the world is now teaching me about the laws of actions and consequences* he thought.

He felt hounded and unsafe. The money in the suitcases had helped him escape from Afghanistan. But now they were weighing heavy as he traveled. The money was his insurance for the future though. Once it was banked, only he would know the account codes, and whoever was chasing him would need to keep him alive.

Since he had taken the money from the boneyard in Herat, he had not relaxed. Now he was jumping at shadows as he headed back to his truck. He looked up and down the deck of the boat, but he could see nobody. But when he turned back to his truck, he noticed that someone had tampered the side of the tarpaulin. Was he being paranoid? How could anyone on the boat know what he was carrying?

He reassured himself that some petty thief had probably been rummaging through all the vehicles, and just happened to have been messing with his truck at the exact moment that Lockhart returned to the hold. All the same, he decided to spent a few hours sleeping in the back of the truck.

So, he grabbed his rucksack from the cab and then clambered into the back. He nestled down in the aisle, concealed by vegetable crates either side of him. The smell of tomatoes hung in the air, wholesome and earthy. Lockhart didn't sleep, but with his head resting on his rucksack, the Caspian Sea gently rocked him from side to side until he felt reassured and calm.

His mind drifted back to the tea shop in Quetta in Pakistan, and the time he had spent sipping mint tea on the old chesterfield. He had been at a fork in the river of fate, and he wondered whether he had made the wrong choice. Had the Chaman Road into Afghanistan been the wrong way to go? He wondered where he would be now if he had chosen the less dangerous road.

It was about an hour later that Lockhart first heard someone scuffling around outside the truck. The tarpaulin was thin, and Lockhart could make out the stranger walking right around the truck. He sat up silently, immediately tense and alert. There was a sound of tearing fabric and a thin line of light began to appear in the tarpaulin at the back of the truck.

Lockhart slowly transferred his weight to his feet and stealthily moved towards the tear in the truck's wall. He could make out a small blade slowly sawing through tough material. Whoever was outside was cutting their way in. Lockhart hadn't been paranoid after all, but that was scant comfort now.

There was nothing for it; he would to have to fight. In with the crates of vegetables were a few wooden stakes which the tomato sellers had used to secure their market stand. Lockhart took one in his hand. It was about two feet long and heavy. He steeled himself, ready to smash at whatever came at him through the rip in the side of the tarpaulin.

The tear was about a foot across when the man withdrew his blade. Lockhart realized at once that the thief would stick his head through to have a look at what was inside the truck. The tarpaulin started to bulge as the stranger's head came through.

Lockhart began to swing the heavy wood towards the target, as the thief's eyes came into view through the slit. He recognized them at once. They were exactly as he had seen them through the burka when the journalist was sitting on the back of the bus in Ashgabat. In an instant, there was enough of the man's head through the hole for his peppered beard to come into sight. Lockhart was struggling with a decision; he recognized the journalist at once, but couldn't decide if that meant he should hit him or not.

It didn't matter either way, because his swing was already in motion and it was too late to stop. Without thinking about it, Lockhart eventually swung harder, like he was swatting an irksome fly.

The journalist did not know what had happened. He fell back out of the truck and hit the cold metal floor of the car deck on the ship. For a moment he tried to struggle against it, to scramble to his feet, but then the injury sunk in, and his body collapsed back onto the floor. A thin cut had opened above his eyebrow and it wouldn't be long before the swelling started.

Lockhart opened the tail of the truck and jumped down. On the floor at the side of the truck, the journalist was out cold, with the small knife still grasped in his hand. Before he could work out what to do, Lockhart heard a commotion at the far end of the deck. A group of three men emerged from between the wooden pallets at the far end, each wearing something which looked vaguely like the ship's uniform.

Lockhart wondered how he could explain what had happened as he stood over the unmoving body of the journalist. He had been trouble ever since Ashgabat, and now he was a problem without even being conscious. Lockhart raised his hands in the air, just in case.

However, as the three sailors approached, the tallest pointed to a camera on the side of the metal hull. There was evidently surveillance on the boat, and they had seen what had happened. Without waiting for him to come around, two of the men grabbed the journalist and half dragged and half carried him away.

"It's your truck?" asked the remaining sailor.

Lockhart nodded and held up the keys.

"My truck, my tomatoes," he replied as he reached into the truck and handed the sailor one.

The sailor took it and bit into the fruit and took a moment to savor its taste. Then he looked back at Lockhart.

"You have more?" he asked.

"I have a truckful."

The sailor offered Lockhart a place at their dinner table for a bag of tomatoes. Lockhart thought it was a good deal, mostly because it would break up the monotony of the long trip.

"Your tomatoes will be safe here" said the sailor, chuckling and pointing to the camera on the wall. Besides, we have thrown your friend in the prison."

*

It was true. When the journalist came around from his bang on the head, he found himself in pitch darkness. It was so black that he blinked several times, unable to be certain whether his eyes were open or closed. He wondered if he had gone blind. He could hear the sound of the engines roaring, and the floor that he was sitting on was vibrating. He remembered that he was on the boat.

He had been making his way back from reporting in Iran, and he had jumped the border into Turkmenistan. Just like in Iran, his orthodox widow's dress had disguised his European features. He remembered noticing a stash of money under the driver's seat as he had caught the yellow bus in Ashgabat.

As a shrewd journalist, it hadn't taken him long to piece together the story. A man driving a makeshift transport from East to West through Turkmenistan would probably have started out in Afghanistan. There must have been at least a million dollars under the driver's seat, and that kind of money would only have come from theft or smuggling. If it was stolen, it was probably government money. A hard-working contractor wouldn't have been careless enough to lose that sort of cash.

So, the money wasn't legit, and the man was on the run. At first, the journalist had thought about writing a story about him. He'd offer the guy anonymity, but he probably wouldn't cooperate. Smugglers didn't like publicity. So, he had considered turning him in for a bounty, but he didn't know who was chasing him.

The journalist heard a scrabbling noise in the corner of the dark room. He wasn't alone in his prison. The ship's rats were running along the skirting. He was still too dazed to stand up, so he waited to see how brave the rats were and how close they'd get.

He had followed the driver after they parted ways at the hospital in Ashgabat. The man had tried to buy him off with five hundred dollars, but it had only made the journalist more curious. He had sat in a cafe near the hospital for a few minutes typing up his notes and staring absently out of the window.

Eventually he focused on the view outside the window and saw a car hire shop opposite the café. *Maybe it was a sign* he had thought. It was certainly an opportunity, so he had hired an SUV for a few of the dollars the bus driver had given him and waited further down the street, keeping the coach visible in his rear-view mirror.

He had tailed the bus for most of the afternoon until just before sunset, when it had driven off the road after almost running down some kid. The journalist has driven on through the cloud of dust and parked up a mile further on.

The truth was, he wanted the money for himself. He had never stolen a cent in his life, but at the moment he was in desperate trouble. Serious people were chasing him. Serious people wanted him dead. It would blow over eventually, but for now he needed to hide. With the millions under the driver's seat, the journalist could hide away easily. He could even change his face if he needed to.

So, he had come back after dark, long after the coast should have been clear. The bus was still there, parked up behind a house across the field. He had tried to break in, but someone had shot at him. Then, as he made his escape in his SUV, another car had chased him and eventually run him off the road. His car rolled several times, but landed back on its tires, ruined. It wouldn't be the first deposit he'd lost with a hire company.

He had walked on slowly through the night towards Turkmenbasy until eventually a lorry driver had taken pity on him and offered him a lift.

He had given up on the money; he had no idea who had shot at him, or who had tried to run him off the road, but it had been enough to warn him off. Then this evening, as he hung around the port in Turkmenbasy he watched the last truck load onto the ferry, he couldn't believe his eyes. He recognized the driver. It was the guy from the bus. The guy with the money.

His hunch about the man heading for Europe had been right, and so he had thrown a few dollars at the gruff woman in the kiosk and got on board as the last foot passenger. Once the boat had set sail, he had had a look through the tomato truck to see if the smuggler still had the cash.

Then, as he had poked his head through the tarpaulin, he had felt an almighty smash. He thought he had been shot as he fell back onto the deck. And now he was here, in the dark.

The wall he was slumped against felt like cold metal; his hands were tied behind his back. The room smelled of engine oil and he had the sense that it wasn't very big. If there was a door, it would take him an age to find it in the dark, and it would certainly be locked. So he rested his aching head on his knees and listened to the sound of the rats scrabbling in the corner.

*

Meanwhile, Lockhart had been taken to one of the noisiest parts of the ship. Below deck, the sailor had led him past the engine room which sounded like hell, and into the nearby crew quarters which sounded like a slightly muffled version of the same.

The ship's cook added the tomatoes to a stew which smelled good, and Lockhart was ushered to sit with eight other men who were playing cards and shouting boisterously at one another around a big table. Several asked him questions in English; Where was he from? Why was he driving tomatoes across the Caspian Sea? Lockhart was charming and evasive in equal measure.

The sailors were good humored, and before too long, the cook started to dish out the stew, along with Azeri bread and sausage. Lockhart was handed a plate just like the others and tucked into the food. As the journey across the Caspian Sea continued, the sailors were happy. They were all Azeri men, and they were on the way back to their homes. At one point the youngest of the men fell off his seat as the boat rocked violently, and everyone laughed.

The sailors' happiness was infectious, and Lockhart remembered that he was a tourist making his way through the world. For the last few days he had felt like a fugitive, except for the few moments when he had prayed with Rosalina and Jeyhun. He wasn't religious, but the moment had been calm and wonderful.

Now these noisy sailors were having the same effect. As the night drew on, they drank tea and smoked cigarettes. The engines rumbled in the background, but their voices became slower and deeper. Then one of the older men began to speak, and all the others listened.

The sailor closest to Lockhart leaned into him and spoke into his ear.

"He is telling a story," he said.

The youngster disappeared into the kitchen and re-emerged with a kettle of tea and several candles. As he went about lighting them and placing them on the table, another sailor turned off the harsh fluorescent light above their heads. The men's hard faces flickered in the soft light, and the sailor began his tale.

"Yüz il əvvəl," the sailor began.

"One hundred years ago," the shipmate next to Lockhart translated. The older guy's deep, rich voice continued in his native tongue.

"A young sailor set off from Baku to seek his fortune" the translator continued quietly. The story was an odyssey about an Azeri boy who had set out to sail to Iran, but was sent off course by a cruel wind which blew him all the way to Russia.

The sailor's tone was hushed as he described the boy's brave fight with bears, how his few belongings were stolen from him by a traveling conman, and how for a time he had been enslaved by an evil witch.

But Azeri boys were made of stern stuff, and the boy soon outwitted the witch who met a grizzly fate with another bear. The sailors cheered at the news, and the translator told the story with so much gusto that Lockhart became captivated by the story too.

The boy had ended up in Moscow, where he was given a job in the Tsar's palace. It was so cold in Moscow that the Tsar's heart was made of ice, and one day the boy spied the Tsar beating a young servant girl. The boy's heart was filled with rage. The sailors growled about the indignity of it all, and the man next to Lockhart shook his head angrily as he translated the story.

The heroic boy took matters into his own hands by rescuing the servant girl and stealing the Tsar's sapphires and rubies. The Tsar's army chased him across the whole of Russia, but he outran them all and ended up back at his little boat on the shore of the Caspian Sea.

The sailor boy lifted the girl into the boat and rowed them out into the break waves. Then he took a sapphire and threw it into the sea, which turned a beautiful blue and offered him safe passage back Baku. Then he threw a ruby into the sky, and the heavens turned red and the sunset far quicker than usual.

The Tsar's army was plunged into darkness. The wind had so much mischief with the blinded army that it forgot to blow the boy off course, and he and the servant girl sailed safely back to Baku with his treasure. The sailors cheered at the news.

The man who was translating gave Lockhart an excited thump on his shoulder as he interpreted the triumphant ending to the story.

Then the sailor who was telling the story held up his hands to call for quiet. The others looked at him across the big table. Most of them were still drinking mint tea, for which they seemed to have an endless thirst.

"İnşa nəhəng bir qala" the sailor whispered in the flickering light, his voice hoarse from years on the sea.

"The boy and the servant girl built a giant fortress, and they were married," murmured the translator. "They bought justice to Azerbaijan and ruled over its people for years."

The final part of the story involved the Tsar trying to overthrow the young sailor's fortress and being beaten and enslaved. He ended his days working for the servant girl, who was kind and fair to him until his icy heart melted and he died.

Eventually, several of the sailors left the table to go back to the engine room and to attend to their jobs on the ship. The translator offered Lockhart a bed in a cabin. He explained that there were always free beds, because some crew were always working.

Lockhart thanked him and offered him the rest of his sack of tomatoes.

The cabin was further away from the engine room, and quieter than the mess that he had been sitting in for the last few hours. The food had been hearty, and the company had been warm, and Lockhart felt relaxed.

He was happy below the deck of the ship as it made its way across the Caspian Sea. The wicked wind had blown him off course, but now in the company of the sailors he felt like he was back on his path. At the dinner table he had felt like a tourist once more and was ready to sleep soundly for a few hours.

The story about the boy and his treasure had been so captivating that Lockhart hadn't thought once about his own treasure, the blue plastic bales of cash hidden under the tomatoes in his truck. If the money in the truck went missing, he would deal with that tomorrow. He felt like a weight had been lifted from his shoulders.

For the last few miles, the money had felt like a heavy burden, and he was looking forward to banking it once he got to Europe. For now, though, the Journalist who had been following him was locked below the deck, and the ship was in the middle of the Caspian Sea, so Lockhart could afford to relax.

He knew that either the giant or his pay masters would come looking for their money, like the Tsar's army chasing their precious stones. While he had been listening to the Sailor's story, Charlie Lockhart had reached a decision. He had been thinking about using the stolen money to keep traveling around the world, to stay one step ahead of his pursuers. But he didn't want a lifetime on the run. There would be no fun in that.

So there in the candlelight in the sailors' mess, Lockhart had decided to head home and prepare for whoever the wicked wind blew across the sea to him. He knew the perfect spot. A house at the top of a hill where he could see people coming. A place he knew well, so he would be ready for whoever came after him.

He would do what the Azeri boy had done and make his way home. And then he would stop and dig in, and wait for them to arrive. As he started to make his plans, lying on the bed in the cabin, Lockhart fell into a deep blank sleep that lasted for hours.

CHAPTER THIRTY-FIVE

Baku Ferry, Caspian Sea.
"I wish I was a fisherman, tumbling on the sea,
heading away from the shoreline and its bitter memories."
- The Waterboys, Fisherman's Blues.

In the dark hull of the ship, the journalist was planning his next move as well. He had spent plenty of time locked up during his career and had never been convicted. Most likely, the sailors would hand him to the port authorities who would hand him to the police as a petty thief. He would phone his editor, who was used to journalists ending up on the wrong side of the law. The editor would bribe the policeman, and the charge would disappear. The journalist would walk the streets of Azerbaijan by lunchtime.

The question was whether the bus driver, the tomato truck and the money would be gone by the time he got out. He hoped not. He wanted his cut of what was hidden under the crates.

Lockhart woke up three hours later to find the whole ship was juddering. The captain was maneuvering the boat towards the quay and she was complaining bitterly. Outside the cabin, the men who had been lazing around the table last night telling stories were up and about, focused and energized.

Each sailor had responsibilities and routine as they arrived at the port and so Lockhart shouted quick goodbyes as they rushed about. Within minutes he was starting up the engine of his truck and slowly rumbling off the ship and onto dry land. Corrugated steel containers sprung up all around him and huge yellow cranes towered higher still.

There was other traffic in front and behind him, and they snaked through the port towards a checkpoint. Lockhart had prepared a few small bundles of cash to see him through customs with a minimum number of questions, but in the end, he didn't need them. It was early morning and he couldn't tell whether the officials on duty were part of the worn-out night shift or the still-bleary-eyed early team. Either way, they were not going about their work with a great deal of gusto.

A man with a dark uniform waved the tomato truck through the customs point, and before he knew it Lockhart was driving through the streets of Baku looking for a plan. The sooner he could get rid of the suitcases hiding under the tomatoes the better. The money was slowing him down, and the giant was catching him up.

CHAPTER THIRTY-SIX

Baku City, Azerbaijan.
"Two thousand miles I've roamed..."
- Otis Redding, Sitting on the Dock of a Bay.

The banker had been sitting at his Formica desk in the back office since the bank had opened for business that morning. It was a slow day, and he was mostly pushing around files so that his two clerks thought he was busy. His seniority meant that he got the biggest desk directly underneath the bank's only ceiling fan, but this was a dubious honor.

The ancient fan groaned and creaked as it spun around. The banker blamed the creaking on the weight of the dust that had gathered on the blades. And he blamed the cleaner for that.

A fly which had been taunting him for the last quarter hour finally landed on a file next to his empty coffee cup. He thumped his fleshy fist hard on the table, missing the fly by two inches but rattling his cup on its saucer.

"More coffee," he called gruffly, to nobody in particular. Nobody in particular rushed to fill his cup. He moaned to the fly about the standard of his staff, loosened his tie, and undid his top button. He scratched away at his beard as the fly resumed its orbit around his balding head. A dark shadow drew across the paperwork on the banker's desk, but he didn't look up immediately. It was only when the air brakes hissed on the other side of the window he realized how closely the lorry had parked.

His first thought was that he was being robbed; the truck blocked up the doorway and prevented any escape. The bank was about seven miles from the ferry port, and not in the best part of town. Then the banker noticed that the back of the truck was full of tomatoes; Unlikely to be a heist, then.

The driver didn't look much like a farmer as he sauntered out of his cab at a leisurely pace. He was nearly six foot tall, but looked friendly enough. He ran his hands through his dark hair and took a good look around before heading into the bank. He pushed through the aluminum swing door and looked around for service. There was an air of confidence about him which marked him out from regular customers. The banker got up from his desk and walked over to greet him, mostly out of curiosity. He held out his hand, and the driver shook it.

"I want to open an account with a cash deposit," the driver said.

One of the two juniors looked up, eager to help. The banker scowled at him and ushered the driver into his office. He was shrewd enough to realize that a guy with an English accent wanting to open a cash account in Baku was probably up to no good. Which meant there would be something in it for him. He flicked a switch on the wall and the filthy creaking fan wobbled to a halt. Then he showed the Englishman to a well-used chair and turned to close over his office door. A bit of privacy would be useful if his instincts were right.

"I'd rather you leave the door open," the stranger said.

The banker shot him a questioning look.

"The cash is on the truck, and I can't carry it all in by myself."

There was a long pause, during which the banker gradually sat up straighter, re-buttoned his collar and adjusted his tie.

"Would you like some coffee?" he asked and shouted an instruction to the juniors without waiting for a reply. The driver was rich, English, and in need of a bank account. The banker's day was getting better by the minute. The coffee arrived with a clatter as the junior's hand shook slightly as he served his boss. The banker sent him out to carry the suitcases in from under the tomatoes. His eyes grew wide as he watched his two staff carrying in suitcase after suitcase, and then opening each one to reveal the blue plastic bales inside. His shirt had started to stick to him and he pulled down his tie and undid his collar again. The driver said nothing.

It had to be drug money, as far as the banker could work out. Dirty dollars which he could wash clean, for a price. His mind was working overtime, trying to work out his best angle. His best pitch. His best scam. Still the driver said nothing. It was unnerving him.

Even with their electronic note counters, it took the two clerks the best part of an hour to slit open the bales, count the notes and add them to the vault. Once, the driver stood up and looked at the vault, as if he was checking how secure the bank was. He needn't have worried; the front office would blow away in a strong gale, but the back room where the money was kept was as strong as any other bank in the world. Thick concrete walls and a modern steel lined safe. Pretty much impenetrable. The driver had taken one look at it, nodded and sat back down.

Eventually, one clerk came back into the banker's office, looking shell-shocked. He handed his boss a small piece of paper, with a total written on it.

$299,997,538.00

The junior walked out without saying a word and closed the door over behind him. After a moment, the banker cleared his throat, and made a pitch. He talked about the difficulties of moving such large amounts of cash. The problems with administration. The suspicions which might be raised. There would need to be an administrative charge to compensate for the difficulties.

"How much?" asked the driver.

The banker heard a soft bleep on the other side of his office door. He glanced for a moment at a tiny yellowing monitor on his desk. A tall woman in a burka had just walked in, but the clerks were dealing with her. This was not the time to get distracted. This was the deal of his life.

"Ten percent," he said gruffly, looking down at the figure in front of him.

"One percent" was Lockhart's reply.

The banker thought about it. Three million, US. It was like he'd just won the lottery. Three million meant a new life, and a luxurious one at that. But one percent seemed low. He pushed for more, but the driver wouldn't budge. He tried to meet him halfway but the driver stuck stubbornly to one percent.

"I could report you to the authorities," he bullied.

Lockhart looked at him calmly and said, "I could strangle you with that cheap tie if I wanted to, and nobody would come running in here to save you. Least of all those two out there."

The banker's eyes flicked back to the black-and-white screen. The clerks were deep in conversation with the woman in the burka. It was true that he treated them badly, and it was also true that they probably wouldn't step in to help. *You reap what you sow.*

"But I will not strangle you, and you will not report me," the driver continued. "You will take one percent, which is more money than you've ever seen in your life until today."

The banker nodded, defeated. The driver was right; it was a lot of money. Even so, he was envious of the other ninety-nine percent beyond his grasp. Then the deal got worse.

"By the way, you will take your one percent, and split it three ways with the two guys outside. They look like they do most of the work around here."

It horrified the banker. He would be a million dollars better off, but somehow it ruined it to know that the clerks would be as rich as him. He called the two clerks in and explained the situation. They hurried off to pack three suitcases with a million dollars each, unable to believe their luck.

The banker kept an eye on them as he bashed angrily at his keyboard validating the transaction, making sure that the driver had two hundred and ninety-seven million dollars in a legitimate European account in the name of Charlie Lockhart.

Once the bulk of the deposit was locked away and the banker's fee was counted out, the clerks and the banker each took a suitcase and locked up for the day. Before they left the office though Lockhart reached forward and swiped the banker's car keys from the desk. In return, he flipped him the keys to the truck.

"One more thing," Lockhart demanded. "I need your car."

No negotiation; it was part of the deal. The banker shook his head miserably. This was the crummiest million dollars he had ever earned.

"It's not all bad news," Lockhart smiled, as the four men walked out of the bank together. "You can keep the tomatoes."

CHAPTER THIRTY-SEVEN

Baku, Azerbaijan
"I'm sticking with you, cos I'm made out of glue."
– I'm Sticking With You, The Velvet Underground.

Lockhart walked out of the bank and into a problem. The journalist was sitting on a bench just outside the bank's aluminum doors. His face was bruised, and he had a cut above his left eye where Lockhart had smashed him with the wooden stake on the Baku ferry. He was eating one of the tomatoes from the back of the truck. It was the journalist's job to track people down, and grudgingly Lockhart had to admit that he was good at it. It was becoming tiresome.

The journalist stood up when he saw the men coming out into the street. His morning had been pretty much as he expected. He had been passed from the boat to the port authorities and then made a call to his editor who had wired enough cash to secure his release. The whole thing had taken about an hour. The journalist had never visited a country where this didn't work; it was only the amount of cash and the speed of release that varied from place to place.

"Hey," he called out to Lockhart in his thick Spanish accent as if he were greeting an old friend. "Charlie Lockhart, how are you?"

Lockhart stared at the journalist. He had revealed his name to the bank staff less than an hour ago, and yet already the journalist had learned it. Lockhart shot a look at the two clerks with their million-dollar suitcases. They'd given away his name for twenty dollars five minutes before they'd become millionaires. They looked uncomfortable and scurried off without another word.

Just then, the banker's frustration boiled over. He leaned over the journalist and took the half-eaten tomato from his hand.

"Nobody said you could eat my tomatoes" he growled, before throwing it to the floor and stamping on it, grinding it into the pavement with his heel. He threw his suitcase into the cab of the truck and climbed in after it. He fired the ignition and roared off towards the highway, presumably to begin a new life in the sun. Lockhart smiled and wondered when he'd calm down and start smiling. Even the angriest of men would have to smile at a million-dollar suitcase, eventually.

Then it was quiet. Lockhart pressed the banker's key fob and a dusty Vauxhall bleeped nearby. He eyed up the journalist for a moment, considering what was best to do with him. He was another problem that needed sorting.

"Need a lift?"

The journalist shrugged, and they both got into the car. Neither of them had thought about a destination, so Lockhart turned the ignition and rolled out onto the highway. He headed vaguely West. He aimed roughly towards England. They drove for ten minutes before either of them spoke.

"So, you bribed someone to learn my name," Lockhart said as the road flattened out for a stretch. He could see scattered tail lights for miles ahead. "Why is that?"

"Because I've been looking for a new name, and I like the sound of yours," the journalist replied.

"You like my name?" he asked. He stole a glance at his passenger. The journalist explained that his editor in Spain had been receiving death threats over the Iran story. Credible, state sponsored threats.

"So, I have to hide out for a while. I need a new place and a new name, and I like yours."

Lockhart was thinking. "Me too. I like my name. And the thing is, *it's mine.*"

Why did the journalist think he could take his identity? What was he missing?

"Yes, but you don't need it," continued the journalist. "You've been hiding your name from everyone. You've got a truckload of dollars and you want to keep your name a secret."

Lockhart began to understand. "So, you thought you could take it?"

"You're smuggling drugs, or guns, or something," the Spaniard explained. "I know you are. You must be. So, you don't need your name; in fact, you don't even want it."

He was wrong about smuggling, but it was true Lockhart would be better off without using his name. David Barr had seen his passport in Kandahar, so whoever came looking for the money would come looking for Charlie Lockhart.

"I need to hide somewhere until my story is published and I'm no longer threatened, so I can hide in England. You have a passport and a social security number and a bank account which are no use to you when you get home, but they would be very useful to me."

Lockhart considered the situation. It was true that he wouldn't use his real identity when he got back to the UK. He had spent hours in the truck trying to remember if he had mentioned his real name to anyone in Kandahar, but he hadn't. Only Barr had seen his passport. But he knew that someone would come after him, and it seemed sensible to use a new name just in case.

"What if I say no?" Lockhart asked.

"You don't want someone like me knowing your business," replied the journalist. "I'm no good at keeping secrets."

It was a threat, and yet Lockhart suddenly felt like maybe the journalist wasn't such a bad guy. He was just streetwise, keeping himself safe and driving a hard bargain. They had a bit in common.

"There's a reason that I won't be using my name" Lockhart warned him, changing through the gears as the traffic slowed up in front of them.

"Whoever is after you cannot be as bad as the Iranians" argued the journalist. Lockhart shrugged. He wasn't convinced about that. He had been battered and bruised and shot at and chased, but he hadn't lost his faith in people. He was still trusting and inquisitive and his heart was still searching for the good things in the world. Rightly or wrongly, he put his trust in the journalist.

CHAPTER THIRTY-EIGHT

Boyukshor Lake, Baku.
"And all the bad boys are standing in the shadows."
– Tom Petty, Free Fallin'

The banker had got two miles from his work before it happened. He had just pulled off the Boyukshor Highway and onto a badly maintained road north of the lake. He was still grumbling to himself about having to share his cut of the money with the two junior clerks and moaning about the broken radio in the lorry cab. He'd taken his eyes off the road for a second to adjust the tuning, and when his eyes came back to the road, there was a man standing in the middle of it.

The man looked tall and solid. He was rooted to the tarmac, with a cell phone in one hand and a pistol in the other. He looked calm despite the lorry hurtling towards him. He knew he was a great shot. He was in a classic weaver stance; feet shoulder width apart, strong leg forward, body leaning into the target.

He burst the tire cleanly with his first shot. The truck veered sideways and into a concrete service drain. Not ideal, but Tyler could improvise. Tomatoes spewed across the tarmac and turned it blood red.

The truck's engine had cut, but the rear wheels were still spinning by the time Tyler got to the back of it. He had ignored the cries of pain coming from the cab at the front. He'd learned a long time ago that guys who shout the loudest rarely die first. He'd seen it in Iraq first hand; back when he was quicker to risk his neck for his colleagues. Before he realized that every man was ultimately out for himself.

He had been patrolling outside Basra with three other guys. The patrol had been ambushed, and one of them ran off the road into the soft cover. Just like you're trained not to do. Just like protocol says you shouldn't. He landed on a mine which ripped his foot off. He screamed like a child. He'd lost nearly everything below his knee.

Tyler and another guy ran into the minefield to help. Just like you're trained not to do. But they couldn't listen to that screaming and do nothing. Couldn't block it out either. So, Tyler and the other guy rushed in. The other guy hit a mine as well. So now they had two casualties. But the second guy didn't scream. He just lay quietly with half of his body gone and a chunk out of his head and life oozing from two bloody stumps just below his waist.

The guy who had fucked it all up was still screaming. When Tyler reached him, he was pissing blood and was trying to tourniquet himself. Difficult to get a tourniquet on yourself back in Iraq because they weren't issuing the one-handed Velcro versions back then. In Afghanistan, there were stories of guys wearing loose tourniquets on each limb before setting out on patrol because the risk of getting something blown off was so high.

Tyler strapped up the guy in the minefield as best he could, got him to apply a bit of pressure to the stump under his knee. Called for medevac. Whacked in morphine, mostly to shut the guy up. Then he took his chances and pulled the casualty out of the minefield and back to the patrol vehicle. He heaved the injured guy into the back. He didn't go back for the quiet guy. Minefields are designed to draw you back in. Besides, there was no point.

Then Tyler had clambered through the vehicle to the cab. And that's when he found the driver with a bullet in his head. Sitting quietly, no trouble to anyone.

So, Tyler had learned to watch out for himself, then watch out for the quiet ones, and to do whatever was necessary with the ones who screamed the loudest.

He and his commanding officer had gone back to the village after dark that same day. Killed everyone they found. Sometimes men, sometimes women, sometimes children. Sometimes in their sleep. And they reported nothing. Just like you're trained not to do. Just like protocol says you shouldn't. It felt great.

Now the road in front of Tyler looked like a war zone. The bright red debris from the tomato truck looked like a bloodbath, and the guy at the wheel was still shouting for help. He could wait. Tyler checked his cell phone, which was beeping like crazy. About an hour ago, the GPS tracker signal he had been tracing had become much stronger. Much more precise.

The last few days had been frustrating because the tracker had been buried deep inside one of the tight blue bales of cash. Burying it away was smart, because it was guaranteed to stay with the money during transit. But by the time the chip had been surrounded by dollar bills, wrapped tightly in plastic, hidden in suitcases, thrown into the back of a truck and covered with tomatoes, the signal had become muffled. Very hard to chase accurately. Each time Tyler had got close, the truck and its fearless driver had rumbled on to the next town.

An hour ago, though, things had changed. When Tyler had gotten off the Ferry earlier he had headed straight for the Highway and torn off towards central Europe. It seemed like the sensible thing for the truck driver to do, so he put his foot down and tried to make up some ground. He stopped for gas after about thirty miles and saw that the tracker was going wild.

The signal had become accurate enough to track its location on Google Maps. It was bleeping next to a bank in Baku when the signal had improved. Not good news. If the driver had banked it, the only way Tyler would get it back would be by *persuading* him to transfer it to him. Not impossible, but Tyler wasn't good with gentle persuasion. He didn't have the patience for it.

By the time he was back on the road and hurtling towards the bank, he could see that the dot on his screen was moving away from the bank, and straight towards him.

So, Tyler had done the obvious thing. Found the first blind corner between them, set up an ambush and waited. He shot out the front tire, and now he had things under control at last. He climbed into the back of the truck and started plunging his hands into the tomatoes. Like a fairground game, trying to find hidden treasure. But there was nothing hiding beneath the fruit. *Where the hell was the money?*

There was no way that all the cash could be in the cab, but Tyler's GPS kept bleeping so he went to investigate. He ignored the driver who was making a racket, begging for help. The guy seemed to have impaled himself on the gearstick just below his chest. The metal shaft couldn't have hit anything vital because the guy was still gurgling and complaining.

Tyler opened the suitcase on the passenger side and rummaged through it. There was maybe a million US dollars inside, but nothing more. Chicken feed. His rough hand groped around inside the case, feeling for the tracker. Bills spilled over the side, falling into the footwell and blowing out of the cab altogether. Some flew into the air, others stuck to the mashed tomatoes on the road.

Tyler found what he was looking for. He grasped the tracker device and pulled it out of the case. It was an unassuming gray box with a tiny red LED blinking in one corner. It was about the size of a deck of cards, but heavier because it was packed with batteries. Tyler threw it hard at the driver.

"I haven't followed you for six days just for a million fucking dollars," he growled. "Where's the rest?"

The banker whimpered, but he didn't answer. He didn't mind bullying his staff, but in his heart, he was a coward. Someone had shot him off the road and now he was dying at the wheel of the crummiest truck he'd ever driven. The day couldn't get worse.

The tracker hit the banker's head, but he didn't react. Too much pain elsewhere for the blow to register. Adrenalin pumping through him to try to deal with his injuries. Tyler jumped out of the cab and walked around the hood over to the driver's side. He opened the door and pulled the driver out by his collar. This time he screamed as he felt the gear stick sliding out of his wound.

His legs didn't work, and they dragged like lead weights out of the cab and through the tomato puddles as Tyler pulled him round to the back of the truck. He threw him inside the canvas trailer with incredible strength so he slammed against the back wall.

Tyler clambered in after him. He needed to know what had happened to the money. The truck had stopped near a bank, so the driver might have deposited the rest of the cash. But Tyler was worrying that he'd been chasing a million dollars across Turkmenistan while David Barr had limped out of Afghanistan in the other direction with the rest of the three hundred million.

The guy in the back of the truck wasn't living up to his nickname.

"Not so fearless now, are you my friend?" Tyler taunted him.

He had hoped that the guy would have reacted to the mention of his name. He didn't. He checked for the tattoo on the guy's wrist. Nothing there. He wasn't Fearless. Tyler didn't know who the hell the guy was. But he definitely had a million dollars, and he definitely had the tracker. So, he knew something.

Tyler grabbed the banker's hair and pulled his head back. The guy was in no condition to fight back. His eyes rolled towards the ceiling and his slack jaw lolled forward. His breathing was labored. Tyler took a tomato from the nearest plywood box. He balanced it on the lips of the guy's partly open mouth, and then whispered in his ear, "Where is the rest of the money?"

The banker whimpered again, but just like in the cab he said nothing coherent. He was frightened and bits of his insides were leaking out from the wound under his chest. He was close to delirious. Tyler smashed his fist down on the tomato, which exploded into the banker's nose and throat, blocking his airway.

The force of it shocked his body back into subconscious action, and his lungs fought back, coughing and rasping the burning juice back out of his airway. Tyler tightened his grip on the hair at the back of the man's head. He was already balancing another tomato. He was already getting into a rhythm.

"Where is the rest of the money?" he asked, louder this time.

Another pause, and then another violent explosion from Tyler. He rammed the tomato down the guy's throat and then replaced it with another. The banker hardly coughed this time. Hardly struggled. His eyes had become bulbous and watery.

Tyler continued to balance the tomatoes and smash them down the guy's throat. He carried on shouting about the money, but now he wasn't waiting for a reply. He was just angrily smashing away. Teeing up tomatoes on his lips like a golfer at a driving range. Swinging his fists down again and again.

Eventually the guy was stuffed with the fruit. Stomach, windpipe, mouth, cheeks, nostrils. Seeds were running down his face and over his blood-soaked shirt. His lips were ripped, and he'd lost a couple of teeth.

Tyler flung the banker to one side, exhausted. He'd been cooped up in the car all day, and he felt better for the workout. He slid out of the back of the truck and round to the cab where he gathered as many dollar bills as he could, and rammed them back into the suitcase. He'd retrieved a million, but it didn't feel great. The rest of it was banked safely in Baku or hidden away with David Barr. Either way, the tracker was smashed, and the trail had gone cold. He made a phone call and then headed for Baku Airport.

CHAPTER THIRTY-NINE

Airport Highway, Baku.
"If I could start again a million miles away,
I would keep myself, I would find a way."
– Nine Inch Nails, Hurt.

Lockhart looked at the journalist. Despite all of his antics along the way, he had only ever been a fly in the ointment. The real problem was Tyler, the giant guy who had chased him from the marketplace in Mary. When he had tried to force his way onto the bus outside the motel, Lockhart had been smart enough to pull his collar up and his hat down. He didn't want the guy getting a good look at him. But their eyes had locked for a moment, and Lockhart knew that the giant had meant business.

He didn't look like the kind of guy who would give up easily either. Especially for three hundred million dollars. The longer Lockhart ran, the longer Tyler would chase him. The longer they chased him, the longer he would live in fear. Lockhart needed to turn and fight. He needed to fight on his own terms, so he was heading home.

After Lockhart and the journalist had come to an agreement, there wasn't much more to say. Occasionally, the journalist would throw out a question as they drove along the highway, but generally he was a mute companion. The plan they had agreed was simple. The journalist would fly into the UK as a tourist. Lockhart would drive back through Europe and meet the journalist later in the month.

Lockhart was looking forward to the trip; a chance to trundle along without the burden of three hundred million dollars on his back. The journalist didn't ask what had been in the back of the truck, and Lockhart didn't tell. He was glad that the money was gone. Now he had a chance to see a bit more of the world.

Lockhart looked over at the journalist, who seemed to be deep in troubled thought. He had ditched the burka and was now wearing jeans and a t-shirt. He was looking forward to a new disguise as an Englishman called Charlie Lockhart. It was a name which meant nothing to the Spanish or the Iranians. He had written an explosive article that implicated members of his government with deals in Iran. There were several factions who would like to keep him quiet at any cost. Until the story was published, and the consequences had played out, the journalist would live quietly in a tiny English village in the middle of nowhere, pretending to be someone called Charlie Lockhart.

Lockhart was glad to offer the journalist refuge, even if it meant lending him his own identity. He knew what it felt like to be hunted. Maybe the journalist had become brutish on his journey simply because the world had forced him to become that way. Forced him into the burka, forced him to become sly. Maybe anyone on the run from Iranian forces would toughen up and seize chances to escape without worrying about the consequences.

As for himself, Lockhart was determined to stop running. Ever since he heard the tale of the Azeri boy on the Baku ferry, he knew what needed to be done. At some point, whoever was chasing him for the money would catch up with him. When they found him, they would try to take the money back.

They wouldn't succeed; Lockhart knew that he had to see the money go safely back to Afghanistan. It was money for roads, sewers and drains. Money to fight disease and poverty. Money to give opportunity to people who had none. Money to help a whole nation had been stolen by a couple of greedy westerners. If the thieves wanted to kill him, let them try. Lockhart would stop running and wait for them to find him. Once they were dealt with, the money was going back where it belonged.

The journalist would be Lockhart's first line of defense. The guy had insisted on taking his name and identity, so Charlie would keep him close by. He would act as an early warning if Lockhart's unseen adversaries should arrive. If they were looking for a man called Lockhart, they'd end up at the journalist's front door. And then Lockhart would spring them from behind. He had no intention of playing fairly; they didn't deserve it.

So, Lockhart and the journalist ironed out the details of the deal as they drove to the airport. Lockhart would buy a house for the journalist to live in, and he would let him use his own name to do his banking and his living. He warned the journalist that the Iranians might not find him, but whoever Lockhart was running from might.

Lockhart was pleased. The journalist might just flush out the giant and whoever he worked for into the open. It would be much easier to deal with an enemy who he could see.

CHAPTER FORTY

Heydar Aliyev airport, Baku, Azerbaijan.
"Don't go chasing waterfalls, just play in the rivers and the lakes that you're used to." – TLC, Waterfalls.

Old habits die hard thought the journalist, as he stood in the North Terminal of the modern airport. He was staring at the departures board and considering his options. He had planned to catch the BMI flight to London Heathrow, which was leaving in an hour. But a flight to Paris Charles de Gaulle had caught his eye, and he was considering taking that instead. He and Lockhart had discussed the BMI flight, and it was not in the journalist's nature to trust anyone else. He didn't like strangers knowing his business. He always worked alone, and he had learned to be cautious about everything.

So, for no good reason, he would wait an extra hour and then catch the flight to France. Once he was on the plane, he would relax. He would take the Eurostar from Paris to London and then meet up with the man whose identity he was borrowing in a tiny village called Woodridge. Even when the Englishman had described several larger towns nearby, none of these had sounded familiar. The middle of nowhere. Perfect.

As he sat in a coffee shop waiting for his flight, he froze. Storming straight towards him was the giant. He was still wearing the black outfit that he had on in Mary when he was rolling through the dust. The journalist tried to relax and reminded himself that he'd been wearing the burka when Tyler had been trying to scramble onto Lockhart's bus. There was no way for the man to recognize him.

The journalist slunk back into his booth and watched with relief as the soldier stormed past. He looked mad as hell, which was probably a good thing. He didn't check in at Air France or BMI either, which was even better. The Journalist finished his coffee and checked in. By the time he was in the air, Lockhart had covered the best part of two hundred miles of ground. He was heading home, more focused on the road ahead than the road behind.

He had forgotten the labyrinth streets of Morocco and his days as the fearless truck driver in Quetta and the dusty heat of Kandahar. Instead, he was focused on what lay ahead. A return to England, and to Woodridge, the tiny village he remembered from when he was young. It would be a good hiding place until he was ready.

He stretched back in the seat as he drove through Azerbaijan and up into Romania, on his own for the first time in a while. No journalist, no passengers, no ferrymen, no market traders and no hoteliers. There weren't even any other cars on the long straight road through the mountains which were looming up on either side. Soon enough Lockhart was twisting through them, as the road snaked left and right trying to find a way through and over the rock.

The higher the road climbed, the worse the weather got, until eventually Lockhart abandoned all thoughts of planning his next move, and focused instead on not hurtling off the edge of the tarmac.

The rain was falling hard on the ground now, golf ball droplets hitting the road so hard that they bounced fiercely back into the air. A couple of times Lockhart hit standing water and aquaplaned towards the edge of the road; lightning flashed and Lockhart caught sight of a frightening sheer drop inches from his front tire.

He eased off the gas. He'd watched *The Italian Job* enough times to know that he didn't want to end up balanced on the side of the cliff, with two wheels hanging off the edge. Lockhart knew that a high number of people survive war zones and then die in car crashes. The reason is simple. They think they're invincible once they've survived bullets and missiles and roadside bombs and bloodshed. Lockhart listened to his subconscious and slowed the car down.

He plowed on, ever west, towards home through the rain and the lightning which eventually gave way to mist and moonlight. He had covered nearly five hundred miles by first light, and he didn't feel like stopping. By midday, the wet roads were steaming, and the smell of wet European vegetation was thick in the air. It was the kind of smell Lockhart had missed without realizing it. Being a tourist had made him notice many foreign sights and smells and sounds and people, and now he was noticing the ones he knew well.

Each mile he drove, people were looking more and more western. Over the next few days, cars became newer, villages became towns and towns became cities. Roads became wider, advertising became more sophisticated, and gas became more expensive. Hotel staff became more professional but less courteous. Lockhart was on his way home.

CHAPTER FORTY-ONE

Alum Rock, Birmingham.
"You can't always get what you want,
but if you try sometimes you'll surely find
you get what you need."
– The Rolling Stones.

The old man was sitting in front of the television in his front room. He was in his usual place on the brown sofa, suspended in time. His past was behind him, enlarged and framed on his wall. A picture of a magic place; a dusty village and a tiny window through which the destiny of his family had flown.

In front of him was his future. A simple Formica table where his grandson was eating. In the corner, a modest television was showing the news, and the boy was watching. There was a global mystery unfolding, and the old man knew that boys loved mysteries almost as much as they loved adventure.

The newscast was showing a chaotic scene of basketball fans and police officers outside the Staples Center in Los Angeles. Twisted on the pavement in the background was the body of the man who had jumped from a nearby roof.

"A soldier who disappeared in Afghanistan thirteen months ago has jumped to his death from the roof of a Los Angeles hotel."

"He jumped while on the airwaves of a late-night radio show. Program host Rachel White says she does not understand what his dying message meant and security services both here and in America are baffled."

The screen showed a rather tacky publicity shot of the radio host standing in front of a giant radio station logo. Meanwhile, the sounds of the soldier's last words were piped into the tiny room in the house in Alum Rock.

"Charlie Lockhart is Fearless."

The boy looked up from his rice. He knew what it meant immediately. It was a message about his brother Ajmal, and Kandahar, and revenge. Daud knew it instantly, the way you know bad news when the phone rings.

"Although his last words mention Charlie Lockhart, the man who jumped has been identified as Captain David Barr who went missing after his last tour of Afghanistan, where he worked Logistics in Kandahar."

"LAPD say that Barr, who was seriously injured serving in Iraq in 2004, might have been living rough in California for the last year. Some people here are speculating that life on the streets, coupled with Post Traumatic Stress, could have bought on an episode of paranoid schizophrenia which led to him changing his name and jumping to his death."

The old man shook his head sadly as pictures of the American Airbase showed on the television, but Daud sat transfixed. *Charlie Lockhart is Fearless.* The man had been an American soldier in Kandahar a year ago. That's when Ajmal was in Kandahar for the last time. That's when Ajmal was handed to the Americans by a man called Fearless.

Daud knew the public report by heart. He had read it again and again, line by line, upstairs in his bedroom. The convoy from Quetta, the incident at the main gate, and the scuffle on the canteen roof. Daud's brow had become furrowed. He refused to believe the report and had decided eventually to blame the only other man on the roof. Now for some unknown reason a soldier had just delivered a message to him.

Daud was one of only three people in the world who understood the message that David Barr had sent. The message wasn't that Charlie Lockhart was fearless. The message was that Fearless was really called Charlie Lockhart.

The official reports into Ajmal's arrest in Kandahar, his interrogation and his subsequent rendition to Guantanamo began with a scuffle on a roof. The man who was supposed to have caught Ajmal in his act of treachery didn't even have a real name. He was simply referred to as "Fearless".

Daud had assumed that the name had been invented, because the mystery contractor vanished soon after Ajmal's arrest. It was all too convenient, and Daud was keen to believe the whole thing was a conspiracy, anyway. But now there was news. The mystery was unraveling. It was just over a year since Ajmal had been arrested on the roof at Kandahar and finally, Daud had a name. Daud had a target. Fearless was Charlie Lockhart.

CHAPTER FORTY-TWO

Crown and Cricket Public House, Woodridge, England.
"I fear rivers over flowing.
I hear the voice of rage and ruin."
— Creedence Clearwater Revival, Bad Moon Rising

The journalist was relaxed. He was in a dark corner of the Crown and Cricket on the top of the hill at Woodridge. It was months since he had arrived in the village and he was still in hiding.

"The change of government will help," he told Lockhart. "It will be much easier for them to publish as soon as the current regime is out of power."

Lockhart hoped he was right. They were growing to respect one another. The journalist had sacrificed a lot to expose corruption in his country's government. It still wasn't safe for him to go home.

"How long do you think it'll be?" Lockhart asked him.

The journalist shrugged and took a sip of his red wine. Lockhart was drinking a dark ale, which the journalist hadn't cultivated a taste for during his time in the village. He winced a little every time Lockhart put his glass to his lips.

"A few more months I hope," he said. His voice trailed off as he thought about the life he had given up for his exclusive investigation. Lockhart gave him a moment lost in thought.

The television in the bar was tuned in to the twenty-four-hour news, and over the journalist's shoulder Lockhart could see a re-run of Rachel White's interview about Barr's suicide. He saw the picture of Barr flash up on the TV screen, and recognized him from Kandahar, months ago. The desert felt like it was another lifetime, but Lockhart had always know that something would happen, and that someone would come. And now he could feel the danger coming back to life.

"Listen," Lockhart urged the journalist. "There's something I have to tell you. There's been a report on the news, and it mentioned my name. It's about Kandahar. And you know that when they come looking for me, there's a chance that they will find you instead?"

It was a risk that the journalist had taken happily. Compared to what the Spanish or Iranian authorities would do to him, he couldn't imagine he had much to fear from whoever was chasing Lockhart.

"I'll be careful," he said. "I'll look both ways before I cross the road."

Lockhart laughed, but he said, "Look, this is serious. If you want to move somewhere else, nobody is making you stay, ok?"

The journalist had been serious all week. He had kept himself to himself, trying not to draw unwanted attention in the village. When it had been necessary to introduce himself, he had told people he was Charlie Lockhart. And nobody had come looking for him. The plan had worked well.

"Where else would I go?" the Spaniard asked, settling back with his wine. Lockhart hoped the Spaniard was making the right decision. Tyler was coming, and he was ready. He just hoped that the journalist was ready, too.

CHAPTER FORTY-THREE

Starbucks, Hope Street Los Angeles.
"I can't get no sleep."
– Faithless, Insomnia.

James Neilson was deep in thought at the end of the coffee counter. The place was humming along busily although the morning commuters had left for work, and the steam had gone out of the service.

Neilson had been woken up by a phone call just before three o'clock and hadn't been back to bed since. The first six hours had been fueled with adrenalin, but now he was tiring and needed caffeine. He glanced over to the woman in the corner. She was staring out of the window, agitated. Her lips were moving as if she was rehearsing a line. She looked like she needed more than coffee.

The call that had woken Nielson had been from the radio station. Something had gone wrong on air. People were upset. More calls would follow. Neilson was a smart guy, and he spent the first hour after he was woken piecing everything together. *Asking questions.* Who took the call? Who put the guy through on air? What had Rachel said to him? Was she culpable? How long was he on the air before he jumped?

The second hour had been spent deep in conversation with the lawyers. They were nervous, but Neilson had been around the block long enough to know that lawyers are always nervous. By dawn he was talking to the LAPD who reassured him they only wanted to talk to Rachel White as a witness. After that, he held a conference with his breakfast news team to let them know how they should report the suicide. Then he called Rachel; he knew she'd be awake.

Coffee arrived; one sweet and creamy, the other black and strong. Nielson swiped both cups from the counter, mumbled his thanks and headed over to Rachel White. She looked worse than he did. Her eyes were red rims and blue shadows. She told him she'd slept, but she hadn't. She told him she was fine, but she wasn't.

She looked up as he sat down.

"I'm going to need a week off, Neilson."

He put the coffee down in between them, as casually as he could. He pushed the latte towards her and said, "Take as long as you want."

Rachel was grateful. She knew that he meant it. Neilson was a good solid guy. He was a contracts man, mostly. He was good with the suits from the network, but he understood the value of creative people. She'd always felt like he was in her corner. Today he was proving it.

"And I could use a plane ticket to Dallas," she said, gazing across the street at nothing in particular.

Rachel White was a good radio personality. People tuned in for her, so she was valuable to the radio station. The executives wouldn't complain if he gave her a ticket to the moon. But Neilson smelled something that he didn't like.

"Dallas? Who do you know in Dallas?"

Rachel had been wrestling with a secret ever since they'd sat down. Something she'd kept from her producer. Something she omitted to tell the LAPD earlier. Something she knew she should keep to herself, but she was going to tell Neilson, anyway. She wasn't sure why she was telling him, except that Neilson was the kind of guy who people told stuff. A good listener.

"I don't know anyone in Dallas," she replied, her eyes coming back to the table. Checking out his reaction. "I will take a drive from there up to Pine Bluff."

Neilson knew that the soldier's suicide had hit Rachel hard, but this was insane. Nobody went to Pine Bluff unless they needed to. The only visitors the place got were biological and chemical weapons experts. People whose job was to dismantle the massive cold war stockpiles locked in the arsenal to the north of the city. Pine Bluff was ugly and broken down and dangerous too. It was a mad place to go.

"Pine Bluff, Arkansas?"

"Pine Bluff, Arkansas." Rachel answered firmly, as if the matter was beyond discussion.

"Who the hell do you know in Pine Bluff, Arkansas?"

"Nobody," Rachel sighed. He would not like the next bit. "Barr's wife and daughter came from there."

"The guy who jumped?" asked Neilson calmly. "You want to see his wife and kid?"

"The cops who spoke to me this morning said he was holding a picture of them just before he jumped" Rachel urged. "They think he'd carried it with him for the last year, but hadn't gone to see them once. Not *once* since he returned from Afghanistan. Why not? They'd filed a missing person report for him."

Neilson looked troubled. Rachel was creating a mystery for herself. He could see it happening, right there in front of his eyes. Creative people go mad if they're left alone with their guilt. She was creating a mystery so she could rush off and solve it, instead of sitting at home blaming herself for Barr's death. Neither option was particularly healthy, but Neilson was weighing up which one would get Rachel back on the radio quickest. He was a compassionate businessman. But ultimately, he was a businessman. And having Rachel White off the air was bad for business.

"There's more," she told him as he took a sip of his black coffee. "David Barr didn't jump off the building last night."

Neilson nearly choked on his coffee, but regained his poise and swallowed before scowling at her. "Rachel, half a million people heard it happen."

Rachel shook her head.

"Something was wrong with it," she said. "Something felt wrong, so I listened back to the tapes this morning."

"When?"

"When it was still dark," she shrugged. "I wasn't sleeping."

No shit.

Suddenly Rachel looked excited. Her tired eyes became sharp and alert as she told Neilson her secret.

"There's a second breath on the tape. I can hear Barr grunting, and a second breath in the background. People can't breathe twice at the same time, so David Barr wasn't alone up there. Someone else was with him. Somebody pushed him off."

Neilson was having none of it.

"Rachel, this Barr guy sat talking to you for five minutes about how he was going to jump off."

"I know," she replied excitedly. "But then he *didn't* jump off. He was pushed. I'm certain of it. Someone pushed David Barr off the roof live on my show. So, I'm going to Pine Bluff, and I'm going to find out who the hell he was."

Neilson told her to leave it to the police, but he could see that she wasn't going to listen. She was stubborn, and the sooner he helped her to work this thing through, the sooner she'd be back on the air. Before he could tell her to be careful, her phone rang. International code. Neilson looked at Rachel and raised an eyebrow.

"Who do you know in the UK?"

CHAPTER FORTY-FOUR

Starbucks, Hope Street Los Angeles.
"Come together right now, over me."
– The Beatles, Come Together

For a split second, Rachel White had considered letting whoever was ringing her cell phone go to voicemail. But she didn't. She picked up on the third ring. The accent on the other end matched the international code, and the voice started talking straight away.

"Rachel White?"

A man's voice. Probably in his thirties. Educated. Confident.

"Yeah. Who's asking?" She flashed her eyes at Neilson across the table. He was still blowing at his damn black coffee. *Always cautious.*

"I just saw your name on a TV report and I thought I should call" the voice replied. "I called the radio station, and they gave me your number when I told them who I was."

"And who are you?"

He thought back to the desert, and what Barr had told him about the safety of anonymity all those months ago.

"I'm Charlie Lockhart," he said. Barr was dead, and the time for hiding was over.

It took Rachel about two seconds to place the name. Only because she was tired. Only because she hadn't slept. Only because she'd listened to someone being killed nine hours ago. Lockhart was the name that David Barr had shouted out as he fell from the roof. *Charlie Lockhart is fearless.* Rachel didn't even know what that meant.

164

"So, are you fearless?" she asked. She was reaching. She stopped performing for Neilson and twisted in her seat, searching for a bit of privacy. Intimacy. She shielded her conversation with a hunched shoulder and a curtain of dark brown hair.

"Yes," replied the voice on her cell. "I'm Fearless."

Honest. Patient. Definitely in his thirties. The fact that he was fearless made no sense to her, but she played along, hoping everything would fall into place.

"What can I do for you, Charlie Lockhart?"

"I need a favor." Lockhart said. "I'm trying to work out what happened to David Barr."

"Well, there's something we have in common," Rachel sighed. "Do you have any idea?"

Lockhart explained that he had met Barr briefly in Kandahar. He described how Barr seemed to have fallen in with the wrong crowd and described Tyler to the woman on the end of the phone. Rachel listened, trying to piece the fragments into a story in her mind. Barr had sounded like a nice guy last night. A nice guy who had run into a lot of trouble.

"I'm going to Pine Bluff," Rachel suddenly blurted out. Christ, she was tired. One minute she was thinking about a trip to Pine Bluff. Steeling herself. The next minute she was telling the guy on the phone about it. A guy who she didn't know at all.

On the other side of the coffee table, Neilson shook his head and dialed a number on his own cell. He started talking quietly to someone on the other end. Making himself busy to give Rachel some space.

"What's Pine Bluff?" Lockhart asked.

"Hell on earth, apparently," she said, watching for Neilson's reaction, but he was busy with his own conversation. "It's where Barr got enlisted and got married and spent half his life, according to the detective I spoke to earlier. His family is still there, and I want to find out who he was."

Lockhart said nothing. A trip to Pine Bluff sounded like a bad idea on all kinds of levels, but he understood why she wanted to go. He'd probably go himself if he wasn't holed up in Woodridge. The snow had been coming down for three days and was piling up against the old stone walls which divided up the livestock and the landscape.

"I guess I just feel bad for him," Rachel admitted. "I just want to know who he was, and what happened to him."

Lockhart leveled with her. She had been fairly open with him.

"I think he may have killed himself to escape a guy called Tyler," he told her. There was a pause while Rachel thought it through.

"I'll go you one better," replied Rachel. "I think your guy Tyler was on the roof with him. I think Tyler pushed him off. Somebody did. And I think I can find out more in Pine Bluff."

Rachel explained the scuffles, and the tapes, and her hour of careful listening. Lockhart looked out across the white field behind the house. The old stone walls which separated the fields had been swallowed by the mist which was rolling up the hill. He visualized Tyler throwing someone off a roof. It wasn't hard to imagine. Rachel might be right.

Opposite Rachel, Neilson had finished his quiet phone conversation. He took a cheap napkin from a chrome holder in the center of the table and then pulled an expensive Parker pen from his jacket pocket. The type of pen you sign million dollar contracts with. He wrote a quick note onto the soft paper and folded it over. Then he slid the folded note over to her along with cash to cover the drinks. She gave him an apologetic wink, and he squeezed her hand stoically. Then he leaned forward over the table and kissed her gently on the forehead in the way that a father would, but a boss shouldn't. Rachel didn't mind at all. Neilson slid out of the booth and through the door onto the street, leaving his troubled employee to her international call.

"So do you think I should go?" Rachel asked Lockhart. "I don't know what good it'll do, but I think his wife should know. I think she should know that her husband didn't jump."

Lockhart thought hard about it and then told Rachel: "People only ask questions like that when they've already decided about the answer."

Rachel knew he was right. It didn't matter what he said, and it didn't matter what Neilson told her either. She'd liked David Barr. She was the last person Barr ever spoke to. And she wanted some answers. She sat chewing it over for a moment. Lockhart interrupted her thoughts.

"Will you let me know where Barr's family are?"

"Why do you want to know?"

"Because I think David Barr was a good man caught up in a bad deal. I think he killed himself to protect his family. And I think his family are owed a payment for a job he was forced to do in Afghanistan. I'm going to cover the debt."

Strong. Caring. *Fearless, actually.* Rachel could imagine how Lockhart had acquired the name. She imagined that he was about six feet tall and in good shape. She was about right.

"Why don't you come as well?" she asked on a whim. "We could be Molder and Scully for a few days. I could use some new company."

Lockhart would have loved to. Right now he was stuck in a one road village that had been cut off by snow for three days. He hated waiting at the best of times. Today he was crawling the walls.

"Well, I hear Pine Bluff is beautiful at this time of year," he said, and Rachel laughed. "But I can't. I'm in Woodridge, the middle of nowhere. And Tyler is coming for me just like he came for Barr. The thing is, I want to make sure I'm here when they arrive."

"You're not going to run and hide?" Rachel asked.

"It didn't do Barr much good, did it?" Lockhart said bitterly. "If you keep running, people catch you when you least expect it. If you've got a plan, you've got a chance. And I've got a plan, so I'm sitting here waiting for my chance."

Rachel told him to be careful, which was pointless but friendly. Lockhart liked the sound of her. She told him she'd find Barr's wife for him. Told him she'd tackle Pine Bluff on her own. Told him she'd deal with Tyler if she had to.

"Look after yourself, Rachel," Lockhart warned her. "He's a big mean guy."

"Who says I'm not a big mean girl?" Rachel asked with a smile, and she hung up the phone. She never said goodbye. Not to anyone. It was one of her rules. She copied Lockhart's number to her contacts and slipped her phone back into her pocket. She threw the cash that Neilson had left into the middle of the table as a tip. Then she unfolded the napkin he had left in front of her. The message was short and sweet:

LAX to Dallas Fort Worth booking ref JX45358
check-in tomorrow morning 07.40
BE CAREFUL!

Rachel White smiled. She was glad Neilson was in her corner. She drained the dregs of her coffee and walked out into the street. And straight into about a million journalists.

CHAPTER FORTY-FIVE

Alum Rock, Birmingham
"Ready or not, here I come. You can't hide."
– Fugees, Ready or Not.

Daud had a simple room. The basics were crammed in; Bed, wardrobe, chest of drawers, desk. Nothing matched anything else and nothing was especially grand. The carpet looked fairly new but the curtains and the bedclothes had seen better days. The worn duvet was pulled taut over the bed, and the room was immaculately clean. The chest of drawers was closed tight, and nothing was poking out from the wardrobe.

The only assault on the tranquility of the room was a crowded desk. Daud ran his life from that desk, and it was spilling over with envelopes, papers, magazines and pens. There were writing pads covered with notes scribbled in different colored inks, coins and business cards. There was a Hajj picture and a French bus ticket and a bottle of sunblock and two coffee cups. His laptop was buried somewhere in the middle of the confusion.

The desk had a drawer, and the drawer had a lock. The key stayed in Daud's pocket at all times. He found himself holding the key inside his pocket whenever he was on the bus, just in case it fell out. He found the touch of it reassuring as the metal warmed up between his thumb and finger.

Until this year, Daud's life had been an open book. Recently though, he had found himself locking more and more of his papers away in the drawer. The official report about Ajmal in Kandahar. The claims he was a terrorist. The claims that Ajmal wanted to kill five hundred men. Somehow seeing the words in black and white made it worse.

Part of Daud burned with shame. When he couldn't bare it anymore, he suppressed it by fueling the other part of him which burned with rage. Rage felt better than shame. He convinced himself of Ajmal's innocence. Busied himself with his plans for justice and revenge.

As well as the official reports about Kandahar and the stark allegations against his brother, Daud also had letters from a human rights charity who had shown an interest in his brother's plight. They spoke about the abuse that Ajmal might be living through, behind the razor wire. They sent letters from high-flying attorneys telling Daud how hopeless Ajmal's case was.

Most of Daud's life sat on top of his cluttered desk, but the letters about Ajmal always went back in a neat pile in the locked desk drawer. Under the letters were Daud's notes. He had seen the report overnight about the suicide in Los Angeles and he had been planning ever since. The reports said that the man who tackled Ajmal on the roof was called Fearless. And now the soldier from Afghanistan had said that Fearless was Charlie Lockhart. He knew he was getting closer to having a target for his rage.

Daud had spent the night trawling through Facebook for the profiles of every Charlie Lockhart. There were about sixty of them, of which nearly half lived in the UK. Five of them were girls, and Daud ruled out another eight on the basis that they were too young or too old to have been in Afghanistan. He rejected another two because they were too fat to have realistically climbed the ladder and run across the roof in the way the military report had described.

That left him with sixteen Lockharts, and none of them had any mention of Kandahar on their profile pages. There was no way of knowing which one had been instrumental in sending his brother to Guantanamo. Daud had printed each profile out, stapled them together and locked them away in the desk drawer, underneath the official report and the human rights letters.

Beneath the printouts was a towel, folded neatly to fit into the space. Inside the towel was the revolver that Daud had bought from the fishmonger in the Crown and Sceptre. He needed it, but he hated it. He owed it to Ajmal to use it. But whenever he was downstairs, listening to his granddad telling stories about the magic that had created their family back in Quetta, Daud could think about nothing but the weapon hiding away in the bedroom upstairs. It was like an ugly heart beating away unseen in the center of a beautiful house.

Tonight Daud was sitting on his bed, scowling at the desk, thinking about the dreadful job that fate had tasked him with. He had narrowed his search down to sixteen men. The time was getting closer. What if he was arrested? What if he had to spend the rest of his life in prison? It would be better than living in freedom while his brother was being tortured on the other side of the world. Revenge was a practical business, and a welcome distraction.

Apart from the warm yellow light bathing the chaotic writing desk, Daud's room was lit only by a flickering television set which was perched on top of the chest of drawers. It was small and old, but it was one of Daud's only luxuries. His father had given it to him on his eighteenth birthday, along with a short lecture about how he should not be seduced by television, and that he should continue to spend his evenings with his family.

He and Ajmal had spent hours watching films together. Sometimes their father would join them, but never for more than a few minutes. Occasionally, their granddad would poke his head around the door and ask questions about what they were watching.

"Who is she? Why is she kissing him? Now why is she crying? And why is she kissing him and crying at the same time?" He would keep going until he had distracted the boys enough to get their full attention. "You know that your grandmother never cries when I kiss her like that? Always she smiles because she knows that she is very lucky."

He would grin from ear to ear. The boys would always shuffle along Daud's bed and implore him to come and join them, but he never did.

Now Daud was on his own. Tonight he sat on the bed feeling distracted, scowling at his desk and listening to the news. Then slowly he became aware the television was talking about the American soldier again. The one who had jumped from the roof. The one who had told him Charlie Lockhart's name as he plunged to his death.

Daud still couldn't work out why the man had shouted out the name as he fell, but there would be time for that later. Today had been a good day because the dying soldier had helped him come closer than ever to knowing the truth. He was closer to finding the man who had ruined his brother's life.

The news report cut to a street scene in Los Angeles. It was daytime. Earlier in the day, all the pictures had been of flashing police lights and pandemonium at the scene of the suicide. Now though, the cameras were focused on a young woman outside a coffee shop. She looked startled, and she looked like she hadn't slept in a while.

"Of course I am sorry that it happened," she was saying. "Wouldn't you be? If you're the last person to talk to someone, then you will always ask if you could have done something to change their mind."

There was a general murmur from the gang of journalists.

"It makes no odds if you are on the radio, or on a helpline, or having a coffee with someone" the girl went on, finding a bit of composure. Beginning to construct an argument. A professional under pressure. Daud recognized her as the DJ who had been talking to the guy when he jumped.

"If you're the last one to talk to them, you'll always wish you could have done more."

She was trying to walk, trying to get away from the press pack without running. The video was picking up the sound of the photographer's shutters snapping away. Lots of them. The camera was shaky, jostling for position.

"Do you know why he did it?" someone called from out of the shot. Random arms with microphones and tape recorders were pushing into the wobbling picture. Rachel White ran a hand through her hair for a second, thinking. Then she decided to give the press pack a story.

"I'm not sure why he did it, or even who he was, really. I know the LAPD are making enquiries, but I think I owe it to David Barr to find out what he was running away from. It's a real life mystery, and it strikes me that if he chose to jump off the roof so publicly after the Lakers game then it's a mystery that he wanted someone to solve. So I'm planning on solving it."

The gaggle of hacks threw out more questions as she came to the end of her sentence.

"How will you do that, Rachel? Will you be on air tonight?"

The shot zoomed in closer, as the cameraman tried to cut all the arms and microphones out of the picture. Rachel White's face filled the screen in Daud's bedroom.

"I'll be flying to Pine Bluff tonight. I'll be back on the air once I've got something to report about David Barr. I'm telling you, there's a lot we don't know about his story yet."

She was holding her cell phone up in front of her.

"I've just had a call from some place called Woodridge in England, you know, a call from the other side of the world. From a stranger. The guy said he was Charlie Lockhart. That's the name that Barr shouted as he fell."

There was an excited reaction from the media scrum.

Daud never heard the end of the interview. He had already taken the warm key from his pocket and was unlocking his desk drawer. He flicked frantically through the sixteen Facebook profiles he had printed out. He found what he was looking for on the seventh sheet.

Name: Charlie Lockhart

Location: Woodridge, UK.

Sixteen became one. Daud had found the man he was going to kill.

He was alone in the house and before he left he spent a few minutes sitting on Ajmal's old bed, talking softly. Speaking to his missing brother like he used to, even though he wasn't there anymore. The room was just like it had been when Ajmal was at home.

Ajmal's clothes were still hanging in the wardrobe. He'd been gone so long that they looked hopelessly out of date. Daud knew that Ajmal wouldn't be seen dead in them now. But nobody had had the heart to throw them out. Daud clung to the hope that Ajmal would be home one day.

Downstairs, he stood for a moment in front of his grandfather's picture of Quetta. He climbed up on the sofa and reached up to the picture. He ran a finger over the window that his grandfather always pointed out. The window that Ajmal had traveled the world to see. He held his lips on the glass for a moment to see if he could feel the magic that his grandfather always talked about.

Then he stepped down and grabbed his car keys. He thrust the fishmonger's revolver deep into his rucksack and covered it with his hoody. Then he set off to search for Charlie Lockhart.

CHAPTER FORTY-SIX

Taynton Hollow, Near Woodridge, England.
"And by five o'clock everything's dead,
And every third car is a cab,
And ignorant people sleep in their beds,
Like the doped white mice in the college lab"
– Del Amitri, Nothing Ever Happens

Taynton Hollow was a sleepy Cotswold village in a county where nothing ever happened. As a kid, Charlie Lockhart had hated it because of its idleness. He was born in industrial Birmingham in a crowded street where everyone knew everyone else's business. There were rows and fights and friendships and opportunities.

His parents were academics. They were wise and calm, always with their heads in books. As a teenager he had found them frustrating. They'd discovered Buddhism and flung themselves into it. They prescribed meditation as a solution to every problem under the sun, the way Catholics hanker after a good Mass whenever trouble is afoot.

Tom Lockhart was a research scientist, always working on a cure for something or other. He was always dedicated, diligent, and selfless. Deirdre Lockhart taught Medieval Spanish in Birmingham, but was poached to run Galician Studies at Oxford University. Teaching English kids about a language of ancient Spanish farmers and fishermen. The whole family moved house to be closer to Oxford and settled into Woodridge.

Despite following his wife's career to Oxford, it was Tom Lockhart who struck gold for the family. A pharmaceutical company paid him a small fortune for a compound he accidentally discovered and the family became fairly rich fairly quickly. Charlie's parents huffed and puffed about how the money wouldn't change them, and it didn't. They were decent folk who turned into decent rich folk. Lockhart respected them for that. None of the extra money came his way, either.

The teenage Lockhart had hated Taynton, because nothing ever happened there. The Lockhart house was serenity itself as his parents continued their new age pursuits of meditation and acupuncture and yoga with a mute vigor. Even more silence gathered momentum across the endless rolling hills surrounding the village and then crashed down like a wave over the family home.

Lockhart knew that his parents were good people, but life was dull. He felt like everything he knew came from books. Lockhart longed to get out of Taynton and see the world. To taste it and smell it. Get scared by it and run away from it if necessary.

Taynton Hollow was tiny compared to the city where Charlie was born. It had a small shop and two pubs. There was a tiny church which was well attended on Sundays; cars traveled in from all the nearby villages and clogged up the narrow country lanes.

But then for his fifteenth birthday his parents bought him a bike which he rode every day. Something told him that there was a lot to explore beyond the monotonous fields and spires surrounding him. He could smell adventure on the wind.

The nearby villages were smaller than Taynton. Some had fewer than fifty houses. No schools or pubs or shops. The smallest of all was the hardest to reach on his bike. It was a tiny place on the top of a huge hill. It was called Woodridge.

Welcome to Woodridge: the middle of nowhere. Years later, when he returned from his travels, Lockhart realized that the middle of nowhere was the perfect hiding place. The perfect place to prepare to deal with Tyler.

Others had hidden in Woodridge before. Years ago, when the teenage Lockhart had returned from his bike ride one evening, his father asked him where he had been.

"I went up the hill to Woodridge," Charlie had replied. "It's the smallest place I've ever seen."

Tom Lockhart folded his newspaper over and gave his son his full attention.

"Did you see the manor house? It was built by a Catholic family at a time when their faith was outlawed by the Queen."

"How old is it, then?" Charlie had asked.

"How old do you think?" his father had replied. He liked his son to do his own thinking.

"Four hundred, maybe?"

"Yes, probably," said Tom, looking pleased. "Maybe older. The Catholic family commissioned the famous lay preacher and architect Nicholas Owen to come to Woodridge and build secret panels and tunnels in their home, so that their clergymen could escape if the priest hunters should come knocking."

"Priest hunters?"

"Yes, they were paid by the Queen to stamp out the Catholics, ," Tom continued. He stood up and wandered over to the family bookcase and started looking for a history text. "Don't forget, the gunpowder plot happened not long after that manor house was built. The Catholics tried to blow up the Houses of Parliament."

"I wonder if Guy Fawkes ever hid out up at Woodridge" Charlie asked his dad. Suddenly, the tiny village seemed more interesting.

"Well, you never know," said Tom, "but probably not. The stakes were very high though. Nicholas Owen himself was discovered in one of his own tunnels a few months later, just after the gunpowder plot. They killed him on the rack in the tower of London, while three of his accomplices were hung, drawn and quartered."

So the manor house proved to be Lockhart's first adventure. His first taste of traveling alone, with his eyes open and his spirit alive. The world had rewarded his adventuring with a glimpse of history and a smell of excitement. Murderous gangs hunting for priests to kill, lowly families outwitting the monarchy, secret panels and gunpowder plots.

CHAPTER FORTY-SEVEN

Pine Bluff, Arkansas.
"I never really gave up on
Breakin' out of this two-star town
I got the green light, I got a little fight,
I'm gonna turn this thing around"
- Killers, Read my Mind

Rachel White was holed up in a place called Lucky Bar on Dollarway Road. Dollarway stretched up towards the US Army Arsenal just north of Pine Bluff. The bar didn't live up to its name. It was functional and unloved. There was a small counter propped up by two deadbeats. The floor was dark and wooden. The varnish had long scuffed off, but the color had been replaced by years of spillages.

Rachel was at a wooden table which was all glued up with decades of beer and nicotine. All the chairs in the place were leather, all different shades of brown. None of them matched. None of them were clean. It looked like years since the place had seen a broom, let alone a lick of paint. Whoever had decorated the dark green walls with horseshoes and railroad memorabilia had long since left. There were wilted flowers in small vases on each table which seemed to be the only attempt at brightening the place up. They probably looked good about a week ago.

All Rachel had known about Pine Bluff when she first headed east was that it ranked as the most dangerous metropolitan area in the United States. Neilson had told her that. Several times. She had flown to Dallas regardless, and then driven another two hundred miles east to Pine Bluff, Arkansas. She'd driven through a town called Hope on her way, and she'd watched

Hope disappear in her rear-view mirror. Neilson had been right; Pine Bluff was a hole.

The sign at the city limits said "Population 55085" but when Rachel had Wiki'd the place last night she had learned that over five thousand residents had left in the last ten years. Ten percent. She looked at the sprawling low-slung place around her. Half of it was boarded up, and half of the boards were scrawled with badly written threats and ghetto slogans. She could see why the population was in decline; there wasn't much worth sticking around for.

Some people called it Crime City. Or Heroin City. The sidewalks weren't swept. The houses had falling in roofs and rotten floorboards. Shop signs were faded and broken. The only things thriving were liquor stores and beatnik bars on every corner. As Rachel headed into the heart of the city, the people she drove past looked ruined and aimless.

She checked in at a Super 8 at midday and headed into town. The guy behind the reception desk had told her that the best place to find army folk would be at Lucky Bar. He made it sound like a busy place. Rachel had expected to have to muscle her way through tightly packed gangs of uniformed men to get near the bar. But it wasn't like that. The place was next to empty.

Apart from the two deadweights drinking at the bar, the only other customer was a grubby-looking Filipino girl who sat in the far corner and looked up hopefully every time the door opened. After a while, Rachel found herself doing the same. The men always shuffled straight over to the girl and spoke quietly before walking out again. Eventually one man struck a deal with her and the girl stood up. She wasn't wearing much of anything and looked like she could do with a good hot meal. She'd lost the way of carrying herself that blossoming young women ought to have. She didn't seem to care that the man didn't wait to hold the door for her. She hadn't been expecting him to.

The woman behind the bar shouted after the Filipino, who turned on her heel and came back in. Without saying a word, she peeled off a couple of notes and left them on the counter before leaving once more. The door rattled shut.

Rachel watched the girl go, and a sadness washed through her. Maybe it was no surprise that the vibrancy of youth had been sucked out of the girl if she hung around in Lucky's all day waiting for business.

The waitress came out from behind the counter and headed over to the far corner where the young girl had been sitting. She looked about six months pregnant, but she was brisk and efficient. Pretty too, in a downtrodden way.

She swung by Rachel's table on the way back over.

"Can I get you something else?" she asked in a soft low voice, totally different to the way she had barked at the young girl a moment earlier.

Her clothes were crisp and well ironed. Starched even, maybe. Rachel thought they must have been unforgiving for a woman as swollen as the waitress, but she looked like pregnancy suited her anyway. She was wearing a name badge pinned to her blouse, which said that she was called Raven. She had undone one button too many on her blouse, and it looked like it was only the top of her apron which was keeping her from spilling out altogether. Rachel wondered if she was enjoying an extra cup size since getting knocked up. Or maybe she was just squeezing the two drunk guys for tips. They didn't look like they had much spare.

"Can I get more coffee, please?"

Rachel could see the waitress trying to figure her out. She felt like a fish out of water with her west coast accent and her west coast tan. She was sitting in a rough bar in a rough town and she'd been there for almost an hour. No wonder the waitress was interested. Rachel looked like she'd been stood up on the worst date of her life.

Raven returned behind the counter and got a fresh pot percolating. There was no music in the place, and the sound of the percolator was the closest thing to atmosphere the place ever experienced. The boys at the bar looked like it was a distraction to their near-slumber. Raven leaned forward and clean the counter in front of them for twenty seconds, which was long enough for both of them to fall into her cleavage and grapple back out again.

Before the coffee had finished percolating though, both men decided that the day would not get any better than their quick glimpse of warm flesh and lingerie. They sunk what remained of their beers and headed back out of the rattling door without saying goodbye to anyone. Raven grabbed the screwed up bills and threw them into the register and shook her head.

There was an open doorway beside the bar which led through to the stores and the restrooms. Raven headed out back while the coffee was on the go, and Rachel was left on her own in the bar. Even when the smell of the coffee overpowered the stench of stale beer, the place was miserable.

Rachel imagined Captain Barr sitting in the place, drinking with his unit. The place would be improved with a few rowdy voices smashing through the silence. She thought about him for a moment; the man who had fallen from the roof while he was on her show. *While he was talking to her.*

Now she was certain that he'd been pushed. And she'd had a phone call from an Englishman who thought she was right. He was Charlie Lockhart, the man whose name Barr had shouted as he fell. He mentioned a man called Tyler who was apparently some kind of giant.

Rachel had checked her mail as soon as she landed back in Dallas. Her newsroom had found out some information about David Barr and his background, and emailed her the details. Probably because their boss

Neilson had squeezed them to get on with it. The email said Barr had been in Pine Bluff for most of his service career. After joining the Army, he had been assigned to protect the perimeter at Pine Bluff Arsenal, which was an important job.

For sixty years, Pine Bluff had squirreled away twelve percent of the country's chemical weapons, although Rachel's notes told her that the place had just finished destroying the last of its stock. The Arsenal had made itself redundant, and the parasitic city around it was dying. Rachel looked around and wondered whether a catastrophic chemical leak could have made the place much worse than it was today.

The waitress came back with coffee and a smile. She leaned over and placed the coffee down on the table, with a fresh cup and saucer and spoon. Rachel could see that she'd fastened her blouse buttons since the men at the bar had left. She smiled to herself. Next to the fresh cup, Raven placed new sachets of white and brown sugar, and a small plastic wrapped biscuit which might well have been a million years old.

Then she took the old cup and saucer along with its unused sugar and uneaten biscuits. Just doing her job, by the book. Rachel noticed she was married. She had dainty fingers, and a silver wedding band. Next to it was her engagement ring, with a huge rock. Very expensive looking. Not the kind of ring you get by working in a down at heel bar. Maybe she was married to a soldier and just enjoyed helping out. Maybe she *was* a soldier, Rachel chastised herself. Maybe she'd come out of the army to have the kid. There was bound to be a connection; there was no way a ring like that belonged in a place like this otherwise.

Rachel thanked her for the coffee and spent the next few minutes thinking about the rest of the email the newsroom had sent. There was a picture of David Barr in uniform and a scan of the photograph he had been holding, up on the roof. It was of a woman in a green dress with auburn hair and a young girl who was about five years old. Barr's family. There was a bloody black thumbprint in the bottom corner. LAPD had superimposed the words "not for publication" over the scan, but the women's faces were clear enough. They were beautiful. Rachel could understand why Barr had clung on to the picture right to the end.

The newsroom had also found details of Barr's military career. He had spent several years protecting the perimeter at the Arsenal, gaining promotions until he was running the unit. What came in and out of Pine Bluff Arsenal was mostly signed off by him. Two years ago the base had begun to wind down, and at the same time Barr had been sent to Afghanistan to run the gate at Kandahar.

Neilson had also asked the journalists to send details of the rest of Barr's unit over to her. As she sat drinking her coffee, Rachel double clicked on the attachment they'd sent to her phone. They'd dug up about twelve other names of soldiers who worked with Barr and who were still based in Pine Bluff. The great thing about journalists is that they can work on rumor and innuendo. They can call in favors and play dirty. They don't have to wait for the official channels. Christ knows how they had gotten the list together for Neilson, but it was impressive for a day's work.

One name stood out as soon as Rachel opened the attachment. It was the name of the man that Charlie Lockhart had warned her to watch out for. The man who he thought could have thrown Barr from the roof. He lived here in Pine Bluff. He must have known David Barr well. The fourth soldier on the list of twelve was Jason Tyler.

Suddenly Rachel felt nervous. Neilson had warned her about Pine Bluff. Lockhart had warned her about Tyler. She'd walked straight into both of them. And yet the picture of David Barr's family kept her focused. He had died on her show. She needed to find out why.

She convinced herself that she was safe in a city of fifty thousand people. Not much chance of bumping into the one guy she was trying to avoid. Even so, it was probably not a good idea to drink in the bar he was most likely to walk into. Just in case. She realized that she had been dumb, shooting her mouth off on the TV yesterday. She'd told the world that she thought Barr had been murdered, and that she was coming to Pine Bluff. So now she needed to be smart. She should find Barr's family and then get the hell out of Pine Bluff. Quickly.

She called over to Raven, who put down a glass that she was drying and walked over to the table. Rachel was still impressed at how quick she was on her feet, considering the size of her belly. She was toned and athletic, which only worked to emphasize her bump.

"Cheque?" she asked.

"No," Rachel faltered. "No, I'm after your help."

"Okay?"

"I'm looking for an old school friend, and I thought you might have seen her. I think she might hang out here sometimes."

Rachel showed the waitress the picture on her phone, trying to put her thumb over the LAPD sign and failing badly. It was a lame story. Rachel knew it and so did the waitress. She didn't pull her up on it, maybe out of kindness.

"I don't think I've ever seen her," she said. "She has pretty eyes though, doesn't she?"

Rachel agreed and smiled. "She was married to a soldier; I heard they hang out here?"

"Well, some of them do," the waitress said as she walked back towards the counter. "My husband used to work up at the facility years ago, he might know them. What's her name?"

Shit. It suddenly occurred to Rachel that she had no idea what David

Barr's wife was called. Maybe she should have listened to Neilson and stayed back home. The waitress was already picking up her cell phone. Rachel thought quickly.

"It's the Barr family I'm after," she called over to Raven. "She's David Barr's wife, if that means anything to your husband."

Rachel wandered over to the counter so she wouldn't have to shout across the room. The waitress had turned her back, partly because her cell was charging on the back shelf and partly because she wanted some privacy, Rachel imagined.

"Hi baby it's me," the waitress cooed into her phone.

Over her shoulder Rachel could see rows of hard liquor and a few postcards, and a staff rota. There was a mirror on the back wall; the waitress was checking her hair in it.

"Baby, did you ever know a guy called Barr? David Barr?"

Just above the postcards on the back wall was a picture frame with a bronze plaque underneath it heralding the Employee of the Month. Sure enough, there was a picture of Raven in the middle of the frame. She had been Employee of the Month, April 2009. Presumably she'd remained unchallenged since then, because the dusty frame was still hanging on the wall. Her picture had sat beaming away while she slaved below. But it wasn't the smile that Rachel was staring at. It was the name below it.

"Sure, sure, yeah I know," the waitress was saying. "It's just that a girl came in asking if they drink in the bar."

Underneath the fading picture, a small sign read:

Lucky's Employee of the month

April 2009: Raven Tyler

It was too much to hope that the name was a coincidence. Rachel's blood froze.

"Well, sure," she heard the waitress say. "No problem. I look forward to it."

The waitress put the phone down and paused for a second before she spun round. She was still smiling. Even so, Rachel felt that it was time to go. If her hunch was right, and Raven had been talking to Tyler on the phone, she didn't want to hang around to meet him. She fumbled in her purse to settle up for the coffee. By the time she looked back up, the waitress was between her and the door. Still smiling. Wiping down the table with a cloth. But definitely between Rachel and the exit.

"So, I need to pay for the coffee?" Rachel said, trying to stay calm.

"Sure, leave it on the counter," Raven Tyler replied, her voice still light and airy. "Don't you want to know what my husband said?"

"Sure, yes. Sorry." said Rachel, caught off guard. If the whole thing got physical, she was wondering how hard she could push past the waitress without damaging her baby. Shoving a pregnant woman was not a good idea.

"Well, he thinks he can tell you what you want to know," she smiled. She took the sad-looking flowers from the vase on the table she had just cleaned. She poured the water from the vase onto the table and then mopped it up with the cloth in her hand. It was sopping.

Rachel was edgy. Things felt weird. The waitress was pregnant and smiling, but she was behaving oddly. It was time to make a break before things got worse so she said, "I'd love to talk to your husband, but it'll have to wait."

She didn't bother with excuses. They both knew that Rachel wanted out, and they both knew that Raven wanted her to stay exactly where she was. Raven turned to the door and turned the sign in the window to "closed."

The gloves were off. But it was tricky. Rachel figured that if she shoved the waitress hard near her shoulders, she wouldn't risk damaging the baby. She didn't want that on her conscience. She walked towards Raven Tyler.

Suddenly the waitress put her hands up.

"Wait a second," she breathed. Rachel only hesitated for a split second, but that was all it took. The waitress smashed her fist hard into Rachel's face. Rachel felt the woman's engagement diamond rip into her cheek, and then numbness as the full force of the blow hit her square in the face. She'd never been hit like that before, and for a split second everything went black. Like her brain had rattled around in her skull and taken a second to reboot.

Then too much was happening at once. As she began to realize that blood was trickling from her nose, Rachel felt herself being pulled backwards. Raven Tyler had grabbed a fistful of her dark hair and was dragging her along the floor by her scalp. Moving quickly. Rachel felt the woman's hand reach round from behind her and clasp the sopping wet cloth across her mouth. She could see the blood running from her nose down across the slim fingers of her captor. Her head was tilted back. She was drowning on the water from the vase. She complied as she was marched choking and spluttering through the doorway into the back room.

It was hard to say how strong the waitress was, but she was lithe. Always twisting, always moving, always better balanced than Rachel. Rachel lashed out at her, no longer caring about the baby inside her. More concerned about herself. Raven Tyler threw her into the storeroom and she hit the floor hard. The waitress stood in the doorway and Rachel sprang back to her feet ready to fight. She hadn't hit anyone in anger since high school, but it wasn't in her nature just to lie down defeated.

She staggered to her feet and grabbed at a couple of bottles from the crates which had scattered as she fell. She smashed them against the concrete floor, and looked up, ready to slash out at the woman who had broken her nose.

Raven Tyler was a step ahead though. She'd grabbed the shotgun from behind the bar and swung it into the storeroom. Her stance was great. Legs just more than shoulder width apart, leaning into the room. It looked odd with her pregnant belly.

The weapon was high, and she was looking straight down the barrel. The smile had gone completely from her eyes. They'd turned dead and gray, like wolves' eyes. Raven Tyler's shape told Rachel that she knew how to handle the weapon. Her eyes told Rachel that she'd be happy to do it in a blink. Rachel put the smashed bottles down meekly, coming back to her senses and realizing how quickly the situation had gone wrong.

The waitress was considering giving Rachel a barrel to teach her a lesson when the door out in the bar rattled. Could be Tyler. Or it could be trouble. The waitress dropped the shotgun behind her back and went to investigate.

As the pregnant silhouette disappeared from the doorway, Rachel realized that she had a few seconds to save her life. She looked about for a weapon but there was nothing to match the shotgun. No exit and nowhere to hide. So she did the only thing she could think of. She hit redial on her phone and hoped to God that Neilson was the last person she'd spoken to. Neilson would know what to do.

CHAPTER FORTY-EIGHT

Woodridge, The English Cotswolds, Winter 2010.
"Oh the weather outside if frightful, but the fire is so delightful, and since we've no place to go, let it snow let it snow let it snow."
– Dean Martin, Let it Snow.

The young couple at the top of the hill took a deep breath and then opened the door. They ran full pelt across the courtyard to the door opposite. It took about thirty seconds to reach it. The bigger of the two banged hard on the door with his flat hand.

"For God's sake open up!" he yelled as the smaller squeezed around him to get some shelter.

As Diane Reed flung open the door, her neighbors spilled into the hallway. Before she could close it, another couple flung themselves in, crashing into the first. The woman behind was screeching, but by now the first couple had burst into fits of laughter. One of them was blowing the water away from his lips and the end of his nose.

The house was warm and homely, and as Diane pushed the door hard against the wind and the hammering of hailstones, the couples ripped their coats off quickly. Diane fussed about with them, helping people out of coats and ushering the couples through. Several other sets of wet clothes were already hanging from the coat rack. She had laid out newspaper underneath them on the stone floor to catch the drips.

Woodridge was a community of about twenty families with a handful of children. Most of the families had been in the village for generations, working the worn out land. There were a few wealthy newcomers, but mostly the fifty or so residents had been born and bred in Woodridge by parents who had been born and bred there too.

The houses were clustered around an old stone farm. The farm was built in the shelter of a small copse at the top of a steep hill. It had been built on the remains of an old Roman settlement next to a track that connected two ancient towns. Opposite the farmhouse was a public house which served the same purpose as the original settlement; to provide rest and shelter for travelers between those towns.

It looked like time had forgotten Woodridge. The exteriors of the stone buildings hadn't changed for hundreds of years. Inside, they had been converted into fairly modern living spaces. The newer families had re-plastered and double glazed and centrally heated the places; the more established residents made do with cozy rustic interiors.

The heart of the village was the old stone manor house. When it had come onto the market recently, it had sold quickly. A brusque Spaniard had snapped the place up and taken to living inside the place like a hermit. He said his name was Lockhart, but apart from that, the other villagers had learned nothing about him at all.

The villagers thought the other new arrival was altogether better. He had moved into the village at almost the same time as the Spaniard but had immediately gone to the trouble of getting to know people. He was a friendly guy. Introduced himself as Ryan Birch. Birch had been the first name that had popped into the real Lockhart's head when he arrived in the village.

Lockhart and the journalist had stuck to the plan they had agreed in Baku. The Spaniard holed himself up in the impressive manor house and used the name Charlie Lockhart. The real Lockhart moved in to a small cottage next door and introduced himself as Birch. At first it had seemed strange, but it had soon become second nature. It worked fine. It was simple. Life was easy. Time dragged like hell.

Most of the villagers lived in the stone barns huddled around a graveled courtyard behind the manor house. In the summer, the gray stone walls provided a simple backdrop for explosions of blossoms and flowers which had been carefully designed over the years. Today, the yard and the roofs and the streets were blanketed in snow. The village sat at the highest point for miles around and as a result it got cut off from the world whenever the snow arrived.

By tomorrow, the settlement would be impossible to reach in anything but a tractor, and nobody was stupid to attempt to go down the hill in any sort of vehicle at all. So when they knew the snow was coming, the residents stocked up their firewood and their larders and made the most of their splendid silent isolation.

Diane Reed's barn had a huge hearth right in the center of the full height lounge, the flames licking away as they flashed heat out into the room. Her neighbors had gathered on the plump deep sofas surrounding the fire.

The group was all rosy cheeks and steamy spectacles, still laughing about the weather outside. Most had taken up Diane's chirpy request that they help themselves to mulled wine. The room smelled of oranges and cloves. Conversations had broken off into small groups, but everyone knew each other well.

Diane's husband Peter jammed another sturdy log towards the heart of the fire and turned to address his neighbors.

"Let's get the Residents' Committee business out of the way," he paused for effect as the neighbors listened up. "And then we can get on with the important stuff, like dinner!"

There was laughter and then general rummaging about for clipboards. The committee met once a month to discuss the mundane business of the village. It was mostly an excuse for a friendly get together.

"I think we are all here, except for our friend, Mr. Lockhart."

The journalist hadn't turned up once. He didn't particularly want people knowing that he was Spanish. He was trying to keep a low profile. But mostly, he didn't want to make new friends in a village he was hiding out in. He had taken on Charlie Lockhart's name but assumed none of his affable personality.

In contrast, Lockhart himself had been involved in everything. The bank in Baku had worked out fine, and he now had a huge amount of money which didn't belong to him. Money that should be building schools and hospitals in a broken country, but was instead sitting in a bank account with his name on it.

He set up a bank account for the Spaniard. Called him Lockhart. Transferred enough money for the Spaniard to buy the manor house. The cottage came as part of the manor's estate, but Lockhart didn't move in until a month after the journalist to ensure that nobody thought they were together.

With three hundred million in the bank, the interest alone was growing at a staggering rate. Lockhart had spent months sitting at the top of the hill trying to work out how to make sure the money ended up in the right place. Doing the right thing. His feet were itching. He wasn't a man designed to stand still. He wanted to get back out and see that the money was given to the people who needed it. But he remembered the sailor's story from the Baku ferry. So he stayed on his hill and waited for his enemy, but nobody came. Summer had become fall and still he waited. And still nobody came. Then fall became winter and now Barr jumped of a building. And somebody was coming.

Peter Reed had rattled through the village agenda while his wife Diane stood behind his mouthing "beef or chicken?" to their various guests.

Everyone was hungry and so business was swift.

"Finally, it's good to see the school in such good order," he said. "It looks like our newest resident has been a guardian angel in recent weeks."

"It must be time for dinner," Lockhart said, deflecting the attention. "Diane, how's that chicken coming along?"

Everyone laughed. He really hadn't done much. The cash in Baku was meant for schools and hospitals and he had tried to distribute some of it while he was waiting in Woodridge. He had started by helping one teenager in the village. She was interested in becoming a farmer, and he offered to take her on as a gardener to pay her way through a famous agricultural college nearby. The school fees cost far more than her family could afford, and far more than a gardener would ever earn. Lockhart paid them anyway.

Since then, the man they knew as Ryan Birch had been one of the best things that had happened to the village. He was courteous and convivial, but private about his affairs. He never took credit, but the villagers started to notice that he was a man who made things happen.

The local school was threatened with closure because of a lack of funds, and three families began to make plans to move house to another village with a more stable school. Within weeks a mysterious benefactor came forward and secured the school funds. There was also money to rebuild the classrooms over the summer break. Ryan Birch himself had turned up on site several times to help with the laboring.

He never took credit. He felt like a fraud. The money in his account should have been saving lives. Educating kids. Helping local kids get a decent school seemed like a tiny gesture compared to what he would need to do once he'd wrapped up his business in Woodridge.

Lockhart had stepped in when the brewery tried to turf out the landlord of the local pub because he wasn't making enough profit. The guy had a wife. He had kids. So the brewery signs had come down, and news that a private buyer had taken over swept through the village. It was Lockhart. He went for a drink once a week and complimented the landlord on the taste of his beer and the shininess of his horse-brasses. He mentioned nothing about owning the place.

But the neighbors seemed to have got wind of what had happened and as they gathered for the residents meeting they seemed determined to let Lockhart know how much they appreciated it. So he was pleased when his ringing phone gave him a chance to escape. He answered and began to head out towards the entrance hall where the wet coats and boots were stacked. Diane began to usher the others to the dining table. The call was muffled and he couldn't make out what the person on the other end was saying.

As he got further away from the others, he could hear the call better. Someone was talking in the background, but not to Lockhart. It was like he was eavesdropping on someone else's conversation. A woman's voice.

Probably someone's phone accidentally redialed at the bottom of their purse. Lockhart waited for the scrunching of car keys and mascara.

He was about to hang up but curiosity got the better of him. He closed over the door between him and the others. Shut out the noise. Then voices started to emerge, like people emerging from the fog. Bit by bit as his ear tuned in. A gruff sounding man. More focus. A woman talking quickly. Demanding. Scratches and scrabbles. The man closer to the phone. Questioning. Lockhart heard the word Fearless. The sounds of a struggle and a second female voice. A voice he recognized. It was Rachel White. Rachel white, whose last dialed number had not been Neilson. It had been Lockhart.

CHAPTER FORTY-NINE

Lucky bar, Pine Bluff.
"She was practiced at the art of deception,
Well I could tell by her blood-stained hands"
– Rolling Stones, You Can't Always Get What You Want.

Rachel was forcing herself not to look at the glow of light emanating from behind the freezer unit on the far side of the room. While Raven Tyler had gone to investigate the noise out in the bar, Rachel had grabbed her phone from her pocket and hit redial. She knew there wouldn't be time to speak to whoever picked up. Instead, she had slid her phone across the rough concrete floor as far away from her as she could, and it had come to rest behind the freezer. In the dark cellar it was a tiny pearl of hope. Every second the glow continued, she could imagine Neilson on the end of the phone. He would know what to do. He was a smart guy.

Suddenly there were two silhouettes in the doorway. The waitress had returned and behind her was a huge man. It had to be Tyler. Rachel knew she was in big trouble. They were both looking at her, as though they were trying to decide what to do with her.

In the corner of her eye Rachel could see her cell phone glowing gently on the other side of the room. Still connected then. Still hope. Neilson was a patient man; Rachel silently prayed that he wouldn't hang up too soon.

Raven seemed relaxed. It was her husband Tyler who was now holding the shotgun loosely by his side. He looked at Rachel like she was a problem he could do without.

"Why are you looking for Lucy Barr?" he asked as he stepped into the room.

Rachel told the truth. She was a radio host from Los Angeles. Barr had killed himself on her show, and she felt compelled to meet his family. She wanted to know why he jumped. As Rachel explained her story to Tyler, his wife patted her down. She checked her pockets and took her purse.

"The LAPD wouldn't give me her address, so I figured I'd ask a few questions here at Lucky Bar being as you soldiers hang out here."

She said the name of the bar as clearly as she dared. She could still see the glow of her cell phone in the far corner. The waitress turned to her husband and shrugged. She hadn't found anything dangerous in the woman's purse.

Tyler made a decision. He spoke to his wife as though Rachel wasn't there.

"The easiest thing is to put her in the freezer until it's over."

Raven looked like she was mulling it over, subconsciously rubbing her pregnant stomach. Then she nodded casually and headed back round behind her husband. She heaved open the lid of the freezer and a cloud of frozen air escaped as the seals gave way. It was lit from inside, and the hard light accentuated the angles of Raven's face. Her nose looked more prominent, and it struck Rachel that maybe she'd had it broken a few times.

"I saw you on the news today," Tyler said. "You said that you didn't think David Barr jumped. You said he was pushed."

Rachel was feeling numb.

"You want to put me in the freezer?" she asked.

It was too surreal to frighten her.

Tyler ignored her question. He fixed her with a hard glare and said, "You think I pushed him, don't you?"

That was exactly what Rachel thought. She was sure of it. The way he was planning to put her in the freezer didn't exactly convince her he was innocent either. She thought about her phone call with Charlie Lockhart yesterday. He had warned her about Tyler. *Christ, she'd mentioned Lockhart on the TV report.*

Lucky Bar didn't have a kitchen, but it had a microwave on the back shelf and a freezer full of pre-cooked meals which could be blasted for a few seconds and then served to the drunks. Raven was making space in the freezer by removing some boxes and tin foil covered plates. The ice clouds continued to steam out into the light behind Tyler as the waitress went about her work. He leaned closer to Rachel so she could feel his breath on her face.

"You spoke to Charlie Lockhart yesterday. Where is he now?"

"England," Rachel replied. There didn't seem much point in lying. "A place called Woodridge is all I know. He said it was in the middle of nowhere. Why the hell would you put me in a freezer? You don't even know me."

Rachel was good with fear. Good with control. She was working hard to keep her voice low and reasonable. She knew that most people needed to get angry before they could kill someone. They need a trigger to start the violence. Something which they can use afterwards to justify their rage to themselves. Rachel stayed calm and tried not to give the big man a trigger. It was a good strategy. Very few people can kill in cold blood. Sadly for Rachel, Tyler and his wife could.

Like all good tacticians, Tyler had the ability to think simply. The girl in front of him was a problem. She would fit in the freezer. He could put her in the freezer, and the problem would disappear. Simple.

"I saved Barr's life."

Rachel looked at the giant guy in front of her. He wasn't making sense, but he was talking. Talking was good. It was better than being locked in the freezer.

"He's dead," she said. "How did you save his life?"

"In Iraq," Tyler replied. "I saved his life in Iraq. There were four of us on patrol. He got one of us blown up and one of us shot. He got his own foot blown off. I was the only one who walked away, and I walked away with Barr on my back."

"So let me get this right," Rachel stared at him. Anger was boiling up inside her. All she could think about was the blood-smeared picture of Lucy Barr and their daughter. "You're telling me that because you saved him in Iraq, you had the right to kill him in Los Angeles?"

Tyler thought about it. "I saved his life and then he stole three hundred million from me. I had the right to kill him anywhere."

He meant it. He believed it. He knew now that Barr had never stolen the money. It changed nothing. He'd saved Barr's life and then he'd taken Barr's life. Tyler and David Barr were quits.

Rachel was getting desperate.

"Lucky Barr," she said loudly.

The waitress turned round abruptly. She'd made a neat pile of boxes and dishes at the side of the freezer, but now she was staring intently at Rachel. Tyler was staring at her too. Rachel knew that she'd pushed it too far.

"Why would you call him lucky?" the waitress asked.

"Where is your cellphone?" demanded Tyler, and he and his wife kicked into action. She threw the contents of Rachel's purse onto the concrete floor. Mascara, bank cards, lip balm, grubby receipts; but no cell phone.

"Where is it?" Raven demanded. Her voice was like ice, her eyes gray and lupine again.

Tyler was already patting Rachel down roughly. Then he spotted the glow in the corner behind the freezer. He grabbed Rachel by the neck and scooped her up. She was tiny in his arms and he manhandled her easily into the freezer. By the time the terror of what was happening to her was dawning, the lid was already slamming down on her like a closing coffin.

Tyler grabbed the cell phone and sat down on the freezer lid. The waitress hopped up and joined him, looking at the caller ID warily.

Rachel smashed into the lid of her coffin with all of her strength, but it might as well have been nailed on. The weight of Tyler and his wife was far too much for her to shift. It was pitch black inside, and the walls were so cold that her skin burned where she touched it. She writhed around inside trying not to keep any one bit of her body in contact with the metal for more than a couple of seconds.

As far as Tyler was concerned, Rachel was in the freezer and she wasn't a problem anymore. But whoever was on the other end of Rachel's phone was a problem. Tyler put the handset to his ear and demanded to know who was on the other end of the line. And Charlie Lockhart told him.

CHAPTER FIFTY

Lockhart's Cottage, Woodridge.
"If I did it fast, you know that's an act of kindness."
– Tori Amos, Waitress.

Tyler's mind was working overtime. The guy on the end of the phone said he was Charlie Lockhart. He sounded English. But it could be a trick. Tyler needed proof.

"Do you know who I am?"

"Yes I do," the English voice said. "You're the man who stole three hundred million dollars in Afghanistan. Then you lost it. Now you want it back. Let me talk to Rachel."

Tyler had forgotten about Rachel. She was beginning to chill in the dark of the freezer beneath him. She wasn't a problem anymore. Tyler ignored the demand.

"Where is the money now?"

"Where is Rachel?" the voice replied. The waitress could hear the tinny sound of the Englishman on the phone as she sat close to her husband on top of the freezer. She could feel the anger building up in Tyler, so she put one arm across her stomach in case he lashed out.

"Rachel is out of the picture. Just like Barr is out of the picture. Just like you will soon be out of the picture if you are who you say you are."

On the other side of the world, Lockhart took a breath. He knew the conversation was bullshit, but he was playing for time. Keeping Tyler talking. Keeping them all in Lucky Barr. Hoping that his plan would work. He looked out of the window across the snowy street to the pub. Snow had started to drift against the side of the walls and icicles hung from an overflowing drainpipe. Lockhart wondered how long a woman could survive in a freezer. He wondered how efficient the Pine Bluff Police Department were.

"You understand that I'm coming for you?" Tyler asked. He was used to intimidating people. He was used to people being afraid. "I'm coming to Woodridge, and I'm going to find you."

"Thank Christ for that," Lockhart replied. "I'm getting bored with waiting for you."

He meant it. Woodridge was friendly enough, but it was dull. It was cut off from the rest of the world, just like Kandahar had been. No razor wire or guard towers, but a huge hill and a million tons of snow. Lockhart felt trapped in the tiny village, lying low waiting for the enemy to arrive. Waiting to deal with Tyler so he could get out on the road again. *It is hard to appreciate the road ahead when you're constantly checking over your shoulder.*

"Listen. I'll make it easy for you. If you wire my money back, I won't need to come and visit you. We could call it quits."

"I can't do that," Lockhart replied. "It's not your money. Now where's Rachel?"

As if on cue, Tyler felt the woman in the freezer thump hard against the lid he was sitting on. He didn't budge. Beneath him, Rachel's body had begun to make decisions for her; shaking and shivering violently. Her skin still burned, but her mind was numbing. She felt sleepy and confused. Losing track of why she was in the cold and the dark.

"Three hundred million for your life, Charlie. It sounds like a good deal to me."

But Lockhart told him, "It's not my money to give. You know where that money came from, and it's going back there. Trust me."

Lockhart was determined that he'd keep that promise or die trying. But he had no intention of dying at the hands of Tyler. Not now he'd got the measure of him. He had been staring out of the window for so long that his breath had steamed up the cold glass. Where the hell were the Pine Bluff police?

Then he heard noises at the other end of the phone.

The front door of Lucky Bar had smashed open and slammed shut again. Tyler and the waitress were out from the back room like a shot. Raven was in the bar first, with Tyler just behind, shotgun back behind his legs, out of site but ready for action.

It wasn't Pine Bluff's finest. In fact, it was Pine Bluff's grubbiest instead. The Filipino hooker was back, and she was angry. Shouting at the waitress and calling the odds. It cost her twenty dollars to work the bar for the day, and now the bar was shut. She was demanding the money back. She had fire in her eyes and was threatening the waitress about what she did to people who jerked her around. Big mistake. Raven hit her hard in the stomach and she snapped like a twig. She was on the floor in a second.

"Stay there," Tyler told Lockhart, and he put the phone on the bar. He stepped out in front of his wife and swung the shotgun round from behind his legs. He rammed both barrels into the hooker's throat as she lay on the floor, tamed. An old chair had crumpled where the waitress had dropped her.

"You'll have to pay for that," Tyler explained, nodding at the broken chair. His wife took the Filipino's purse and emptied it onto the bar. A couple of hundred dollars fell out, bundled. Three hypodermics, a couple of wraps, cotton balls, a change of underwear, a spoon, and a bottle of water. Her worldly possessions.

"That's my spoon," was all that Raven said. She shoved the underwear back into the purse and threw it back at the girl on the floor. Then she grabbed her by the ankle and dragged her across the filthy wooden floor and out into the street. She was just turning back into the bar when she heard the sirens in the distance.

CHAPTER FIFTY-ONE

Lucky bar, Pine Bluff
"Now that you know what I'm without, you can't just leave me. Breathe into me and make me real" - Evanescence, Bring Me to Life

Charlie Lockhart felt a rush of relief when he heard the sirens on the line. Rachel White's cell phone was still glowing on the end of the bar where Tyler had left it. Tyler himself was watching through the rickety front door of Lucky Bar. The Filipino had limped off like a wounded animal as the police arrived. The two officers in the wailing squad car glanced at her bleeding knees as they drove past, but she wanted nothing to do with them, and they wanted nothing to do with her. It would only mean paperwork.

The cop car pulled up at the curb outside Lucky's. Siren off, lights off, engine off. The two officers got out of the cruiser stretching, as if they'd been sitting down all day. Then they sauntered over to Raven Tyler, who was standing square in the doorway. She smiled as demurely as was plausible for a woman who had just dragged a girl out of her bar by her ankle. She didn't invite them in.

The guy who had been driving the cruiser looked the waitress up and down. The top button of her blouse had come loose again during the struggle with the prostitute, but he pretended not to notice. He furrowed his brow a little and tried hard to keep his gaze above her neckline.

"Trouble?" he asked, nodding down the street.

"Nothing I can't handle," the waitress replied. "Although it's getting harder every day."

She rubbed her hand over her stomach and courted a bit of sympathy.

"How's Mary?" she asked the officer. He wasn't a regular at the bar, but he popped in from time to time. The waitress knew his wife casually. She made small talk long enough to buy Tyler some time, and then she said, "Where are my manners? Would you boys like to come in for coffee?"

Inside, Tyler had taken a moment to store the shotgun back behind the bar, well out of sight. Then he'd straightened the chairs and got fresh coffee brewing. The officers greeted him as they came in.

"You guys are getting faster," Tyler said with a smile. Kept his head down, pouring the coffee.

"Well, someone called it in a few minutes ago," the second officer explained. "Problems with some girl at Lucky Bar, the dispatch said, so we came here as quick as we could, because the coffee's always good."

Tyler nodded and handed both officers a mug.

"That was her, I guess? Dispatch said she wasn't local."

The waitress nodded this time. She explained that there had been a disturbance, but that she didn't want to press charges.

"Let's just say I don't think she'll be in a hurry to come back" she smiled. The cops chuckled as they slurped their coffee.

And then suddenly there was an almighty crash. And the cops stopped chuckling. And they put their mugs down. And they drew their guns.

Rachel White had lurched through the doorway, knocking over the chairs. She was wet and dazed. Her hair was matted and her lips were blue. She could not control her muscles, and she was shaking violently. But she was out of the freezer, and she was standing in front of two cops.

Lockhart had been pacing around the tiny front room of his cottage in Woodridge. It was like a prison cell. He'd called Neilson at the radio station in Los Angeles and he'd called the cops. But he was five thousand miles away from the action. Five thousand miles from an innocent woman fighting for her life. And there was nothing he could do to help her. When he heard her burst through the door and into the bar, relief flooded through him. She was still alive; there was still hope for Rachel White.

Rachel stumbled forwards and grabbed hold of the bar. She hung on for dear life while her muscles seized and cramped. She remembered that Tyler tried to kill her. *Tried to freeze her.* He was a monster, and he was still there in the bar. But now the police were here. Now she'd be okay. She couldn't stop shaking though. And she couldn't get her lungs under control. She couldn't talk.

It was the waitress who broke the silence. She needed to defuse the situation quickly. She'd noticed that Tyler had edged behind the bar towards the shotgun, but the cops had already drawn their weapons in the confusion, and even Tyler wouldn't beat both of them in such a confined space. So she threw the cops a line.

197

"My sister," she said. "Look at her. This is what this place has done to her."

Tyler cottoned on. He showed the cops the contents of the Filipino's purse, still lying on the bar. Needles and spoons and little brown wraps. The cops shook their heads. They'd seen it a million times before.

Rachel looked down at the bar, horrified. She tried to talk, but her chest was cramping too tightly. She sounded incoherent. She sounded like a junkie.

"Cold fucking turkey," the waitress shook her head too. "It breaks my heart, but God help me I will put her straight."

Rachel's legs went. She clawed at the bar to stay upright. Her hand landed on her phone. It was still lit up. But the ID on the screen was wrong. She hadn't rung Neilson in her hour of need. She'd rung an Englishman who she'd never even met. Disaster. Even so, the phone was still lit up. Silently, Rachel prayed for the strength to talk. Nothing happened.

Five thousand miles away, Lockhart could hear Rachel's slurred sounds. He knew exactly what was going on, but he could do nothing about it. She was hypothermic and confused. Raven was playing her, and she was losing.

At least Tyler's days were numbered. Their conversation earlier had made it clear that he'd be coming to Woodridge. Coming for the money he'd stolen and coming to deal with Lockhart like he'd dealt with Barr. But Lockhart would be ready for him.

"We'll have to take her in," the cop who had been riding passenger was saying. "For possession, at least."

There was no way that the waitress could let that happen. Not now. Not after everything that had happened in the cellar. The second cop was less scrupulous that the first and was stealing glances at her cleavage every time she looked away. She took a deep breath and watched him swallow, losing his train of thought for a moment.

"She's my sister," she implored. "If you take her in, she'll deal inside and get hooked again. I won't see her for a year, and when I do it'll probably be at her funeral."

She took in another gulp of air. The cop was swayed. It sounded melodramatic, but he'd seen it happen a lot in the last few years. Broken girls, devastated families. He looked at the pregnant waitress and her junkie sister. She'd be an auntie soon enough. Maybe that would keep her straight for a while at least.

The cops looked at each other, and then the one who had been driving said "Look, strictly speaking we didn't find her in possession. What's on the bar was on the bar when we walked in. It wasn't in any of your possession, I guess."

The waitress stepped forward and hugged the cop closest to her.

Pressed her three lumps into him, to seal the deal. Rachel made an angry gurgling sound, but her lips were cracking and her tongue felt about six times bigger than normal. She could hear the Englishman saying something down the phone. Shouting, in fact. She slumped forward on the bar, covering the phone with her hair. Put her ear near enough to hear what he was saying.

The snow had whipped up outside Lockhart's window so that he could hardly see the pub across the road. The flakes were heavy and mesmerizing, but his mind was sharp and his pulse was racing. The cops were leaving. They were leaving Rachel with Tyler. She'd be dead within an hour.

"Punch him" he was shouting down the phone. "Hit him now, before it's too late. Rachel, this is your only chance, can you hear me?"

He was rooting for her, willing her to do it. He knew she could save herself if she had the strength. But she didn't have any strength. Everything hurt and ached, and she looked up at Tyler with dread in her eyes. He was taught and muscular, not to mention enormous. She might as well hit a mountain for all the good it would do.

She lifted her head, but could still hear the voice shouting from five thousand miles away, encouraging her to sock him in the eye. *Yeah, thanks for the advice, chump.*

The younger cop had drained his mug and was already at the door. No arrests, no paperwork; job done. His partner was still frowning, wondering if he was making the right decision. He walked over to the bar and leaned over Rachel.

"Your sister is giving you a second chance here," he said, nodding at the heroin on the bar. He took the two wraps and folded them into an official looking bag. Stuck them in his pocket. He put a hand on Rachel's shoulder and wished her good luck. She tried to tell him. Tried desperately to explain that he was leaving her to be killed. Frozen, for God's sake. She heard the Englishman's tinny voice rattling the earpiece on her phone. The cop heard it too, leaned over with her. Tyler had noticed too. Lockhart was roaring now. Telling Rachel that she had to find the strength to hit him.

She looked at the cop, and she looked at the phone. And in her head, she apologized to Lockhart. He had worked out the one thing she could do to save herself. Her one chance to get free. He wasn't telling her to hit Tyler. He was telling her to hit the cop.

She took every ounce of strength she had left in her frozen body. She forced herself up from the bar as hard as she could, ramming her head straight into the cop's face. His lip bust. It was superficial, but it would count as battery. Assault on an officer. While he was working out the charges, Rachel clasped both of her hands together and swung hard at the cop again. His partner had turned around and was running back into the bar by now. Between then they wrestled Rachel White to the ground.

They cuffed her and marched her out of the bar, the older guy dabbing away at his bleeding lip. The second cop turned back as he reached the doorway with a smirk on his face. The whole episode had been kind of bizarre.

"Even *your* tits won't save your sister from those charges," he said to the waitress. Then he seemed to remember that Tyler was in the room and he stopped smirking. He nodded at the giant and mentioned something about due respect, before heading outside and joining his partner in the cruiser. Engine on, siren on, lights on. And they drove Rachel White to safety.

Tyler had one hand on the shotgun behind the bar. He would have blasted the smirk off the cop's face if he didn't have more pressing issues to deal with. He glared at Rachel White's cell phone and snatched it up off the bar.

"I'm coming for you, " he growled at Lockhart.

"I'm waiting, " Lockhart replied.

CHAPTER FIFTY-TWO

Woodridge, English Cotswolds.
"Come back to what you know, take everything real slow."
- Embrace

It was five hours later that the footballer and his agent arrived in Woodridge. Lockhart was watching the clock. The snow was still falling, and he was surprised they had made it up the hill. It must have been a struggle. Lockhart was glad to see their car pull up outside the cottage, though. It would be a welcome distraction.

The footballer thought the place looked pretty. The houses were all old and worn. The place was in the middle of nowhere and there was a blizzard on. It was like stepping bank a hundred years; Ivy-clad walls protected well established gardens, and the roads were not used much judging by the condition of the pure white snow the agent's car was plowing through.

The footballer thought it was a strange place to have a meeting, but his agent reassured him that sometimes it was good to get away from prying eyes. The footballer remembered the hill they'd just struggled up. Only the most kamikaze paparazzi would have followed them in this weather.

The player's contract prevented him from talking to other football clubs, so conversations about his career had to happen in places where the media wouldn't be snooping. Somewhere like Woodridge. The agent had told him that if the meeting went well, he could be on a plane to Asia by the evening. But the whole thing was shrouded in mystery and it wasn't until they arrived at the house that the two men found out what the deal involved.

The house itself was tiny. The footballer lived in a mansion in the North of England, and he couldn't understand why a man who was apparently far richer than him would live in an unassuming cottage in a village in the middle of nowhere. The perimeter was protected by a traditional stone wall which was about three feet high. Immediately behind the wall were thick evergreen bushes which hid the modest lawn from prying eyes.

Beyond the evergreens, the short approach to the house was immaculate. Everything that poked up above the carpet of snow was manicured. A girl from the village was busying herself in a greenhouse as the footballer's BMW came to a halt in front of the house. There was a path in the snow where the girl had walked between the main house and the greenhouse. The wind was up and the snow was starting to drift.

The cottage originally belonged to the manor house next door. Four hundred years ago it had been sharply hewn from local stone, but time and weather had smoothed its edges and softened its color.

At the end of the driveway, the BMW parked up outside the cottage. The footballer and his agent stepped out into the snow and looked around. Despite its age, the cottage was in good order. The chimney was billowing smoke and the smell of burned firewood hung in the air. A man appeared on the road back beyond the stone wall, followed by the sound of muffled hooves. He was leading two horses; it was too treacherous for riding. They peered over the evergreens, their nostrils steaming in the cold air. Soon enough they lost interest, and they continued to plod along behind the man as he led them to their stables on the edge of the village. The footballer felt like he had stepped back a couple of centuries.

It was too cold to stand around. The glow from the windows matched the smoke from the chimney. There was a roaring fire going inside the place and the windows cast an orange light over the monochrome garden. Next to the greenhouse the footballer spotted a huge wood store with a forest full of cut and chopped logs ready to be thrown onto an impressive fire at the heart of the house. The agent was about to bang on the solid oak door when it opened.

Heat rushed out to greet them, and a confident looking man who was standing in the doorway. It was Lockhart. He looked tanned and relaxed as he greeted the player and his agent. He shook their hands and ushered them inside. He asked them about the intricacies of their journey through the narrow lanes in the snow.

The footballer had been right; there was a blazing fire going in the main room in the house. Lockhart invited them to sit, and they all took seats in front of the fire.

The meeting didn't take very long. Lockhart asked the footballer if he would be interested in a trip to Turkmenistan. The agent went through the process of explaining that the footballer had a very good contract and was happy at his club. He mentioned that the fans loved the player and that he had no reason to leave. All the same, he didn't rule out the trip.

"There is no rich sheik at the other end of the flight," Lockhart told him, "and I am not asking you to leave your club."

Despite their protestations moments earlier, both the agent and the player looked crestfallen. Why the hell had they battled through the snow to meet some guy in a tiny cottage if he wasn't offering him a lucrative new deal?

"What I want to know," Lockhart continued, "is whether you've thought about what you're going to do when you finish playing football?"

The footballer thought about little else. He filled his days training hard, eating well, scoring goals, being chased by the press and mixing with the glamorati. But at night he lay awake thinking about the inevitable end of his playing career. It terrorized him the way other men worry about being shoved in a box and buried under six feet of earth.

He figured he had two seasons left to play at top level before his legs started to give up. Beyond that his life was a blank. Since he was fourteen years old, his days had been mapped out by agents and managers and chairmen and coaches. In two years' time, he would have to fill his days for himself. People wouldn't want his autograph. People wouldn't stare at him in bars anymore. He had no idea what he would be doing in two years' time, and that scared the hell out of him.

"I wanted to talk to you because I have an opportunity for you," Lockhart continued.

Suddenly there was a loud banging on the window. Lockhart looked up at the window, ready to react. It would take Tyler another twelve hours to get to Woodridge, even if he had set off as soon at he'd put the phone down. And Lockhart knew that when he arrived in Woodridge, all the villagers would send him to the manor house next door. It was much too early for Tyler to be knocking.

He could have sent someone else to do his work. So when there was a bang at the window, Lockhart was up like a flash. As soon as he saw it was the girl from the greenhouse, he relaxed. She was staring through the window, her eyes transfixed on the footballer. Lockhart smiled and went to let her in.

"I just came to let you know that I'm off for the night," she said. She sounded distracted and kept looking over Lockhart's shoulder. She told him she'd have trouble getting back tomorrow if the snow continued, but she didn't seem to be concentrating much on what she was saying.

"Don't worry," Lockhart told her. "There's not much growing in this snow, so don't break your neck getting up here tomorrow."

She headed back out into the snow, hood and scarf protecting her from the cold. But before she headed off down the path, she turned round and stole one more glance over Lockhart's shoulder to the man behind.

"Here," she said, lowering her voice. "Is that who I think it is?"

"Depends who you think it is" Lockhart chuckled and watched as she trotted off down that path, bewildered. No doubt there would be some stories in the pub tonight. He closed the door on the cold and returned to the footballer and his agent.

"What do you know about Turkmenistan?" he asked them. The agent knew nothing, but the footballer answered.

"South of Russia, I think. Near Afghanistan."

The agent shot him a suspicious look.

"Hey, I'm not just saying that because they sound similar."

The agent laughed and held his hands up as he apologized.

"They're outside of Europe anyway," continued the footballer. "Why are you asking?"

Lockhart explained his journey through Turkmenistan and his chance meeting with the young boy called Nazar. He told the footballer how he'd nearly run him over because he was playing in the street. Then he explained how Rosalina, his mother, had encouraged him to play football as a way of improving his education. She made him count his kicks in English, Lockhart remembered.

The agent wasn't looking too interested in the story, but the footballer asked how many keep-ups the boy could do. Lockhart explained that Nazar had been on the verge of beating his own record when he almost got run over. The footballer laughed.

"My dad used to go crazy at me for playing in the street," he said. "I loved it though. I never felt so free."

"How about setting up schools for kids who play football in the street?"

"Soccer schools?" asked the footballer. He liked the idea. It would be something worthwhile to do after he retired from top flight soccer. Something with a bit of soul, rather than a few years of gradually sliding down the lower leagues until he got fat and fell out of love with the game.

"Well, schools where they teach a bit of soccer and a bit of everything else," Lockhart said. "Like Rosalina wanted for Nazar."

The footballer's agent interjected, his brow slightly furrowed.

"How much are you asking us to invest?" he asked.

"Just time," Lockhart replied, watching the footballer's response.

"My client's time is precious," the agent replied.

The footballer said nothing.

"Of course it is," Lockhart agreed. "For the next year, at least."

A cloud passed across the footballer's face. *Two more years, and then what?* He had more money than he would ever need, but life had to be about more than money. He was a shrewd man with a big heart, and he knew that his career boiled down to a cabinet full of trinkets. He had won more medals than most, but what did that mean? What would he leave behind?

"Don't you think it's amazing," Lockhart interrupted his thoughts, "that somewhere in the middle of the desert in a country you've never even heard of, there's a kid called Nazar wearing a shirt with your name on the back of it?"

The footballer thought about it earnestly. He didn't think it was amazing. He just thought it was good marketing. But he understood what Lockhart meant. He was being offered an opportunity to help people. He was being offered a purpose.

"So you'll pay to build some sort of academy, and I'll help set it up and publicize it?"

"More than help publicize it. I'd like people to think of them as your academies. We can name them after you, if you like?"

The footballer liked it a lot. He liked the idea of training kids, and inspiring them. Helping them to respect themselves and to work hard. He liked the idea of not withering away once his contract expired.

"You said academies?" the footballer noted. "How many?"

"The first two would be in Turkmenistan" Lockhart told him. Of course, he wanted to build some in Afghanistan in time, but there was no need to worry the footballer with that just yet.

The footballer thought about it. He liked the idea, and he liked Lockhart. Lockhart was an easy man to trust. He seemed inspiring.

"What if I put in half?" he asked suddenly. His agent coughed.

Lockhart smiled gratefully. He told the footballer that he could put in as much or as little money as he liked. He reached forward and shook his hand.

"I'm afraid that there is no way in which you should see that handshake as legally binding" the agent told Lockhart, glaring at his client as though he should know better.

"Well, you can definitely consider it morally binding" the footballer smiled, as though he had just taken his first step away from a world that the agent would never escape. Then Lockhart made a final request.

"I nearly ran Nazar over because he was playing football in the road last year, and then his parents helped me out when I needed somewhere to stay. He was wearing a shirt with your name on it. I thought it would be a nice way to say thanks if you flew out to meet him. You'd get a feel for the country that way too."

The footballer looked at him.

"So you want to pay me to travel halfway across the world to have a kick about with a kid who lives in the middle of the desert?"

Lockhart grinned.

"Yeah, all right then," laughed the footballer. "I'll do it."

CHAPTER FIFTY-THREE

Taynton Hollow, England.
"The wolves they howled for my lost soul
I fell down a deep black hole."
– Paloma Faith, New York.

Two days after the footballer left the top of the hill, Daud arrived at the bottom. He was having second thoughts. His heart was full of anger at the man who had sent his brother to Guantanamo. Day after day he had sat quietly after morning prayers, imagining the horrors that his brother Ajmal would be facing in the camp, far away from the gaze of justice. Far from freedom or hope.

He had gone through the motions of worship, but his mind was always elsewhere. He had begun to imagine how he would finish the man called Fearless. He would have to tell him who he was and how he was avenging his brother. He had fixated on the words he would use and imagined the terror in the man's eyes.

But not far from the surface, Daud was a good man. No matter how hard he focused on his plan, a voice in his head continued to question him. Why had Ajmal been on the roof? What explanation could there be other than the one the Americans had assumed? *Was it impossible that his young brother was on the roof directing a missile to kill hundreds of men?* Daud refused to believe it.

He and Ajmal had gone to Mosque together since Daud could remember. They knew each other inside out. When they had gone out to Pakistan together for the wedding, Daud had been pleased that his brother had headed off to Quetta to find the old house from the family picture, it felt like a good-hearted thing for him to do. He was looking forward to his brother returning home full of stories of the old town and the magic window through which his family's fate had flown. How could that wholesome journey have ended up with Ajmal languishing in Guantanamo? How could he contemplate his brother as a terrorist? It was crazy.

Daud's sense of duty buried his doubts, and he committed himself to revenge. But the closer he got to his target, the more obstacles Allah seemed to put in his way. The weather was bad as he headed away from Birmingham, but as he drove along the motorway, the snow had got heavier, and the flakes had got bigger. Driving had become difficult as the traffic thinned out and the slush under his tires thickened.

The cars in front slowed to a crawl, but the heavy trucks kept a threatening pace behind him. By the time he saw the turning for Woodridge he was clenching the steering wheel and peering forward into the white.

Things didn't get better once he was off the main road. As he came to the first junction, he hit the brakes and nothing happened. The car sailed on into the merging traffic as if he hadn't touched the brakes at all. He turned the wheel but it made no difference, and he slid out across two lanes of slow traffic. He braced for impact, but somehow nothing hit him so he tapped at the gas and got the car moving again. It was slow work as he watched the miles to Woodridge gradually count down.

He was four miles from the village when he started to notice the road getting steeper. Either side of the road the bright paintwork of recently abandoned cars stood out against the otherwise white backdrop. The owners of the cars had hurried off into the blizzard and were nowhere to be seen. Daud took the car as far as it would go, but eventually he came to a halt. Each time he pushed the gas, the spinning tires dug deeper into the now thick snow, and he was forced to bail out.

The heater had been on full blast, and the cold air hit Daud as he opened the door and stepped out into the best part of a foot of snow. It was crisp and new, and it clung to the bottom of his trousers and caked around his feet. Daud was wearing jeans and walking boots and he grabbed his thick jacket from the boot of the car. He pulled a balaclava over his head and put his hoodie on top of that. He slung his rucksack over his shoulder and started up the hill.

The cold was still biting, and Daud cursed as he realized that he had forgotten his gloves. Within minutes his hands were red raw, but he needed to keep his balance so he kept them out of his pockets.

The doubting voice in his head was getting louder. Many times during his preparations, Daud had justified his anger by grasping at signs that fate was helping him to gain revenge for Ajmal. He had learned his target's name, found his address and obtained his weapon easily, as though some higher power knew that the injustice bestowed on Ajmal needed to be balanced out.

But now the doubting voice told him that the opposite was true. He was being beaten back by the snow and the cold. His eyes were screwed up and his face was numb. Maybe Allah wanted him to go home, think again, and show mercy.

Daud ignored the nagging voice. He had come too far now to turn back. Besides, he was a thoughtful man, and nerves were a natural response to a difficult decision. He couldn't feel his feet anymore, and his calves were aching as he trudged uphill through the thick virgin snow. There were no cars now, and the animals seemed to have abandoned the skies and the wide open fields. Apart from the muffled crunching of his boots, silence had descended around the solitary young man. Only his doubts grew louder.

He reached Woodridge at the top of the hill about half an hour later. There was a stone-built bus-stop on the edge of the village, and he took shelter in there from the wind. After a moment, he let the ruck sack slip from his shoulders and fall to the floor behind him. He pulled up the balaclava and looked out from the shelter.

Apart from his own, Daud could see no other footprints around the bus-stop, and in fact there were none along the road at all. His own were already being erased by the rough wind and fresh flakes. He knew that there would be no car tracks; the road he had just ascended would have been lethal even for the sturdiest vehicles. He sat down at the back of the shelter and rummaged through his bag. First, he pulled out a can of coke, which he opened and gulped down. The sugar was good.

Next he removed a towel from his bag, and from beneath it he pulled the ancient revolver and a small box of bullets. His eyes flicked back to the road for a moment, and then he unlatched the chamber and opened the box. His raw hands shook violently as he tried to control their movement, the tips of the bullets scratching across the revolver before eventually slotting into their holes.

Then he folded the towel back around the gun, and put it back at the top of his rucksack, and buckled up.

From his shelter on the edge of the village, Daud could make out the grand pub on the main road. Its windows were warm and welcoming and there was the muffled sound of music coming from within. The snow had masked the white lines on the car park tarmac, and the cars were parked in a free-for-all. Most looked grateful to have made it off the road, and their drivers had clearly headed into the bar for a hot coffee or a warming whiskey.

According to the electoral register, Charlie Lockhart lived in the oldest house in the village which was called Woodridge Lodge. Daud found it almost directly opposite the pub which was unfortunate because the rest of the village seemed deserted. Still, it was unlikely that anyone would be heading out into the storm now, and even if they did, their heads would be bowed against the swirling flakes and they wouldn't pay much attention to a passing stranger.

The place looked impressive. The rest of the village seemed to consist of the stone barns at the back of the Lodge, and the main house imposed itself on everything around it. The windows were mostly dark although there was a glow coming from a doorway in one of the rooms, and Daud could smell the smoke coming from the chimney even before he saw it. Charlie Lockhart was at home.

CHAPTER FIFTY-FOUR

The Crown and Cricket, Woodridge.
"In the shithouse a shotgun, praying hands hold me down.
Only the hunter was hunting in this tin can town"
– U2, Silver and Gold

Tyler was happy enough. He could sense that he was getting closer to the ever elusive Fearless, and he had taken the time to prepare. He felt fresh from flying first class into Heathrow. The food had been good and he had slept well, so by the time he arrived in London he was ready to act.

He hired a right-hand drive Audi Q7, a full size luxury SUV, on the recommendation of the salesman. He was going to choose a powerful BMW, but the salesman was insistent that most of the country would be under snow by the end of the day, so Tyler had taken his advice and gone for the Audi. It had been the right decision, but now the snow had arrived he wasn't sure that anything was going to be getting through the storm in a hurry.

He followed the SUV's built in navigation to a small village in the middle of the country. It wasn't much more than a pile of stones at the top of an impressive hill. There was a pub opposite the address he had typed into the sat nav, and he had pulled in there and swung the Audi around so that it was facing the house on the other side of the road.

The snow had proved ideal cover as his car had been gradually consumed by white camouflage. He was used to waiting, and he had grabbed plenty of supplies at a sportsman's store on his way. He had water, warm clothes, a new burner phone and some night goggles.

It was next to impossible to buy a firearm in England. He had considered waiting until nightfall and raiding the nearest farmhouse, but knew he'd only find a decrepit shotgun and an annoying dog to deal with. And there was no guarantee of a kill with a shotgun. If Fearless ran, Tyler wanted to be sure to put him down.

So he had bought a crossbow and bolt. Hardly his weapon of choice, but he was calm and steady enough to kill with it, even when the red mist descended. It also made him think of the old English stories of Robin Hood, running through the ancient stone village with a bow and arrow in his hand. Stealing from the rich and giving to the soon-to-be richer.

Every fifteen minutes he turned the engine, blew the heaters, and ran the wipers. It was just enough to allow him to keep an eye on the house without anyone noticing him staring. When darkness fell, he would grab his goggles and the crossbow and break into the manor house over the road. Fearless would probably have stashed the cash there. Once Fearless led him to wherever the dollars were stashed, or told him the account codes, Tyler would silently put a boot on his throat and a bolt through his eye and have the rest of the night to quietly head off into the anonymity of the snow.

It was about four PM. Tyler noticed an Asian guy out in the street, looking furtive. He was smart enough to know that normal people didn't hang about in biting cold snow, so he couldn't be up to much good. When the guy slunk into the gloom of the bus shelter, Tyler grabbed his night goggles, and switched them on. He turned up the magnification and pointed them at the shelter. The mysterious stranger was pulling a weapon out of his rucksack and loading it. By the way his hand was shaking, he wasn't exactly a pro.

Tyler smiled. This place looked like it hadn't changed for a thousand years; the last place you'd find a hit man. *What were the odds?* Clearly Fearless had built up a few enemies along the way. Tyler pulled on his jacket and pulled his kit together. The guy was heading out of the bus shelter and straight for the house that he had been watching. Tyler couldn't take the chance that someone would silence Fearless before he'd found out where the money was stashed.

As Tyler got out of the SUV, the cold air hit him, but he sucked it in. Luxury cars and first class flights had helped him get where he needed to be, but he was a warrior, and he liked the feeling of the cold on his skin. His eyes were alert and his strides were long as he headed out of the car park and crunched over the road, following Daud's footprints towards the back of Woodridge Lodge.

CHAPTER FIFTY-FIVE

Woodridge, England.
"Like a cat in a bag, waiting to drown"
– The Verve, The Drugs Don't Work.

Lockhart was moving around his tiny cottage like a wasp in a jar. It was nearly a year since David Barr had asked him to drive the Mastiff from Kandahar to Herat, and it was nearly a week since David Barr had been killed.

Lockhart missed the road. He missed not knowing what would happen next. When he was traveling, every day was a new adventure. For the last few months he'd been standing still, and it was boring. Now he knew Tyler was coming, and he couldn't wait for it to be over. He remembered the story that the ferrymen had told him. He was as ready now as he would ever be.

The fire was roaring in the oversized hearth and Lockhart watched it for a moment, the licking flames transfixing him. For a few seconds he thought about nothing but the way they rose and fell like fall leaves caught in the wind. Then suddenly questions crashed back into his mind and he began pacing again. What had happened to Rachel White after the police had taken her away from Tyler? Part of him wanted to get on a plane and head for Pine Bluff to find her and talk to her. Check she was okay. He wanted to ask her about David Barr and his family too. He felt that he owed them.

He turned from the fire, frustrated. There was no point going to Pine Bluff when Tyler would soon be arriving in Woodridge. Lockhart had to hold his nerve and wait. As he felt the warmth of the fire on his back, he paced over to the window, resting his clenched fists on the cold stone of its frame. He imagined Rachel's fear back in Lucky Bar. What kind of man could lock a woman in a freezer?

Lockhart's cottage was simple. The solid front door opened straight onto the main room of the house with its huge stone hearth. There was a sofa and a couple of chairs gathered around the fireplace, and a wooden staircase on the back wall which led to the only bedroom and a bathroom upstairs. It was all he needed. He hadn't planned on staying so long. Below the staircase was a wooden door beyond which was the kitchen. Lockhart walked through and turned on the kettle, absent mindedly.

There was a MacBook on the kitchen table, which he used to check his emails and to do his banking. He felt guilty every time he checked the Baku account. The interest kept stacking up at an astonishing rate. Over the year, the three hundred million dollars had grown by another twelve million. This meant nothing to Lockhart at all. Just numbers on a page. The money should be spent, building schools and hospitals, helping kids like Nazar and his family.

But there was nothing he could do until Tyler was dealt with. If the money paid for a school on the other side of the world, Tyler would find out and raze it to the ground. So Lockhart would wait for Tyler, and then he would deal with the money. The kettle clicked off as the kitchen filled with steam. Lockhart ignored it and paced back through to the fire.

As he looked out of the picture window, Lockhart could see the distant glow of the lights in the pub on the main road. The wind had blown fresh snow over the main path. The tire tracks from the footballer's car had disappeared. Nothing stirred in the garden or the street beyond. Lockhart was alone.

*

Opposite the Crown and Cricket, the journalist was walking purposefully through Woodridge Lodge. Although it was grand from the outside, the inside of the house was like a museum. Since he had arrived in the village, the journalist had done very little to make the place his own. The curtains were half velvet and half dust; the ceilings were high and the rooms were light, but the place felt musty and unloved.

The village had proven to be the perfect place to hide while his Iranian story was published. It was going to make him famous, and probably rich as well. The downside was that the Iranian secret police and Spanish special forces would probably be trying to track him down to silence him. Maybe even to kill him. Once his whole story was published, and the glare of the media spotlight was on him, they wouldn't dare attack him, but until then he was staying out of sight in Woodridge.

He had been smart to latch on to Charlie Lockhart. After a rocky start, they seemed to have worked each other out. Lockhart wasn't a bad guy. He had given the journalist his name and opened a bank account for him.

Now everyone in the village believed that his name was Charlie Lockhart. None of his neighbors knew his real name, and neither did the banks or the people who sent him bills. They all thought he was Charlie Lockhart, and he felt safer than he had done for a long time. Life had been calm, with him bolted up in the big house and the real Lockhart living quietly in the small cottage next door.

Now though, someone was ringing on his ancient doorbell, which was worrying. He had been careful not to make friends, and he never invited anyone to visit. True, he was on the main road, and there was a snowstorm, but there was no reason for anyone to be stranded, needing help, at the top of the hill.

The journalist had worked on explosive stories and made enemies before. He had been taught to be cautious. So now, as he strode through the farmhouse kitchen, he grabbed a knife from the block as he passed. He held it firmly in his hand behind his back as he reached the strong oak door. *Why didn't it have a spyhole?*

He part opened the door and was met by a young guy with his hood up. He looked Asian rather than Spanish or Iranian. Probably a good sign. The journalist said nothing, in case his accent gave him away. He stared at the stranger, waiting for him to speak.

"My car is stuck on the hill,' Daud said. 'Can I use your phone?"

The accent was not one which the journalist recognized, but he sounded fluent enough in English to be native. He kept his grip on the knife, but opened the door wider, and invited the man in. Daud walked through the door, focused on the job ahead of him. The time for questioning was over, and the time for doing was upon him.

Daud had reasoned the argument through a hundred times, weighed the consequences again and again, but now he had chosen his path.

"There is a telephone in the kitchen" said the journalist, and so Daud walked blindly through the narrow hallway into the heart of the house. He felt like he needed more space to get the job done anyway. The journalist left the back door ajar, hoping that his guest wouldn't stay long.

The kitchen had an earthen tiled floor, which was as old as the house. There was an old oak table in the middle of the room which had documents and photographs spread across it. There was a small laptop in the middle of the mess, and a solitary chair in front of it.

Daud turned and looked at the man who had followed him into the kitchen. The man who had betrayed his brother and sent him into the arms of the Americans.

"Your name is Charlie Lockhart?"

The journalist kept the knife gripped in the hand behind his back. The Iranians and the *Centro Nacional de Inteligencia* were not looking for Charlie Lockhart, so the guy in his house wasn't a threat to him. But still it made no sense why he had arrived here, caked in snow.

"I'm Lockhart," said the journalist cautiously, trying to disguise his Spanish accent and waiting to see what the man wanted.

It didn't take long to find out. Daud pulled something from his pocket and thrust it hard into the center of the Spaniard's chest. He kept pushing until the journalist toppled backwards and fell against the wall, winded.

The journalist looked down and saw that Daud was twisting a photograph into his chest. A photograph of a man who he had never seen before. The whole thing was as bizarre as it was alarming. He took the picture from Daud with his free hand and studied it carefully.

Daud was breathing hard, angry, waiting for a response.

"You might as well have killed him," he spat.

Daud was past doubts or questions now. The man in front of him had sold his brother to the Americans. He was responsible for his brother's torture, and he didn't even seem to recognize him.

The journalist's mind was racing. He had no idea what this guy wanted, what the photograph was, or what to say to calm him down.

Daud snatched at his hood, and pulled it down. The kitchen felt hot after the hike through the snow. His blood was pumping hard and his brow was furrowed. He had always been the elder brother, the sensible one. He was always measured, and fair, and reasonable.

Not today.

*

Outside, Tyler had reached the back gate and was moving stealthily through the garden of the Lodge. His eyes swept across the windows of the other houses nearby. It was getting dusky and warm lights were glowing from inside. No silhouettes. No prying eyes. The back door was still off the latch.

Tyler thought it was unfortunate that the snow would give away his tracks, but his boots were new today and he could burn them once the job was done. Plus, the snow was still falling so the imprints might be erased within an hour. The synthetic material of his jacket was making a lot of noise, so he slipped out of it, and moved silently through the back door.

In the kitchen, Daud's usual control had slipped. He wasn't thinking straight; he was just building himself up to finish the job. To avenge Ajmal by killing the man who had sent him to Guantanamo.

"You know what you did," he spat menacingly. "You know *exactly* what you did."

The journalist had absolutely no idea what he had done, or more to the point what Lockhart must have done. Stealing Lockhart's identity was supposed to have protected him, but now it had bought trouble to his door.

"Listen, I'm not Charlie Lockhart, " he said, contradicting what he said before.

This only made Daud angrier. The very least the man could do was to admit what he had done. The guy had showed no interest in the picture of Ajmal, and now he was changing his mind about who he was. Daud stepped forward and punched the man hard in the stomach.

This was enough for the journalist. He had been calm and diplomatic until now, but this guy wasn't Iranian or Spanish Intelligence. He was a scrawny, angry Englishman.

His face hardened, and he pulled out the kitchen knife from behind his back. His brow furrowed, and generations of animalistic darkness welled in his eyes. Coldness ran through his veins. He convinced himself that he could ram the knife into the stranger's stomach. He hoped that the stranger would be convinced too, so he wouldn't have to prove it.

Daud took a step back, reached into his rucksack, and pulled out his revolver.

Scissors, paper, stone.

Daud won.

The journalist was at a loss. He didn't know Daud, or Ajmal his brother, and he had no idea why the guy was so pissed off with Lockhart. It made it hard to argue his case.

Daud aimed the gun straight at the Journalist's forehead.

"I'm not Charlie Lockhart," the journalist repeated, his voice cracking slightly. He had been trained for this kind of situation; his kind of work usually meant being held captive at some point. His job had often been dangerous, and he had prepared for the worst.

He had learned how to keep his hotel room secure and he had agreed standard protocols for checking in with his editor while he was on assignment. He had left alarm words with his family, which he would embed in any message he was forced to make. He had been taught to identify different weapons, and to spot whether the safety catches were on or not. He had been shown how to avoid being hijacked, and he had been told how to negotiate and behave if he was taken hostage.

Now he was at gunpoint, none of the training seemed helpful. He should keep eye contact, he remembered that. Refuse to kneel down. Be a pain in the ass. Talk lots.

Despite all the things the journalist had learned, a strange resignation washed over him. The man with the gun didn't look like he wanted to reason, or chat.

Daud was ready. Ready to kill the man who had sent Ajmal to the Americans. Deep in his soul Daud knew that there was no simple explanation for what had happened, other than the obvious one. The fact that Ajmal was guilty. There was no story which would be comforting to hear, so instead Daud had blamed the man he read about in the official reports. The man who had wrestled his brother to the ground and sent him into captivity. Fearless, the man who had disappeared from Kandahar soon after his brother's arrest.

It was much easier for Daud to imagine killing Fearless than to imagine his brother in distress. And much easier than considering that Ajmal might be guilty. Daud aimed the revolver at the journalist's forehead and squeezed on the trigger.

CHAPTER FIFTY-SIX

Woodridge Lodge, England.
"Crazy skies all wild above me now, winter howling at my face,
And everything I held so dear disappears without a trace."
– David Grey, Sail Away With Me.

As Daud pulled the trigger, the journalist had instinctively closed his eyes, realizing that death was coming. But it didn't arrive. There was a faint whistle and Daud released the gun which clattered to the floor. The next thing the journalist felt was a sharp stabbing pain in his shoulder.

As he opened his eyes, he realized he was toppling backwards as the weight of Daud slumped forward onto him. The heavy oak table in the middle of the kitchen stopped the journalist from falling further, but Daud's body twisted around him and continued to fall to the hard stone floor.

As Daud twisted, the pain in the journalist's shoulder increased, and as he looked down, he saw that his shirt was torn and blood was pouring from it. A movement in the corner of his eye made him look up from his wound, and he saw with horror a giant of a man wearing black clothes blocking the doorway. *Why hadn't he bolted the back door?*

It was the guy he had seen back in Mary, trying to claw his way onto Lockhart's bus. He had a small crossbow hanging nonchalantly by his side, and his broad shoulders filled most of the doorframe. For a moment the journalist thought he must have been hit by the crossbow, but then he looked down at Daud. He was lying on the floor on his back, his eyes bulging open, and a steel tip emerging from his forehead.

Evidently Tyler's crossbow bolt had smashed through his temple and exited through the front of his forehead, giving him a steel horn, which had pierced the journalist's shoulder as Daud had slumped forward onto him.

Having expected to die a few seconds ago, the unexpected turn of events gave the journalist a lease of life. Daud had released the revolver as he fell, and it was lying on the wooden table in front of him. Almost within reach.

Tyler saw the journalist's eyes move towards the gun, and years of training kicked his body into action before any conscious thought caught up. He sprang forward, his first step landing heavily on top of a frail wooden chair. The chair skidded on the tiled floor and started to splinter apart under his bulk, but it gave him enough leverage for his second step to land on top of the oak table.

One foot kicked away the weapon while the other landed with all of his weight on top of the Journalist's arm. There was a dull crack, and the journalist cried out as his arm snapped.

Tyler acted on impulse, standing on top of the table with his back crammed against the low ceiling above him. He looked down at the arm which he had pinned to the table with his boot and fired the crossbow again. The bolt pierced straight through the journalist's outstretched hand and lodged into the wooden table. The journalist screamed as his hand was pinned to the oak.

Tyler climbed down and picked up the gun from the floor. He placed it carefully back on the table and caught his breath. The man stuck to the table stopped screaming, but had broken into gentle sobs. Beneath the table, the Asian guy was dying noisily, coughing and drowning on blood.

Tyler pulled the splintering chair back towards the table and sat down close to where the journalist had sunk to his knees. He rested his black boot on Daud's throat and applied some pressure. The noise stopped, and Tyler turned his attention to the journalist. The man who he had chased right around the world. The man who had stolen three hundred million dollars. The man who was about to pay it back, with interest.

"Hello, Charlie," Tyler said, and he grabbed the sobbing man by the throat.

Beneath Tyler's boot, the edges of Daud's world were turning black. He was aware of a third person in the room, and he knew that something had gone badly wrong. He was pretty sure that he was injured, but nothing seemed to hurt.

The Journalist denied being Charlie Lockhart at third time. Despite the overwhelming pain in his hand, the irony of his situation didn't escape him. He had taken Lockhart's identity to keep himself safe from people who wanted him dead, but hadn't thought that Lockhart's pursuers might be worse than his own.

"I'm not him. I can take you to him, but I'm not him. He lives next door."

It sounded like a desperate lie. Tyler grabbed at the documents on the table. Many of them were in Arabic, but there was a small pile of official-looking English letters; they were bills. They all had Lockhart's name on them.

Under the table, Daud knew that bad things were happening. Thoughts were slipping from him, breaking up in his mind as he tried to grasp onto his last precious moments of consciousness. He remembered that it had something to do with Ajmal. He was in trouble. He had to save his brother.

Beneath Tyler's boot, Daud had started to shake violently. The last gasps of air exploded from his lungs as his chest contracted, and the blood which had begun to congeal in his mouth was thrown into the air. Then suddenly, Daud stopped and went limp and silent. The journalist looked down at Daud, knowing that he would be next to die.

Tyler had not looked down at Daud during his final spluttering. He was inconsequential compared to the other man in front of him.

"Have you banked it?"

The journalist understood at once. It was about the money. The blue bale which he had seen under the driver's seat of the yellow bus in Ashgabat.

"I have some of your money. Maybe nearly half."

Tyler demanded to know where the money was. The journalist was smart enough to know that he was in no position to bargain. If the giant was going to kill him, then it was better to get the ordeal over with quickly.

"This house is worth nearly a million and there's another two hundred thousand in the bank" he said. That was about the truth of it. He was as honest as he could be because this would be the worst time to be caught in a lie.

Tyler held his throat tighter.

"You drove out of Kandahar with three hundred million dollars, and that's what I want back."

Suddenly the journalist understood. *That's why Lockhart had been driving a bus.* There must have been more than one blue bale. A lot more.

Tyler had considered shooting the man's knees to convince him to talk, but the snowscape outside was so quiet that he didn't want to risk the noise. He stood up and towered over the journalist who remained pinned to the table. Then he stooped down to the floor and grabbed Daud's corpse by the hair. His blank eyes were still open, and the bolt was still protruding from his forehead as Tyler lifted him from the floor.

"Where is the money?" Tyler asked the journalist gently.

The Journalist remained mute, partly because he couldn't think of an answer which wouldn't get him killed, and partly because he was mesmerized by the sickening way that the giant man had lifted the dead guy from the floor by his hair like a marionette. Daud's slack jaw had dropped, and he was drooling blood. His unfocussed eyes were staring at the journalist without seeing anything.

There was silence while Tyler waited for the journalist to reply. Then suddenly, without warning, he rammed the dead guy's head straight into the journalist's face, horn first. Before the journalist could react, the bolt protruding from Daud's head ripped through his cheek. Instinctively he tried to pull away, and pain instantly shot up his arm as he ripped at the hand which was pinned to the kitchen table.

"Where is it?" Tyler asked quietly. His slow measured question was a contrast to his explosive physical violence.

After a few seconds, Tyler lost patience and thumped Daud's head into the Journalist's chest again and again, until the bolt ripped through his shirt and pierced his skin. The journalist couldn't take any more, and in a moment of desperation he ripped his hand from the table and was instantly sent dizzy with pain. He was losing a lot of blood, but now that he was free, he stumbled towards the gun resting at the other end of the table.

He reached it at the same time as Tyler. He got his hand around it, but the barrel was pointing towards him. Tyler had dropped Daud to the floor and was trying to prize the journalist's fingers from the weapon. The journalist didn't have the strength to turn the gun back towards his adversary. Tyler was the stronger man, and he knew that he would win out. The journalist knew it too, and he knew that he was finished. The man in the black outfit would torture him until he gave him an answer, and he didn't know the answer. So the journalist took the best option he had left. He couldn't turn the gun, but he could pull the trigger, so he leaned forward and put his head to the cold metal.

He squeezed before Tyler could disarm him, and a shot rang out through the kitchen. He died instantly, and fell to the floor next to Daud.

The cockerel in the yard crowed twice, and then Woodridge fell silent again.

CHAPTER FIFTY-SEVEN

Guantanamo Bay, Cuba.
"When I'm dead and hit the ground a love back home, it unfolds"
– Coldplay, Violet Hill

Ajmal was thinking about his school days. The spring of his life had gone well. His parents and grandparents had worked hard to ensure that he and his brother Daud grew up in a world of opportunity. As he grew up, he prayed hard at the Mosque every day, thankful for the luck that Allah had bestowed on his family. He was diligent at school, and always hungry to learn.

Ajmal's grandfather reminded him every day how lucky he was. He told them how different life would be if they were still in Quetta. He told the boys that when he was as young as them he was out in the fields feeling hungry each day.

"Hungry for food, hungry for knowledge, and hungry for adventure," he told them. "My head and my heart rumbled almost as much as my stomach. You are lucky to have all of these chances around you, but you must work hard to grab them when they come your way."

Then he would smile at them and his eyes would twinkle, and Daud and Ajmal were filled with the desire to impress their grandfather. After school, the brothers would play hockey opposite the Mosque. They were simple, happy times. He imagined where all the kids from the mosque might be now. He imagined how they would look now that they were grown up, with their wives and their children and their beards.

Ajmal grew up in the shadow of his brother Daud. Daud looked after him at school and in the street. Sometimes he would help him with this homework, other times Daud was the person he turned to when he needed advice. Early on, Daud had showed signs that one day he would be the head of the family. He was clever and reasonable and caring. He seemed wise beyond his years. And whenever there was trouble, somehow Daud was always there to save the day. With anger in his eyes and fists flying, mild-mannered Daud would stop at nothing to fulfill his role as the family's protector.

Ajmal missed Daud. He missed having a big brother protecting him. When he was younger, he had wanted to step out of Daud's shadow. He wanted to prove that he was a man too, and that it wasn't always going to be Daud who made the family proud. That was why he set out to find his grandfather's old house in Quetta. That was why he organized the convoys to trade with the Americans. That was why he tried to keep the townsfolk unscathed on the journey by making deals with the militia in Afghanistan.

He hadn't stood on the roof of the canteen in Kandahar because of some ideological battle. Afghanistan was a huge desert, apart from a few cities. Not much had ever thrived there, but the bits that had flourished had since been decimated by war. Ajmal didn't care who ran or raped the place.

He just wanted to go home a hero who had made things better in his grandfather's old home. He wanted to be more than just Daud's younger brother. His heart had led him to Quetta, to see the house that his grandfather had talked about. But once he had arrived and saw the NATO convoys driving down the Chaman Road, the smell of money and opportunity had drawn him in. The chance to make money had led to danger, and the chance to bargain a way through the danger had led to him standing on the roof guiding a missile into the camp.

He was ashamed. Compared to the drivers he had led into Afghanistan he was rich and privileged. At the time, he had justified his actions because he was buying the safety of the men driving behind him in the convoy – but he knew that he had no right to trade one man's life for another. He had been standing on the roof to protect his fledgling empire. He was there through greed, and now he was in Cuba, in the devil's house, for exactly the same reason. Whatever his fate turned out to be, he deserved it.

It was at least three days since he had slept. He was naked, hanging from a beam in a dark concrete room. They wouldn't give him a lawyer or a phone call. There were no rules. There was no trial or parole or schedule. He had no release date to fixate on. He had no future.

He remembered the window in the house in Quetta. Life's delicate journey measures itself out in such tiny moments. If his grandfather had been born somewhere else, things would be different. If his grandmother hadn't walked past the tiny window all those years ago, Ajmal wouldn't be where he was right now. If his cousin hadn't got married, Ajmal might never have come to Pakistan or Quetta. If he hadn't driven his truck through the archway at the end of the Chaman Road, and into Afghanistan, he wouldn't have ended up in Cuba. He wouldn't have faced the torture. He would have had a clearer conscience too.

An inky black hopelessness had soaked through Ajmal's heart as he hung in the cell in Guantanamo. He could feel nothing of his arms, and his wrists hung loosely from the cutting metal restraints attached to the concrete ceiling. He hung his head in despair.

Thousands of miles away, Tyler had just dragged Ajmal's brother unceremoniously away from the other man he had killed. It was the other man he was interested in. Charlie Lockhart. *Fearless.* He was in Lockhart's house, and wherever the money was hidden, he would find it. He pulled off the dead guy's watch to check for the famous tattoo. Just to be sure.

It was a messy job, as blood had run down from the hole in the man's palm. It had congealed around his watch and smeared around his wrists. Tyler spat on the man's skin and rubbed vigorously. Nothing. No tattoo. Not Fearless. Not Lockhart. *For fuck's sake.*

Tyler put his head in his hands. Why the hell had the man said he was Lockhart if he wasn't? It made no sense, and he could feel his anger rising. He kicked the dead man hard in the chest, which released some of his rage.

Then Tyler sat and thought. The imposter had said something about the real Lockhart being nearby. He had said that the money was nearby, and he had mentioned another house in the village. Maybe it was true. He left the crossbow on the kitchen table and grabbed the revolver, thrusting it into the pocket of his jacket as he headed back out into the snow.

CHAPTER FIFTY-EIGHT

Lockhart's Cottage, Woodridge.
"On candystripe legs Spiderman comes, softly through the shadow of the evening sun. Stealing past the windows of the blissfully dead, looking for the victim shivering in bed." – The Cure, Lullaby.

Something was in the air. Lockhart was not prone to paranoia, but he felt as though Tyler was getting closer. It had been over twenty-four hours since the giant had threatened that he was on his way. The light was dying outside, and the firelight was now reflecting off the window in front of him. Moments ago, Lockhart thought he heard gunfire coming from the Lodge next door. But it could have been a car backfiring. Or just his imagination.

Even so, it had spooked him, and he felt like he was on his guard. Still, he could see nothing in the dusky street beyond the evergreen hedge, except for the glow from the Crown and Cricket on the other side of the road.

Since the moment he took the money from the Mastiff in the boneyard in Herat, Lockhart had known that someone would come looking for him. Now David Barr was dead, and he was alone in the house on the hill, and the snow had cut him off from the world. Lockhart felt like the time was now. The river had flowed to here, to now. And that was why he was ready.

Outside, Tyler was looking both ways along the deserted road. Dusk was falling, and the street was deserted. He scissored over the low dry stone wall and crouched down, looking through the evergreen bushes over the grounds to the tiny cottage in the distance.

Inside the cottage, Lockhart grabbed a couple of tumblers and found a bottle of twelve-year-old Glenlivet. It was a decent single malt. He walked back through to the main room and sat down on one of the chairs near to the massive stone fireplace. It was much too big for the house. He poured himself a glass, and had a swig. Then he grabbed a second glass and filled it with more whiskey. He placed it on the opposite side of the table. He was certain that Tyler would be coming.

There was no way Lockhart would give Tyler three hundred million dollars which didn't belong to him. And there was no way that Tyler would take no for an answer. Stalemate. Lockhart knew that it would turn ugly, but even so he wasn't going to make the first move. He would give the giant the chance to walk away. Otherwise, he figured that he would be no better than Tyler himself. Lockhart knew that he had a job to do. He had to get Tyler off his back, and he had to ensure that the money ended up where it was meant to be. Where it was needed most. He also owed it to Rachel, and David Barr to put Tyler straight.

There was no option for Lockhart to be afraid. His old university friend Laurent had once convinced him that death was nothing to be afraid of, anyway. Laurent was French, and borderline insane. Lockhart shared a flat with him for almost a year, and there was never a dull moment. After a few bottles of wine he would fly into a rage about the indignity of his life, and the terrible choices which had led him to where he was today. Most times, the end of his sentences would descend into French profanity accompanied by the sound of breaking glass. Laurent had a penchant for the dramatic and enjoyed throwing things around.

Lockhart had taken to him immediately. He was all Camel cigarettes and Pastis and philosophy. Looking back, it was all a sham, but Lockhart had been barely out of his teens and knew next to nothing about the world.

Girls had loved Laurent's brooding looks and his drunkenness. Lockhart suspected that half the reason for his cigarettes and his red wine and his disheveled appearance was to lure women to his boudoir. In reality, his dad was rich and utterly bourgeois. He was ready to welcome his son into the family firm as soon as he tired of being a romantic.

But Laurent's philosophy was genuine enough. He would quote Sartre and Camus at will, and rant about the futility of life. In quieter moments, he would listen endlessly to Jacques Brel, and fret over the nature of everything. Lockhart found his restless soul enjoyable company. It was during one of those quiet moments that Laurent had said to Lockhart, "Death is the most frightening of all the bad things, but is nothing to us. When we exist death is not yet here, and when death arrives, then we do not exist anymore. You will never know death."

Laurent was an Absurdist – he thought it was stupid that people spent their lives scrabbling about trying to make their place in the universe seem significant. They were kidding themselves. The universe was cold and empty and couldn't care less about them. It was a fairly bleak conclusion.

Lockhart didn't believe in Absurdity any more than he believed in Bahá'í book of Hidden words, but he enjoyed listening to the theories that people clung to as they tried to find their place in the order of everything.

Laurent had explained that people looked towards the future for hope of better times, but deep down they know that the future is death. So their lives were an absurd paradox. Lockhart felt like he was in the middle of that paradox as he waited for Tyler to arrive.

"Reject fear of death, because death is inevitable" Laurent had told him. "Don't try to make sense of the universe, because there is no grand plan to understand. Do whatever you want, because actually none of it matters very much. Ignore the usual rules, and play by your own."

Tonight, that was exactly what Lockhart was planning to do. Outside in the snow, Tyler had reached the outside of the cottage and was skirting low around the sandstone exterior, trying to find an easy way in.

Lockhart smiled to himself about how certain Laurent had been about everything. Lockhart felt like he was still searching for his place in the world. He was still a tourist. Maybe his destiny was to travel, and never to find a place to rest. Since David Barr had died, he had known that his days in Woodridge were numbered. He could feel the river trying to dislodge him again. That suited him fine.

He stood up and went back to the window. It was dark now. Maybe the Giant wouldn't come tonight after all. The snow had stopped suddenly, and a few of the brightest stars were trying to pierce their way through the blanket of cloud. Lockhart was about to go back to his chair when he happened to look down and notice the set of prints in the snow. They were massive, and pushed tightly against the stone wall. They were fresh too. Somebody big had been skimming the cottage. Tyler had arrived.

Lockhart paced briskly out to the kitchen and picked up his mobile. Time to go to work. He grabbed the phone and called the number which he had preset for when this day arrived. It rang twice before a woman's voice answered.

"Reservations?"

Lockhart explained he needed to book a flight, and went through the process of getting the seat reserved.

"Just me" he told the woman at the end of the phone.

"Gatwick to Hong Kong. Six hours?" he looked at his watch. "Yes that should be fine."

He paid and thanked the woman before putting the phone down. He never traveled first class, but he knew that the airline would put up with him arriving at the last minute if he'd paid more. With his Gatwick flight booked, he took a pen and paper from the kitchen table and wrote "Heathrow, 10.34pm". It looked random enough. He left the bogus note in plain view on the kitchen table.

Tyler was having no luck. The front door looked too solid to break down. There was no point smashing a window at the front because it might be seen from the road. He skirted round the back of the house, still staying close to the stone wall that surrounded the cottage. He had covered two thirds of the building, and he hadn't found a weakness. A familiar frustration was starting to build as he felt the handle of the old revolver smooth and cold in his hand.

Inside, Lockhart had returned to his own sofa, and was rolling his tumbler in his hand, watching the whisky coat the inside of the glass. The trap was set. It was up to Tyler now whether he chose to walk into it. Lockhart heard a smash in the kitchen as the back door caved in. Tyler was nothing if not predictable. Lockhart took another sip of his whiskey, and stayed exactly where he was.

CHAPTER FIFTY-NINE

Lockhart's Cottage, England.
"If I have a bag of rocks to carry as I go,
I just want to hold my head up high"
- REM Walk Unafraid

Tyler had broken into houses all over the world. Sometimes in training, sometimes in combat. The basics were always the same. Assess the situation before you rush in. Find the weakest spot for entry. When you go in, go in hard and fast. Keep moving and act decisively, and always know the quickest way out. Just in case.

Once Tyler had made up his mind, he pulled the revolver from his jacket pocket, and stepped out to face the back door. It was away from the road, and less solid than the oak door at the front. He guessed where the lock would be, and smashed his foot into it with all of his might. It felt like the whole house shook as the door gave way. Tyler had put all of his weight into the blow, and a less experienced man might have tumbled into the kitchen when the door gave way. But not Tyler. He was well balanced and he stepped into the house deftly, keeping low and strong.

The kitchen was clear, so Tyler moved forward into the cottage. He spotted a note on the kitchen table. It was a flight time. He smiled and ripped the top sheep of the pad of paper and scrunched it into his jacket pocket. *Final call for passenger Lockhart.* He expected to find the living room empty too, but it wasn't.

There was a tall guy sitting in a comfy chair staring at him. The man was in his early thirties, looking as if he had been expecting him to drop in. Tyler could have saved himself some trouble and just rung the doorbell.

Most men would have sprung up the stairs to get away from the danger, but the tall guy just sat there looking relaxed. Tyler's expert eye swept the room, and noticed the second whiskey glass in front of Lockhart. One man, two full glasses.

"Where's your friend?" he asked, pointing the revolver up the stairs to cover himself. He kept his eyes on the guy near the fire though.

"The drink's for you," Lockhart replied. He wondered how the hell Tyler had got his hands on a weapon in such a short space of time. "I had a feeling you would be on your way. Why don't you sit down?"

Tyler took a moment to weigh up the options. The man in front of him hadn't flinched. He didn't need to check for the tattoo. He knew he'd found Fearless, and he could see how he had picked up his nickname. He had the revolver in his hand and the man on the sofa looked unarmed, so he took a seat and sniffed at the glass.

He was more used to bourbon than scotch, but he was cold to the bone and he wasn't fussy. He took a gulp. It was earthier than the malts at home. As the man in front of him raised his glass, Tyler caught a flash of a tattoo on the underside of his wrist. Lockhart saw him looking, and reached over the table, pulling up his sleeve.

It was there; the tattoo describing the man's blood type and his Arabic name. David Barr's ghost driver was alive in the flesh. Tyler was closer to the prize than he had been since Kandahar.

"You've come for your money."

Tyler looked up and nodded. *Why was the man so calm?*

"You've probably come to kill me too."

Tyler shrugged at this. It was probably true.

"Do you have it?" he asked.

Lockhart has spent a long time planning this moment. Depending on the next few seconds, things could be really good, or really bad. In truth, he knew they would go bad. But he had to give Tyler a chance to walk.

"The money is banked," he said simply. "It's not here and you can't get it without my help, so you might as well put the weapon away because you can't use it."

Tyler scowled, but he believed what Lockhart said. He was living in a tiny house, and didn't look afraid, and he was obviously a smart guy. He put the gun down on the table between the two men, closer to himself than Lockhart. Daring him to try and snatch it.

Lockhart knew the easiest way to get rid of Tyler would be to give him the money, in return for him leaving and never returning. But it wasn't his money to give. He hadn't asked for the three hundred million dollars, but he'd ended up with them. It wasn't his place to hand them to some crooked soldier. So instead, he offered Tyler a deal.

"There is three hundred and twelve million dollars in the account"

Lockhart told the massive guy who was crammed into the seat in front of him. "I don't want any of it because it's not mine. Three hundred million belongs in Afghanistan and I'm taking it back."

Tyler's face hardened.

"That leaves twelve million. And that's my deal. If you give me an account number, I'll wire you twelve million dollars right now, and then you walk away."

"So you stole three hundred million dollars," the giant told Lockhart, and now you're offering me twelve million, and I'm supposed to just walk away?"

"You followed me to Herat?" Lockhart asked, taking a sip on his whiskey. Tyler nodded.

"Well then you must have seen what happened on that road. You must have seen the scorch marks and the burnt out vehicles. I was hijacked by three jeeps, and then nearly burned by some trigger-happy Thunderbolts."

Tyler had heard as much from General Lang.

"So I'm stuck in the middle of the desert with no credentials and a truck full of stolen cash. What option did I have?"

As Tyler sat in front of the open fire, he could see what Lockhart was driving at. He and Lang had worked hard to stay anonymous, and this was the first chance the guy had been able to offer to repay the money.

"I got stuck with the money that you stole," Lockhart explained to him. "And now I'm giving it back to the schools and hospitals that need it."

He gave Tyler a hard stare, but the hulking American didn't seem to have any crisis of conscience.

"So you give me the interest and think that we're all square?" Tyler asked.

Lockhart nodded and said, "You stole a load of money, and you lost it. What I'm offering you is twelve million to disappear. One-time offer, take it or leave it."

Things seemed to be going ok. Tyler couldn't get at the money in the Baku bank without Lockhart, so he wasn't about to kill him. The game had begun. After a year stuck in Woodridge, Lockhart was enjoying the adrenalin rush.

Tyler reached into his pocket and pulled out his phone. Not much signal. He sent a text to Lang explaining the situation. If it was up to Tyler, he would check the money was wired, and then leave the country. He would be rich enough not to care about what happened to the man and his whiskey and his fire and his tiny house. But it wasn't up to Tyler. It was Lang's call.

The two men sat in front of the huge fire in silence. There was nothing to talk about until the text came back. Lockhart threw another log into the flames, more to pass the time than anything else. He used a heavy poker to prod away at the heart of the fire and to move the log into a good position. The wood was dry and seasoned, and it caught quickly. The poker glowed red, and Lockhart left it lying on the stone hearth.

As Lockhart sat down again, Tyler's phone bleeped. The message was simple:

KILL HIM.

Tyler had no idea how they would access the money in the account without Fearless to type in the codes. But he had long ago learned to trust Lang. His boss hadn't been wrong yet. His boss had made them rich, until they lost the truck.

Lockhart hoped for Tyler's sake that he didn't play poker. He would have been the worst. His brow had furrowed, and he had shifted in his seat. He hadn't looked up since he had read the text. Lockhart knew bad news when he saw it, and in his mind he wondered if he could reach the hot poker in one lunge.

He watched Tyler carefully as he leaned forward and picked up his whisky. He took a sip, just enough to wet his lips. Before he got a chance to grab the poker, Tyler looked up, pulled out the revolver, and aimed it straight at him. Without saying a word, he pulled the trigger.

Nothing happened. The change in temperatures between the freezing cold snow and the hot fire had jammed the weapon. Lockhart remembered his dad once saying to him that if life offers you a second chance, you should grab it with both hands. On instinct, Lockhart threw the heavy whiskey glass straight at the man in front of him.

Lockhart had aimed well, and the heavy base of the glass smashed square into the middle of Tyler's face. The man was a brute, but even so he was momentarily stunned. Lockhart was instantly up and away before Tyler had stumbled to his feet. He ignored the poker and ran straight into the fire.

Tyler had been aware of Lockhart moving towards the hearth. He saw his shadow as he was instinctively wiping blood and shards of glass from his face. His nose was broken but the cuts were superficial. He looked up towards the fireplace in confusion. Lockhart wasn't there. It was an impossible escape. The solid oak door was still firmly in place, and for Lockhart to escape out of the back door he would have to have passed Tyler, which he definitely didn't.

Tyler looked at the fire, and then moved closer with his revolver back in his hand. He looked up the huge chimney, as if Lockhart might be hiding up there. He wasn't. Then Tyler notice that there was a cupboard built into the side of the massive hearth. There was a solid oak door which was out of sight when you looked at the massive stone surround from the front. It looked as ancient as the house itself, and as solid as the front door.

Tyler laughed at the futility of a grown man hiding in a cupboard. He gave it a kick but it didn't budge. So he took the poker from the hearth and began to lever the burning logs out of the grate. He piled them up in front of the oak door, and soon it began to smolder. Tyler would smoke him out or burn him out. He didn't really care which.

Lockhart had slammed the thick oak door behind him and slid three bolts into place. Even Tyler wouldn't be able to kick it down. Then he had turned around and started down the steep stone steps at the back of the cupboard which led to a damp narrow passageway below. His shoulders brushed either side of the corridor as he rushed along.

The corridor was just broad enough for Lockhart. He was fairly confident that even if Tyler managed to break through the wooden door, he wouldn't fit down the stone staircase. The tunnel stretched on in a straight line for about two hundred meters. There were lights every few meters in the wall, and occasionally another passage would join the main corridor. About half way along there was a doorway which Lockhart went through. It opened out into a spacious room which had once been a chapel. The original Catholic owners of the Lodge had built it so that they could practice their religion away from the state's prying eyes.

Deep underground, Lockhart remembered his cagey conversation with Rosalina about her Bahá'í religion which was outlawed in Turkmenistan. Back in Elizabethan England, the Catholics had been forced underground. Nearly every house in Woodridge had a secret hole in the fireplace or under the floorboards. They built tunnels to keep priests safe in their houses, and escape routes in the walls, so that if the Queen's men raided, the priests could always escape.

Lockhart had made the underground chapel more comfortable since he discovered it nearly a year ago. He realized at once that it would be useful when Tyler finally arrived. He had furnished it with a couple of sofas, and a low table with magazines on. There was a thick rug on top of the bare stone floor.

He turned on the laptop which was sitting on the low coffee table. He powered up Skype, and dialed in to the laptop on his kitchen table. The video link popped up on the screen, and he could see Tyler through the doorway standing next to the fireplace. He was trying to burn down the oak door. It would take him forever. In the foreground was the pad of paper that he had written on earlier. The top sheet was blank. Tyler must have ripped up the flight details as he walked through earlier.

Lockhart dialed the journalist's number on Skype, and another kitchen table popped onto the screen. He needed to check that Tyler didn't have an accomplice waiting for him in the Lodge. The kitchen was still, but Lockhart's spirit sunk when he saw the two bodies on the kitchen floor. The journalist was dead. He didn't recognize the other man, but he was completely still and the coast was clear.

The problem was going to be the snow. Lockhart picked up his grab-bag from underneath the coffee table. There wasn't much in it. Ten thousand pound sterling and ten thousand Euros, various bank cards, a passport and a bottle of water were all he needed. He grabbed a thick coat and strong boots and the keys to his Range Rover. He bought it new but then had it shipped up to Scotland to be modified.

There was an article on the front of the magazine on the coffee table next to the car keys. Lockhart had read it a few weeks ago and it had given him an idea. A way to deal with Tyler. Lockhart couldn't kill him; it wasn't in his nature. But he was going to finish him once and for all. He had given the giant the chance to walk away, and Tyler hadn't taken it. Instead, he had tried to shoot him in the head without warning. Now Tyler was going to pay.

Lockhart walked out of the chapel and continued down the corridor towards Woodridge Lodge. Back in the cottage, Tyler was pacing like a caged tiger, confused and spoiling for action. The oak door was beginning to smolder, but patience was not Tyler's strong point. He took the poker back out of the fire. It was glowing hot. He began ramming it with all of his might into the wooden door in the side of the hearth. A combination of the heavy poker, Tyler's enormous strength and the fire-weakened door meant that it slowly began to yield.

A small fissure began to appear, and Tyler worked the poker into it, jimmying the door off its ancient hinges. He barged into it with his shoulder and it gave way. As he smashed through the door, Tyler fell into the cupboard, ready for action. He looked like an animal, his face dripping with blood from his broken nose and the hot poker held high, ready to strike at whatever he found in the room behind the door. But he found nothing.

The cupboard was pokey and there was a small light coming from the floor in the back corner. Tyler squeezed his broad shoulders through the smoldering doorway and pushed his way into the dark. Where the hell was Lockhart? As his eyes adjusted to the dark, he realized that there was a small hole in the back corner. It was a tiny stairway down. He couldn't fit. He tried to force his shoulders into the gap, but he was just too big. He roared his frustration down into the passage instead, and then came back out into the cottage.

Lockhart was right at the other end of the tunnel when he heard Tyler's voice echoing fiercely along the stone passageway. Lockhart wondered if he had managed to squeeze himself down the stairs. He climbed another set of steep stone steps and emerged from the passageway through a trap door in the floor of the kitchen in Woodridge Lodge.

The first thing he saw was the journalist lying dead on the floor. Lockhart took a moment to close over his eyes. The other man looked familiar, but Lockhart couldn't place him. He had been shot through the head with a crossbow and his face was bloodied. Again Lockhart closed his eyes , and then he pulled the heavy oak table over the trap door. Tyler's strength was incredibly but the weight would at least slow him down if he tried to come through. Then Lockhart moved to the back door and out into the snow before he became a third corpse on the pile.

CHAPTER SIXTY

Woodridge, England.
"Because I'm a million miles away and at the same time
I'm right here in your picture frame."
– Jimi Hendrix, Voodoo Chile.

The cold air hit Lockhart as he moved outside. He was drunk on adrenalin, and the temperature sobered him up for a moment. He didn't allow himself to think about what would have happened if Tyler's revolver hadn't jammed. He didn't allow himself the luxury of mourning the journalist either. He just focused on what he had to do next. After a year of waiting, it was time to leave Woodridge and start the journey again.

He would miss the people: The friends who came round to eat most nights. The gardener and the painter and the sculptor that he had supported. The school and the pub he had saved. But he wouldn't miss the isolation and the boredom. The waiting and the stillness. He wouldn't miss that at all.

But now the waiting was over. It was all about the next twenty seconds. Lockhart started walking through the snow over the two sets of prints heading back into the house. One set belonged to a dead man, the other to his killer. Lockhart emerged onto the street and kept walking towards the carpark outside the Crown and Cricket. He was ten seconds away. His key fob unlocked the Range Rover. The hazards flashed and it double-bleeped. Tyler was at the cottage window in a fraction of a second.

With blood still dripping from his broken nose, he saw Lockhart crossing the street outside, coming from a completely different direction. He went for the front door but it was locked. His temper was rising fast. He could feel his heartbeat banging in his temples. He ran through the kitchen and in a fit of anger, he threw the jammed revolver across the room into the porcelain sink with all of his might. The weapon discharged and shattered the sink, with bits of white shrapnel flying across the kitchen.

"For Christ's sake," he yelled. He retrieved the now functioning revolver and grabbed a meat cleaver from the knife block on the worktop. If the gun jammed again, he'd hack the guy to pieces instead. Then he sprinted out of the back door and around to the front of the house.

He jumped, then forced himself through the evergreen and over the wall where he had first come in, and set off at full pelt towards the carpark. But he was too late. He had gone about twenty meters before his body started to react to the cold. His lungs felt like they were splitting as the snowy air filled them. His muscles were reacting to the change in temperature too, but he forced his body forwards at full speed, his knees slicing high through the air as he cut across the white lawn.

Lockhart turned the ignition, then flicked on the main beams and the windscreen wipers. They were powerful, and the white landscape came into view straight away. The flakes had started up again, and the carpark was caked in four inches of powder. Nothing the Range Rover couldn't handle. He had seen Tyler, of course. The black outfit in the white snow couldn't be less camouflaged.

He locked the doors and put his foot on the gas, pulling out of the carpark at a steady pace. He didn't want to rush into a mistake. His plan was a good one, and he just needed to stick to it. He needed Tyler to follow him. It shouldn't be too hard. He'd told him where he was going.

Tyler's rage was spilling over. As he reached the road, Lockhart's black Range Rover was driving towards him. His body was moving before his mind caught up. He ran straight into the middle of the snow-covered road, heading for a spot a few meters in front of Lockhart. The road curved and the Range Rover would have to slow down.

Lockhart was doing about twenty miles an hour by the time the man in black got into the street. He watched as Tyler took up a braced position and aimed the revolver with both hands straight at him. He aimed at the windscreen on the driver's side. Head height. He waited for as long as he could, until the kill was inevitable, even with the ancient weapon. He pulled the trigger and this time the gun fired; the bullet flying from the muzzle directly toward the driver's head. Tyler watched in disbelief as the bullet bounced straight off the windscreen without breaking it.

Lockhart pushed the gas and the Range Rover's four liter V8 engine roared. It was sluggish compared to the standard model, because Lockhart had paid for it to be modified by a company called Wright International in Scotland. He had guessed that whoever came after the money would be armed, so he had commissioned the company to armor the SUV. Now the windows were 39mm thick, and there were stitch welded ballistic plates in every panel. The suspension had been reinforced to allow for the extra weight. The Hutchinson tires would run flat, and the fuel was cased in steel. Lockhart was driving a tank. He had used his time waiting well, and the trip up to Scotland to get the Range Rover modified had been worth it.

Tyler was still staring at Lockhart as the Range Rover hit him and he bounced off into the snow. As he lay on the ground, he spotted the blast plate under the chassis. *Who was this guy?*

He was up in a flash, sprinting after Lockhart, but it was too late. He was pulling away. He wanted to shoot at the vehicle, but he knew he was wasting his time. He got back to his Audi and started the engine. He flung it out of the pub car-park and slammed through the gears, ignoring the snow on the road.

Within a minute he could make out taillights in the distance. Lockhart wasn't hanging around, but the Audi was quicker, and slowly Tyler made up ground. It was a good feeling. Eventually he was right on Lockhart's tail. He couldn't decide what to do. If he rammed the armored car, he would come off worse. If he shot at it, it would be futile. There was only one option for now, which was to stick as closely to the car in front as possible. His chance would come if the car in front ran out of fuel before he did, or if the pressure of Tyler following caused Lockhart to make a mistake.

Otherwise, he would wait until they reached wherever they were going, and then take him out. He wondered if the man in front had any idea where he was leading them, or whether he was running blind. His respect for Lockhart was growing as quickly as his hatred. He guessed Lockhart would probably have a plan. He was right.

CHAPTER SIXTY-ONE

Pine Bluff, Arkansas
"I was blind, but now I see"
– Primal Scream, Moving On Up

Ben Lang was trying to piece everything together. None of it was adding up. Since Tyler had texted to confirm he had located Fearless, he assumed the job would have been done by now. While he was waiting for confirmation from Tyler, he had set about his own tasks. Now that he had learned Lockhart's real name, he had requested security details from a contact in the British Government, who owed him a favor. Within the hour, he got an email from an anonymous-looking address. It contained the address, bank details, phone bills and other public records for Charlie Lockhart. He had requested CCTV images covering the roads near Lockhart's house, but there were apparently none; Fearless was either smart or lucky. Maybe both. He'd certainly done a good job evading Tyler so far.

While he waited for Tyler to phone in the kill, Lang had poured over the guy's bank records. The document contained the account number, sort code, and pass codes for Charlie Lockhart's bank account. Lang had everything he needed to hack into the millions. Lockhart had become disposable.

The next set of documents in the envelope showed details about the manor house in the village, Woodridge Lodge. It had been paid for in cash from Lockhart's bank account and had cost nine hundred thousand pounds. The owner of the deeds was listed as Charlie Lockhart, with no previous address noted. He had registered to vote and there were no other listed occupants in the house.

Tyler still hadn't confirmed the kill. There was no reason for it to be taking so long. Although there was no CCTV footage in the email, the British contact had attached a JPEG file of a photograph of Lockhart. Lang double clicked out of curiosity, wondering what the guy who Tyler had chased across Turkmenistan looked like. He studied the screen for a moment, looking at the man on the screen. Something wasn't right. His eyes swept across the screen and slowly his blood started to freeze. He flew across the room to his jacket and grabbed wildly at his mobile phone.

The guy in the photograph wasn't Fearless. He was wearing a short-sleeve shirt and his wrists were visible in the shot. There was no tattoo on either wrist, which meant Tyler had been chasing the wrong guy. And if the guy was a decoy then the bank account would be a decoy too. Which meant they were back to square one; he needed Lockhart to unlock the bank account. Tyler was about to put a bullet through three hundred million dollars.

The phone rang out. He needed Tyler to pick up.

CHAPTER SIXTY-TWO

M4 Southbound, 30 Minutes from Heathrow
"Don't stop me now 'cos I'm free wheeling, and I can't steer"
– Wonderstuff, Can't Shape Up.

The snow was not helping the pursuit. Tyler had been close enough to touch his bumper against the back of the Range Rover at times, but he knew that any tussle with the armored car would see him come off worst, so he held back and followed Lockhart from a few meters behind as they made their way through the blackness of the night and the blinding snow flying against the windscreen. Fog cut across the motorway at times, and Tyler found himself following tail lights, squinting through the flakes to concentrate on his prey.

In front, Lockhart was worried. An orange light on his dash told him that he needed fuel. Badly. There was a petrol station about ten miles ahead, but he wasn't planning on getting out of his bulletproof Range Rover if he could help it. Suddenly, out of the snow he saw a huge black bull, its eyes staring at him as he hurtled towards it. Another car had skidded on the ice straight off the blacktop, and crashed through the wooden fence at the side of the road. Its tail lights were visible in the middle of the field. The bull had come through the gap in the smashed fence, and was now standing on the road. Lockhart stamped on the brakes and hit his horn, and the Range Rover slowed enough for the startled bull to bolt. Lockhart released the brake before his tires lost traction, and continued along the motorway in a straight line.

Instinctively, he glanced at his mirror to see if he was going to be shunted. Tyler was following too close, and knew that he'd come off worst if he rear-ended the heavy Range Rover, so he hit the brakes too hard, and swerved violently. A truck behind him plowed into the side of him, and as Lockhart drove on, the headlights in his mirror disappeared. This was his chance.

He hit the gas and within a few minutes arrived at the petrol station. He saw it from the road, lit up harshly with strong fluorescent lights. The forecourt was empty as there were few other drivers on the road. He wasted no time, pushing his card into the pump; it would be quicker than paying inside. The tank was almost full when he saw headlights coming off the motorway. For a moment he panicked, until he saw that it was a truck and trailer, probably pulling off until the storm had gone. It was hard enough keeping the Range Rover in a straight line; The truck was an accident waiting to happen.

The truck pulled up on the far side of the forecourt, and the driver opened his door and tumbled out as if he was drunk. He fell straight to the floor, face down. Then a huge black figure pushed through the door behind him. By the time Lockhart realized that Tyler had hijacked the truck, it was too late. He stormed out of the cab, his revolver already pointing at Lockhart.

Without thinking, Lockhart raised his hands. Tyler had pulled a cap down to his brow, and zipped his coat up high. There were security cameras on the forecourt, and he was careful not to look up. He was well trained. He kept his back to the main building. He was within five meters of Lockhart when his phone rang. He picked up with his free hand, without ever taking his eyes off Lockhart or lowering his weapon.

Lockhart could hear the voice at the end of the phone shouting at Tyler. He picked up two words which told him a lot:

"Stand down!"

Tyler definitely wasn't alone. He wasn't the boss. He was being given an order and the order was not to kill him. So he wasn't allowed to shoot. Lockhart took a chance, guessing that Tyler wouldn't fire the revolver, least of all on the oil soaked forecourt of a petrol station. Tyler was five meters away, and the sanctuary of the bulletproof Range Rover was less than two.

Tyler was nodding his head in compliance as he listened to new instructions from Lang. Lockhart imagined what he was about to do, energizing his muscles, ready to spring. He swallowed his nerves and exhaled. He was ready to make a move.

Whether it was a twitch or a look in Lockhart's eye, something gave him away. Tyler lunged towards him, arms outstretched, even before Lockhart felt himself moving. He was twisting towards the Range Rover, but he could feel Tyler's shadow falling across him before his feet had moved from the spot. By the time his body began moving towards the driver's door, Tyler was already closing the gap.

Some primal program buried deep in his brain was forcing his back to arch, avoiding the swiping grip of his assailant, and before he knew it, he was in, and clutching at the heavy door, trying to lock the huge soldier out.

As the door swung, it connected with Tyler's solid forearm. His fingers grasped wildly for any purchase on Lockhart, but he slammed the door again, until eventually the arm retreated, and the door slammed. Through the thick glass, Lockhart watched as Tyler's rage exploded. He grabbed at the fuel nozzle and began smashing it against the side of the Range Rover. There was no way he could come through the ballistic panels, and he knew it. But he stood there, venting his anger at having lost his target again.

Tyler shouted something into his phone, and then threw that at the Range Rover too. Lockhart saw the handset flying straight for the center of his forehead, and he ducked even though the phone bounced straight off the windscreen. Even in a rage, Tyler had impressive control. It seemed that the angrier he got, the more deadly his accuracy became.

Lockhart had seen enough though, and started up the Range Rover. He drove off at a steady pace. Behind him, he saw Tyler tower over another man on the forecourt who had been watching what was happening in amazement. He took the keys from the man and climbed into his Saab, driving after Lockhart with his cap still pulled low over his eyes.

As he caught his breath, Lockhart wondered what had happened to the bull back on the motorway. Proud in his field, wide eyed and confused outside his usual territory. As the snow fell, Lockhart thought about Ajmal, the Englishman who had traveled so far from his comfort zone. He wondered what he would be doing if fate hadn't pulled him to Quetta. He wondered the same about himself.

There were no other cars on the road now, except for the Range Rover and the set of headlights following menacingly behind, about fifty meters back. Lockhart had sped up to about eighty, and the lights in the mirror kept in touch. The miles ticked down towards Heathrow. With fewer cars on the road, the surface was becoming ever more treacherous, but the snow plows had been out and the surfaces were just about passable. The Range Rover plowed towards the Airport, and the Saab followed in its tracks.

In the Saab, Tyler was trying to identify a noise emanating from the dashboard. A small button with a phone icon had started flashing, and he pressed it.

"Tyler?"

It was Lang. For a moment Tyler was impressed that the General had procured the forecourt CCTV footage, traced the Saab's registration and cross referenced it with the owner's phone records all in the space of fifteen minutes. Then he realized that in fact the Saab's Bluetooth had picked up the signal from his own mobile. Its cracked screen was illuminated on the passenger seat.

"He's just ahead," Tyler reported. "Bad visibility, but I'm sure he's heading for Heathrow."

Lang was already typing, checking outbound flights from London's busiest airport. It was impossible to know where Fearless could be headed. So he made a decision.

"We need him to make the bank transfer. Do you understand?"

Don't kill him. Don't let him leave. Tyler understood. He had a hundred million dollar cut riding on getting the job right. He hung up, and focused on the tail lights in front of him.

It wasn't long before the Range Rover was turning off. Tyler chuckled to himself. He was heading to Heathrow alright, just like the notepad in the kitchen had told him. *Amateur.*

As the Range Rover pulled onto the Heathrow slip road, Lockhart hit a wall of snow. The slip road hadn't been cleared by the plows in the way that the main road had been, and he approached the junction far too quickly, sailing across it with his wheels unable to grip, despite the weight of the modified car. He gripped the steering wheel tighter and willed the car to come round, which it did. He straightened up and continued round the airport ring road.

About thirty seconds later, Tyler did exactly the same. The Saab was lighter and made more of a meal of the turn, and although Tyler was an expert driver, it took all of his concentration to bring the car under control. As he looked up from the spin, he saw that the Range Rover had accelerated and was already pulling away from him. The eerie, unnatural light of Terminal Five was looming up through the snow, and Lockhart was getting away.

But Lockhart was fishing. Reeling in his opponent. If he could draw Tyler into his trap he could be rid of him for good. Lockhart had no claim on the three hundred million dollars and no desire to keep it. But Tyler hadn't agreed to the deal, so Lockhart had made a decision. Run and hide, or find a way to deal with Tyler. He was going to deal with him.

The river was pushing him along, round the ring road and straight to the front entrance of the departure terminal. The Saab was further behind now, but still within sight. The blood was still in Tyler's nostrils. Lockhart estimated that he would have about forty seconds after getting out of the Range Rover before the man with the gun arrived behind him. He figured he could safely leave the 4x4 parked in the red zone for about ten minutes before it was clamped or towed.

He kept one hand on the wheel, and began to dig about in his pockets with the other. He pulled out his loose change, and put it on the passenger seat. Then he unbuckled his belt and began to slip it from his jeans. He took off his watch and removed his mobile phone from his jacket. It was almost time.

Every moment the world was getting brighter. The tall buildings stopped the snow from swirling around the vehicle, and back-lit billboards were looming up on either side. Low lights skirted the carriageway, and the roads because gritted and slushy.

It was all too public for Tyler, but he couldn't back down now. This was what everything had been building towards. Dangerous days in Nahr-e Saraj, making deals and threatening locals. Heading out into Taliban desert strongholds to squeeze an extra ten percent from local traders. He and Lang had been shot at, and one group had even been stupid enough to take them hostage. Tyler remembered the occasion well.

There had been nine people in the compound where he and Lang were taken prisoner. Tyler had been hooded and tied in a car for four hours, but when they arrived at their sordid destination, he could have pointed to their position on a map and been within a couple of hundred meters. He had kept his eyes and ears open, and he knew the names of five of the men, and who was in charge.

He had worked out who was the weakest member of the group, and he had established which of them had weapons, and who knew how to use them. They had been captive at the compound for less than two hours when the second in command had come to question them, with three men along side him. The General sat calmly, knowing that he had a more impressive weapon by his side than an AK 47.

And so it proved. Tyler refused to talk, simply holding out his hands in silence, indicating that he would talk if his cable ties were removed. One of the henchmen hit him with the butt of his gun, and Tyler doubled over, as though in pain. The truth was, he was all muscle and it hadn't hurt in the slightest. Eventually, he straightened up and held out his hands again.

The second in command spoke to one of the others, and Tyler's restraints were removed. Within thirty seconds all four insurgents were dead. Tyler didn't miss a beat as he felled each of them in turn with his fists knees elbows and boots, like some venomous cage-fighter. It was frightening to watch. Then calmly he took a pistol from the side of one of the men and methodically shot each of the dazed men in the head, showing no mercy and no hesitation.

The remaining five men came through the door one after another, like the keystone cops, and Tyler picked the first three off with bullets between the eyes. It was like target practice. The fourth man came flying into the room, his eyes wild. Tyler grabbed him by the throat and slammed him against the wall, turning just in time to shoot the remaining fighter.

The man pinned against the wall looked around the room. Lang was still sitting at the desk, his hands cable tied in front of him. There were eight dead men on the floor. Tyler turned back to the man on the wall.

"You have to understand that things have changed now, Mr. Houshmand," Tyler said quietly to the frightened looking man. "Do you understand?"

Houshmand nodded without speaking. He was the most feared warlord in that part of Helmand, but with all eight of his close protection team killed in the space of a minute, he was alone and scared. He had no idea how the huge man looming over him had learned his name. He wasn't about to ask.

Lang stood up, and Tyler rummaged among the dead until he found a pocket knife which he used to remove the General's cable ties. Lang stood up, and directed Houshmand to sit in the chair which he had vacated.

The terror was done. In a room full of eight dead bodies, the last man standing will always be compliant. So Lang spoke quietly while Tyler stood behind him. He dictated terms about who would be granted safe passage through the territory, which factories would be left to flourish and which would be razed to the ground. By the time they left, Houshmand was clear about who was in charge in Nahr-e Saraj.

This was how Tyler had earned his money. Dangerously and slowly. The millions of dollars at stake tonight were not legitimate, but he had worked hard for them. The man who held the key to his money was not about to walk out of sight through a well lit airport. No way. He pushed a little harder on the gas.

The Range Rover came to a fork in the road. Without hesitating, Lockhart took the restricted lane which led straight to the drop off point outside departures. He stayed within the speed limit and pulled up as close to the doors as possible, without drawing any undue attention to himself. He pushed the hazards and bleeped the central locking. Then without looking back he walked up to the huge glass structure and through the automatic doors.

The inside of terminal five was just like any other large airport; the same check in desks and hushed atmosphere, the same harsh lighting and stone floors, and the same vain efforts to look different. In Heathrow's case it was a ceiling made of large round sound buffers and an ice cube sculpture in the lounge. Lockhart ignored it all and headed for the escalators to the first floor.

According to the huge screen, all of the fights were delayed. No doubt the runway was frozen with snow. It wouldn't matter. He was almost at the top of the escalators by the time Tyler screeched to a halt behind his Range Rover. A few people looked up but the place was almost deserted; it was past midnight, and the snow had prevented most people from setting out. A recorded message on Heathrow's main switchboard was telling people that the snow was leading to severe delays and that the runway would be closed until at least six A.M. Tyler grabbed the revolver from the passenger seat and thrust it back into his jacket pocket. He jumped from the Saab and rushed to the main doors.

He knocked a suitcase from a Korean tourist who shouted bitterly after him, shaking his fist. Another time Tyler would have turned and silenced the guy, but today his mind was focused on his target. His eyes scoured the departure terminal, and caught sight of Lockhart heading across the walkway on the first floor, making for the departure gates.

Tyler had done his best to wipe his blooded nose and face as he drove, and the black clothes disguised the blood, but all the same the screeching brakes, the yelling Korean, and the pace at which he was rushing towards the escalator were drawing some attention.

None of it mattered now. All that mattered was making sure that Lockhart, and his hard earned dollars, didn't disappear to some place on the other side of the world. Tyler had always been a ruthless hunter, but after a year of close calls and near misses, he just wanted the prize. One hundred million dollars would put him beyond the reach of the law, or the Army. It would mean sunshine and success and palm trees and women and all of the things he had done without for the last twelve months. And all that stood between him and his new life was the man about thirty seconds in front of him.

Lockhart had reached the security checks. With so many flights canceled, there was no queue, and he walked as quickly as possible through the cordon and into the scanning space between two plain black boxes as directed by the uniformed guard. This was it, the scanner he had seen in the magazine article. It was a new generation X-ray machine which could see pretty much everything beneath passenger's clothes. A small sign lit up with the words *Scanning In Progress* for about five seconds after which a guard called him through. He stole a glance behind him as he walked on and glimpsed Tyler almost at the machine.

Tyler saw nothing except for his prey. His work. His hundred million. Tunnel vision. He swept through the area ignoring the man in the uniform and squeezing his huge frame between the black boxes. Inevitably, an alarm sounded.

At once, Tyler realized his mistake. The shrill alarm cut through his thoughts and changed his focus. A man in uniform stepped out in front of him, and was asked him to return to the scanner. He was about six foot two, and he was staring hard at Tyler. Noticing his broken nose and traces of blood on his face. Noticing his heavy breathing and agitated state. Perhaps he was on drugs? Perhaps he had a heavy metal belt and a fear of flying. The security man doubted it, somehow.

Tyler was aware of a lot of movement in his peripheral sight. On a screen somewhere nearby, an astounded analyst had just noticed a gigantic man trying to get through the body scanner with what seemed to be some type of weapon. The revolver showed up brightly compared to the dull silhouettes around it.

The analyst hit the panic alarm, and now the two guards were being replaced by several well-trained police officers from the SO-19 anti-terror branch. They wore police badges with dark combats, thick protective vests, and Heckler & Koch MP5 semi automatics.

Tyler's blood began to boil. Confined between the black boxes, tricked by Lockhart, and surrounded by flat-footed British policemen, his rage exploded. He was a far better shot than any of the officers and as he whipped out the revolver they were slow to react. He was a warrior while they were mostly family men who became firearms officers because it paid a few more pounds towards family Christmases. Tyler had emptied two of his chambers before any of them had even raised their weapons to their shoulders.

Even under pressure his shot was excellent, and both bullets hit home; head shots which felled the police officers. But there were four officers on either side, and they opened fire. The first hit Tyler in the leg as a shocked policeman fired wildly, reacting to his colleagues dropping. As Tyler turned towards the man, a second bullet hit him in the back of the skull. The other bullets didn't matter. Tyler was dead before his giant frame hit the floor.

Lockhart had heard the gunfire behind him in disbelief. He had hoped that the revolver would show up on the scan and that Tyler would be arrested. They idea that the man would have been psychotic enough to try to take on an airport full of armed policemen simply hadn't occurred to him.

Judging by the fact that the gunfire had stopped, and the police were calling for medics, he guessed Tyler was apprehended or worse. The airport would be in lockdown in seconds. Lockhart looked around and spotted a fire alarm and smashed it with his elbow.

The second alarm of the night confused an already difficult situation for the police sergeant in charge of the scene around the scanner. They were administering first aid to the two officers who had been shot, which was hopeless. They had handcuffed the huge man slumped in the scanner, which was pointless.

She assumed that the alarm was a false one, but she knew that even with the airport almost empty there would still be a couple of hundred travelers stampeding past the scene any moment. She instructed a couple of officers to direct tourists through an adjacent corridor as they made their way out of the restricted part of the airport and back out onto the cold snowy street as the management worked out what the hell was going on. The whole airport needed shutting down anyway.

Lockhart was one of the first to walk back past the scanner, and down the stairs into the main entrance. He stepped out through the automatic doors and into the cold air. He could hear distant sirens as he walked towards the Range Rover, which hadn't been clamped. The plan had worked well.

He drove off at a sensible speed as the first of the passengers spilled out onto the street behind him. Emergency vehicles were streaming as he left. He punched *Gatwick Airport* into the sat nav, and stole a glance in the rear view mirror, more out of habit than anything. Nothing was following him.

Thousands of miles away, Ben Lang was staring at his screen in disbelief. The live news pictures were showing a dead man slumped in a heap. The body was too big to be anyone other than Tyler. It was clear that all hell had broken loose around him. The mission had failed, and he was too close to Tyler to be sure that the trail wouldn't lead back to him. He shut off the laptop and began to close down the office.

CHAPTER SIXTY-THREE

"You want it all but you can't have it, It's in your face but you can't grab it" Faith No More – Epic.

Lockhart exhaled. The snow had stopped and the sky was black as tar. There was nothing else on the road, and he had three hours to get to Gatwick. He took his time, never getting above fifty. He didn't see another set of headlights for an hour.

When he arrived at Gatwick, he took the Range Rover to the long stay car-park, and tucked it away in a corner. He checked to see that he wasn't being watched and then he tucked the keys under the wheel-arch. He would work out what to do with it later.

His grab bag contained his passport and as a first class passenger he was ushered through security. As he stepped airside, Lockhart felt free. The hiding and the plotting were over. The house at Woodridge had never been home, and he wouldn't miss it. He had always known that it was just a stopping point on his journey.

His flight was delayed because of the snow, and so he spent a couple of hours shopping for the things he would need in the next few days. He was traveling to Dallas, but he wouldn't stay there for long. He bought a new shirt and suit for the city, and then a rucksack and a few cotton shirts for wherever he headed next.

After, he headed for the upper lounge, took a shower, and changed into the new suit. The bar in the upper lounge was exclusive and opulent. Lockhart sank back into a leather sofa in the darkest corner and watched the room. After a while he ordered a mint tea, and relaxed. He had no suitcase to check in, and he was carrying his new rucksack as hand luggage.

He pulled out his beaten copy of *The Hidden Words*, which he had kept in his grab bag.

O YE RICH ONES ON EARTH! The poor in your midst are My trust; guard ye My trust, and be not intent only on your own ease.

There was little chance that Lockhart would become religious; during his travels he had spent time in churches and chapels and shrines, but none of the great doctrines had turned his head or stirred his heart. He relied much more of fate and feeling, and yet something appealed to him about this beaten up little Bahá'í book which he had picked up in a marketplace in Baghdad. Each time he opened it and flicked to a verse, it seemed to tell him something important. Maybe he was becoming superstitious, like those middle aged suburban housewives who become obsessed with star signs and tarot cards, twisting the readings to suit their heart's desires.

Just before first light, his flight departure was announced, and he stood up and stretched. There would be plenty of time to sleep on the plane. He made one last call from the UK, transferring two million dollars into his personal account. The three hundred million would go back to Afghanistan, but Lockhart figured he'd earned the right to do what he wanted with the interest. So he transferred two million, slung his bag over his shoulder and headed down to the gate.

Minutes later, the heavy plane accelerated into the sunrise and Lockhart felt the tide slowly beginning to pull through waters which had been tranquil for a year. Gently, insistently, the river was pulling him forward again.

CHAPTER SIXTY-FOUR

Fort Worth Airport, Dallas.
"If I had a million dollars, I'd buy you a green dress."
– Bare Naked Ladies, If I had a Million Dollars.

The journey to Dallas had been uneventful. Lockhart's tatty copy of the Hidden Words had remained unread in front of him on the plane. The rising sun had chased his flight across the ocean and he'd been distracted by the vivid oranges and pinks which had stained the clouds beneath him. Eventually the daylight crashed in like a wave over a surfer, charging forward towards America more quickly than the Airbus. Once the light was up the view of the Atlantic became monotonous and he settled back into his seat.

Lockhart had driven all night with Tyler on his back, and now at last he was free of him. Sleep came easily, and when he woke, the ocean had been replace by land, and he was heading south east across Indiana. The silver-black of the morning ocean had been replaced by a wintery green.

Two hours later, the Airbus landed in Dallas, and Lockhart breezed through Fort Worth in next to no time. He had no luggage to collect, and he was through immigration and into arrivals within minutes. He came through the sliding doors and into the main atrium. It was humming and people were rushing by.

There was a stainless steel barrier with a small crowd of expectant relatives waiting behind it. Rachel White was in the middle of them, holding up a small sign saying "Fearless". He smiled and made a beeline straight for her.

"Tyler's dead" was the first thing he said to her. He knew she'd want to hear it. Tyler had almost killed her, and she had heard him kill David Barr. She wasn't a vengeful person, but Tyler was someone the world could manage without. She smiled.

"Barr's wife and daughter want to meet you," she said. Lockhart told her that he wanted to meet them too. It was a weird way for strangers to start a conversation, but they were up and running. Rachel had already hired a car and soon they were out of Fort Worth International, and into the Dallas traffic. She headed out of the urban sprawl and into the open farmland beyond for the second time in a week. Drove through Hope again and watched it disappear in the rear-view mirror again. But this time she had company.

They spent the journey filling each other in on the past couple of days. Lockhart told what had happened to Tyler at Heathrow. She told Lockhart about the freezer and the waitress and how she had taken his advice and bust the cop's lip. Lockhart smiled apologetically.

"It was all I could think of at the time," he said.

"It saved my life," Rachel replied. She looked round and stared at him in the passenger seat. "You saved my life."

Lockhart shook his head and said "just keep your eyes on the road, will you?"

Rachel turned back around, and grinned. He liked her. After they'd passed through Hope, she explained what had happened to her once she was arrested. Explained how she'd slowly warmed up in the squad car to the point that she found her voice. She'd asked for coffee at the police station which had worked like a miracle cure. No signs of any lasting damage. The older cop told her what her rights were, and she made her phone call. Called Neilson, obviously.

His advice had been simple. The cops knew Tyler, and probably wouldn't like her story about him trying to kill her. They probably wouldn't want the hassle. Plus, Tyler probably wouldn't have hung about. If she pushed the story about Tyler, she'd have ended up stuck in Pine Bluff arguing with cops and lawyers for a week.

So she took Neilson's advice; she kept quiet and put her hand up to the assault charge instead. Neilson spoke to the cops and the radio station's Los Angeles lawyer had the whole thing straightened out within the hour. Neilson wired the money for the fine and before the day was over she was released back into the city.

"Were you worried about bumping into Tyler again?" Lockhart asked her as they drove closer to Pine Bluff.

"No," said Rachel and then she paused, watching the cars in front of her. "Yes. A little bit."

Lockhart smiled again. Rachel explained that she had called Neilson from a payphone outside the police station. He had told her the news team had found Lucy Barr's address. It had been too late to go calling on her that night, so she had decided to stay in Pine Bluff. She went back to the Super 8 for the night. The helpful guy on the desk asked her if she'd found what she was looking for at Lucky Bar.

"Not exactly," she'd told him.

Storm clouds were gathering over Pine Bluff as Rachel and Lockhart crossed the city limits. They met up with Lucy Barr in a homely coffee shop in the middle of town two hours later. The rain had really started to come down, and Lockhart and Rachel ran full pelt from the parking lot under a copy of the Dallas Morning News. By the time they burst into the coffee shop the newspaper was a soggy mess. Lockhart slung it into the nearest bin as the pair of them blustered and gasped and laughed.

Then they noticed Lucy Barr and her daughter at a table right in the middle of the shop, taking up two of the four seats. David Barr's funeral was tomorrow. Lockhart and Rachel straightened up and calmed down. Showed some respect.

Lucy and Rachel exchanged easy waves; they'd obviously got the measure of each other over the past couple of days. Lucy stood up and smiled, hugged Rachel and shook hands with Lockhart. Lockhart took to her quickly. He was a good judge of character. She seemed like a gentle soul, taking it all in her stride. Her daughter said hi to Rachel, and Rachel introduced her to Charlie Lockhart.

"Charlie Lockhart, this is Charlotte Amelia Barr who is aged eight and a half years and lives here in Pine Bluff in Arkansas."

Charlotte laughed at Rachel's deliberately formal introduction. She seemed like a sparky kid.

"Hi Charlie," she said, and she looked like she was measuring him up. "You know, sometimes my friends call me Charlie too."

Lockhart smiled at her.

"I don't like it much" she shrugged, and pulled a mischievous face.

Lockhart and Rachel both laughed as her mother gave her a look that was approving and disapproving all at the same time. She had good manners, and a bit of fight, probably a bit like her dad. She had a Coke while the other three drank coffee. The windows had steamed up, and the chairs were comfortable. The place was warm and the conversation was easy.

Lucy spoke openly about Barr in front of her daughter. She explained that she and Charlotte had done their mourning a year ago when he disappeared in Afghanistan. She told them stories about him which were full of warm memories. Sometimes Charlotte would chip in with a detail or two. They both spoke naturally about him in the past tense. Rachel explained again what she had told Lockhart and Lucy Barr separately. How she had become convinced that Barr hadn't jumped, how he was holding the photograph before he died, and how Tyler had attacked her. From time to time Rachel would glance at Charlotte, and then at her mother.

"It's fine," Lucy would say. "She's going to hear about it someday, so it might as well be today."

Lockhart described his first meeting with Barr. The truck with the grenade stuck on the side of it. The tussle with the Afghan Guards. The moment that Barr had pulled his leg off in front of him as he sat down at his desk.

"Yeah, he did that," Lucy smiled. "He used to weigh people up doing that. He made a man in a shoe shop scream once."

They all smiled. His girls missed him. Lockhart told them about Tyler. How he had come to Woodridge to kill him, just like he had hunted down Barr. He didn't tell them about the journalist or the other guy Tyler had killed at the top of the hill. But he did tell them about the airport, and how Tyler had shot at the police. How his blind rage had bought on his own downfall. Lockhart told them that the man who had killed Barr was definitely dead, and how he wasn't coming back. He knew that they needed to hear it.

After an hour of so the conversation wound up, and Lucy invited Rachel and Lockhart to the following day's funeral. Then they all braved the rain as they ran back to their cars. Lockhart could hear Charlotte squealing as she and Lucy dashed for cover. He and Rachel headed back to the Super 8. He checked into a room on a different floor to Rachel, and she booked them a table in the restaurant.

"My treat," she said. "You saved my life remember."

"Well, you won't let me forget it," Lockhart replied. They hit the bar for an hour before eating and shared a bottle of red with their meal and eventually wondered up to their rooms around midnight.

The funeral was reasonably well attended. It was brief and not religious. After it was done, Lockhart pulled Charlotte to one side while Rachel thanked Lucy for her hospitality.

"I need you to do me a favor," he said.

He looked at her. She was bearing up well, considering. He handed her an envelope from his jacket pocket. He asked her to give it to Lucy when they got home. He made her promise.

"And don't go opening it either," he teased. She put it into a little black purse and held it close to her chest.

"I promise," she said.

Lockhart and Rachel White traveled back together from Pine Bluff to Dallas, flew Dallas to LAX, and then hired a car and took it up north to Oxnard. They traveled the whole way wearing their tired funeral outfits, not caring who stared. *Strangers taking pity.* A week since they first spoke on the phone, they felt like old friends.

She drove through Los Angeles up to her place in Oxnard. He stayed awake, soaking up the billboards and the traffic and the newness of it all. It was dark by the time they reached Oxnard and the day had beaten them. She didn't have to invite him to stay; it just sort of happened. It was the kind of day which could have led to them accidentally tumbling into bed together, but they didn't.

Rachel grabbed a couple of beers from the fridge and they sat watching TV. They sat close, and didn't talk too much. Eventually, she wandered off and came back with a blanket for Lockhart. Then she wandered back out again with half a beer in her hand, and didn't come back. Lockhart lay back on the sofa and was asleep in minutes.

Miles away, Lucy Barr's day was coming to an end too. She had taken forever to say goodnight to Charlotte. Tucked her up, stroked her hair, kissed her forehead. They talked about everything and nothing. It seemed to Lucy that she was growing up too quickly. She was sadder and wiser than a young girl should be. But she was tough as her dad. She'd be ok.

Lucy finally dimmed the light and closed over Charlotte's bedroom door. Left it open just a crack. Reluctantly she headed back downstairs with her daughter tucked up and her husband buried. She poured a glass of Shiraz and settled back into her end of the sofa. Sat staring at Barr's end for a while. It looked very empty.

After a while she remembered the envelope that Charlotte had given her upstairs. She said it was from the Englishman. Said it was a surprise. It was thoughtful of Lockhart. He must have realized how she'd be feeling at the end of the day. Lucy wondered who else Lockhart had buried. Who he had mourned for. Who he had sat aching for on an empty sofa. Lockhart had seemed like a good guy who understood the world.

She took a gulp of red and listened for noises from upstairs. She hoped Charlotte had found sleep quickly. Then she opened Lockhart's envelope. There was a sympathy card inside, along with a note. The note explained what Lockhart had already told her over coffee; he believed that Barr was a good man, he was sorry for her loss, and he believed that the man who had killed her husband was now dead himself. He was sure that she and Charlotte were safe.

Then the note explained that Lockhart was planning to make right what had happened in Kandahar, returning the three hundred million dollars, so that schools and hospitals would thrive there. Lucy smiled. It was the right thing to do, and she believed that he would make it happen. He had that effortlessly determined way about him.

Finally he explained he was planning to make sure the interest accrued from the stolen money would also go to good use, and that he hoped that the enclosed cheque would put Charlotte through college. He hoped it would make sure that they were both comfortable in David Barr's absence.

Lucy checked inside the envelope. Sure enough, there was a small white slip inside. Her delicate fingers fished inside and pulled it out. She took another sip of her Shiraz and unfolded the cheque. She sat staring at it for a moment. Put her glass down. Stared some more. It was signed by Lockhart for two million dollars.

It's always the kindness that brings the tears. Alone on the sofa, Lucy Barr sat and wept.

*

Lockhart didn't hang around in Oxnard for long. He didn't like it any more than he'd liked Pine Bluff. He had spent a year of his life stuck in one place and he needed to keep moving. Rachel understood. His plan was to head for Hong Kong, and then to plow on back into Asia, to put the three hundred million dollars back where they belonged.

Lockhart eyed up the distant horizon and set off down the 101 towards Los Angeles and its busy airport. Smiled as he eased into the Ventura traffic. There was no need to worry about his destination. His destination would come soon enough. Right now he was back where he wanted to be. Back on the open road.

MORE BY LEE STONE

Charlie Lockhart Thriller Series

Fearless
The Smoke Child
Helter Skelter
The Road North

Bookshots (with James Patterson)

Break Point
Dead Heat

ABOUT THE AUTHOR

Lee Stone is a thriller writer from Gloucestershire who has collaborated with James Patterson to write two Bookshots - Break Point, a fast paced thriller set at Wimbledon, and Dead Heat, set at the Rio Olympics.

More recently he's released the first four books in the Charlie Lockhart Thriller Series, which he began writing at Camp Bastion in Afghanistan while reporting for the BBC.

Lee spends his time between London, Birmingham and the Cotswolds, and is married with a young daughter.

Printed in Great Britain
by Amazon